HI SCORE GIRL

WATCH OUT SISTER...
HERE COMES THE TWISTER!

Story and Art by
Rensuke Oshikiri

W9-AOQ-975

D0123696

Translation: Alexander Keller-Nelson
Lettering: Bianca Pistillo
Cover Design: Phil Balsman
Editor: Tania Biswas

HI SCORE GIRL CONTINUE Volume 1
© 2016 Rensuke Oshikiri/SQUARE ENIX CO., LTD.
First published in Japan in 2016 by SQUARE ENIX CO., LTD.
English translation rights arranged with SQUARE ENIX
CO., LTD. and SQUARE ENIX, INC.
English translation © 2020 by SQUARE ENIX CO., LTD.

ISBN: 978-1-64609-016-7

Library of Congress Cataloging-in-Publication
data is on file with the publisher.

Printed in the U.S.A.
First printing, February 2020
10 9 8 7 6 5 4 3 2 1

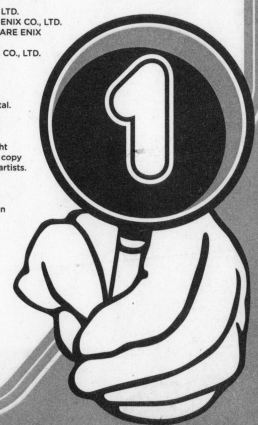

SQUARE ENIX
MANGA & BOOKS
www.square-enix-books.com

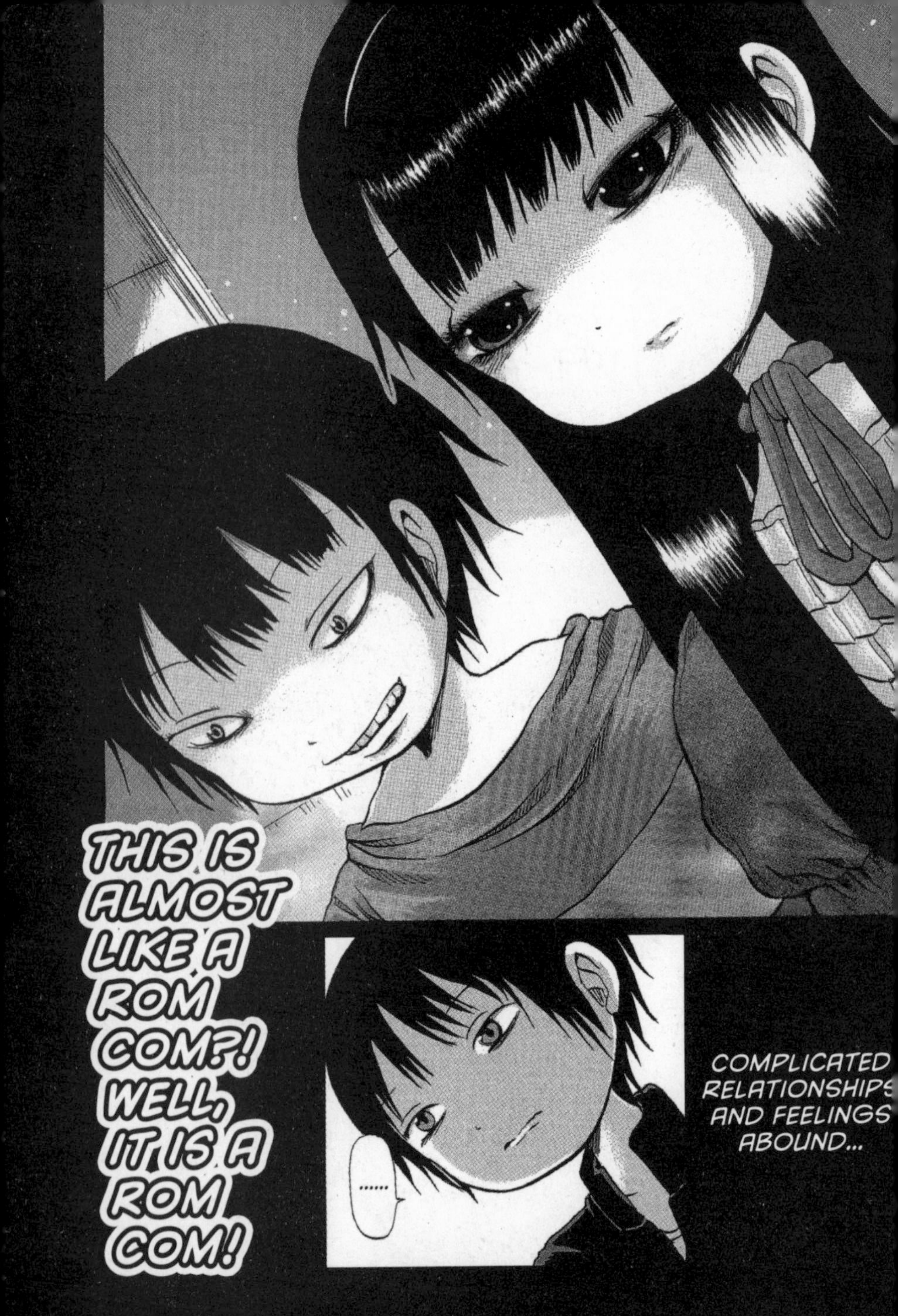
COMPLICATED RELATIONSHIPS AND FEELINGS ABOUND...
......
THIS IS ALMOST LIKE A ROM COM?! WELL, IT IS A ROM COM!

VOLUME 2 COMING SOON!

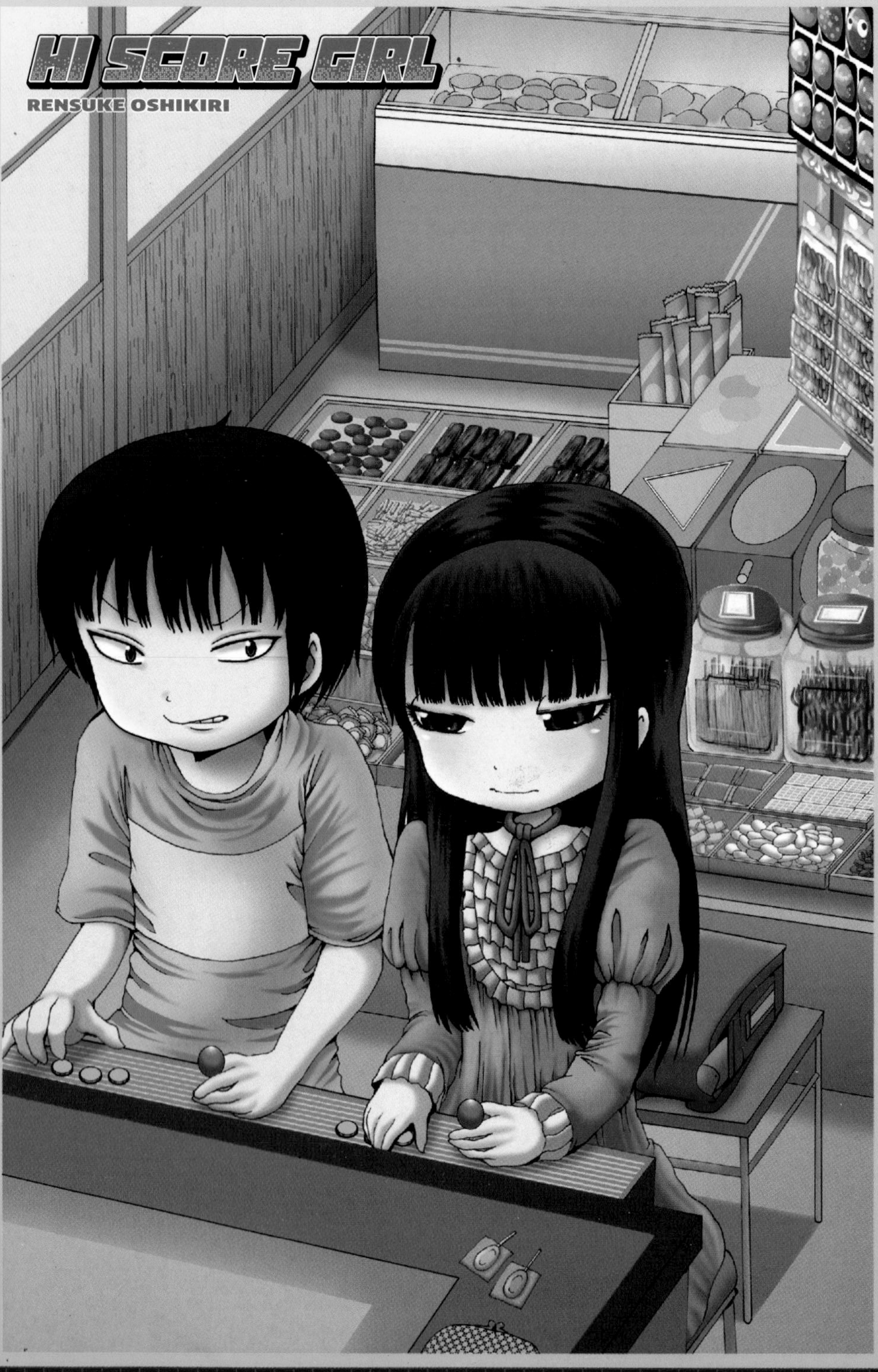
HI SCORE GIRL
RENSUKE OSHIKIRI

hi score girl

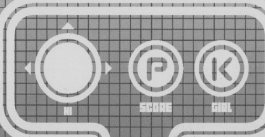

HI SCORE GIRL

SPECIAL MOVES

SAMURAI SPLASH
▽ △ + K or K K

SAMURAI HEADBUTT
◁ ▷ + P or P P

MASALA FIRE
▽ ◁ ▷ + P or P 2x

MASALA TELEPORT
▷ ▽ ◁ + P 3x or K 3x

ROLLING ATTACK
◁ ▷ 2x + P or P P

RENSUKE OSHIKIRI
PRESENTS

hi SCORE GIRL

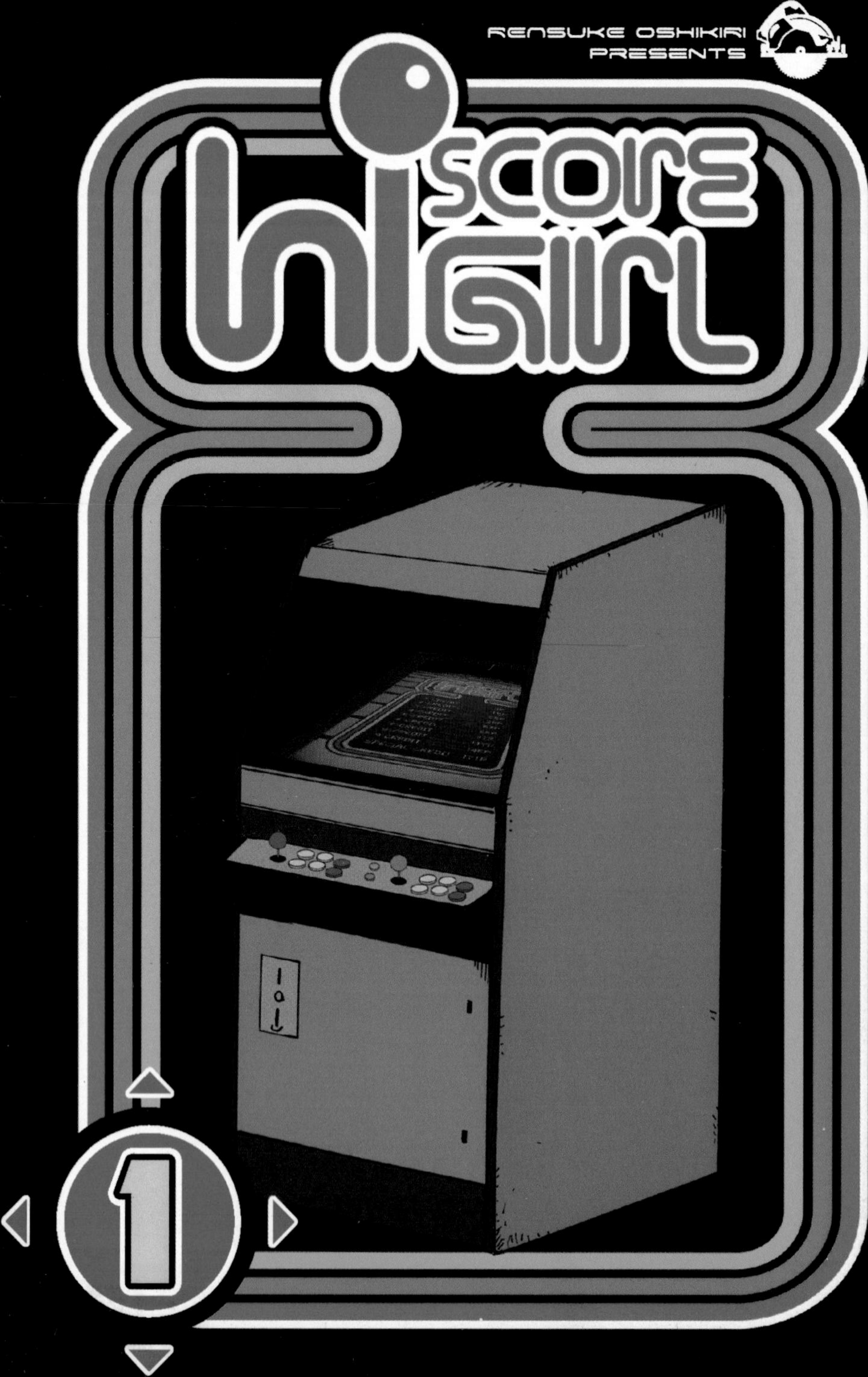

1

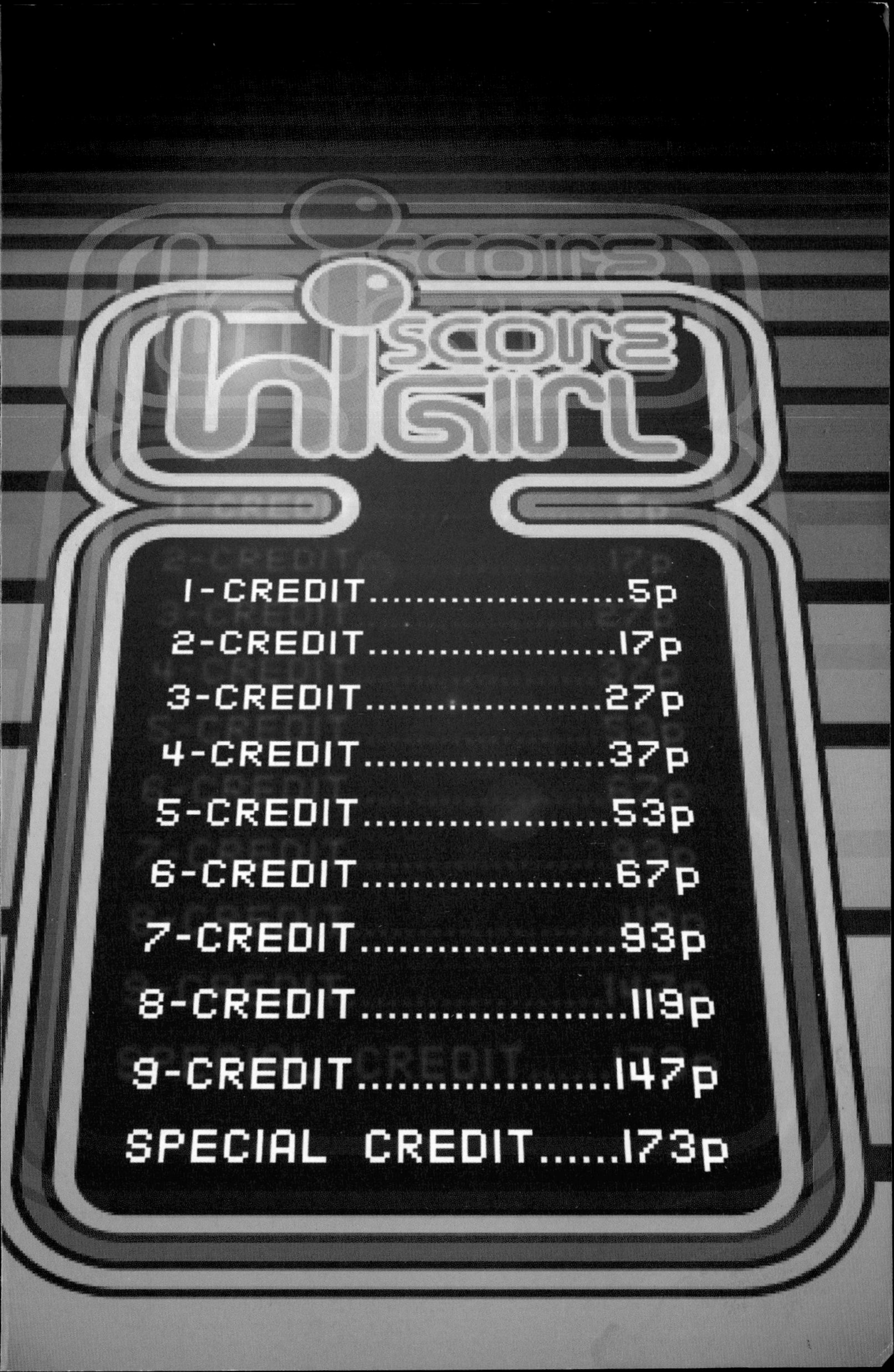
hi score girl
1-CREDIT........................5p
2-CREDIT......................17p
3-CREDIT......................27p
4-CREDIT......................37p
5-CREDIT......................53p
6-CREDIT......................67p
7-CREDIT......................93p
8-CREDIT......................119p
9-CREDIT......................147p
SPECIAL CREDIT......173p

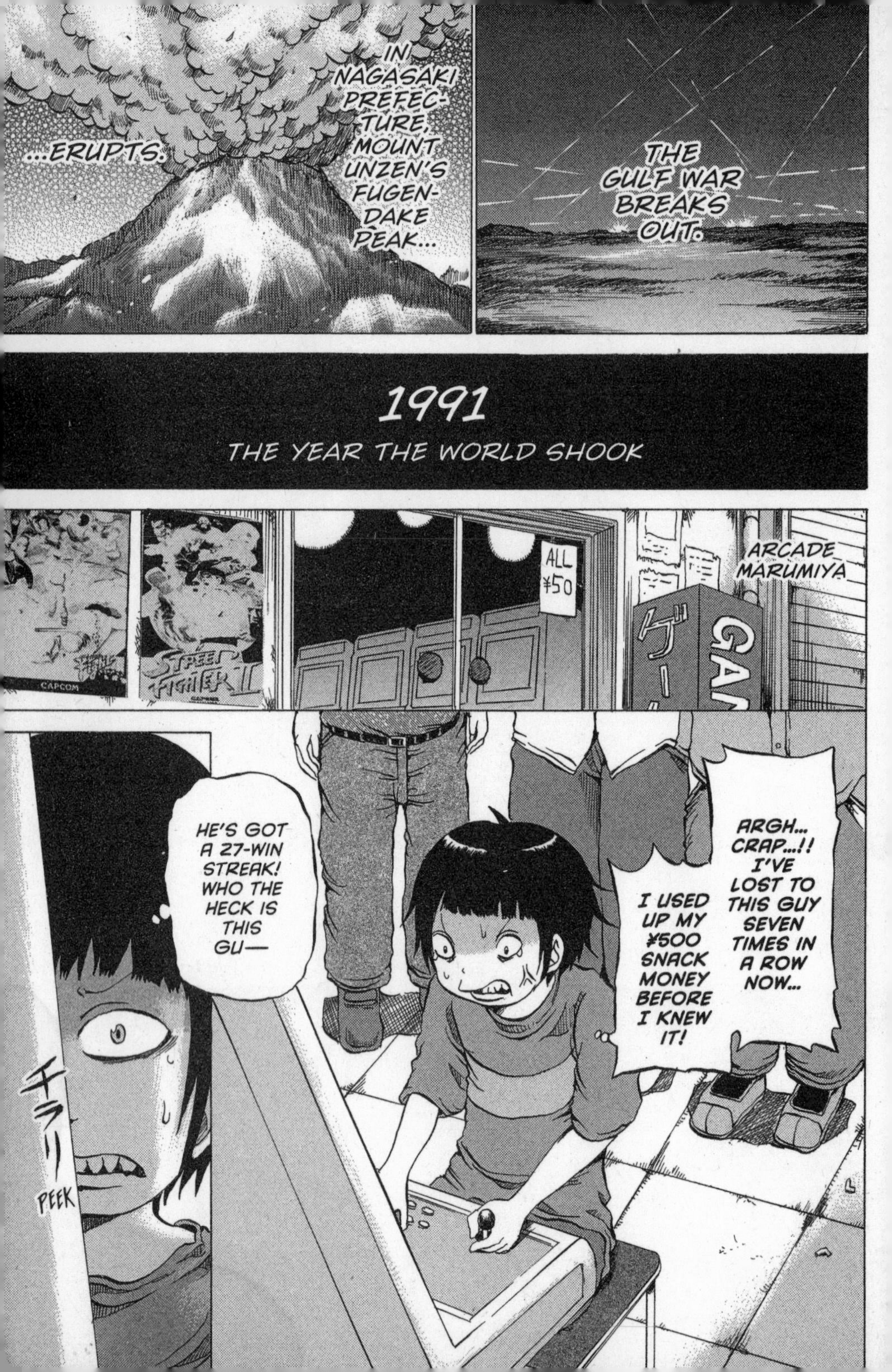
THE GULF WAR BREAKS OUT.
IN NAGASAKI PREFECTURE, MOUNT UNZEN'S FUGEN-DAKE PEAK...
...ERUPTS.
1991
THE YEAR THE WORLD SHOOK
ARCADE MARUMIYA
ALL ¥50
STREET FIGHTER II
CAPCOM
ARGH... CRAP...!! I'VE LOST TO THIS GUY SEVEN TIMES IN A ROW NOW...
I USED UP MY ¥500 SNACK MONEY BEFORE I KNEW IT!
HE'S GOT A 27-WIN STREAK! WHO THE HECK IS THIS GU—
チラリ
PEEK

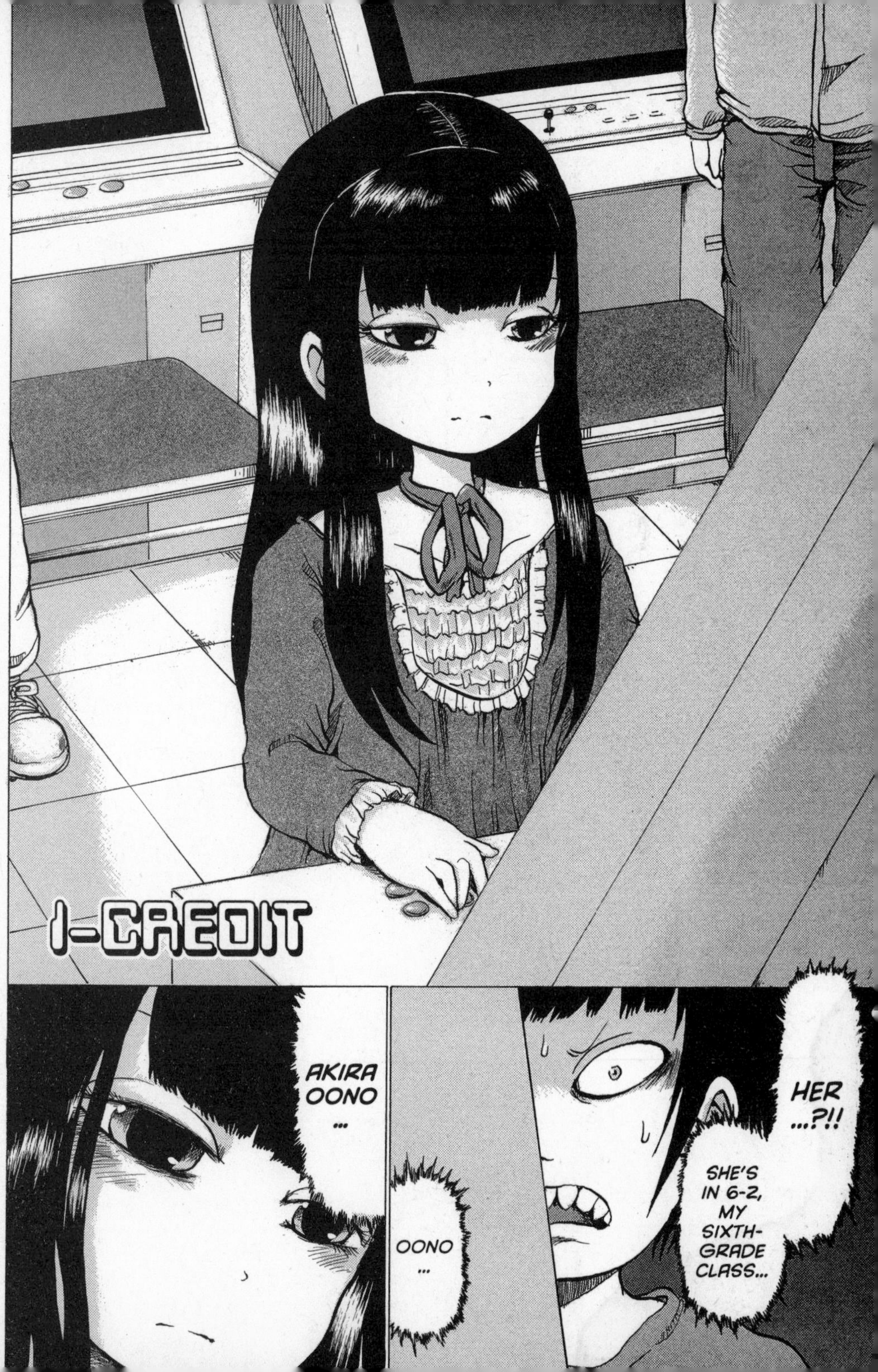
1-CREDIT
HER ...?!!
SHE'S IN 6-2, MY SIXTH-GRADE CLASS...
OONO ...
AKIRA OONO ...

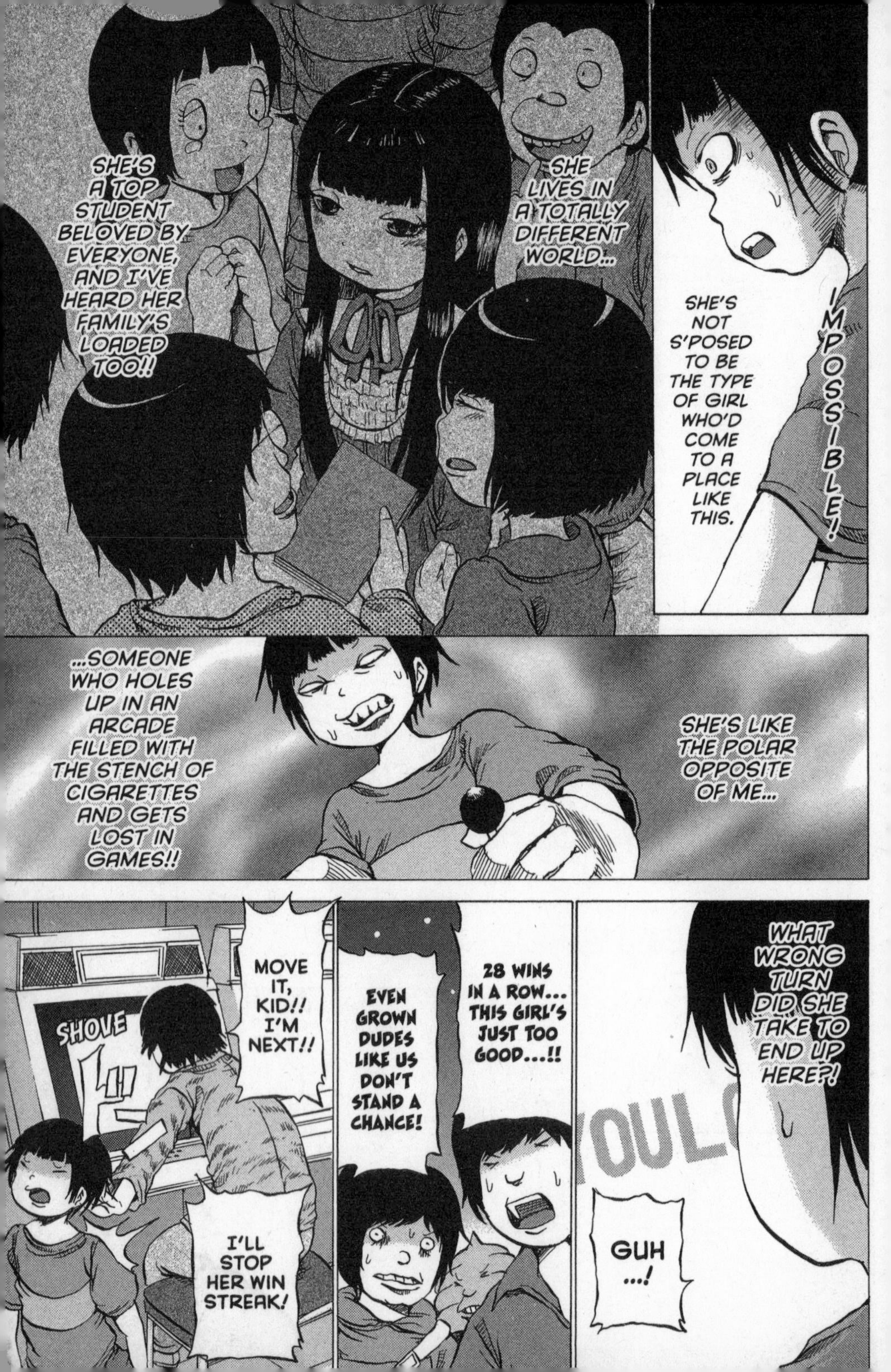
IMPOSSIBLE!
SHE'S NOT S'POSED TO BE THE TYPE OF GIRL WHO'D COME TO A PLACE LIKE THIS.
SHE LIVES IN A TOTALLY DIFFERENT WORLD...
SHE'S A TOP STUDENT BELOVED BY EVERYONE, AND I'VE HEARD HER FAMILY'S LOADED TOO!!
SHE'S LIKE THE POLAR OPPOSITE OF ME...
...SOMEONE WHO HOLES UP IN AN ARCADE FILLED WITH THE STENCH OF CIGARETTES AND GETS LOST IN GAMES!!
WHAT WRONG TURN DID SHE TAKE TO END UP HERE?!
GUH ...!
28 WINS IN A ROW... THIS GIRL'S JUST TOO GOOD...!!
EVEN GROWN DUDES LIKE US DON'T STAND A CHANCE!
MOVE IT, KID!! I'M NEXT!!
SHOVE
I'LL STOP HER WIN STREAK!

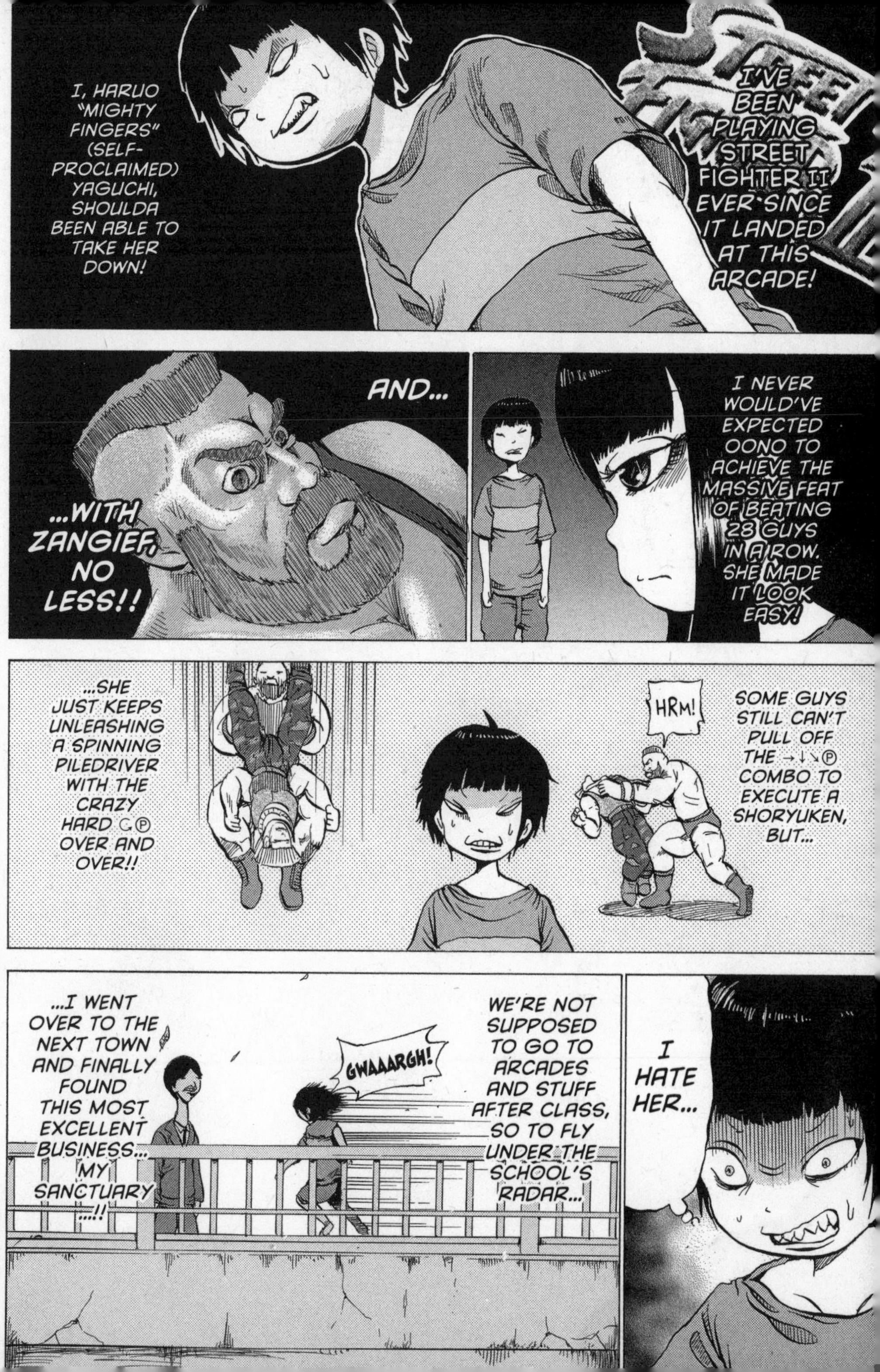
I'VE BEEN PLAYING STREET FIGHTER II EVER SINCE IT LANDED AT THIS ARCADE!
I, HARUO "MIGHTY FINGERS" (SELF-PROCLAIMED) YAGUCHI, SHOULDA BEEN ABLE TO TAKE HER DOWN!
I NEVER WOULD'VE EXPECTED OONO TO ACHIEVE THE MASSIVE FEAT OF BEATING 28 GUYS IN A ROW. SHE MADE IT LOOK EASY!
AND...
...WITH ZANGIEF, NO LESS!!
SOME GUYS STILL CAN'T PULL OFF THE →↓↘Ⓟ COMBO TO EXECUTE A SHORYUKEN, BUT...
HRM!
...SHE JUST KEEPS UNLEASHING A SPINNING PILEDRIVER WITH THE CRAZY HARD ↻Ⓟ OVER AND OVER!!
I HATE HER...
WE'RE NOT SUPPOSED TO GO TO ARCADES AND STUFF AFTER CLASS, SO TO FLY UNDER THE SCHOOL'S RADAR...
GWAAARGH!
...I WENT OVER TO THE NEXT TOWN AND FINALLY FOUND THIS MOST EXCELLENT BUSINESS... MY SANCTUARY...!!

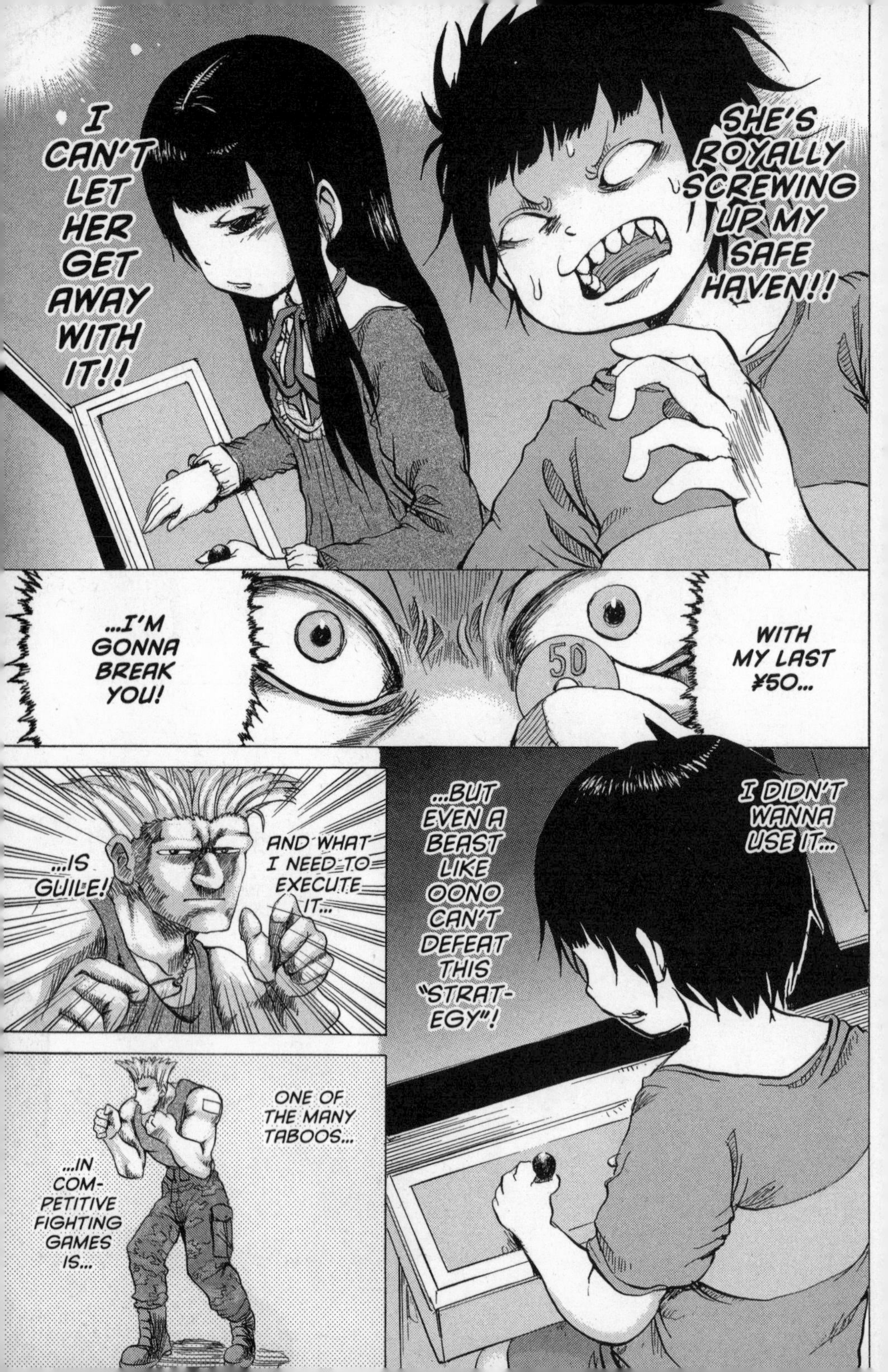
SHE'S ROYALLY SCREWING UP MY SAFE HAVEN!!
I CAN'T LET HER GET AWAY WITH IT!!
WITH MY LAST ¥50...
...I'M GONNA BREAK YOU!
I DIDN'T WANNA USE IT...
...BUT EVEN A BEAST LIKE OONO CAN'T DEFEAT THIS "STRATEGY"!
AND WHAT I NEED TO EXECUTE IT...
...IS GUILE!
ONE OF THE MANY TABOOS...
...IN COMPETITIVE FIGHTING GAMES IS...

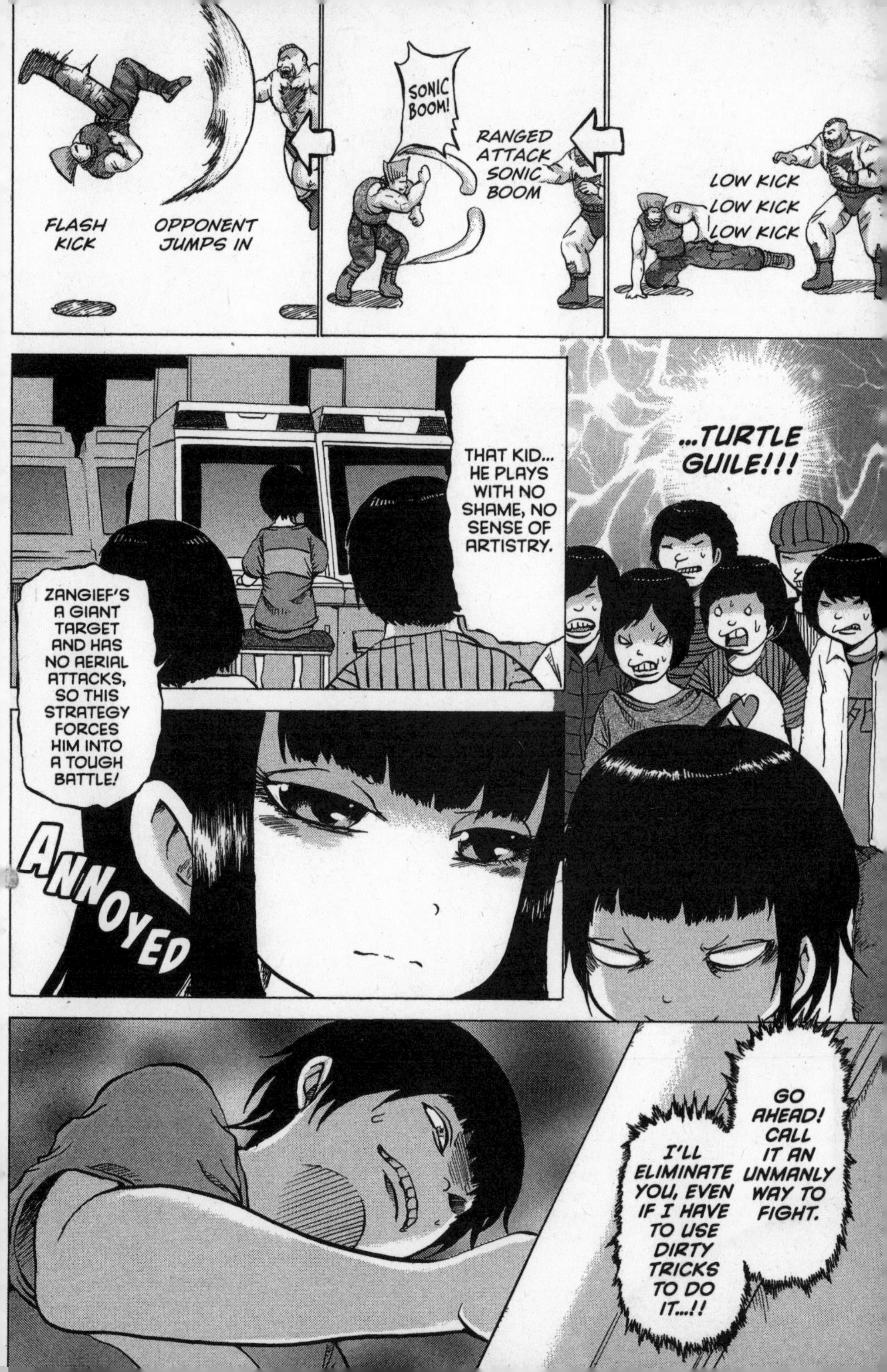
LOW KICK
LOW KICK
LOW KICK
SONIC BOOM!
RANGED ATTACK SONIC BOOM
OPPONENT JUMPS IN
FLASH KICK
...TURTLE GUILE!!!
THAT KID... HE PLAYS WITH NO SHAME, NO SENSE OF ARTISTRY.
ZANGIEF'S A GIANT TARGET AND HAS NO AERIAL ATTACKS, SO THIS STRATEGY FORCES HIM INTO A TOUGH BATTLE!
ANNOYED
GO AHEAD! CALL IT AN UNMANLY WAY TO FIGHT.
I'LL ELIMINATE YOU, EVEN IF I HAVE TO USE DIRTY TRICKS TO DO IT...!!

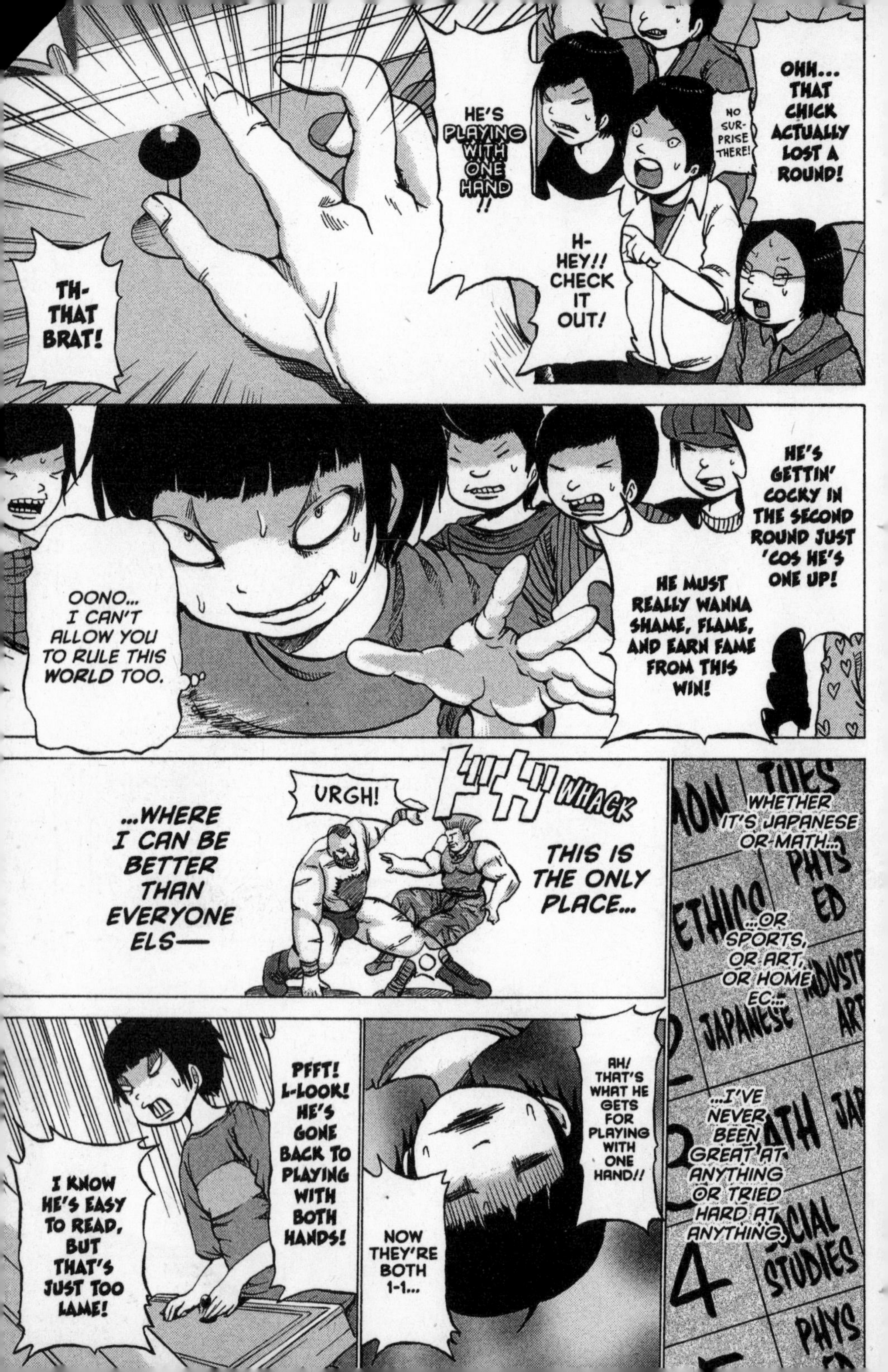
OHH... THAT CHICK ACTUALLY LOST A ROUND!
NO SURPRISE THERE!
HE'S PLAYING WITH ONE HAND!!
H-HEY!! CHECK IT OUT!
TH-THAT BRAT!
HE'S GETTIN' COCKY IN THE SECOND ROUND JUST 'COS HE'S ONE UP!
HE MUST REALLY WANNA SHAME, FLAME, AND EARN FAME FROM THIS WIN!
OONO... I CAN'T ALLOW YOU TO RULE THIS WORLD TOO.
WHETHER IT'S JAPANESE OR MATH...
...OR SPORTS, OR ART, OR HOME EC...
...I'VE NEVER BEEN GREAT AT ANYTHING OR TRIED HARD AT ANYTHING.
THIS IS THE ONLY PLACE...
WHACK
URGH!
...WHERE I CAN BE BETTER THAN EVERYONE ELS—
AH! THAT'S WHAT HE GETS FOR PLAYING WITH ONE HAND!!
NOW THEY'RE BOTH 1-1...
PFFT! L-LOOK! HE'S GONE BACK TO PLAYING WITH BOTH HANDS!
I KNOW HE'S EASY TO READ, BUT THAT'S JUST TOO LAME!

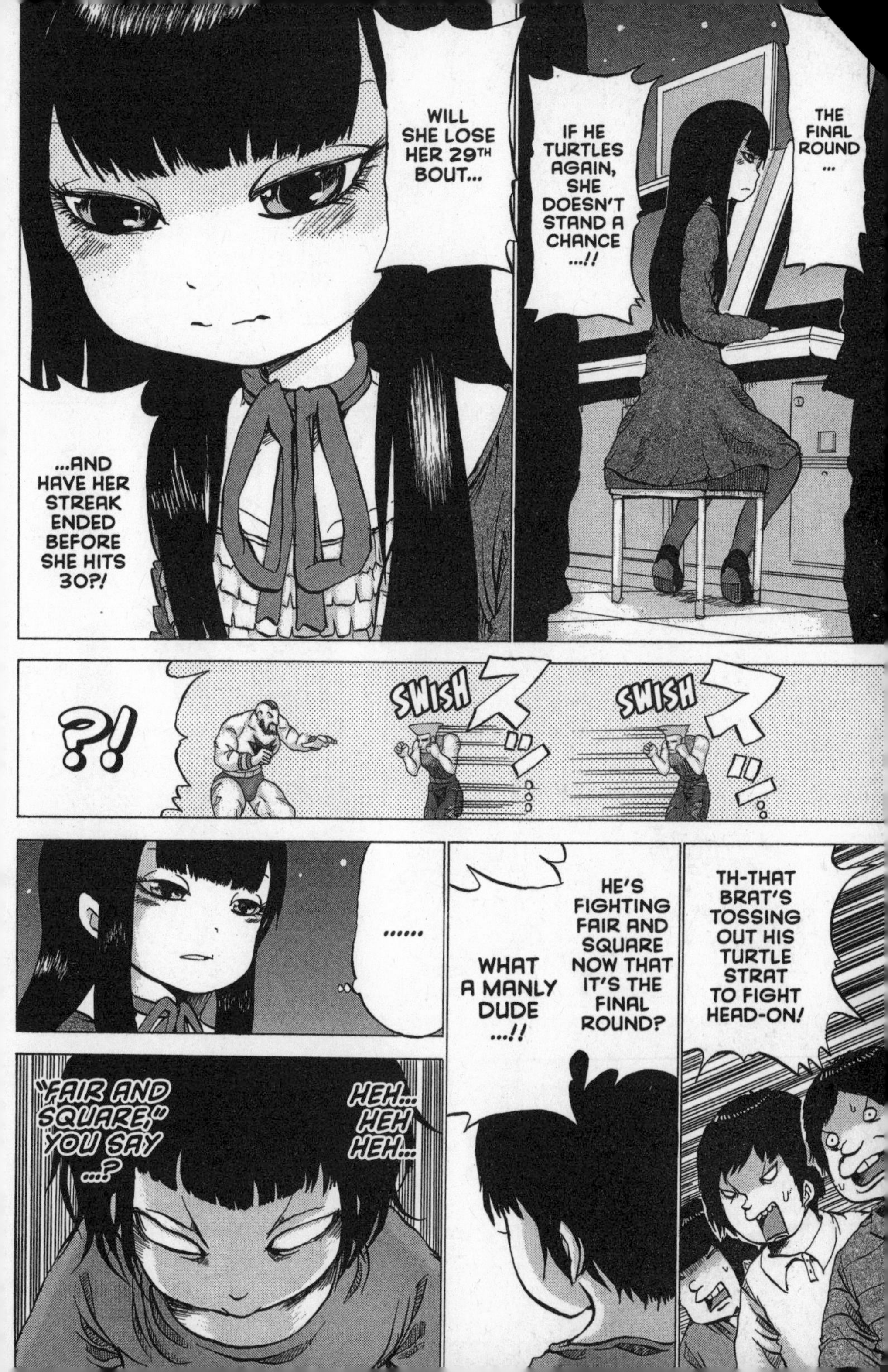
THE FINAL ROUND ...
IF HE TURTLES AGAIN, SHE DOESN'T STAND A CHANCE ...!!
WILL SHE LOSE HER 29TH BOUT...
...AND HAVE HER STREAK ENDED BEFORE SHE HITS 30?!
SWISH
SWISH
?!
TH-THAT BRAT'S TOSSING OUT HIS TURTLE STRAT TO FIGHT HEAD-ON!
HE'S FIGHTING FAIR AND SQUARE NOW THAT IT'S THE FINAL ROUND?
WHAT A MANLY DUDE ...!!
......
HEH... HEH HEH...
"FAIR AND SQUARE," YOU SAY ...?

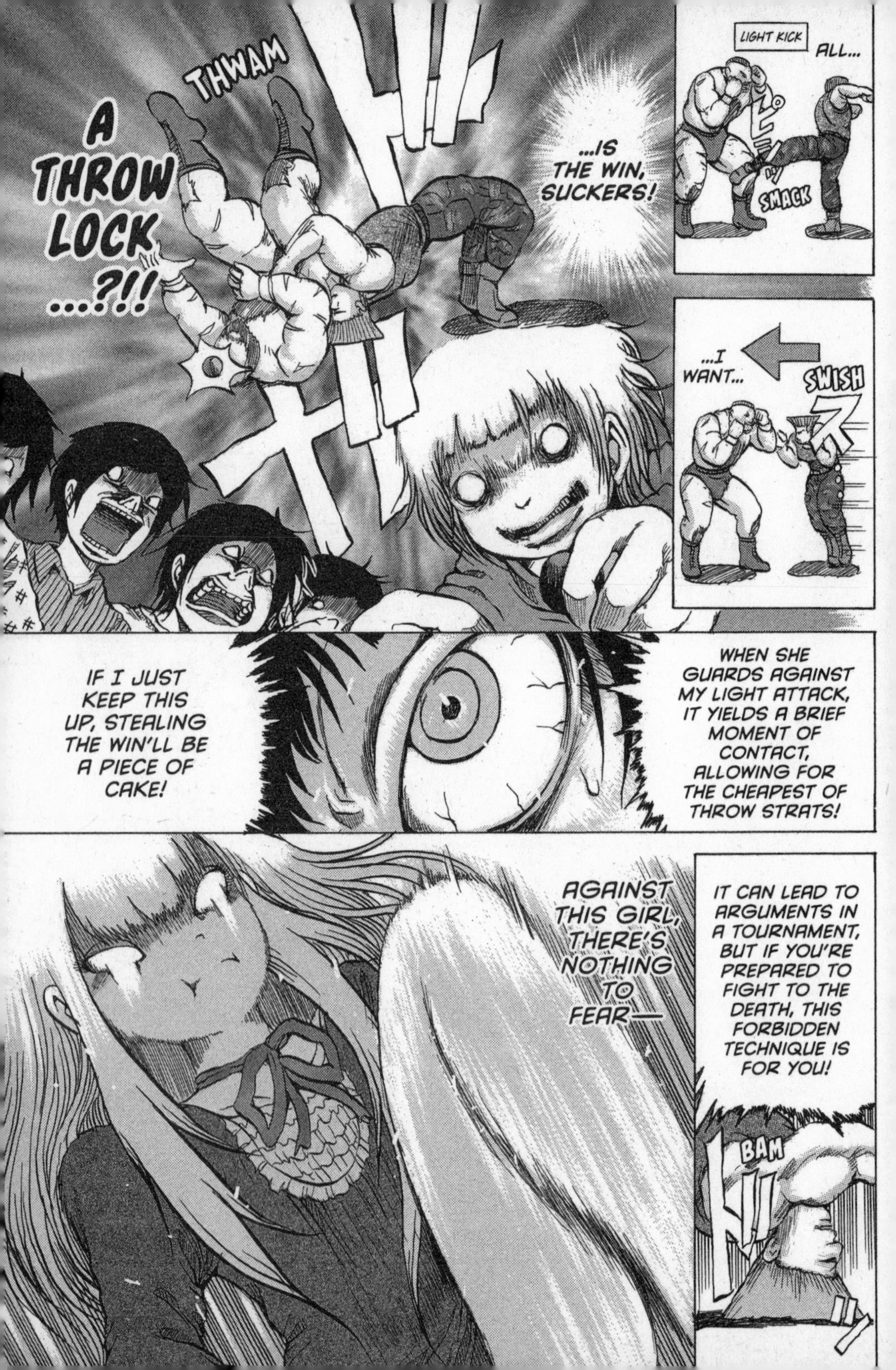
LIGHT KICK
ALL...
SMACK
...I WANT...
SWISH
...IS THE WIN, SUCKERS!
THWAM
A THROW LOCK ...?!!
WHEN SHE GUARDS AGAINST MY LIGHT ATTACK, IT YIELDS A BRIEF MOMENT OF CONTACT, ALLOWING FOR THE CHEAPEST OF THROW STRATS!
IF I JUST KEEP THIS UP, STEALING THE WIN'LL BE A PIECE OF CAKE!
IT CAN LEAD TO ARGUMENTS IN A TOURNAMENT, BUT IF YOU'RE PREPARED TO FIGHT TO THE DEATH, THIS FORBIDDEN TECHNIQUE IS FOR YOU!
BAM
AGAINST THIS GIRL, THERE'S NOTHING TO FEAR—

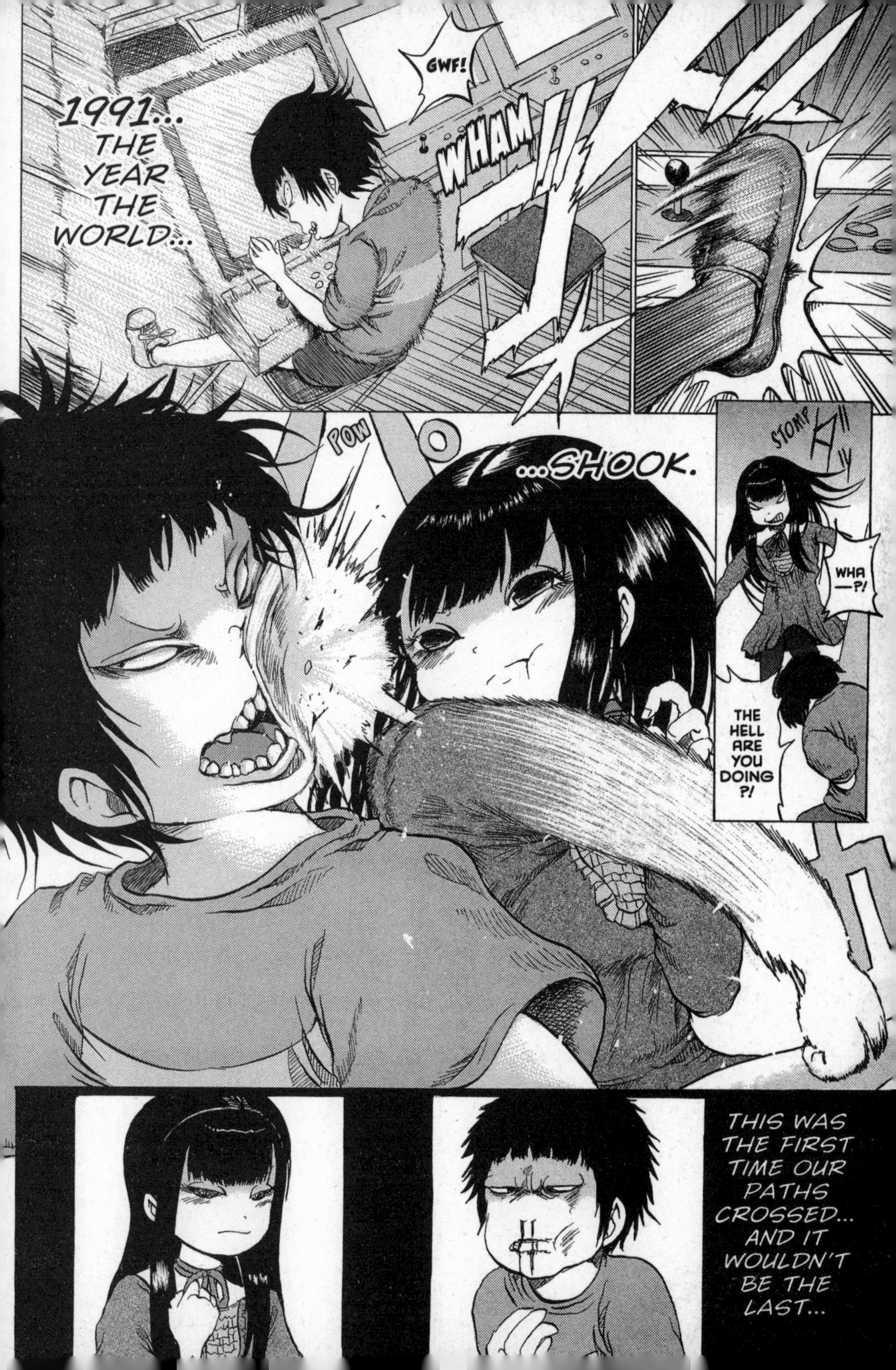
GWF!
WHAM
1991... THE YEAR THE WORLD...
STOMP
WHA—?!
THE HELL ARE YOU DOING?!
...SHOOK.
POW
THIS WAS THE FIRST TIME OUR PATHS CROSSED... AND IT WOULDN'T BE THE LAST...

HI SCORE GIRL

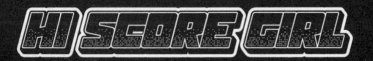

HI   SCORE   GIRL

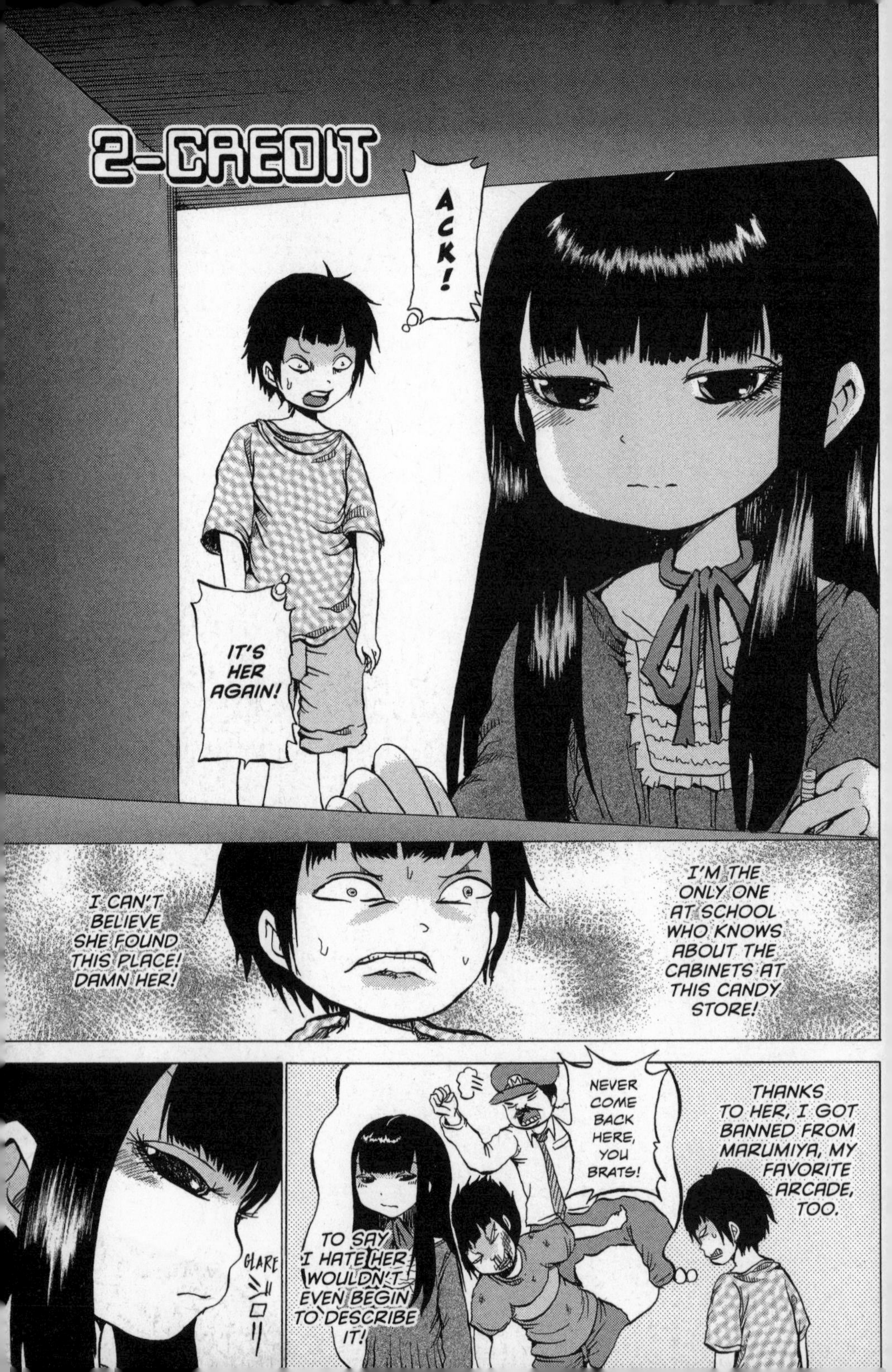
2-CREDIT
ACK!
IT'S HER AGAIN!
I'M THE ONLY ONE AT SCHOOL WHO KNOWS ABOUT THE CABINETS AT THIS CANDY STORE!
I CAN'T BELIEVE SHE FOUND THIS PLACE! DAMN HER!
THANKS TO HER, I GOT BANNED FROM MARUMIYA, MY FAVORITE ARCADE, TOO.
NEVER COME BACK HERE, YOU BRATS!
TO SAY I HATE HER WOULDN'T EVEN BEGIN TO DESCRIBE IT!
GLARE

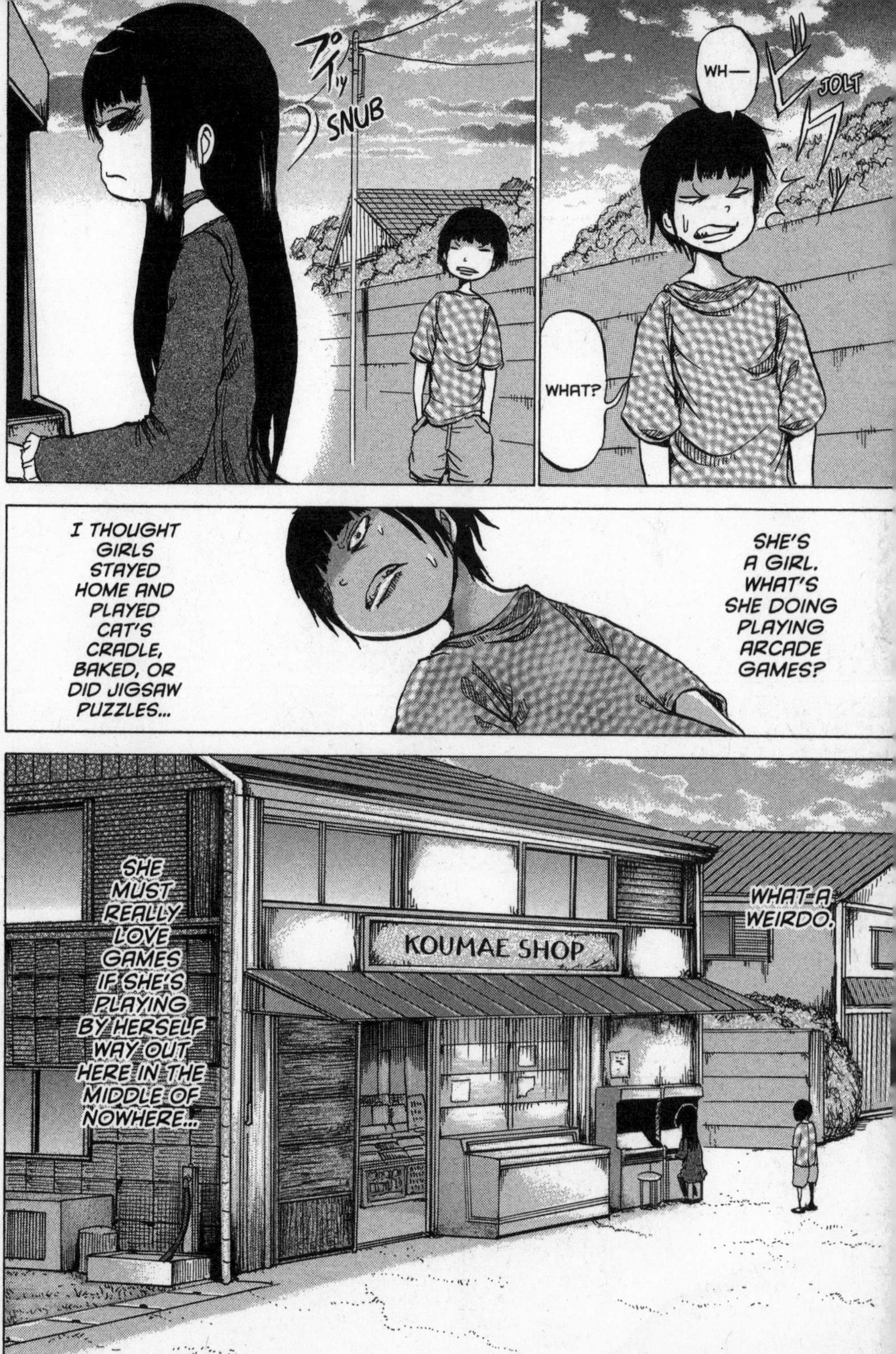
WH—
JOLT
WHAT?
SNUB
SHE'S A GIRL. WHAT'S SHE DOING PLAYING ARCADE GAMES?
I THOUGHT GIRLS STAYED HOME AND PLAYED CAT'S CRADLE, BAKED, OR DID JIGSAW PUZZLES...
WHAT A WEIRDO.
KOUMAE SHOP
SHE MUST REALLY LOVE GAMES IF SHE'S PLAYING BY HERSELF WAY OUT HERE IN THE MIDDLE OF NOWHERE...

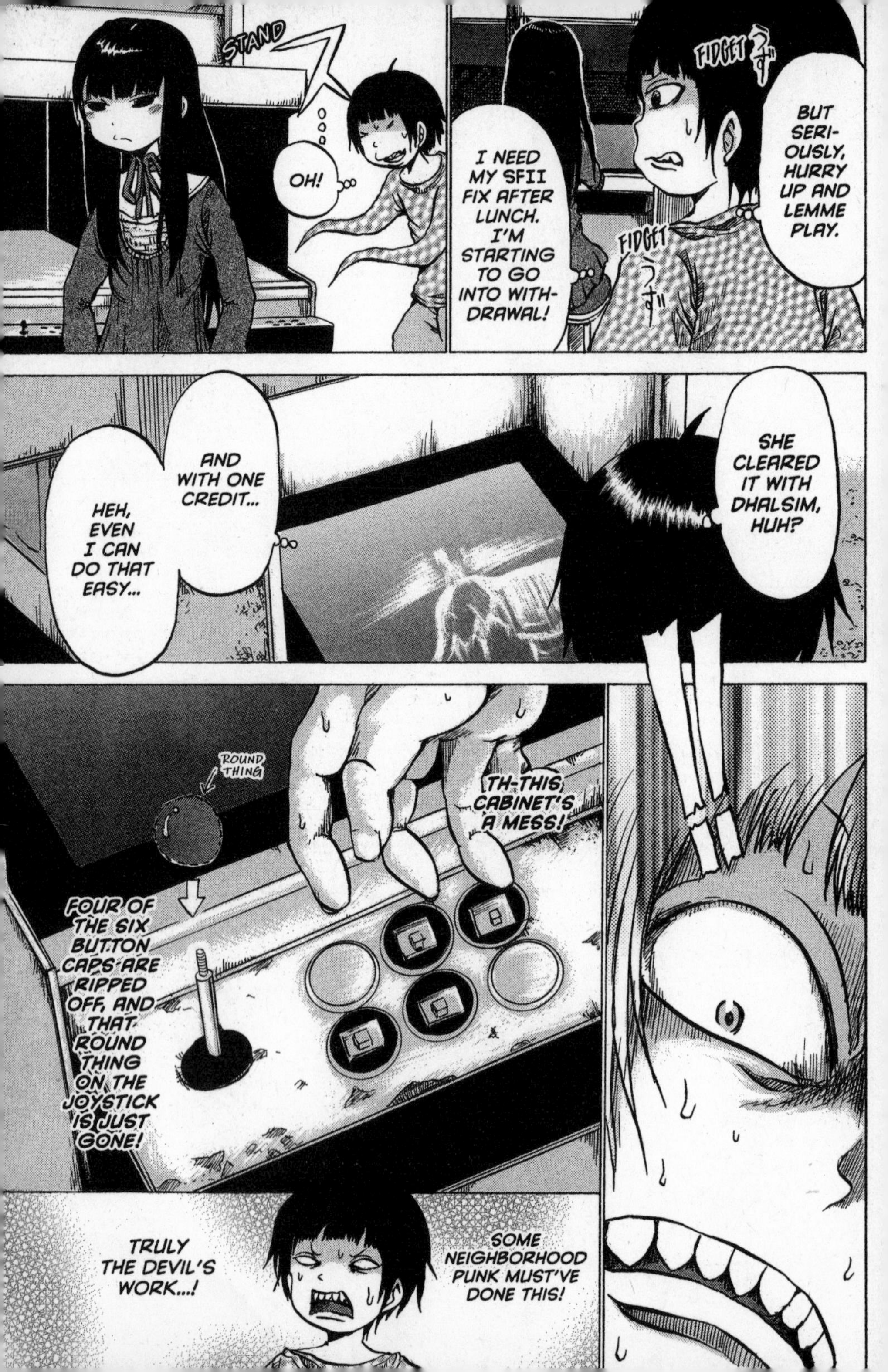
FIDGET
BUT SERIOUSLY, HURRY UP AND LEMME PLAY.
FIDGET
I NEED MY SFII FIX AFTER LUNCH. I'M STARTING TO GO INTO WITHDRAWAL!
STAND
OH!
SHE CLEARED IT WITH DHALSIM, HUH?
AND WITH ONE CREDIT...
HEH, EVEN I CAN DO THAT EASY...
TH-THIS CABINET'S A MESS!
ROUND THING
FOUR OF THE SIX BUTTON CAPS ARE RIPPED OFF, AND THAT ROUND THING ON THE JOYSTICK IS JUST GONE!
SOME NEIGHBORHOOD PUNK MUST'VE DONE THIS!
TRULY THE DEVIL'S WORK...!

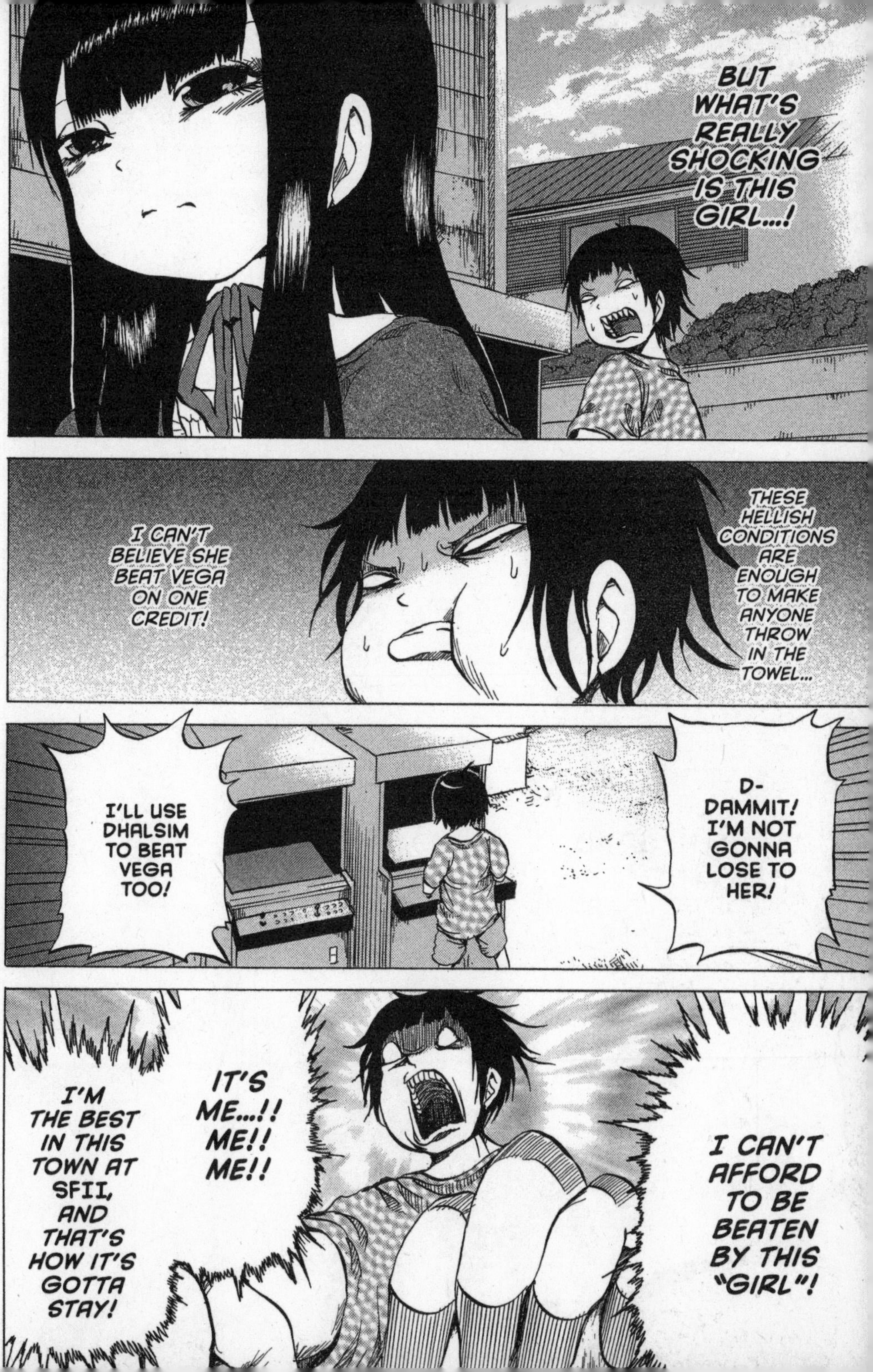
BUT WHAT'S REALLY SHOCKING IS THIS GIRL...!
THESE HELLISH CONDITIONS ARE ENOUGH TO MAKE ANYONE THROW IN THE TOWEL...
I CAN'T BELIEVE SHE BEAT VEGA ON ONE CREDIT!
D-DAMMIT! I'M NOT GONNA LOSE TO HER!
I'LL USE DHALSIM TO BEAT VEGA TOO!
I CAN'T AFFORD TO BE BEATEN BY THIS "GIRL"!
IT'S ME...!! ME!! ME!!
I'M THE BEST IN THIS TOWN AT SFII, AND THAT'S HOW IT'S GOTTA STAY!

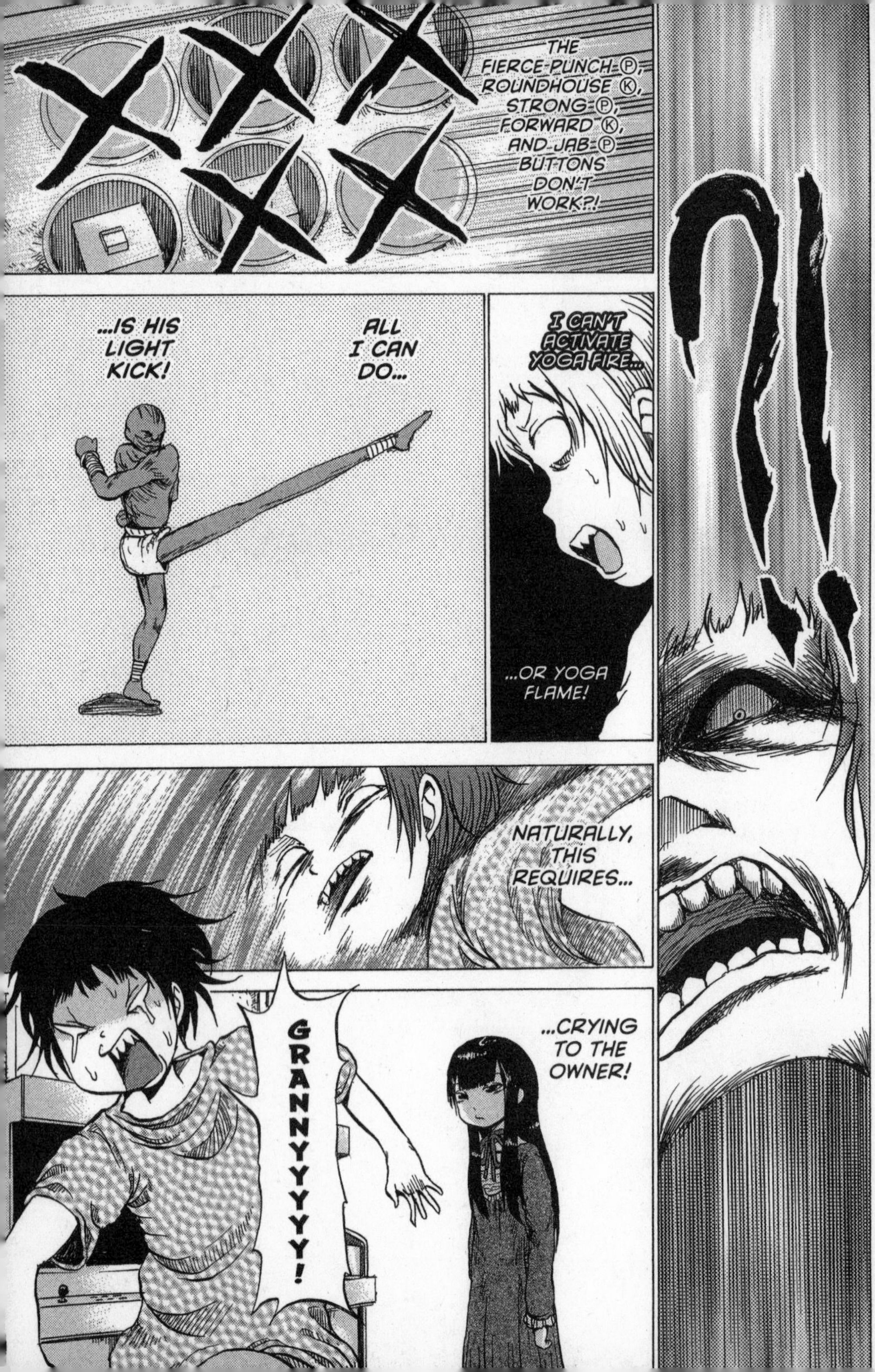
?!!
THE FIERCE PUNCH Ⓟ, ROUNDHOUSE Ⓚ, STRONG Ⓟ, FORWARD Ⓚ, AND JAB Ⓟ BUTTONS DON'T WORK?!
I CAN'T ACTIVATE YOGA FIRE...
...OR YOGA FLAME!
ALL I CAN DO...
...IS HIS LIGHT KICK!
NATURALLY, THIS REQUIRES...
...CRYING TO THE OWNER!
GRANNYYYYY!

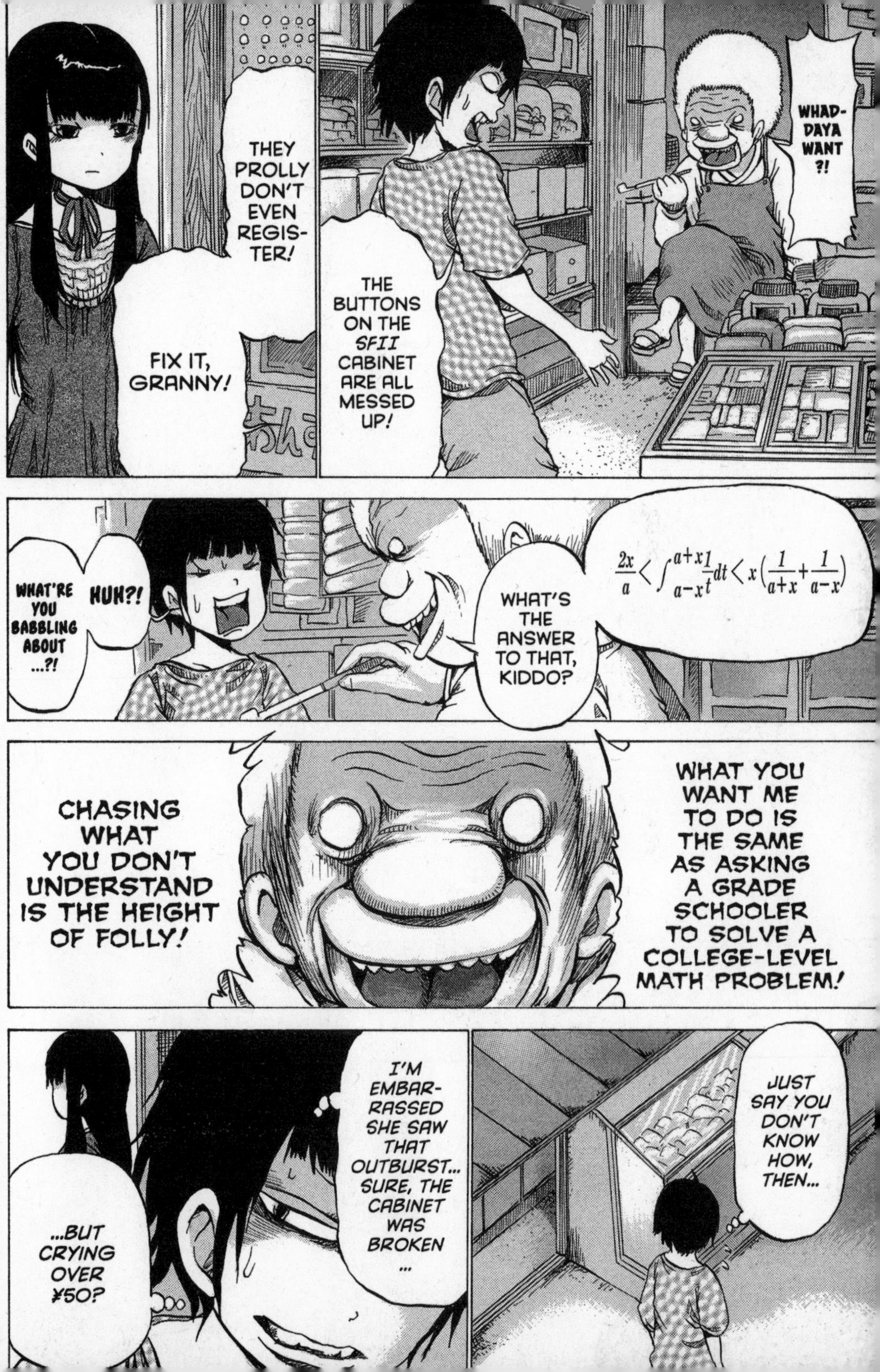
WHADDAYA WANT?!
THE BUTTONS ON THE SFII CABINET ARE ALL MESSED UP!
THEY PROLLY DON'T EVEN REGISTER!
FIX IT, GRANNY!
$\frac{2x}{a} < \int_{a-x}^{a+x} \frac{1}{t}dt < x\left(\frac{1}{a+x}+\frac{1}{a-x}\right)$
WHAT'S THE ANSWER TO THAT, KIDDO?
HUH?!
WHAT'RE YOU BABBLING ABOUT...?!
WHAT YOU WANT ME TO DO IS THE SAME AS ASKING A GRADE SCHOOLER TO SOLVE A COLLEGE-LEVEL MATH PROBLEM!
CHASING WHAT YOU DON'T UNDERSTAND IS THE HEIGHT OF FOLLY!
JUST SAY YOU DON'T KNOW HOW, THEN...
I'M EMBARRASSED SHE SAW THAT OUTBURST... SURE, THE CABINET WAS BROKEN...
...BUT CRYING OVER ¥50?

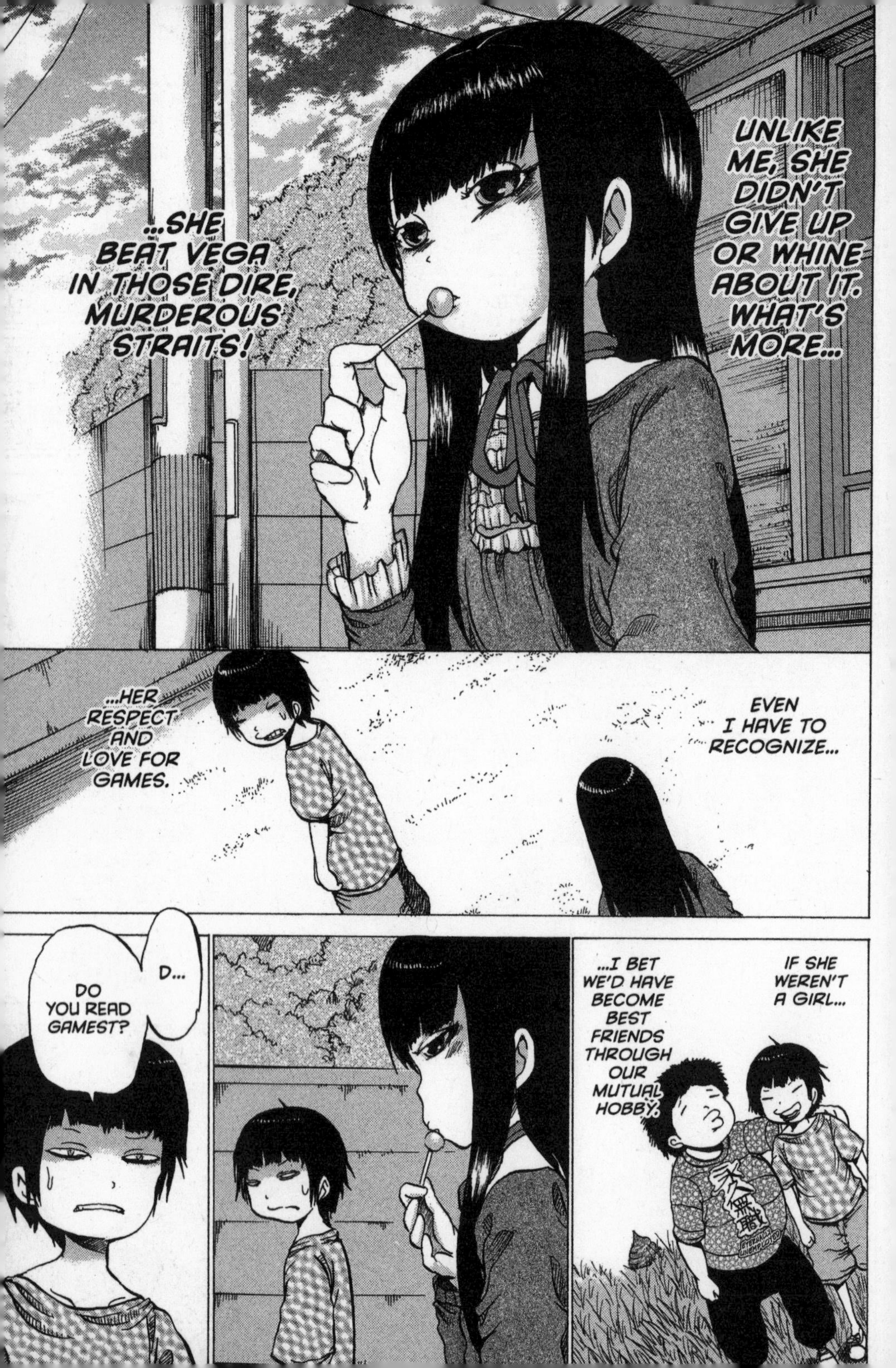

UNLIKE ME, SHE DIDN'T GIVE UP OR WHINE ABOUT IT. WHAT'S MORE...
...SHE BEAT VEGA IN THOSE DIRE, MURDEROUS STRAITS!
EVEN I HAVE TO RECOGNIZE...
...HER RESPECT AND LOVE FOR GAMES.
IF SHE WEREN'T A GIRL...
...I BET WE'D HAVE BECOME BEST FRIENDS THROUGH OUR MUTUAL HOBBY.
D...
DO YOU READ GAMEST?

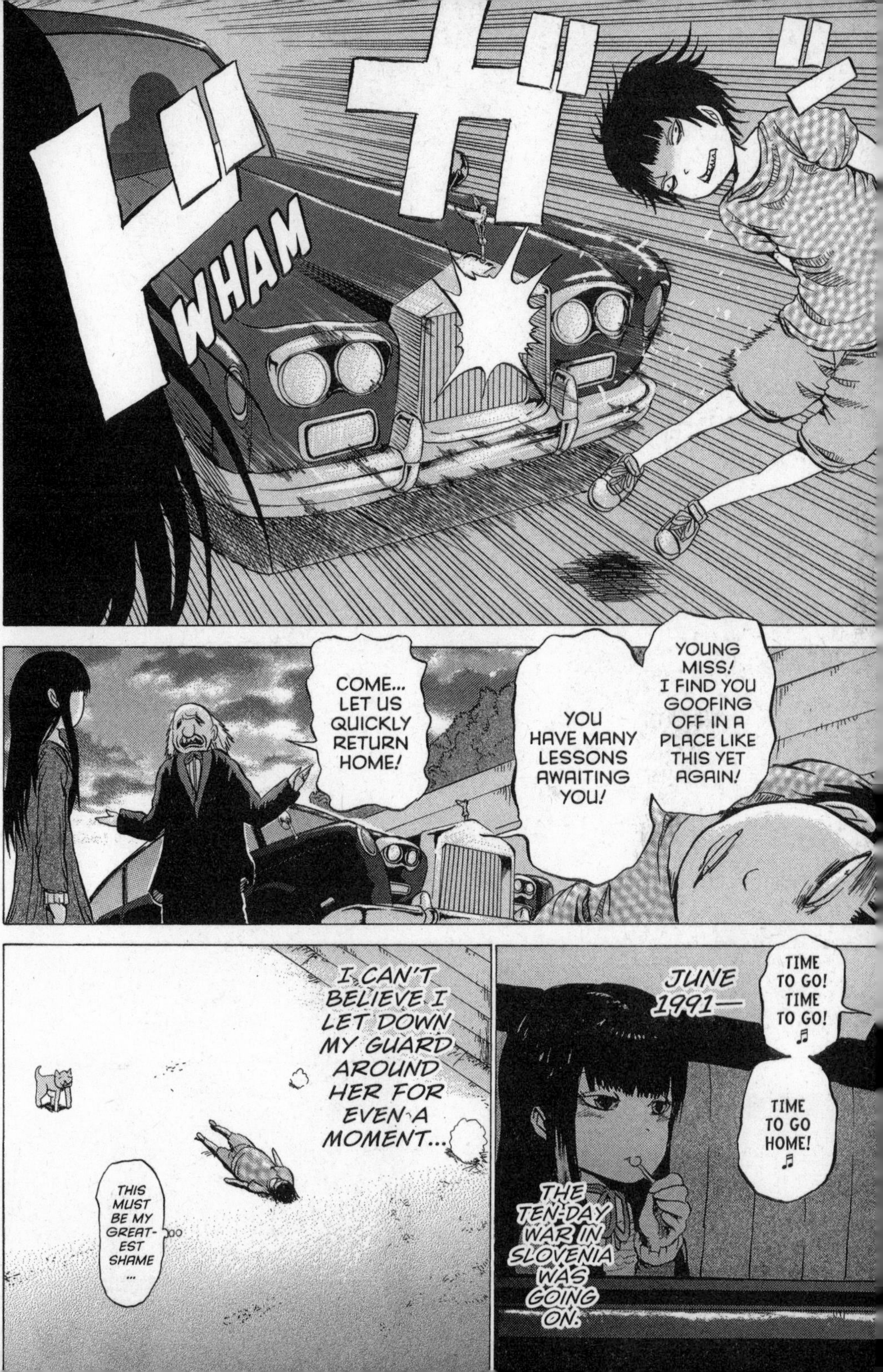
WHAM
YOUNG MISS! I FIND YOU GOOFING OFF IN A PLACE LIKE THIS YET AGAIN!
YOU HAVE MANY LESSONS AWAITING YOU!
COME... LET US QUICKLY RETURN HOME!
TIME TO GO! TIME TO GO! ♬
JUNE 1991—
TIME TO GO HOME! ♬
THE TEN-DAY WAR IN SLOVENIA WAS GOING ON.
I CAN'T BELIEVE I LET DOWN MY GUARD AROUND HER FOR EVEN A MOMENT...
THIS MUST BE MY GREAT-EST SHAME ...

HI SCORE GIRL

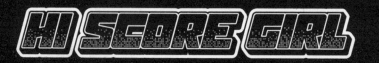

HI SCORE GIRL

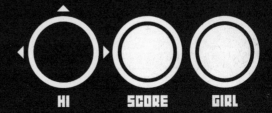

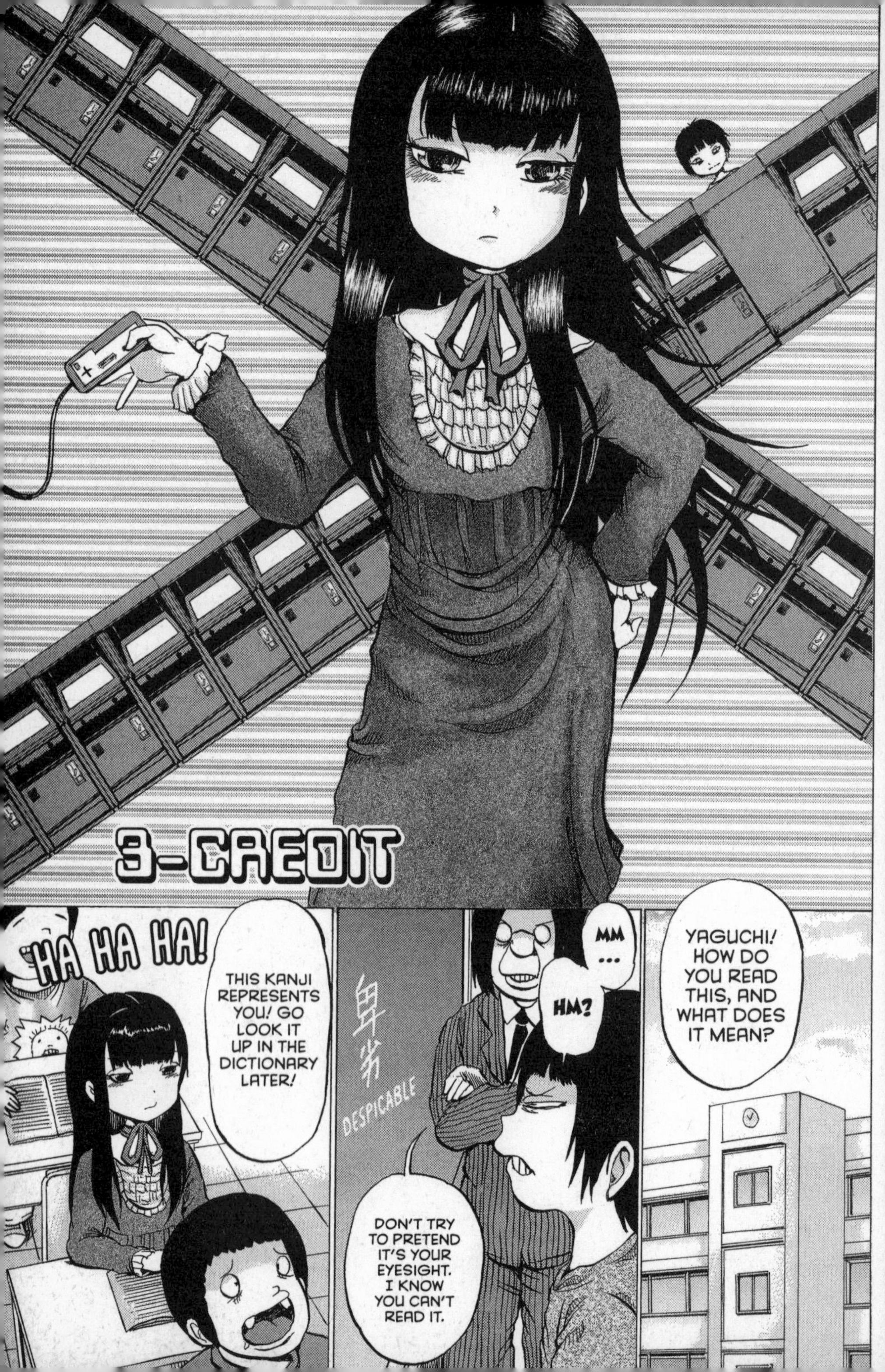
3-CREDIT
YAGUCHI! HOW DO YOU READ THIS, AND WHAT DOES IT MEAN?
MM ...
HM?
DON'T TRY TO PRETEND IT'S YOUR EYESIGHT. I KNOW YOU CAN'T READ IT.
卑劣
DESPICABLE
HA HA HA!
THIS KANJI REPRESENTS YOU! GO LOOK IT UP IN THE DICTIONARY LATER!

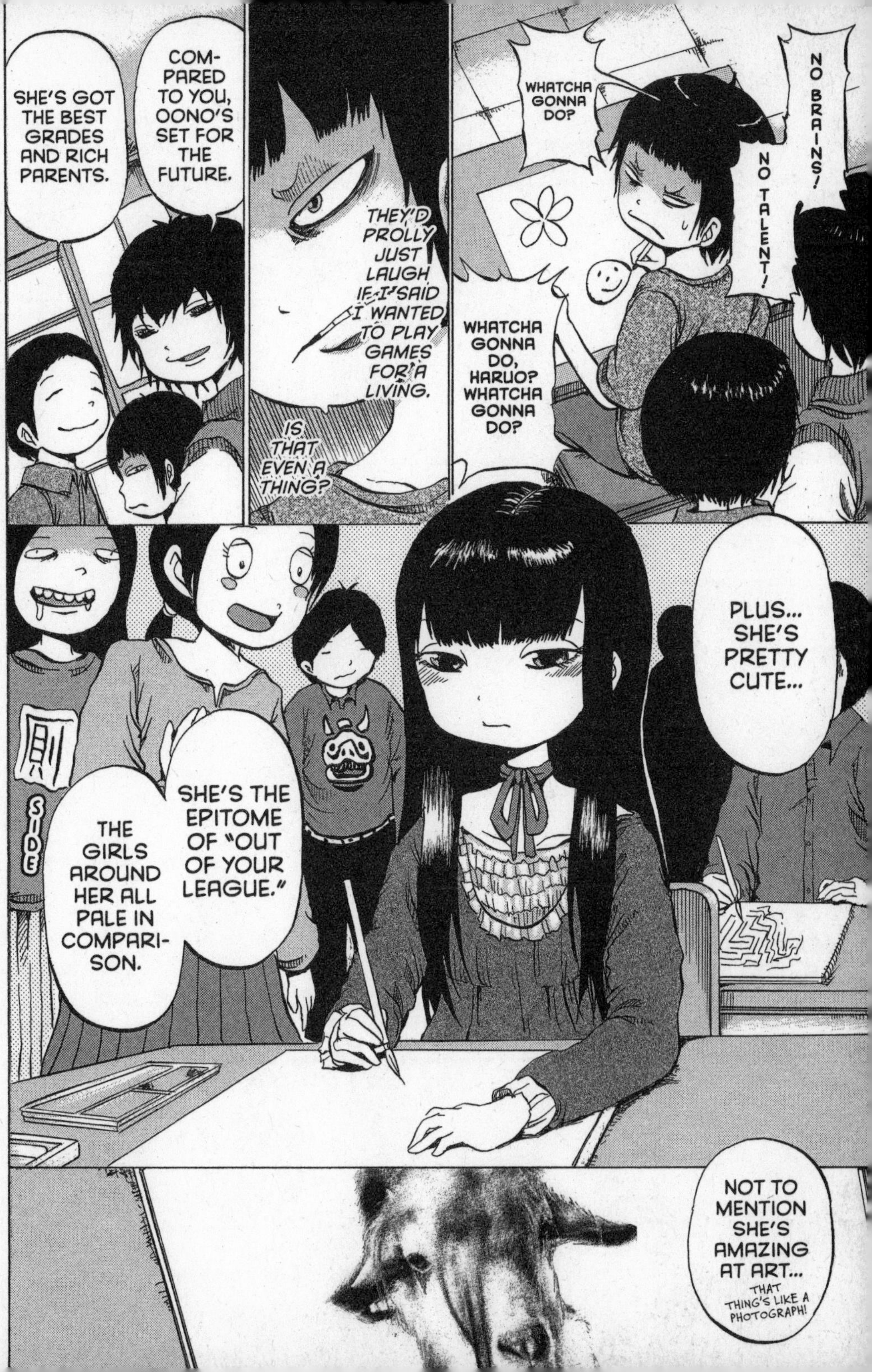
NO BRAINS!
NO TALENT!
WHATCHA GONNA DO?
WHATCHA GONNA DO, HARUO? WHATCHA GONNA DO?
THEY'D PROLLY JUST LAUGH IF I SAID I WANTED TO PLAY GAMES FOR A LIVING.
IS THAT EVEN A THING?
COMPARED TO YOU, OONO'S SET FOR THE FUTURE.
SHE'S GOT THE BEST GRADES AND RICH PARENTS.
PLUS... SHE'S PRETTY CUTE...
SHE'S THE EPITOME OF "OUT OF YOUR LEAGUE."
THE GIRLS AROUND HER ALL PALE IN COMPARISON.
SIDE
NOT TO MENTION SHE'S AMAZING AT ART...
THAT THING'S LIKE A PHOTOGRAPH!

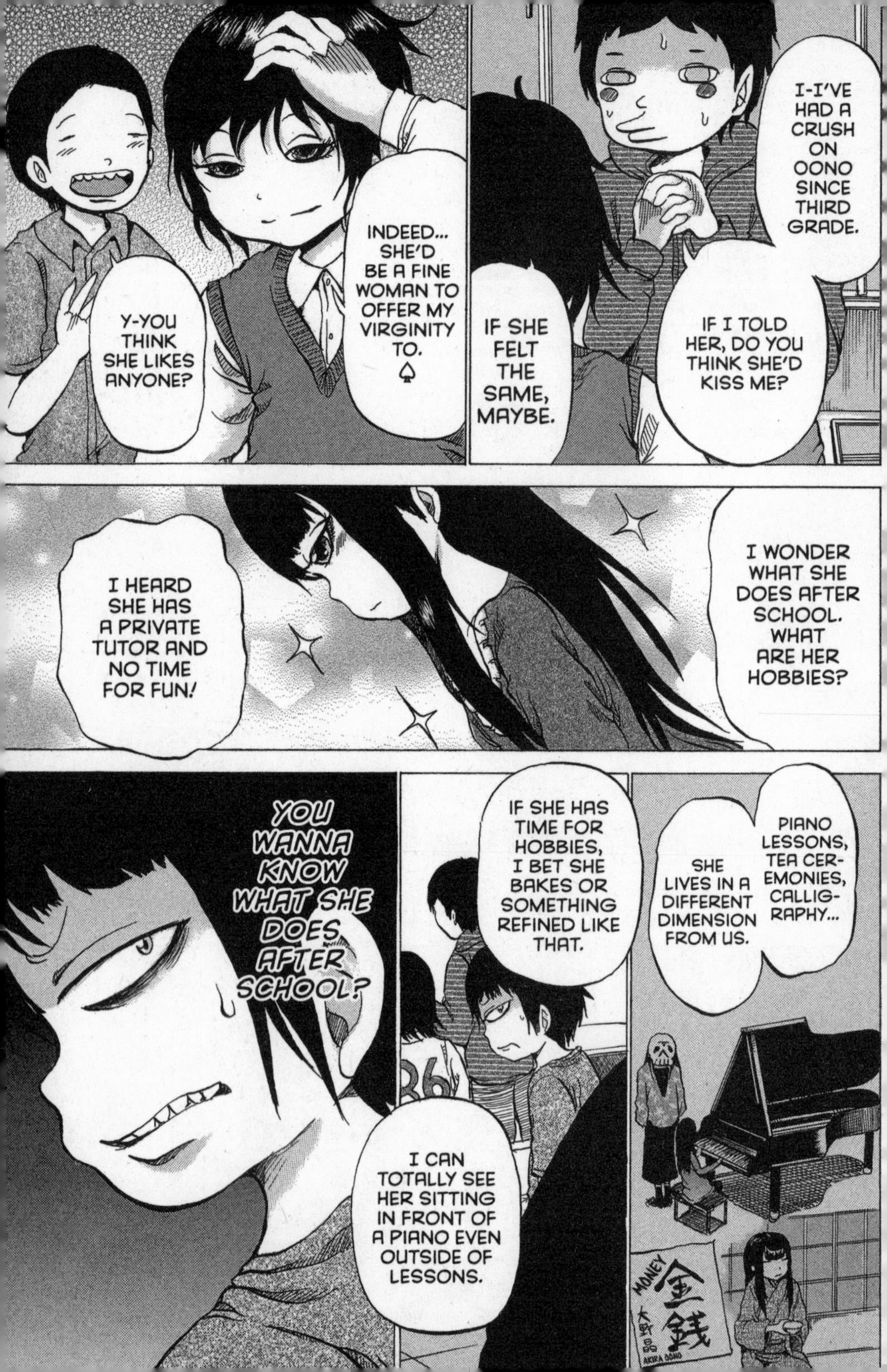
I-I'VE HAD A CRUSH ON OONO SINCE THIRD GRADE.
IF I TOLD HER, DO YOU THINK SHE'D KISS ME?
IF SHE FELT THE SAME, MAYBE.
INDEED... SHE'D BE A FINE WOMAN TO OFFER MY VIRGINITY TO. ♤
Y-YOU THINK SHE LIKES ANYONE?
I WONDER WHAT SHE DOES AFTER SCHOOL. WHAT ARE HER HOBBIES?
I HEARD SHE HAS A PRIVATE TUTOR AND NO TIME FOR FUN!
PIANO LESSONS, TEA CEREMONIES, CALLIGRAPHY...
SHE LIVES IN A DIFFERENT DIMENSION FROM US.
MONEY
金銭
大野晶
AKIRA OONO
IF SHE HAS TIME FOR HOBBIES, I BET SHE BAKES OR SOMETHING REFINED LIKE THAT.
I CAN TOTALLY SEE HER SITTING IN FRONT OF A PIANO EVEN OUTSIDE OF LESSONS.
YOU WANNA KNOW WHAT SHE DOES AFTER SCHOOL?

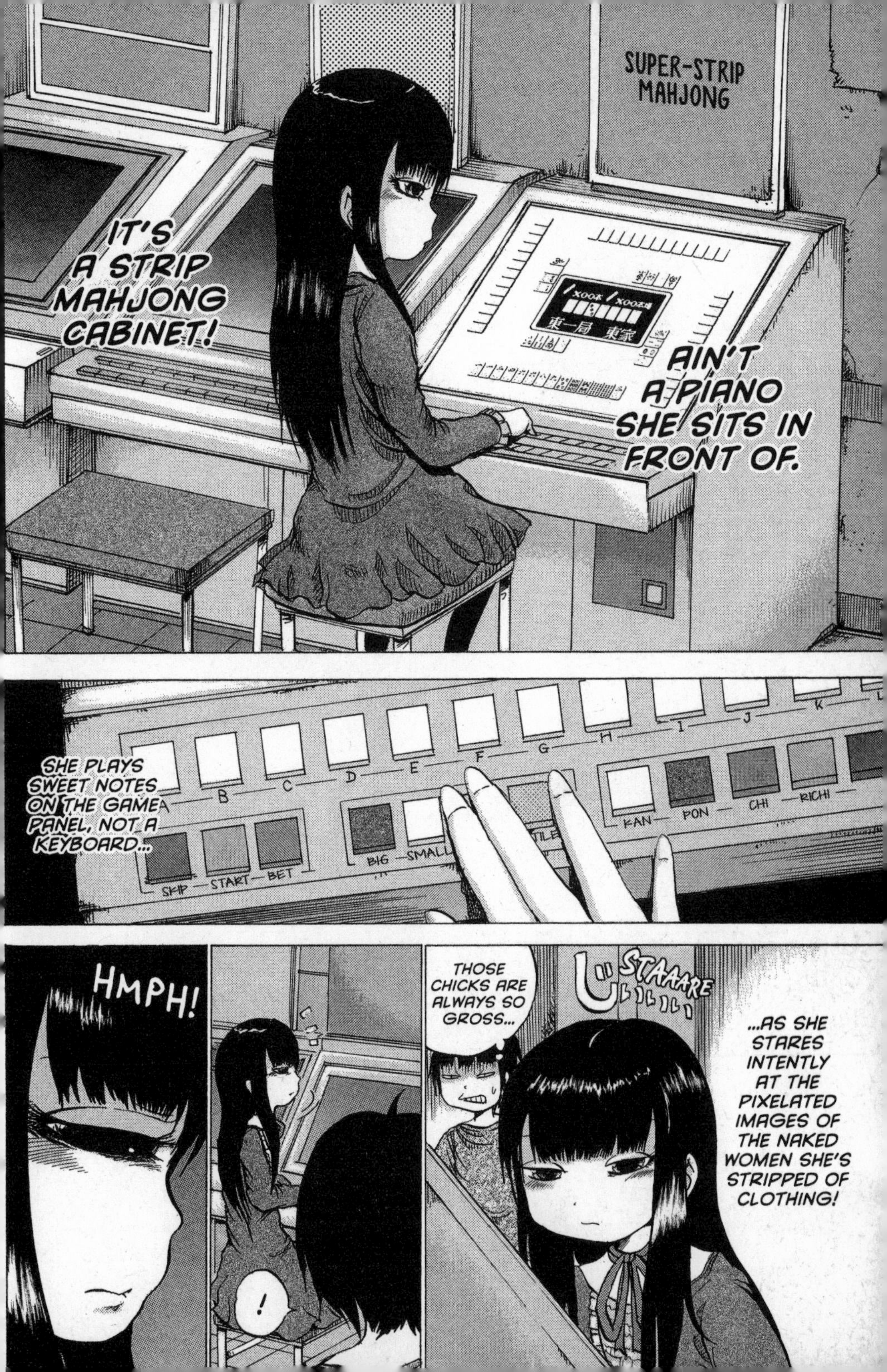
SUPER-STRIP MAHJONG
東一局 東家
AIN'T A PIANO SHE SITS IN FRONT OF.
IT'S A STRIP MAHJONG CABINET!
SHE PLAYS SWEET NOTES ON THE GAME PANEL, NOT A KEYBOARD...
A B C D E F G H I J K
KAN PON CHI RICHI
BIG SMALL
SKIP START BET
じーーー STAAARE
...AS SHE STARES INTENTLY AT THE PIXELATED IMAGES OF THE NAKED WOMEN SHE'S STRIPPED OF CLOTHING!
THOSE CHICKS ARE ALWAYS SO GROSS...
!
HMPH!

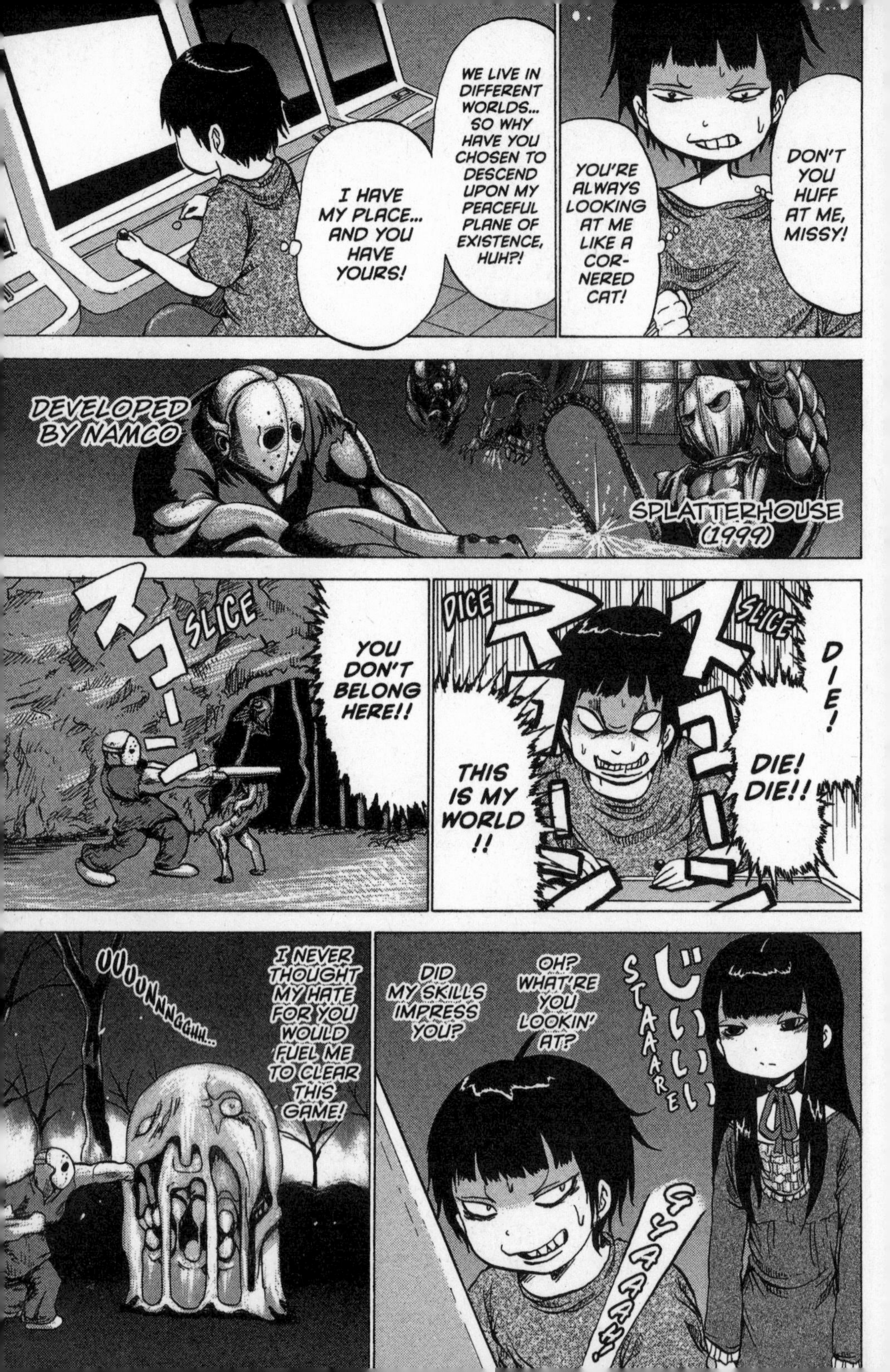

DON'T YOU HUFF AT ME, MISSY!
YOU'RE ALWAYS LOOKING AT ME LIKE A COR-NERED CAT!
WE LIVE IN DIFFERENT WORLDS... SO WHY HAVE YOU CHOSEN TO DESCEND UPON MY PEACEFUL PLANE OF EXISTENCE, HUH?!
I HAVE MY PLACE... AND YOU HAVE YOURS!
DEVELOPED BY NAMCO
SPLATTERHOUSE (1999)
DICE
SLICE
DIE!
DIE! DIE!!
THIS IS MY WORLD!!
SLICE
YOU DON'T BELONG HERE!!
STAAARE
OH? WHAT'RE YOU LOOKIN' AT?
DID MY SKILLS IMPRESS YOU?
GYAAAH!
I NEVER THOUGHT MY HATE FOR YOU WOULD FUEL ME TO CLEAR THIS GAME!
UUUUNNNGGHH...

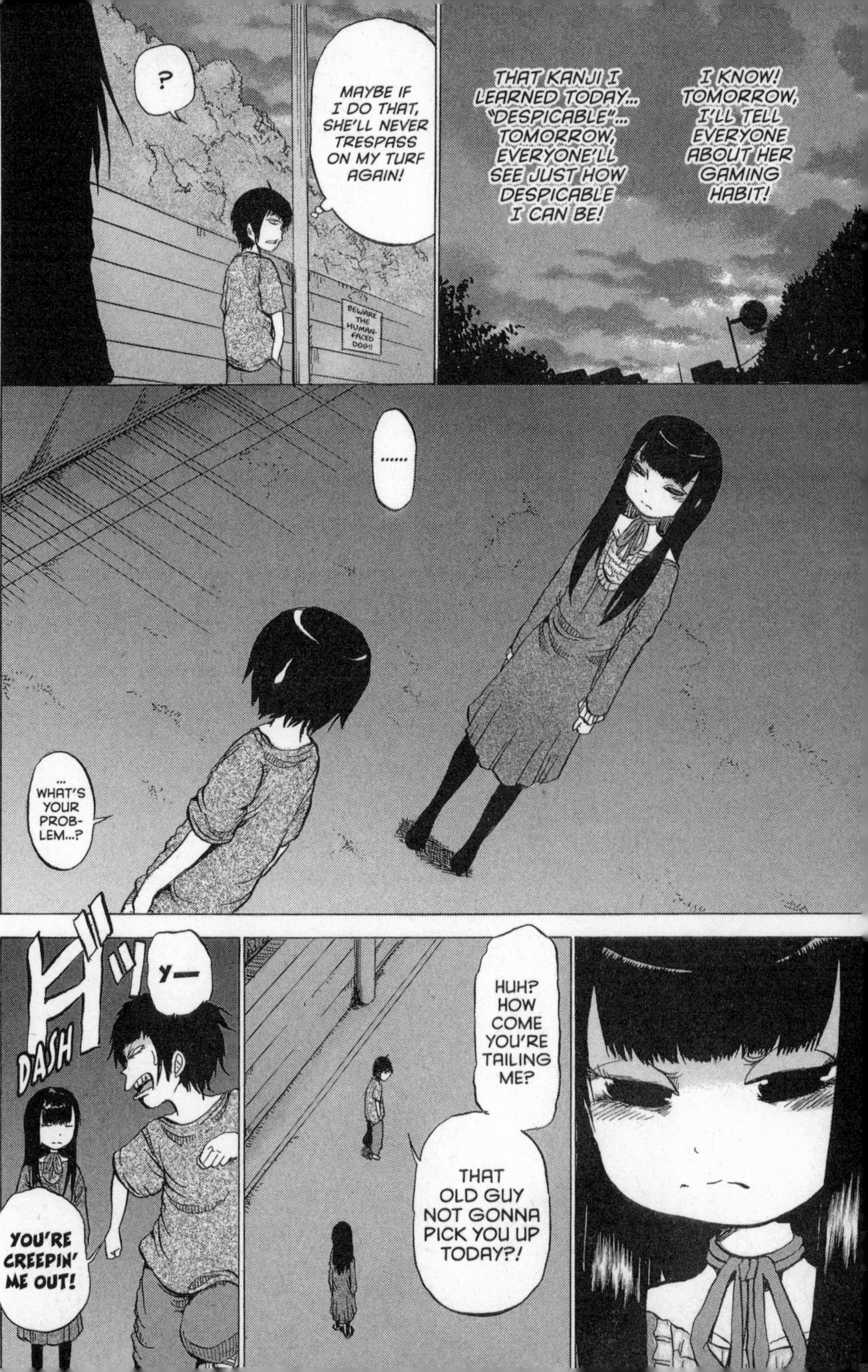
I KNOW! TOMORROW, I'LL TELL EVERYONE ABOUT HER GAMING HABIT!
THAT KANJI I LEARNED TODAY... "DESPICABLE"... TOMORROW, EVERYONE'LL SEE JUST HOW DESPICABLE I CAN BE!
MAYBE IF I DO THAT, SHE'LL NEVER TRESPASS ON MY TURF AGAIN!
BEWARE THE HUMAN-FACED DOG!!
?
......
...WHAT'S YOUR PROB-LEM...?
HUH? HOW COME YOU'RE TAILING ME?
THAT OLD GUY NOT GONNA PICK YOU UP TODAY?!
Y—
DASH
YOU'RE CREEPIN' ME OUT!

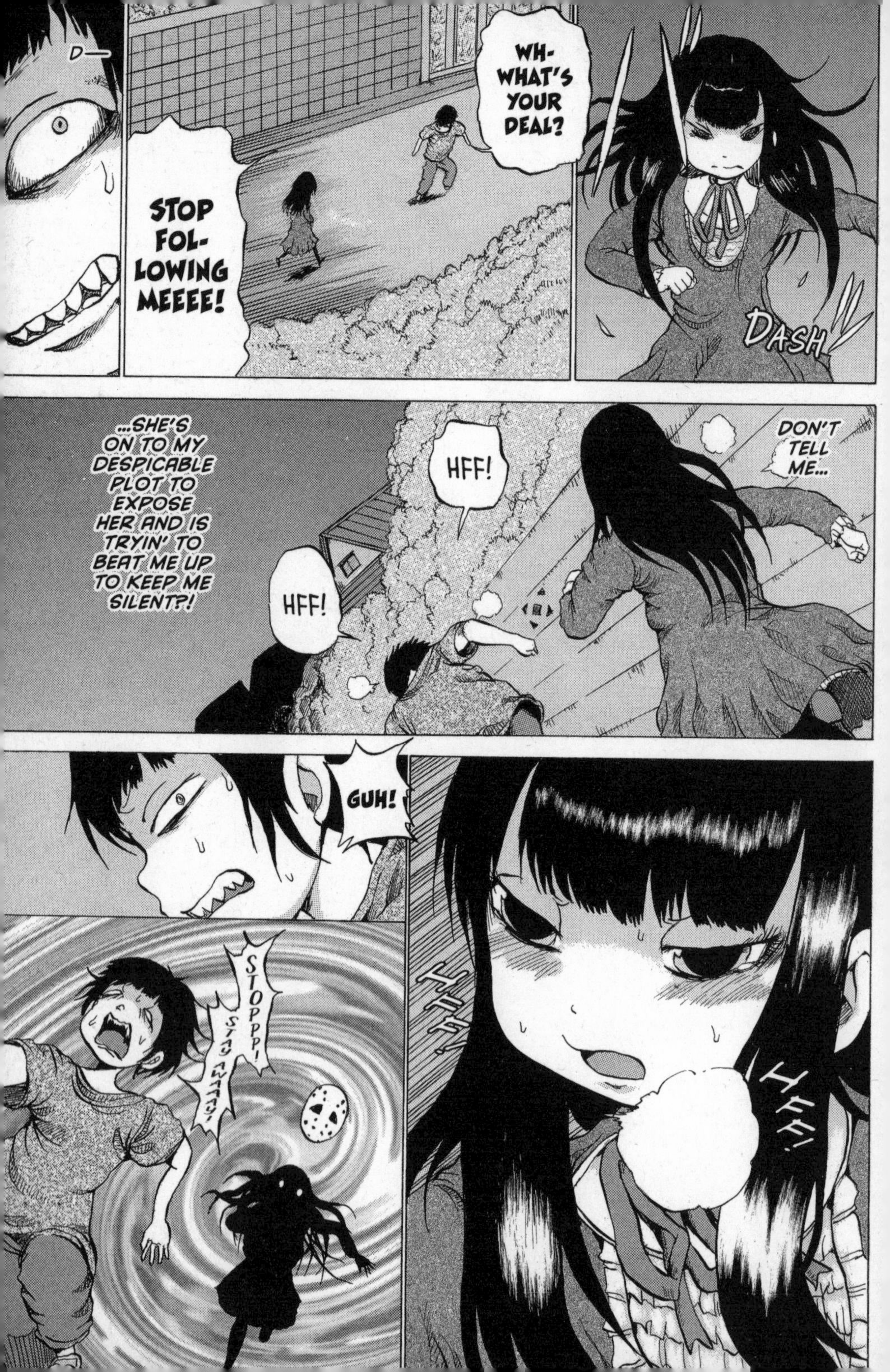
WH-WHAT'S YOUR DEAL?
DASH
STOP FOL-LOWING MEEEE!
D—
DON'T TELL ME...
HFF!
HFF!
...SHE'S ON TO MY DESPICABLE PLOT TO EXPOSE HER AND IS TRYIN' TO BEAT ME UP TO KEEP ME SILENT?!
HFF!
HFF!
GUH!
STOPPP!
STAY AWAAAY!

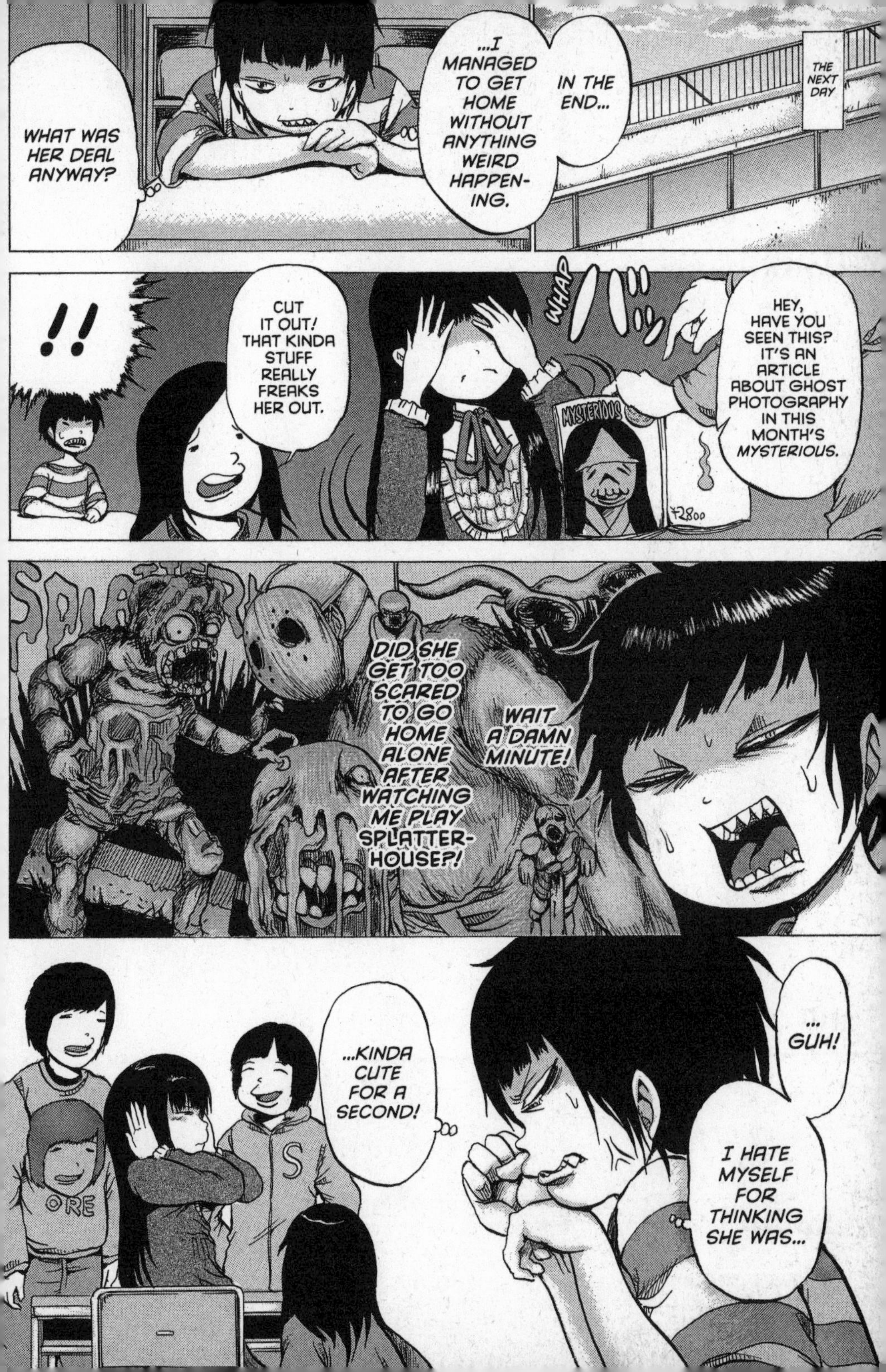
THE NEXT DAY
IN THE END...
...I MANAGED TO GET HOME WITHOUT ANYTHING WEIRD HAPPEN-ING.
WHAT WAS HER DEAL ANYWAY?
HEY, HAVE YOU SEEN THIS? IT'S AN ARTICLE ABOUT GHOST PHOTOGRAPHY IN THIS MONTH'S *MYSTERIOUS*.
MYSTERIOUS
WHAP
CUT IT OUT! THAT KINDA STUFF REALLY FREAKS HER OUT.
!!
WAIT A DAMN MINUTE!
DID SHE GET TOO SCARED TO GO HOME ALONE AFTER WATCHING ME PLAY SPLATTER-HOUSE?!
... GUH!
I HATE MYSELF FOR THINKING SHE WAS...
...KINDA CUTE FOR A SECOND!
S
ORE

HI SCORE GIRL

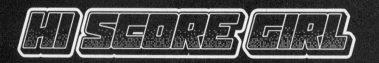

HI SCORE GIRL

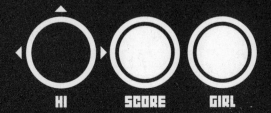

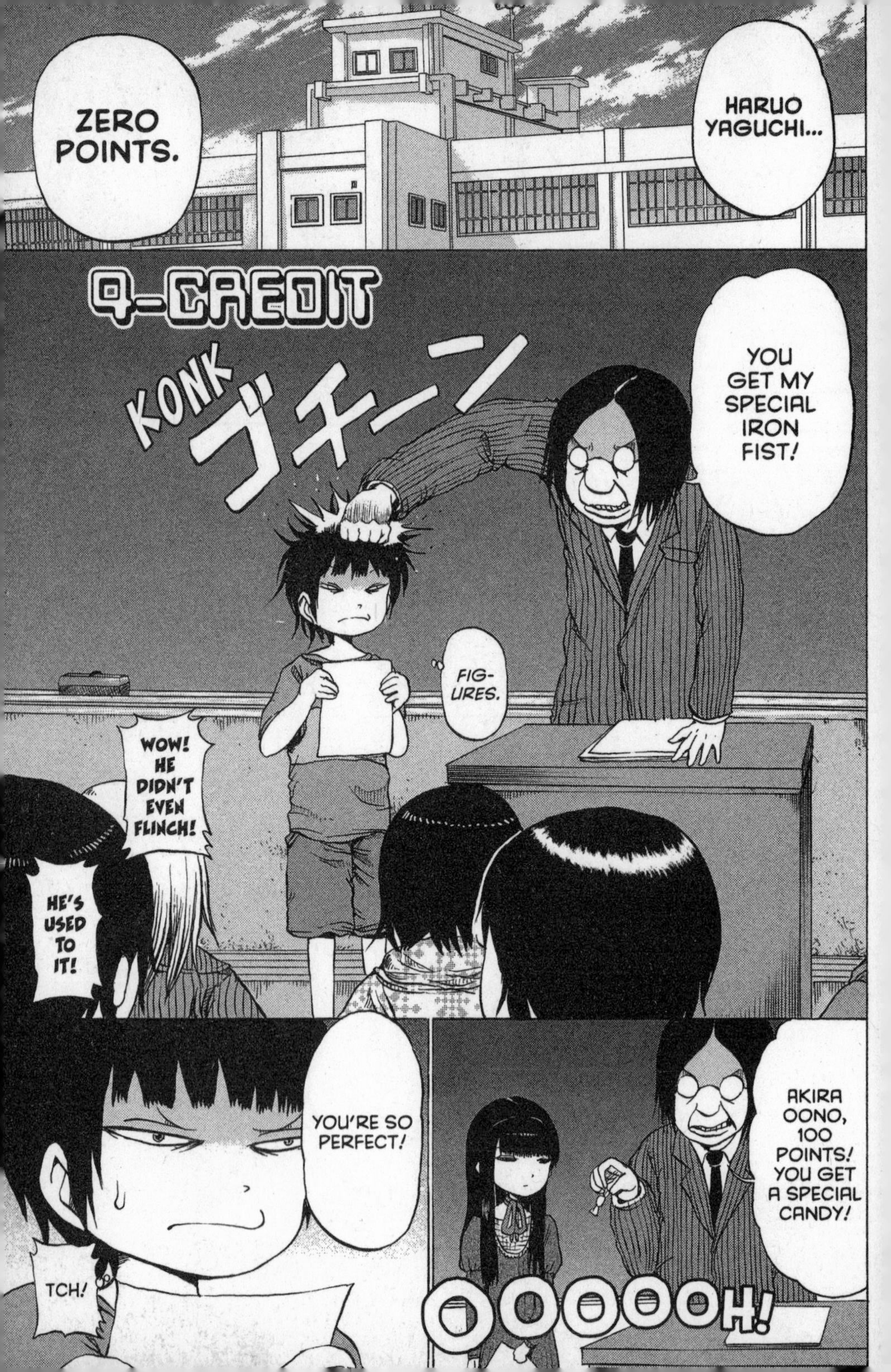
HARUO YAGUCHI...
ZERO POINTS.
9-CREDIT
YOU GET MY SPECIAL IRON FIST!
KONK
ゴチーン
FIG-URES.
WOW! HE DIDN'T EVEN FLINCH!
HE'S USED TO IT!
AKIRA OONO, 100 POINTS! YOU GET A SPECIAL CANDY!
OOOOOH!
YOU'RE SO PERFECT!
TCH!

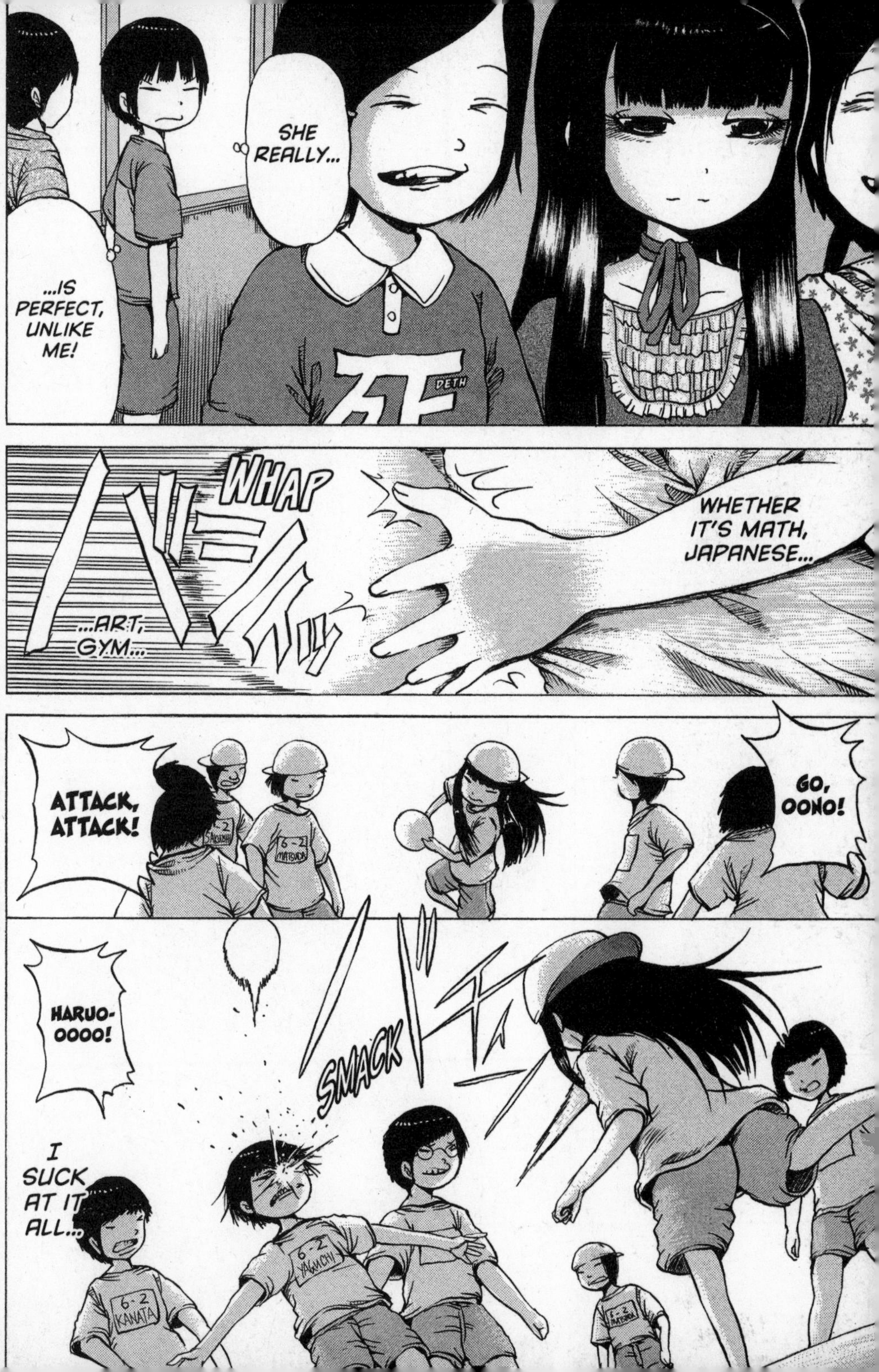
SHE REALLY...
...IS PERFECT, UNLIKE ME!
WHETHER IT'S MATH, JAPANESE...
WHAP
...ART, GYM...
GO, OONO!
ATTACK, ATTACK!
SMACK
HARUO-OOOO!
I SUCK AT IT ALL...

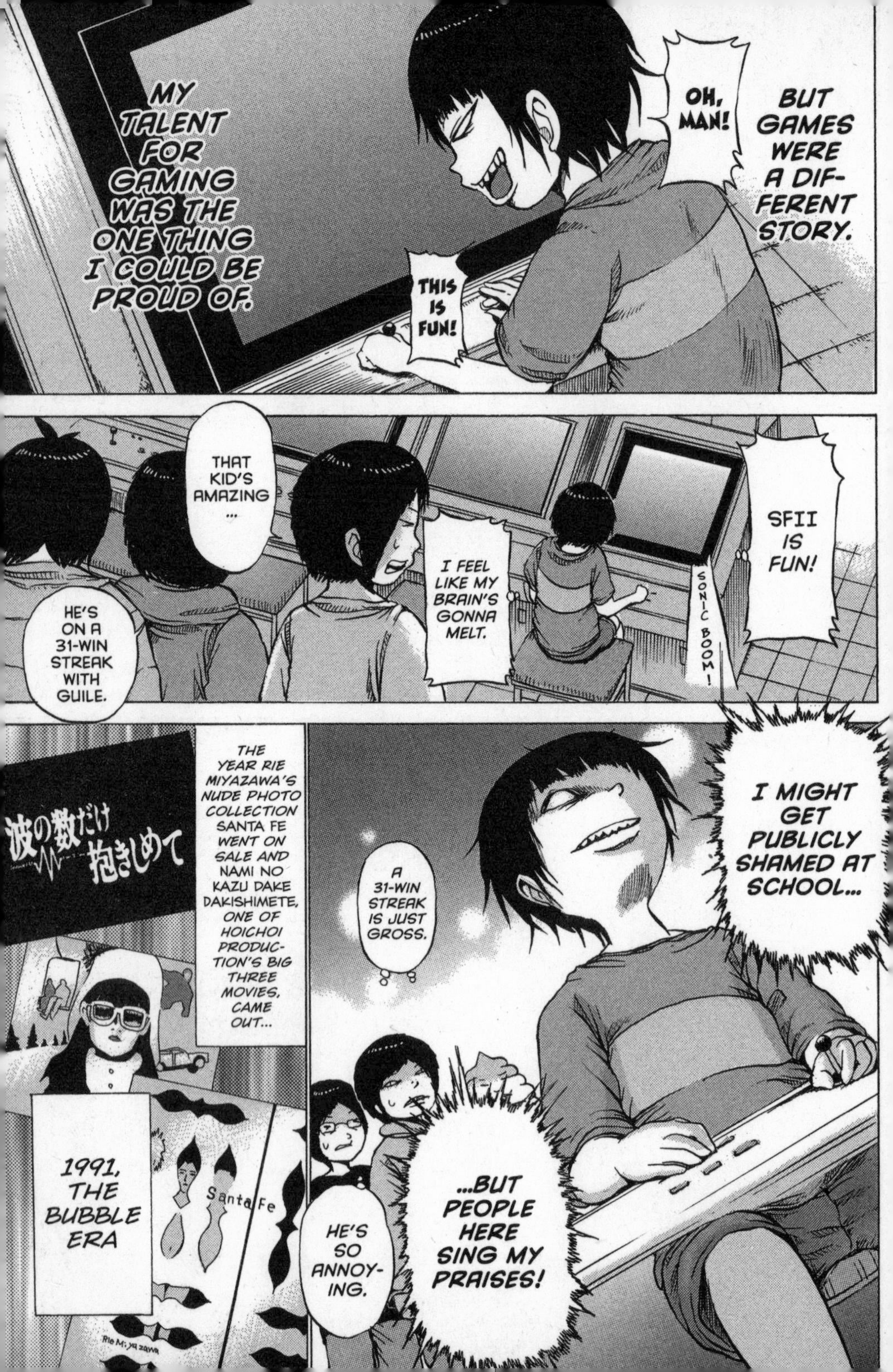
BUT GAMES WERE A DIF-FERENT STORY.
OH, MAN!
THIS IS FUN!
MY TALENT FOR GAMING WAS THE ONE THING I COULD BE PROUD OF.
SFII IS FUN!
SONIC BOOM!
I FEEL LIKE MY BRAIN'S GONNA MELT.
THAT KID'S AMAZING...
HE'S ON A 31-WIN STREAK WITH GUILE.
I MIGHT GET PUBLICLY SHAMED AT SCHOOL...
A 31-WIN STREAK IS JUST GROSS.
...BUT PEOPLE HERE SING MY PRAISES!
HE'S SO ANNOY-ING.
THE YEAR RIE MIYAZAWA'S NUDE PHOTO COLLECTION SANTA FE WENT ON SALE AND NAMI NO KAZU DAKE DAKISHIMETE, ONE OF HOICHOI PRODUC-TION'S BIG THREE MOVIES, CAME OUT...
波の数だけ抱きしめて
Santa Fe
1991, THE BUBBLE ERA
Rie Miyazawa

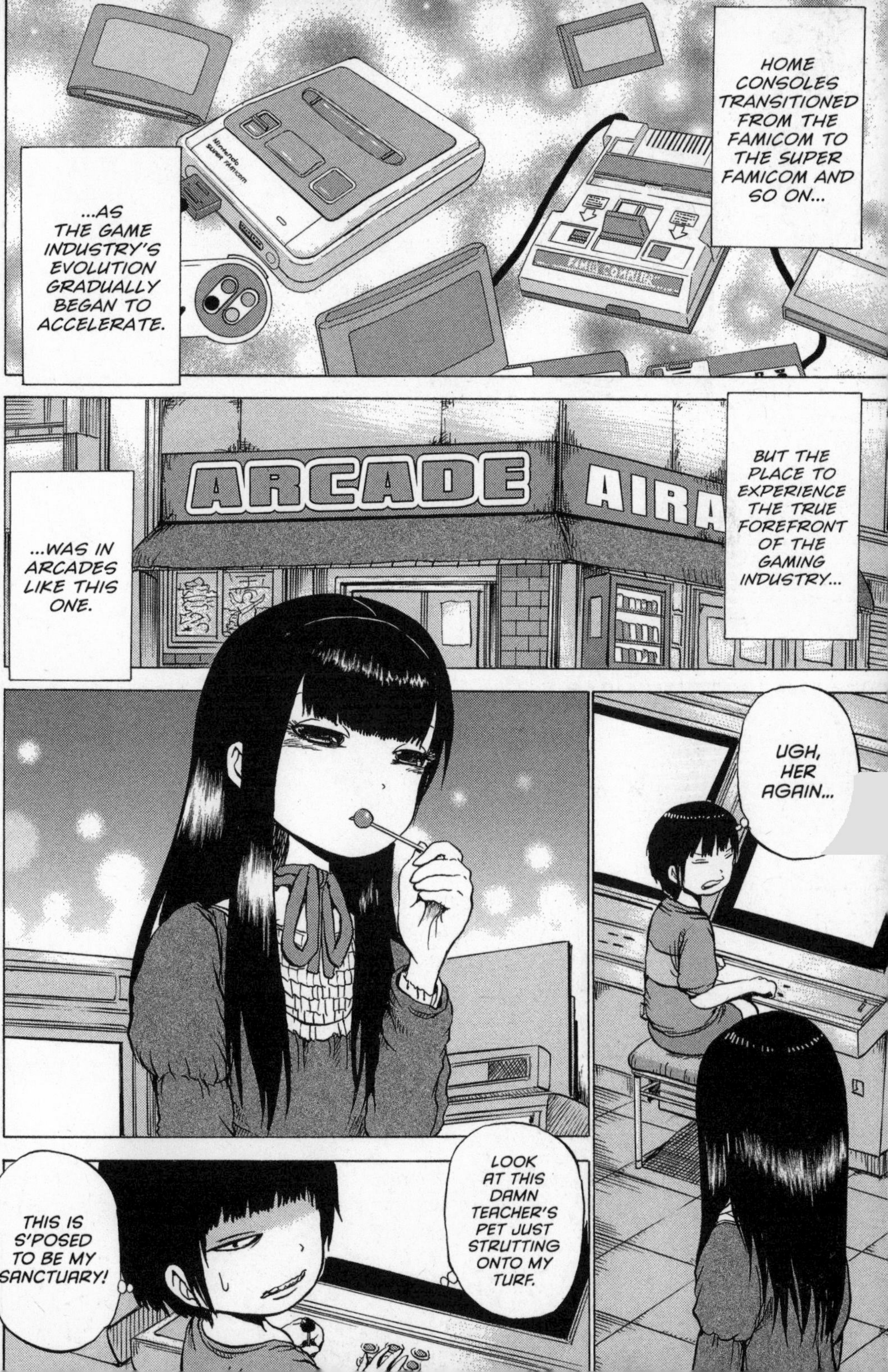
HOME CONSOLES TRANSITIONED FROM THE FAMICOM TO THE SUPER FAMICOM AND SO ON...
...AS THE GAME INDUSTRY'S EVOLUTION GRADUALLY BEGAN TO ACCELERATE.
BUT THE PLACE TO EXPERIENCE THE TRUE FOREFRONT OF THE GAMING INDUSTRY...
ARCADE
AIRA
...WAS IN ARCADES LIKE THIS ONE.
UGH, HER AGAIN...
LOOK AT THIS DAMN TEACHER'S PET JUST STRUTTING ONTO MY TURF.
THIS IS S'POSED TO BE MY SANCTUARY!

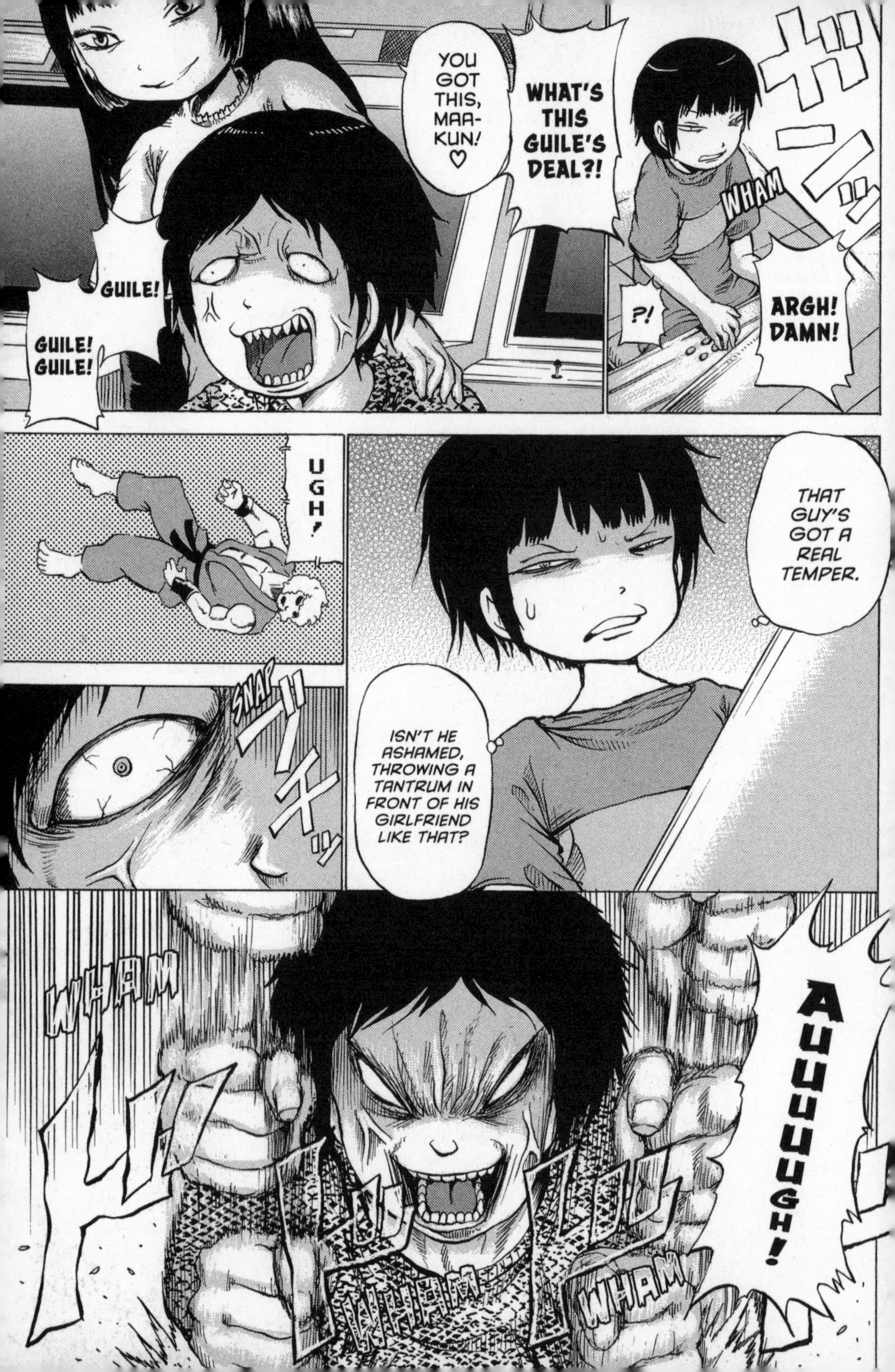
ARGH! DAMN!
WHAM
?!
WHAT'S THIS GUILE'S DEAL?!
YOU GOT THIS, MAA-KUN! ♡
GUILE!
GUILE! GUILE!
THAT GUY'S GOT A REAL TEMPER.
ISN'T HE ASHAMED, THROWING A TANTRUM IN FRONT OF HIS GIRLFRIEND LIKE THAT?
UGH!
SNAP
AUUUUUGH!
WHAM
WHAM
WHAM

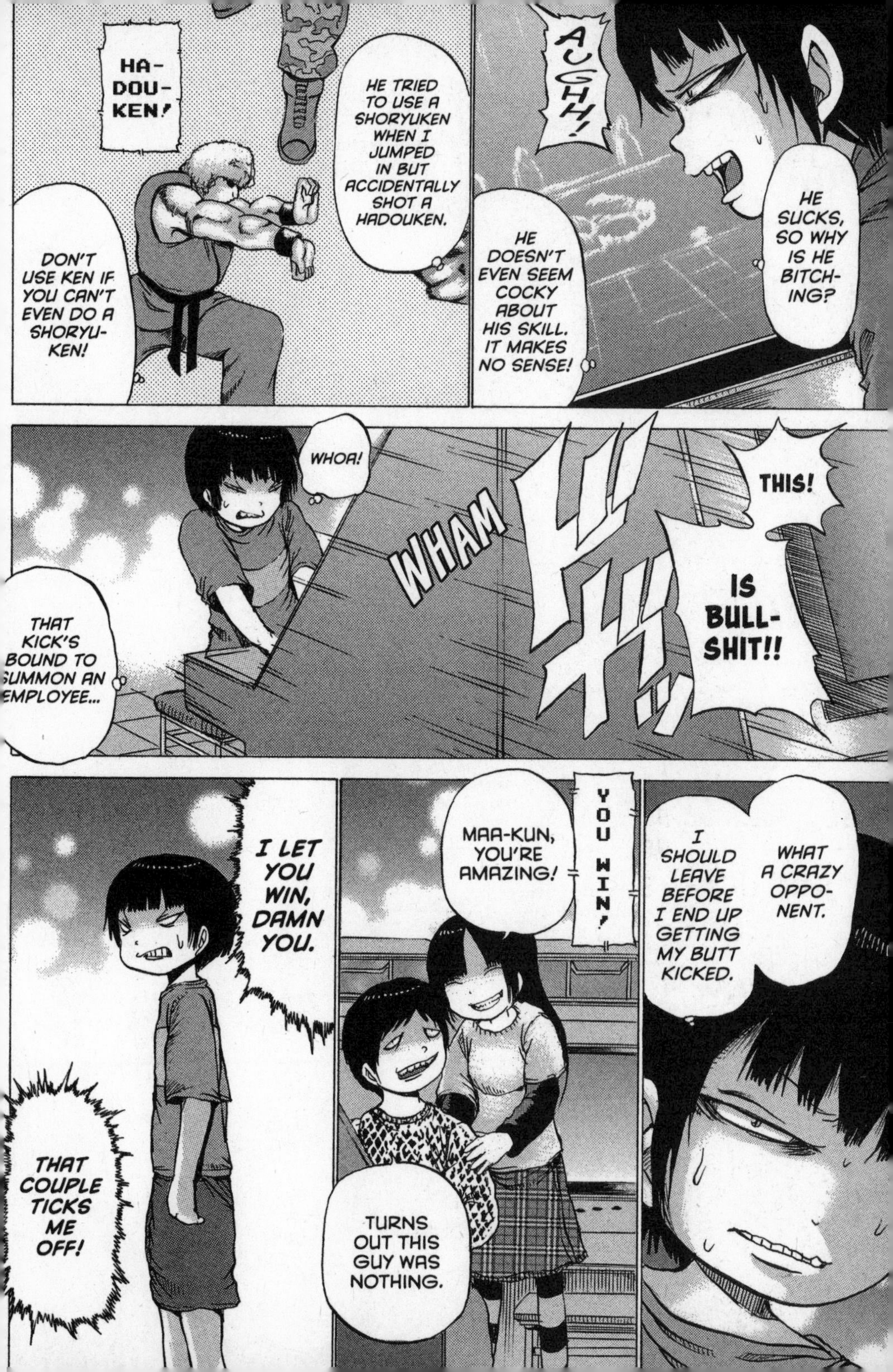

AUGHH!
HE SUCKS, SO WHY IS HE BITCHING?
HE DOESN'T EVEN SEEM COCKY ABOUT HIS SKILL. IT MAKES NO SENSE!
HE TRIED TO USE A SHORYUKEN WHEN I JUMPED IN BUT ACCIDENTALLY SHOT A HADOUKEN.
HA-DOU-KEN!
DON'T USE KEN IF YOU CAN'T EVEN DO A SHORYU-KEN!
THIS! IS BULL-SHIT!!
WHAM
WHOA!
THAT KICK'S BOUND TO SUMMON AN EMPLOYEE...
WHAT A CRAZY OPPO-NENT.
I SHOULD LEAVE BEFORE I END UP GETTING MY BUTT KICKED.
YOU WIN!
MAA-KUN, YOU'RE AMAZING!
TURNS OUT THIS GUY WAS NOTHING.
I LET YOU WIN, DAMN YOU.
THAT COUPLE TICKS ME OFF!

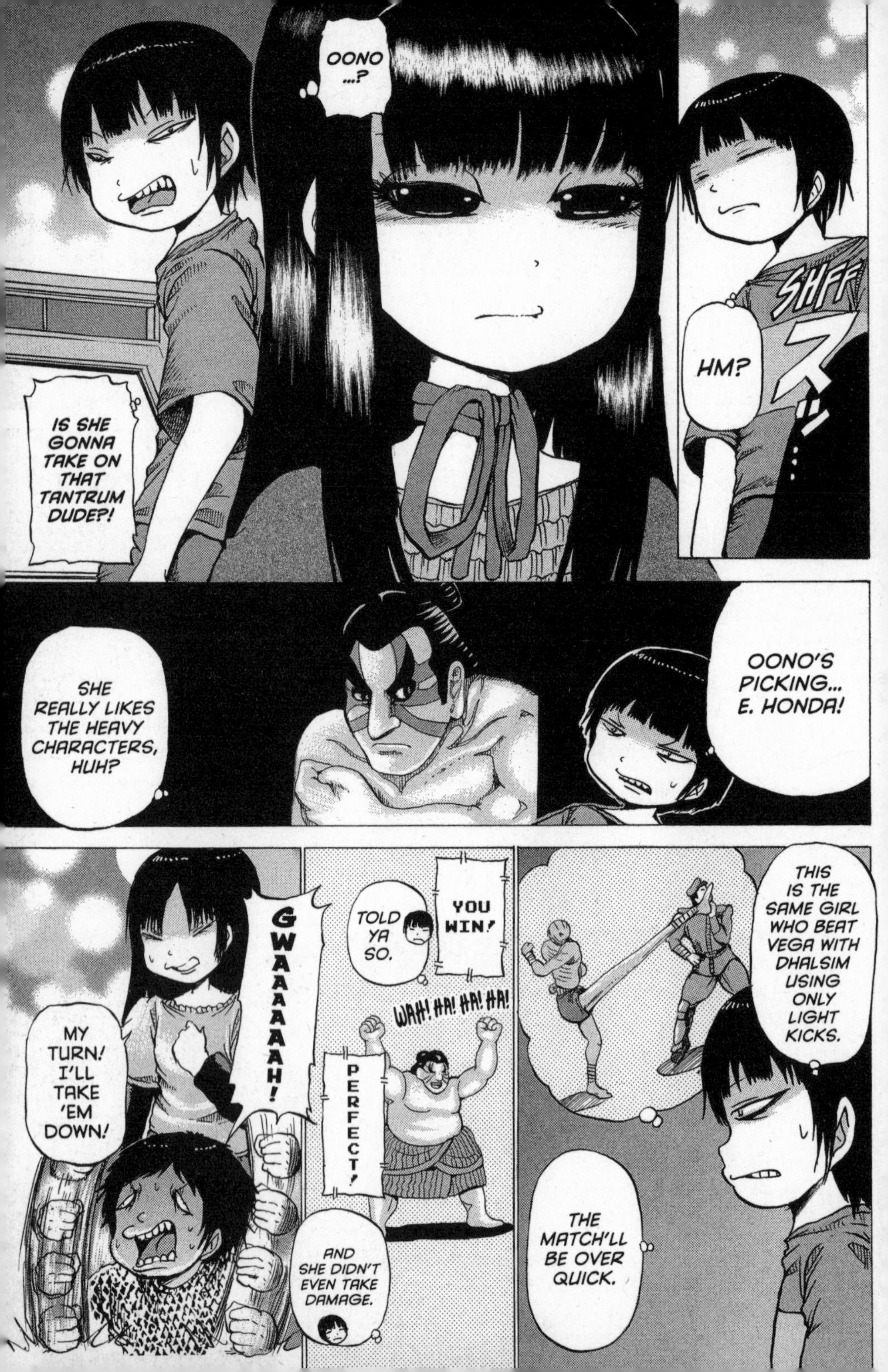
SHFF
HM?
OONO ...?
IS SHE GONNA TAKE ON THAT TANTRUM DUDE?!
OONO'S PICKING... E. HONDA!
SHE REALLY LIKES THE HEAVY CHARACTERS, HUH?
THIS IS THE SAME GIRL WHO BEAT VEGA WITH DHALSIM USING ONLY LIGHT KICKS.
THE MATCH'LL BE OVER QUICK.
YOU WIN!
TOLD YA SO.
WAH! HA! HA! HA!
PERFECT!
AND SHE DIDN'T EVEN TAKE DAMAGE.
GWAAAAAAH!
MY TURN! I'LL TAKE 'EM DOWN!

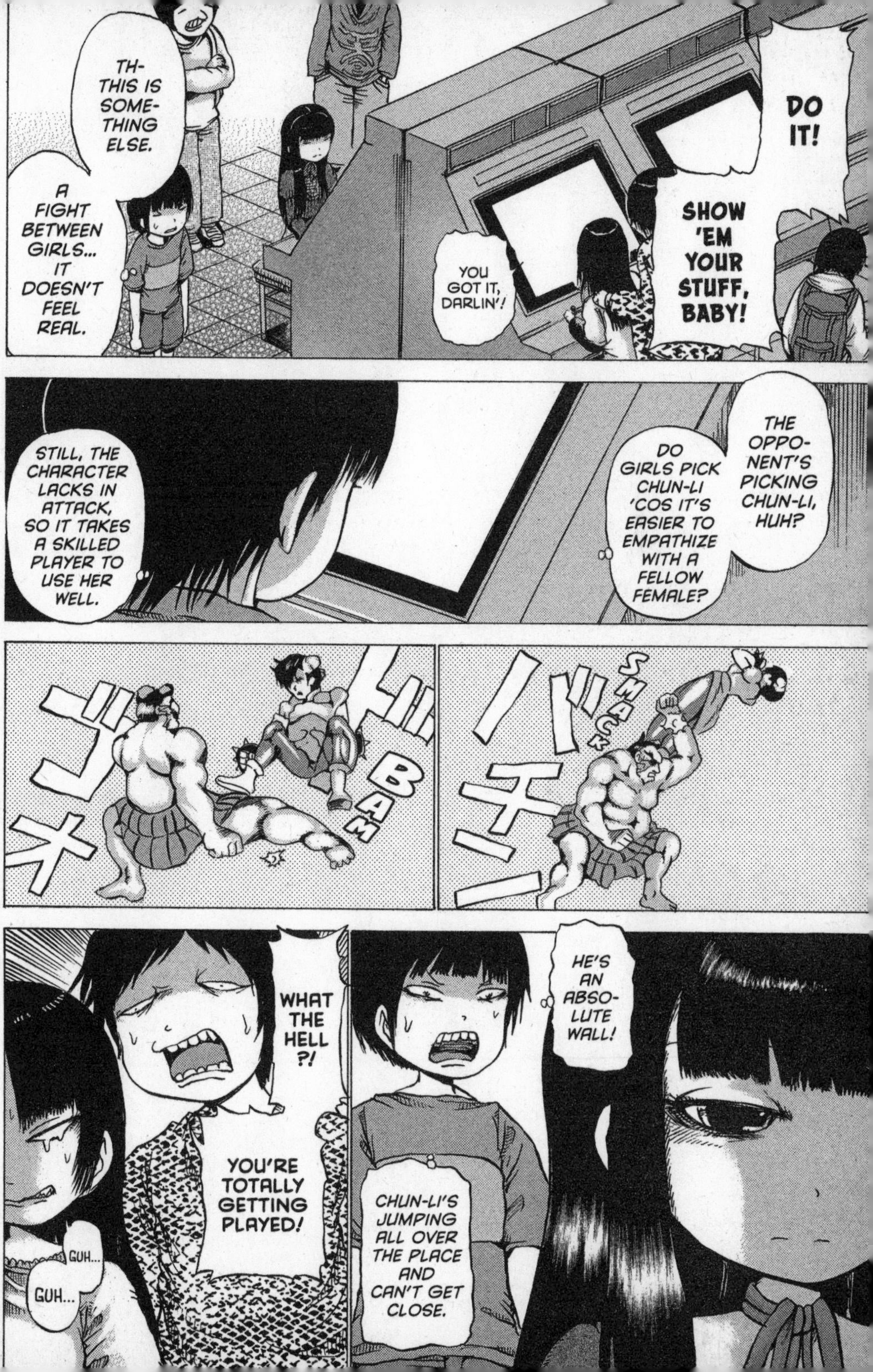
DO IT!
SHOW 'EM YOUR STUFF, BABY!
YOU GOT IT, DARLIN'!
TH- THIS IS SOME-THING ELSE.
A FIGHT BETWEEN GIRLS... IT DOESN'T FEEL REAL.
THE OPPO-NENT'S PICKING CHUN-LI, HUH?
DO GIRLS PICK CHUN-LI 'COS IT'S EASIER TO EMPATHIZE WITH A FELLOW FEMALE?
STILL, THE CHARACTER LACKS IN ATTACK, SO IT TAKES A SKILLED PLAYER TO USE HER WELL.
SMACK
BAM
HE'S AN ABSO-LUTE WALL!
CHUN-LI'S JUMPING ALL OVER THE PLACE AND CAN'T GET CLOSE.
WHAT THE HELL ?!
YOU'RE TOTALLY GETTING PLAYED!
GUH...
GUH...

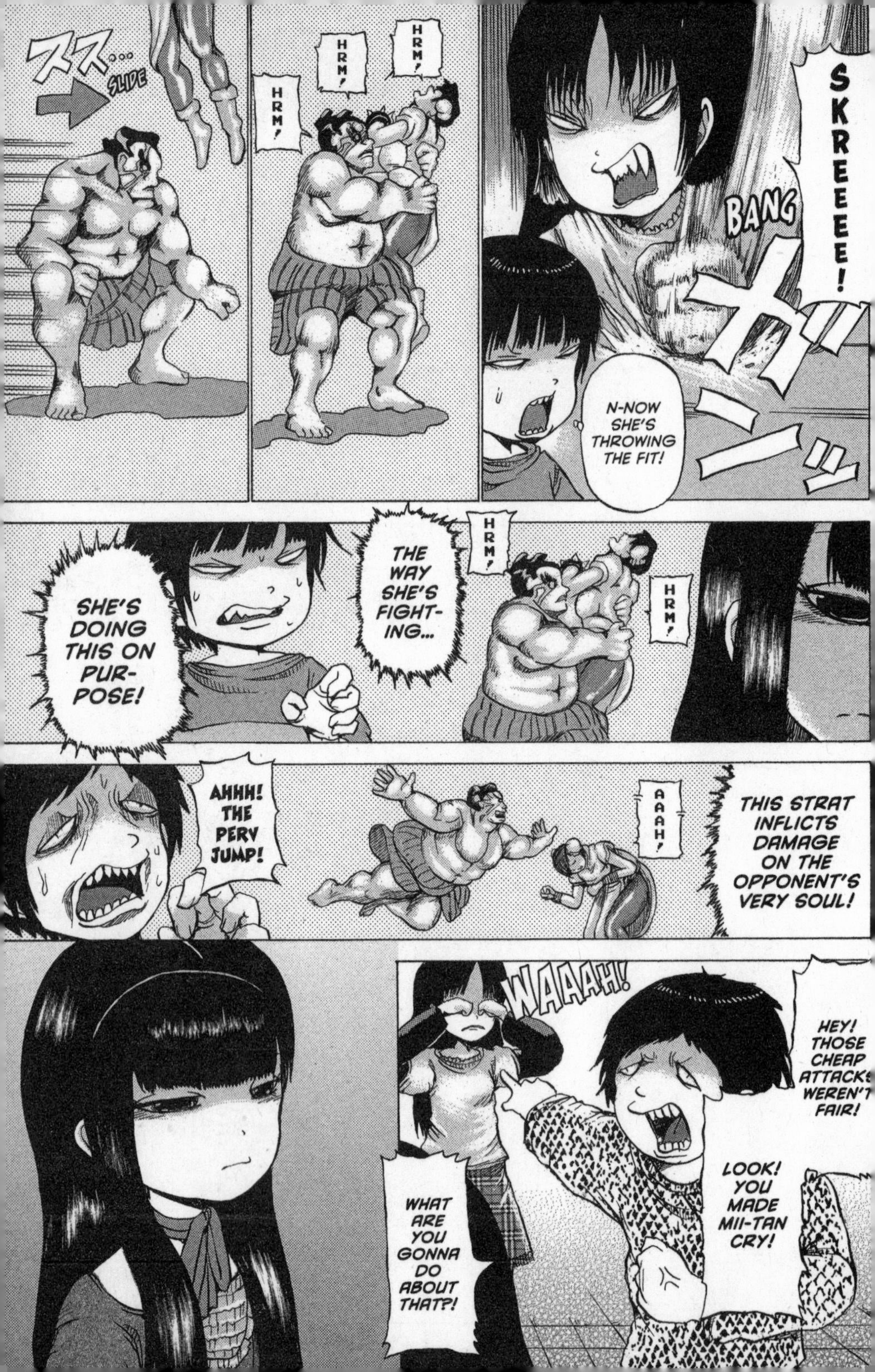
SKREEEEE!
BANG
N-NOW SHE'S THROWING THE FIT!
HRM!
HRM!
HRM!
スス...
SLIDE
HRM!
HRM!
THE WAY SHE'S FIGHT-ING...
SHE'S DOING THIS ON PUR-POSE!
THIS STRAT INFLICTS DAMAGE ON THE OPPONENT'S VERY SOUL!
AAAH!
AHHH! THE PERV JUMP!
WAAAH!
HEY! THOSE CHEAP ATTACKS WEREN'T FAIR!
LOOK! YOU MADE MII-TAN CRY!
WHAT ARE YOU GONNA DO ABOUT THAT?!

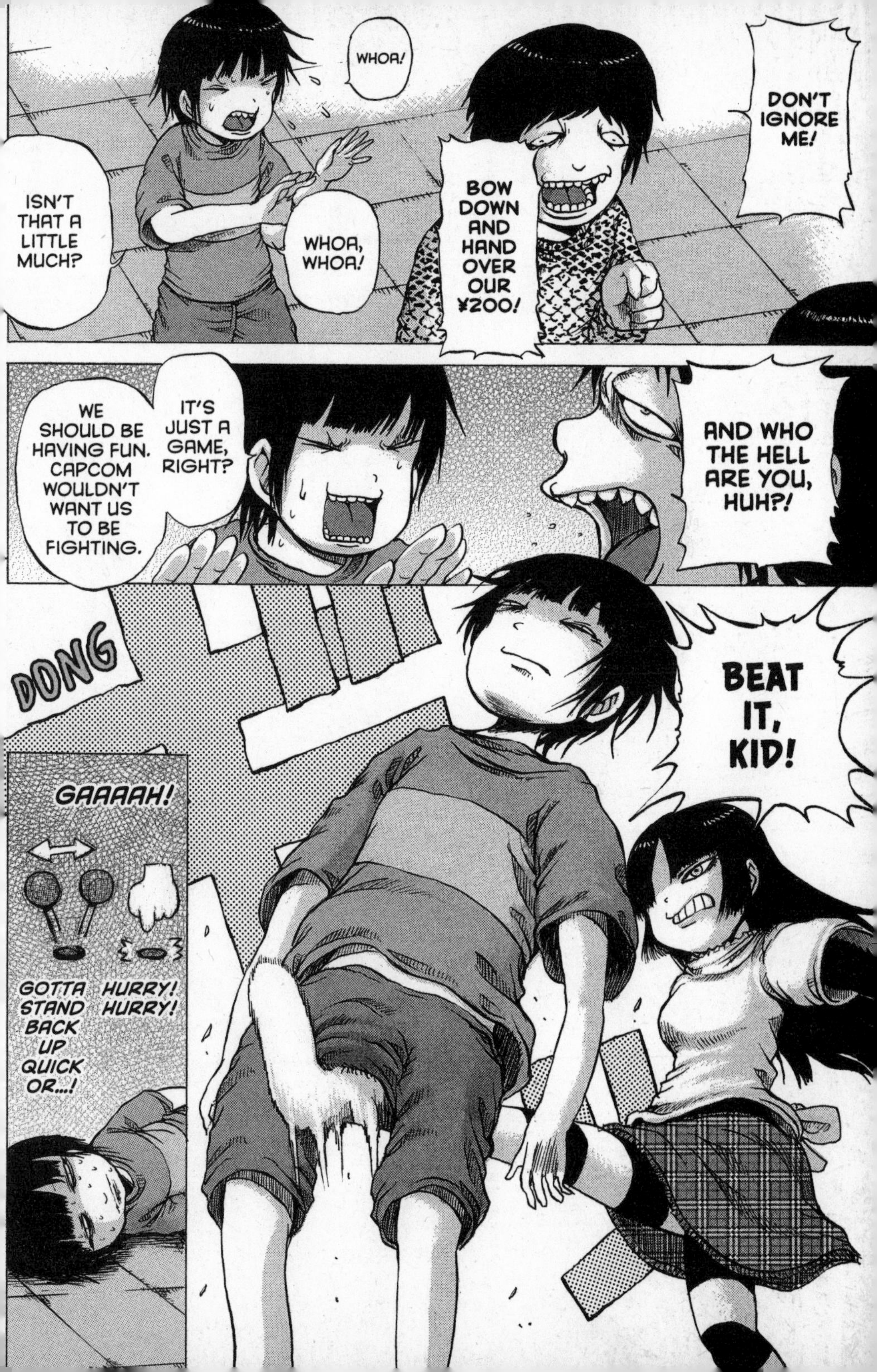
DON'T IGNORE ME!
BOW DOWN AND HAND OVER OUR ¥200!
WHOA!
WHOA, WHOA!
ISN'T THAT A LITTLE MUCH?
AND WHO THE HELL ARE YOU, HUH?!
IT'S JUST A GAME, RIGHT?
WE SHOULD BE HAVING FUN. CAPCOM WOULDN'T WANT US TO BE FIGHTING.
BEAT IT, KID!
DONG
GAAAAH!
HURRY! HURRY!
GOTTA STAND BACK UP QUICK OR...!

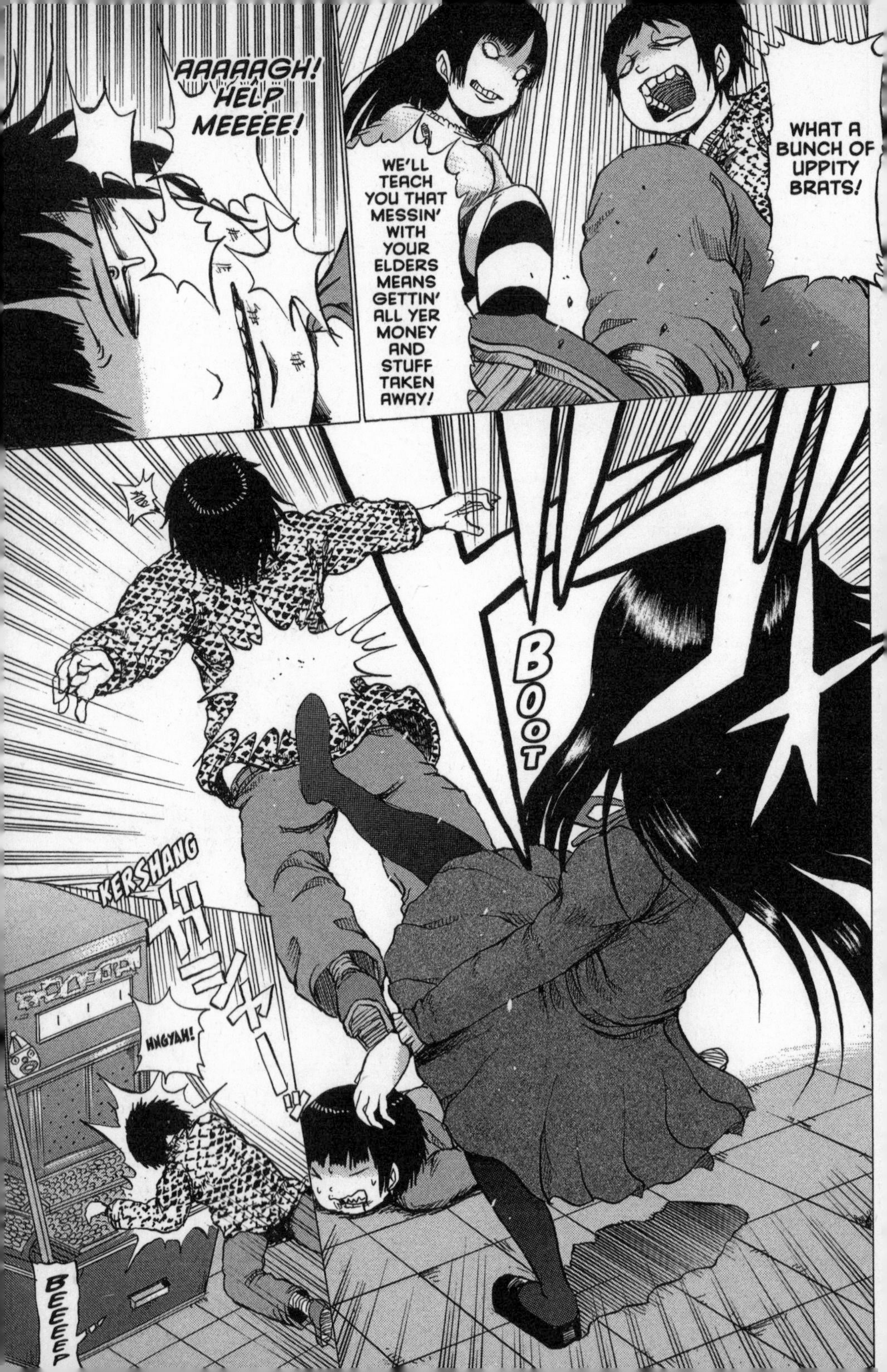
WHAT A BUNCH OF UPPITY BRATS!
WE'LL TEACH YOU THAT MESSIN' WITH YOUR ELDERS MEANS GETTIN' ALL YER MONEY AND STUFF TAKEN AWAY!
AAAAAGH! HELP MEEEEE!
BOOT
KERSHANG
HNGYAH!
BEEEEP

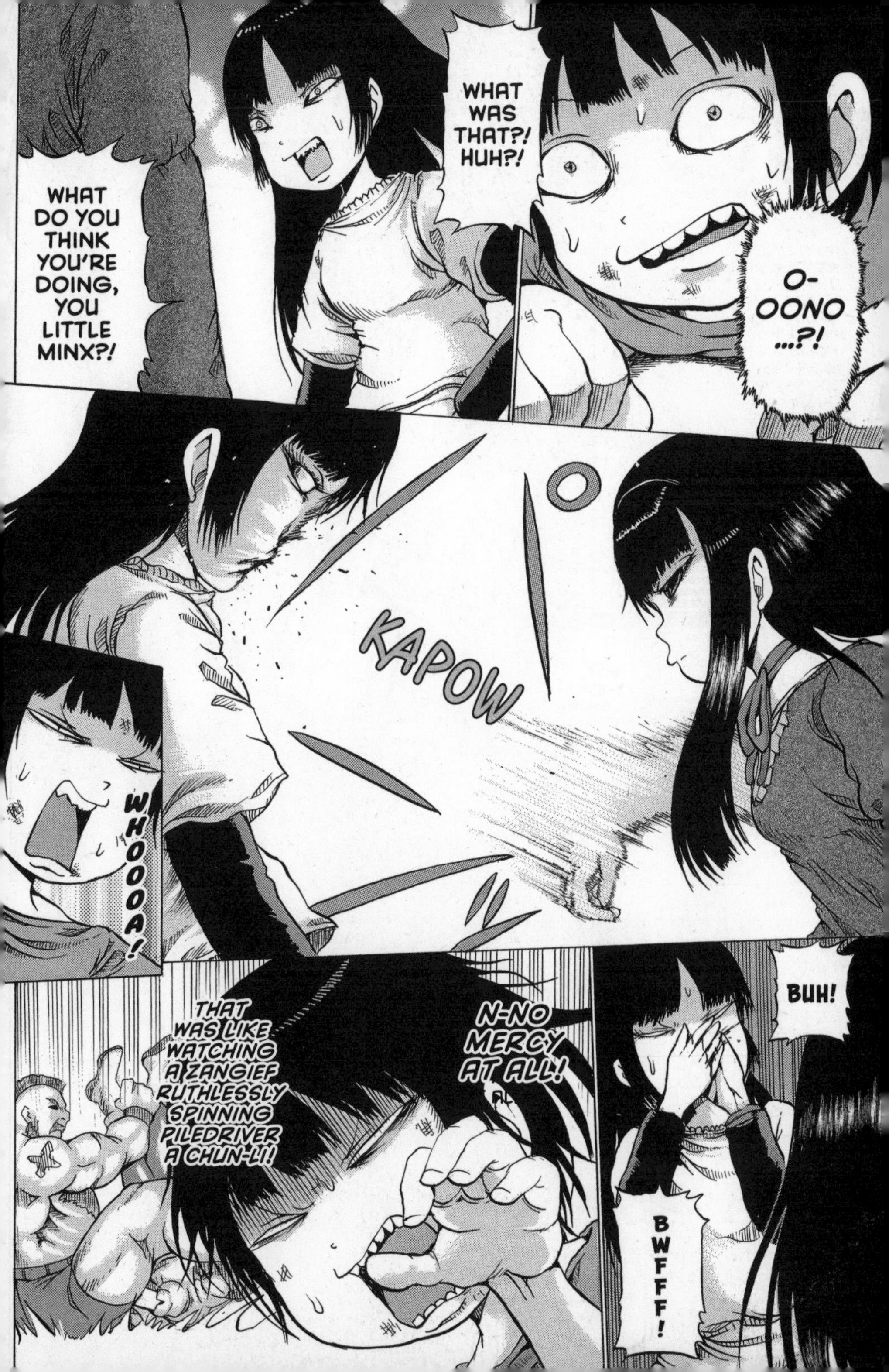
WHAT WAS THAT?! HUH?!
O-OONO ...?!
WHAT DO YOU THINK YOU'RE DOING, YOU LITTLE MINX?!
KAPOW
WHOOOOA!
BUH!
BWFFF!
N-NO MERCY AT ALL!
THAT WAS LIKE WATCHING A ZANGIEF RUTHLESSLY SPINNING PILEDRIVER A CHUN-LI!

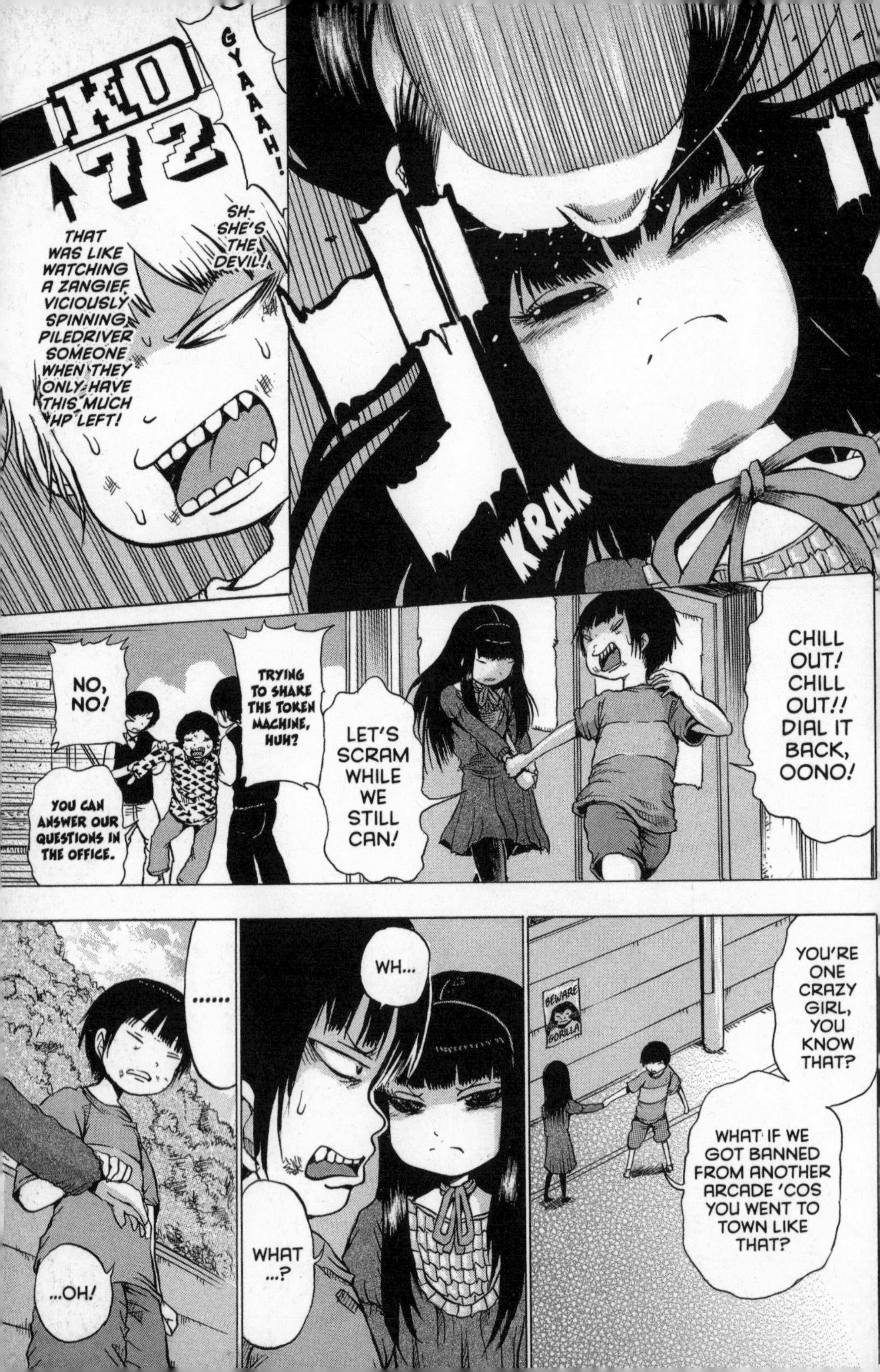
KRAK
GYAAAAH!
SH-SHE'S THE DEVIL!
KO
72
THAT WAS LIKE WATCHING A ZANGIEF VICIOUSLY SPINNING PILEDRIVER SOMEONE WHEN THEY ONLY HAVE THIS MUCH HP LEFT!
CHILL OUT! CHILL OUT!! DIAL IT BACK, OONO!
LET'S SCRAM WHILE WE STILL CAN!
TRYING TO SHAKE THE TOKEN MACHINE, HUH?
NO, NO!
YOU CAN ANSWER OUR QUESTIONS IN THE OFFICE.
YOU'RE ONE CRAZY GIRL, YOU KNOW THAT?
BEWARE GORILLA
WHAT IF WE GOT BANNED FROM ANOTHER ARCADE 'COS YOU WENT TO TOWN LIKE THAT?
WH...
WHAT ...?
......
...OH!

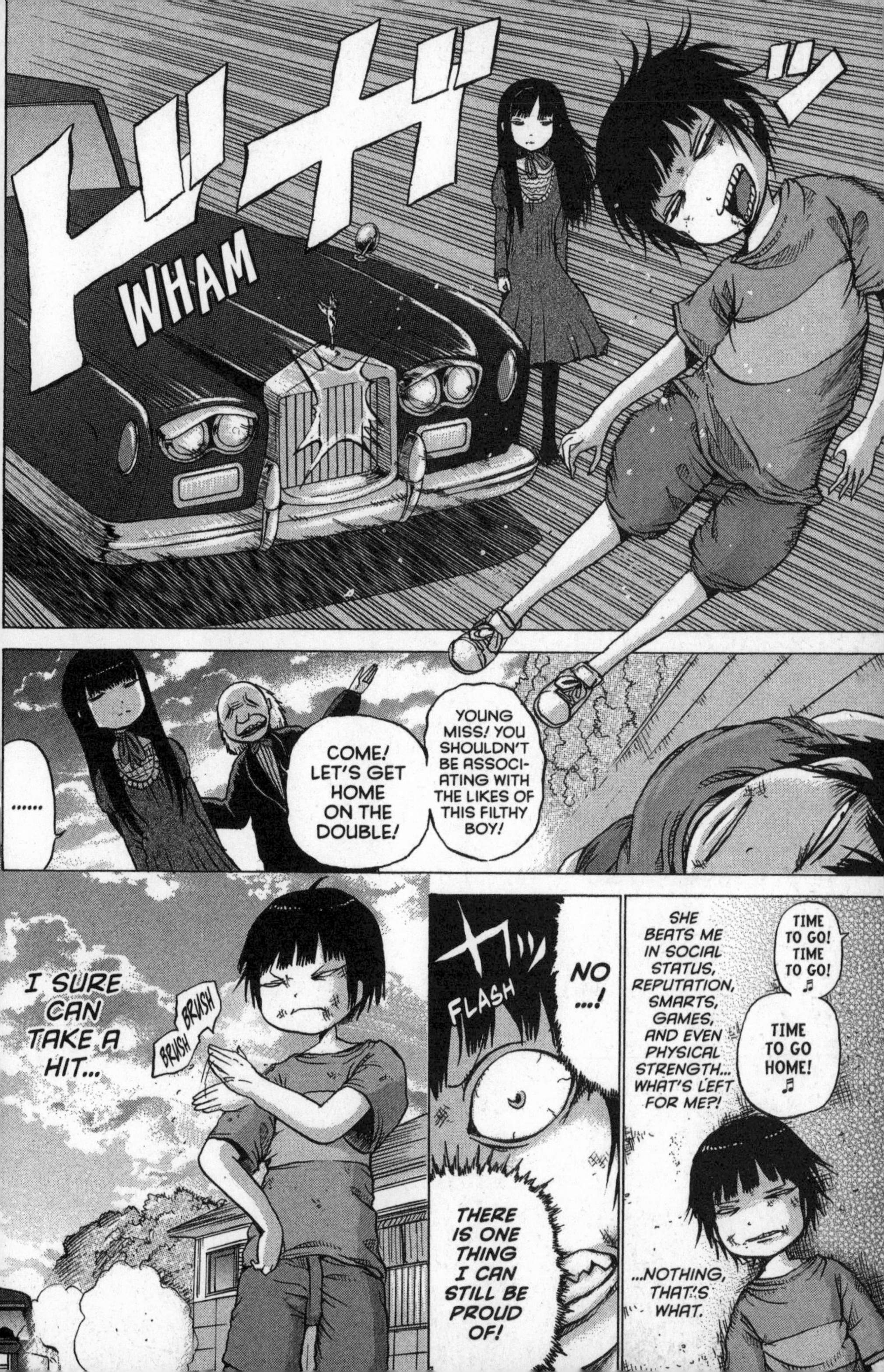
WHAM
YOUNG MISS! YOU SHOULDN'T BE ASSOCI-ATING WITH THE LIKES OF THIS FILTHY BOY!
COME! LET'S GET HOME ON THE DOUBLE!
......
TIME TO GO! TIME TO GO! ♪
TIME TO GO HOME! ♪
SHE BEATS ME IN SOCIAL STATUS, REPUTATION, SMARTS, GAMES, AND EVEN PHYSICAL STRENGTH... WHAT'S LEFT FOR ME?!
...NOTHING, THAT'S WHAT.
FLASH
NO ...!
THERE IS ONE THING I CAN STILL BE PROUD OF!
I SURE CAN TAKE A HIT...
BRUSH
BRUSH

HI SCORE GIRL

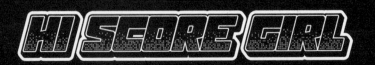

HI   SCORE   GIRL

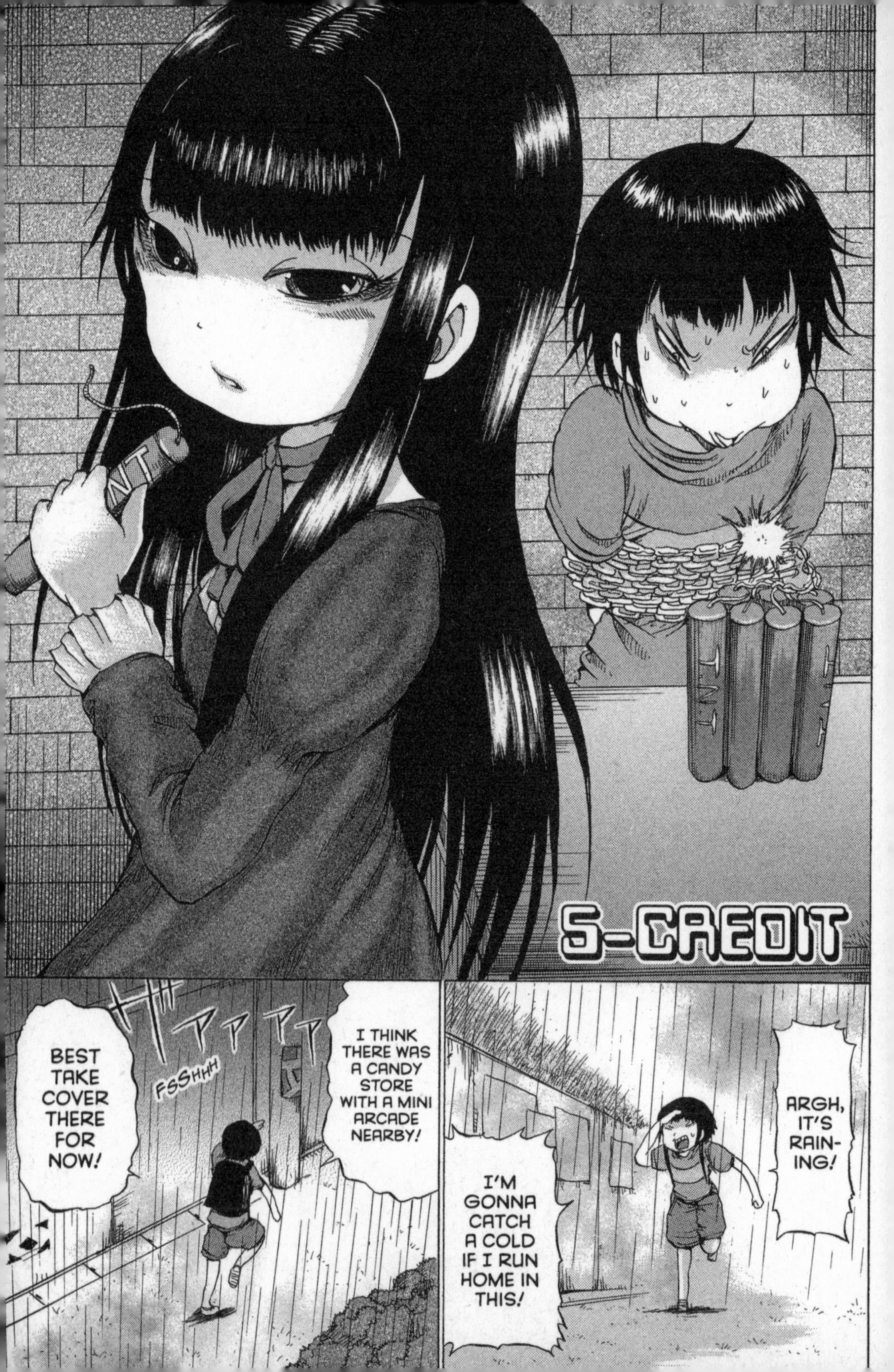
5-CREDIT
ARGH, IT'S RAINING!
I'M GONNA CATCH A COLD IF I RUN HOME IN THIS!
I THINK THERE WAS A CANDY STORE WITH A MINI ARCADE NEARBY!
BEST TAKE COVER THERE FOR NOW!
FSSHHH

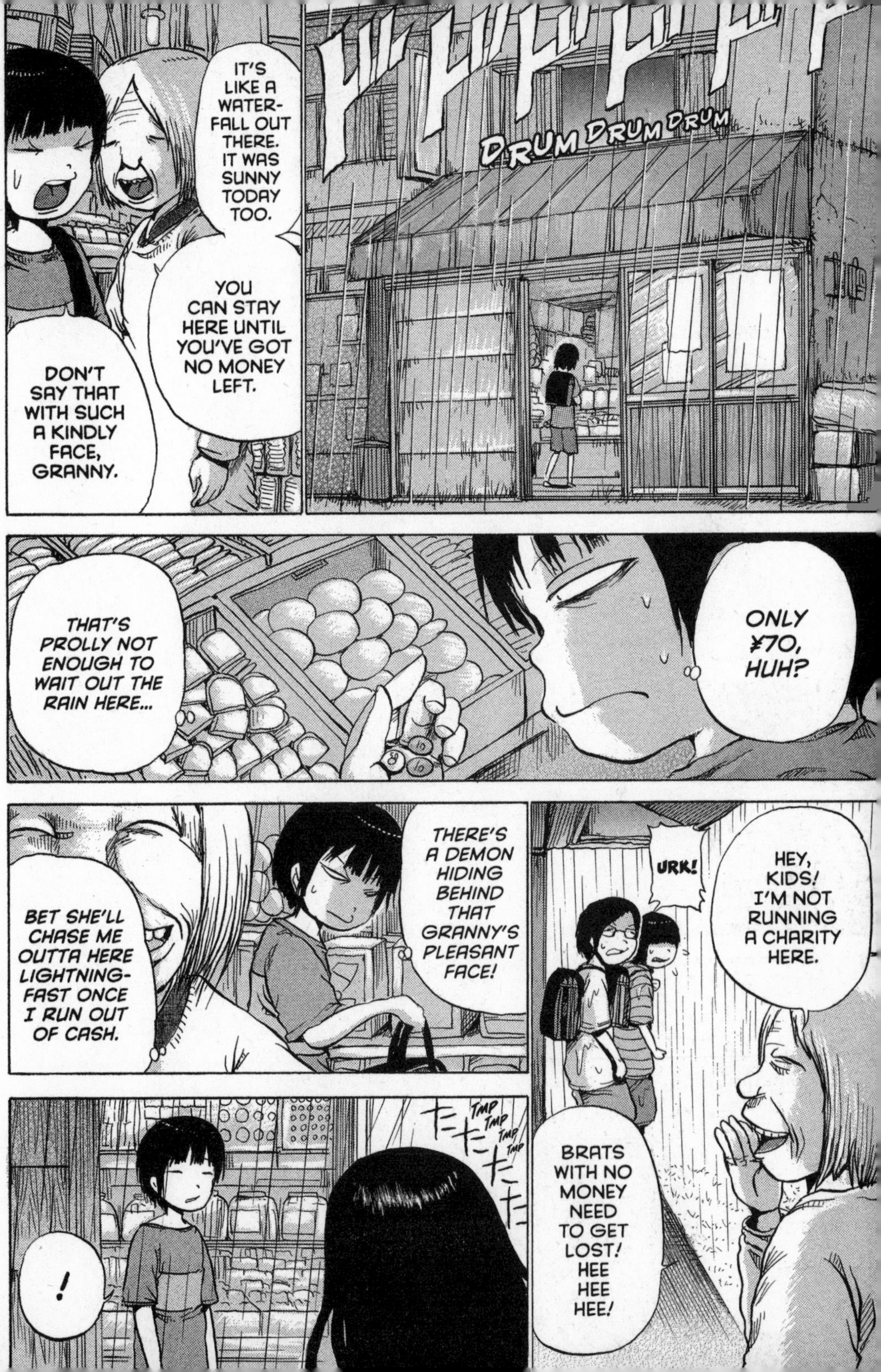
DRUM DRUM DRUM
IT'S LIKE A WATER-FALL OUT THERE. IT WAS SUNNY TODAY TOO.
YOU CAN STAY HERE UNTIL YOU'VE GOT NO MONEY LEFT.
DON'T SAY THAT WITH SUCH A KINDLY FACE, GRANNY.
ONLY ¥70, HUH?
THAT'S PROLLY NOT ENOUGH TO WAIT OUT THE RAIN HERE...
HEY, KIDS! I'M NOT RUNNING A CHARITY HERE.
URK!
BRATS WITH NO MONEY NEED TO GET LOST! HEE HEE HEE!
THERE'S A DEMON HIDING BEHIND THAT GRANNY'S PLEASANT FACE!
BET SHE'LL CHASE ME OUTTA HERE LIGHTNING-FAST ONCE I RUN OUT OF CASH.
TMP TMP TMP TMP
!

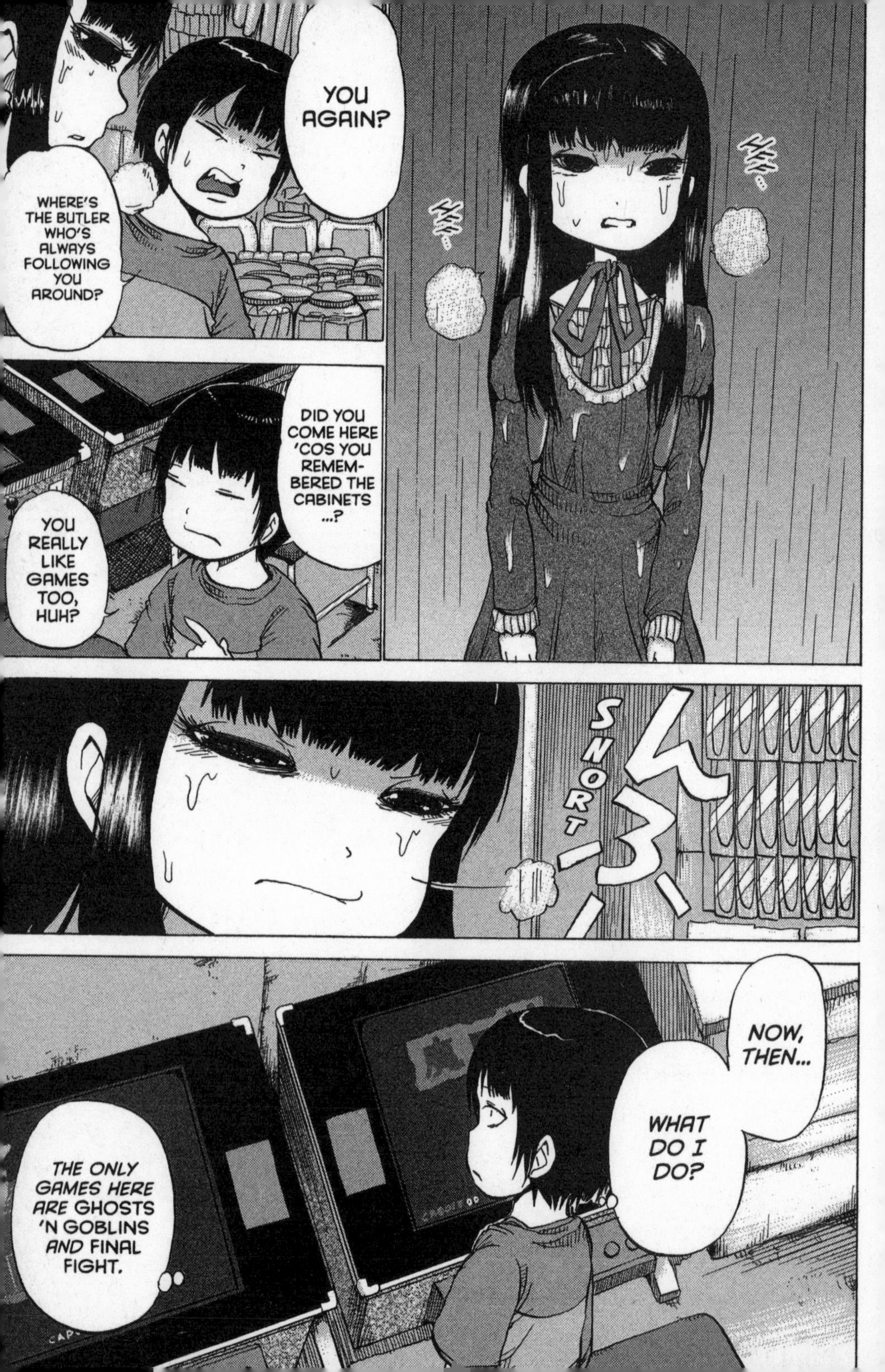
HFF...
HFF...
YOU AGAIN?
WHERE'S THE BUTLER WHO'S ALWAYS FOLLOWING YOU AROUND?
DID YOU COME HERE 'COS YOU REMEMBERED THE CABINETS ...?
YOU REALLY LIKE GAMES TOO, HUH?
SNORT
NOW, THEN...
WHAT DO I DO?
THE ONLY GAMES HERE ARE GHOSTS 'N GOBLINS AND FINAL FIGHT.

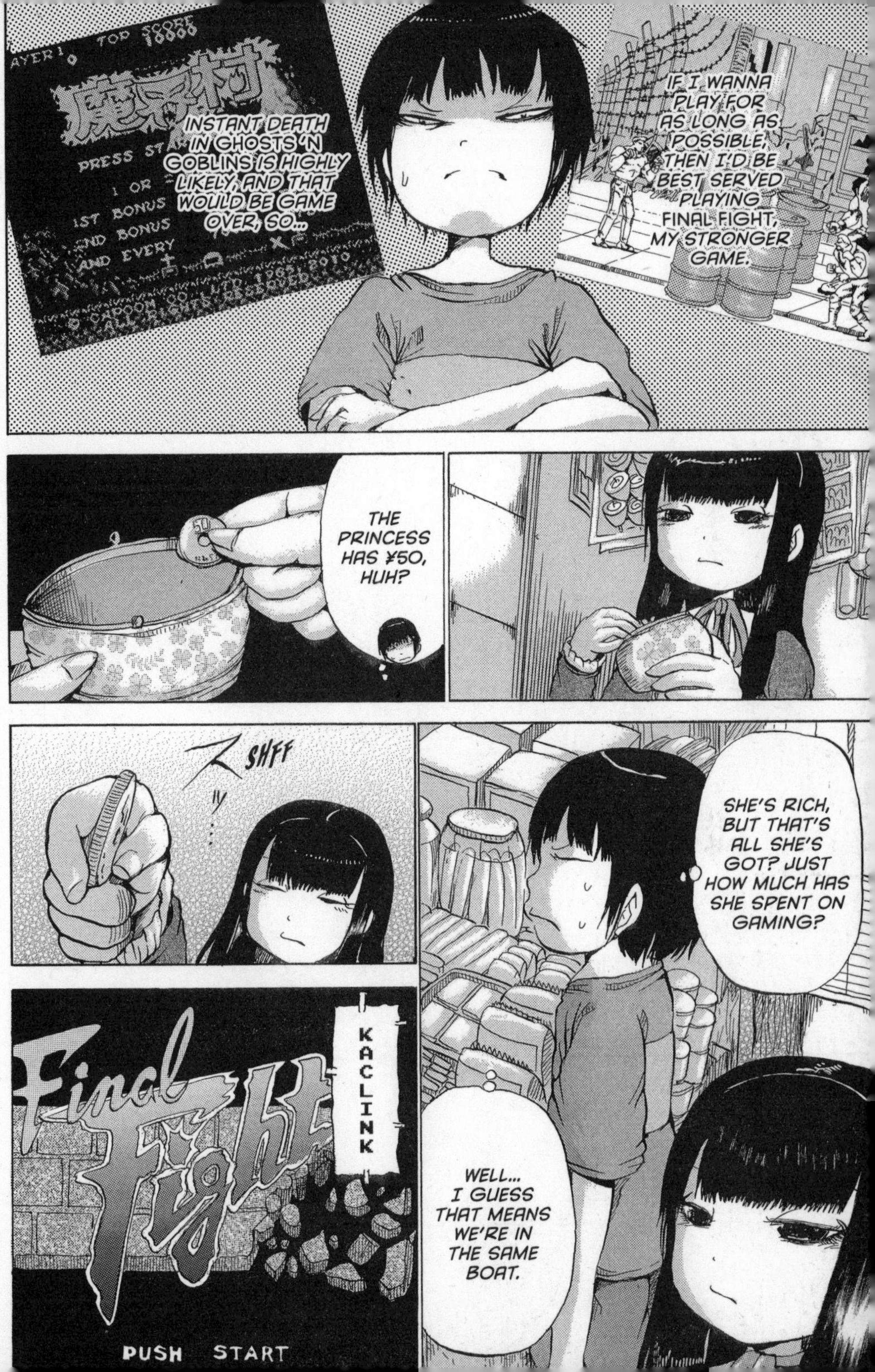
IF I WANNA PLAY FOR AS LONG AS POSSIBLE, THEN I'D BE BEST SERVED PLAYING FINAL FIGHT, MY STRONGER GAME.
INSTANT DEATH IN GHOSTS 'N GOBLINS IS HIGHLY LIKELY, AND THAT WOULD BE GAME OVER, SO...
TOP SCORE 10000
1ST BONUS
AND EVERY
THE PRINCESS HAS ¥50, HUH?
SHE'S RICH, BUT THAT'S ALL SHE'S GOT? JUST HOW MUCH HAS SHE SPENT ON GAMING?
SHFF
WELL... I GUESS THAT MEANS WE'RE IN THE SAME BOAT.
KACLINK
Final Fight
PUSH START

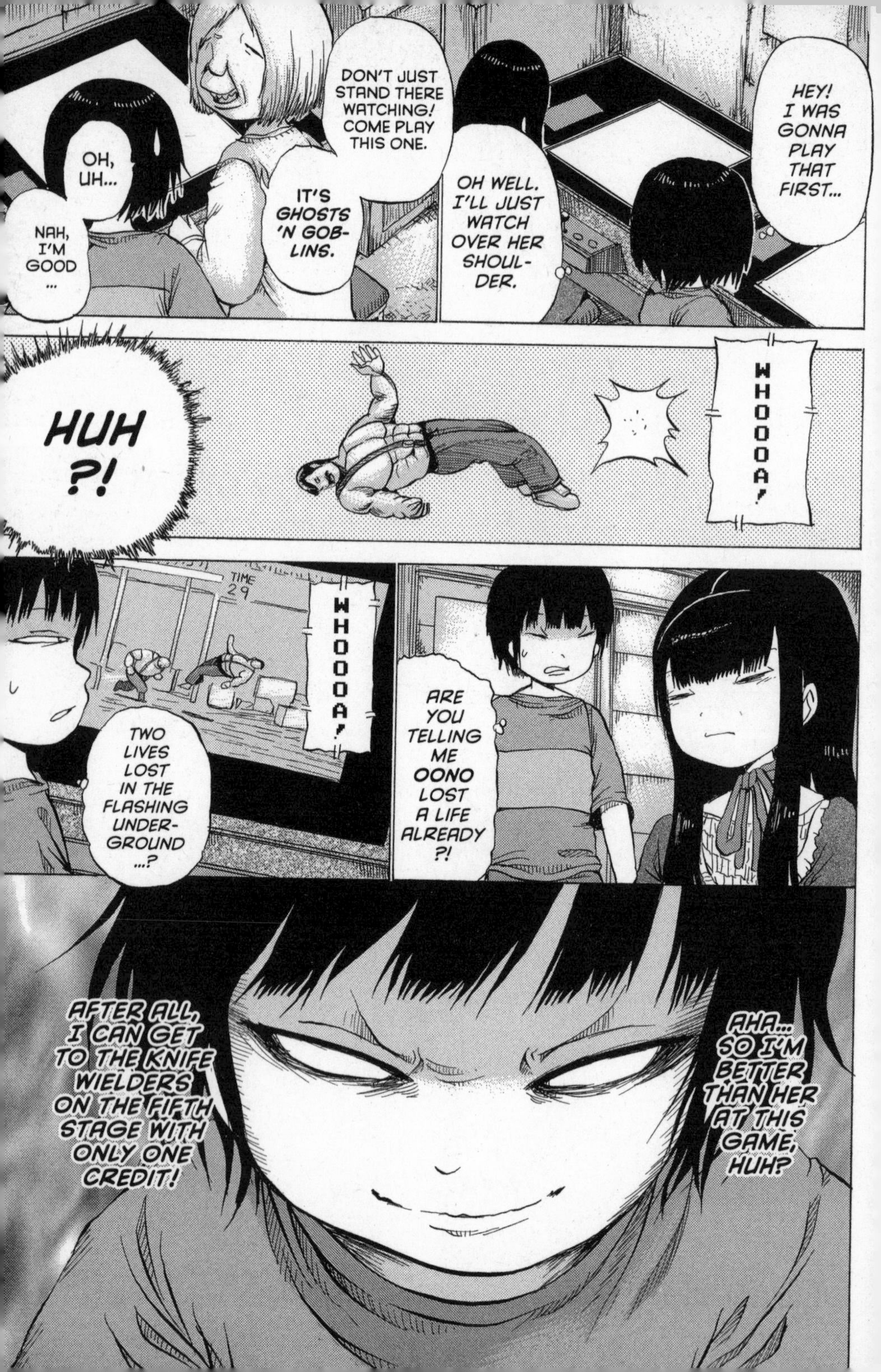
HEY! I WAS GONNA PLAY THAT FIRST...
OH WELL. I'LL JUST WATCH OVER HER SHOULDER.
DON'T JUST STAND THERE WATCHING! COME PLAY THIS ONE.
IT'S GHOSTS 'N GOB-LINS.
OH, UH...
NAH, I'M GOOD ...
WHOOOOA!
HUH?!
ARE YOU TELLING ME OONO LOST A LIFE ALREADY?!
WHOOOOA!
TIME 29
TWO LIVES LOST IN THE FLASHING UNDER-GROUND ...?
AHA... SO I'M BETTER THAN HER AT THIS GAME, HUH?
AFTER ALL, I CAN GET TO THE KNIFE WIELDERS ON THE FIFTH STAGE WITH ONLY ONE CREDIT!

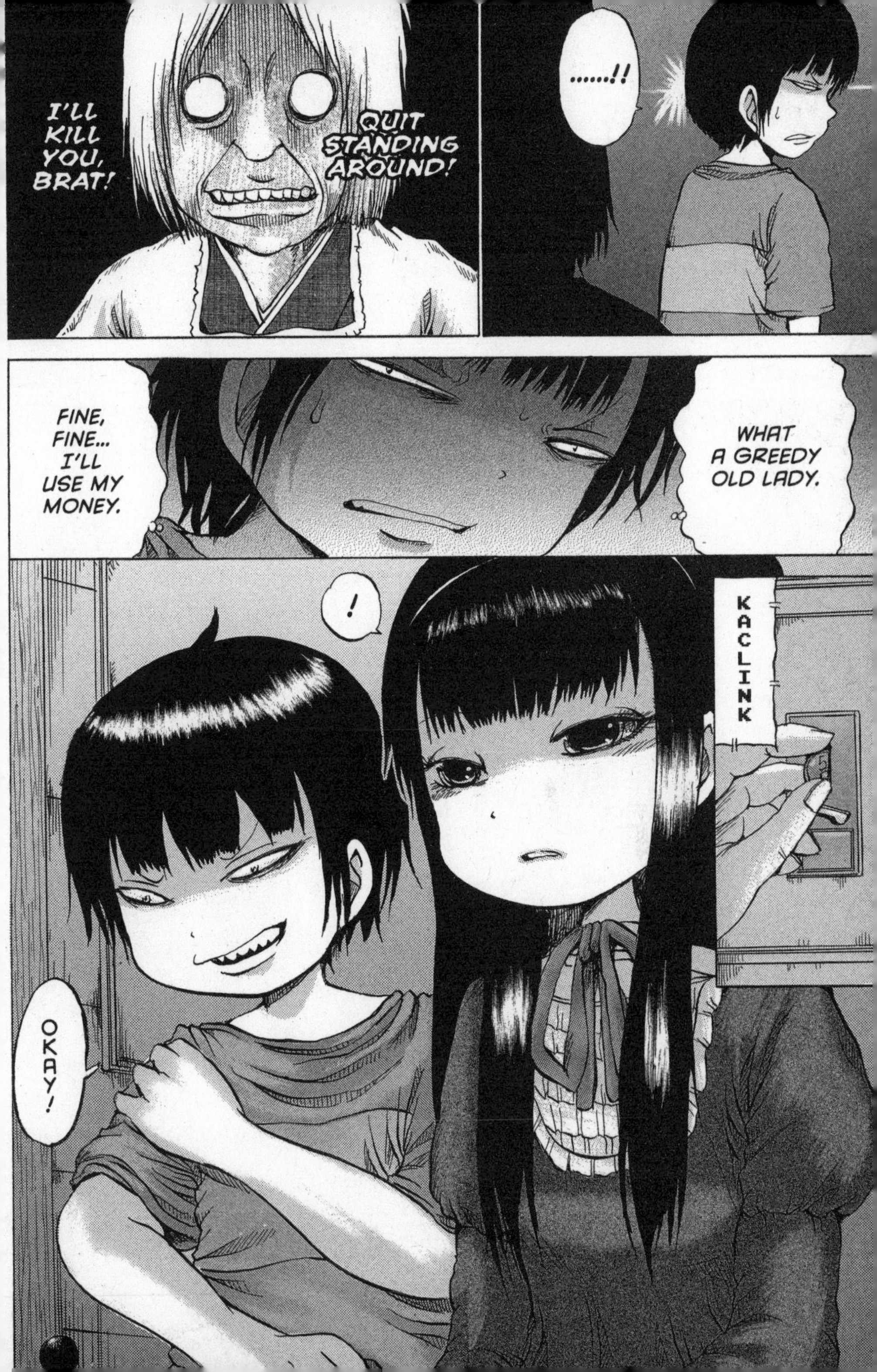
......!!
QUIT STANDING AROUND!
I'LL KILL YOU, BRAT!
WHAT A GREEDY OLD LADY.
FINE, FINE... I'LL USE MY MONEY.
KACLINK
!
OKAY!

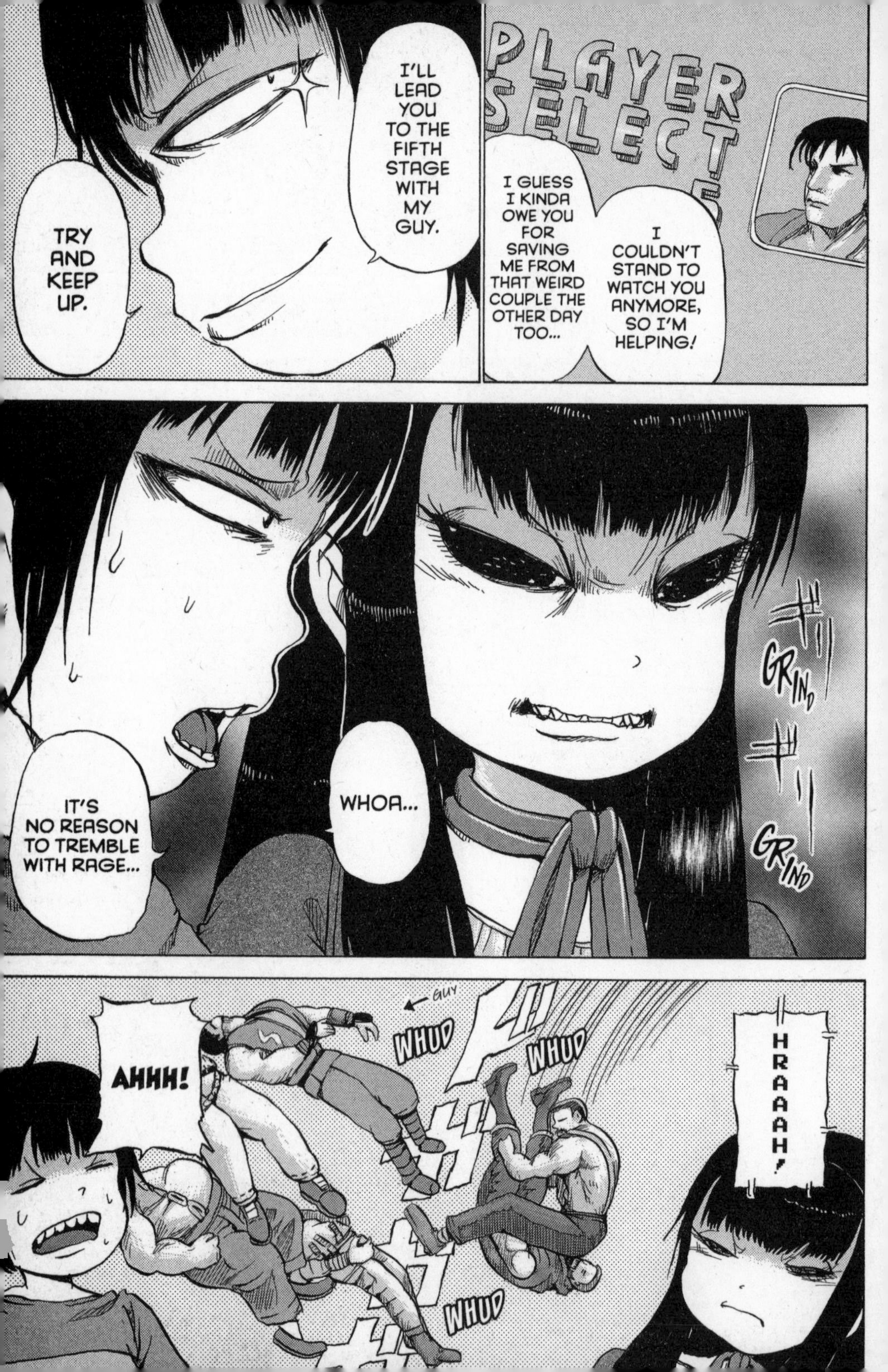
PLAYER SELECT
I COULDN'T STAND TO WATCH YOU ANYMORE, SO I'M HELPING!
I GUESS I KINDA OWE YOU FOR SAVING ME FROM THAT WEIRD COUPLE THE OTHER DAY TOO...
I'LL LEAD YOU TO THE FIFTH STAGE WITH MY GUY.
TRY AND KEEP UP.
GRIND
GRIND
WHOA...
IT'S NO REASON TO TREMBLE WITH RAGE...
HRAAAAH!
WHUD
WHUD
GUY
WHUD
AHHH!

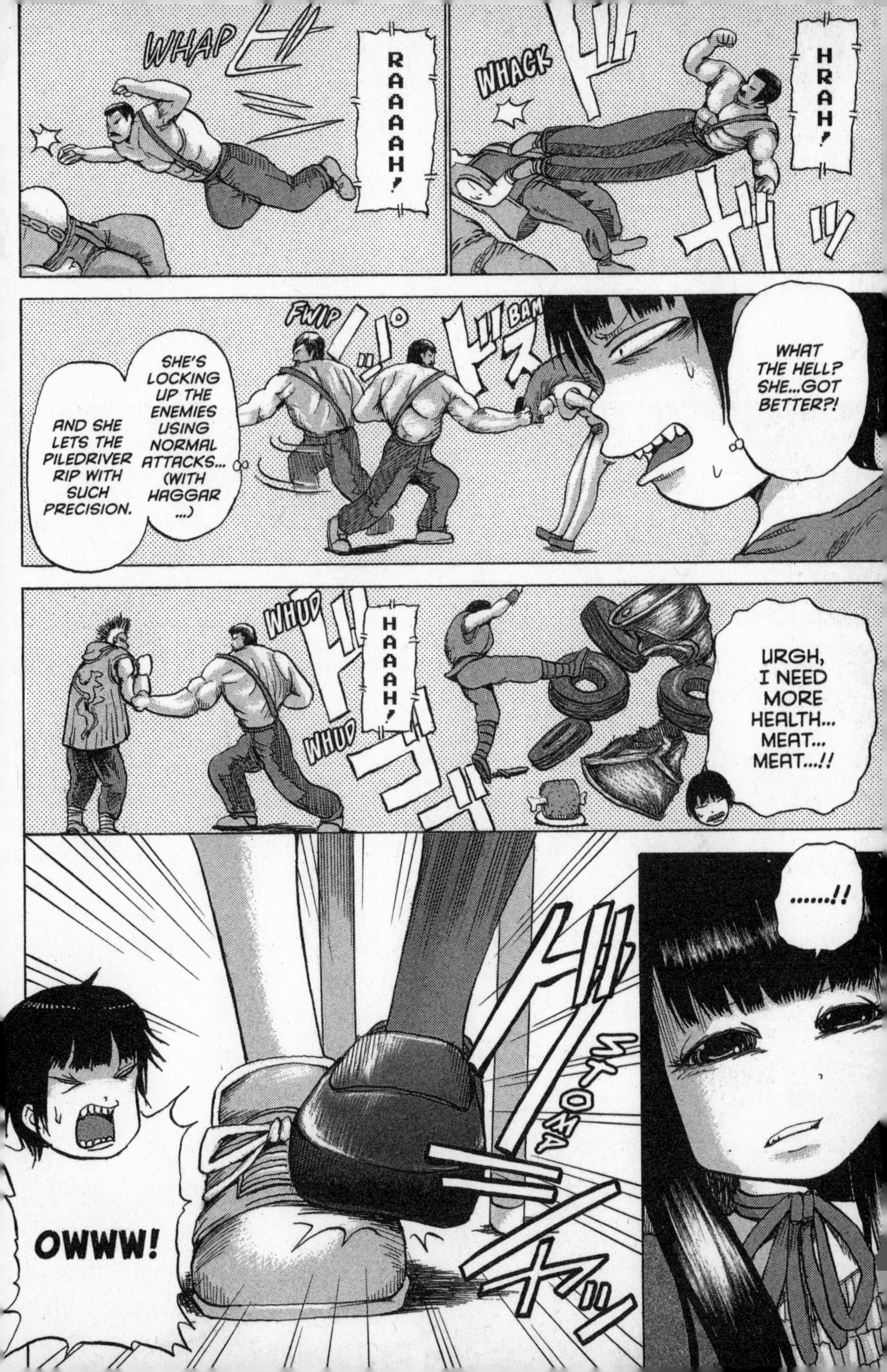
HRAH!
WHACK
RAAAAAH!
WHAP
WHAT THE HELL? SHE...GOT BETTER?!
BAM
FWIP
SHE'S LOCKING UP THE ENEMIES USING NORMAL ATTACKS... (WITH HAGGAR ...)
AND SHE LETS THE PILEDRIVER RIP WITH SUCH PRECISION.
URGH, I NEED MORE HEALTH... MEAT... MEAT...!!
HAAAAH!
WHUD
WHUD
......!!
STOMP
OWWW!

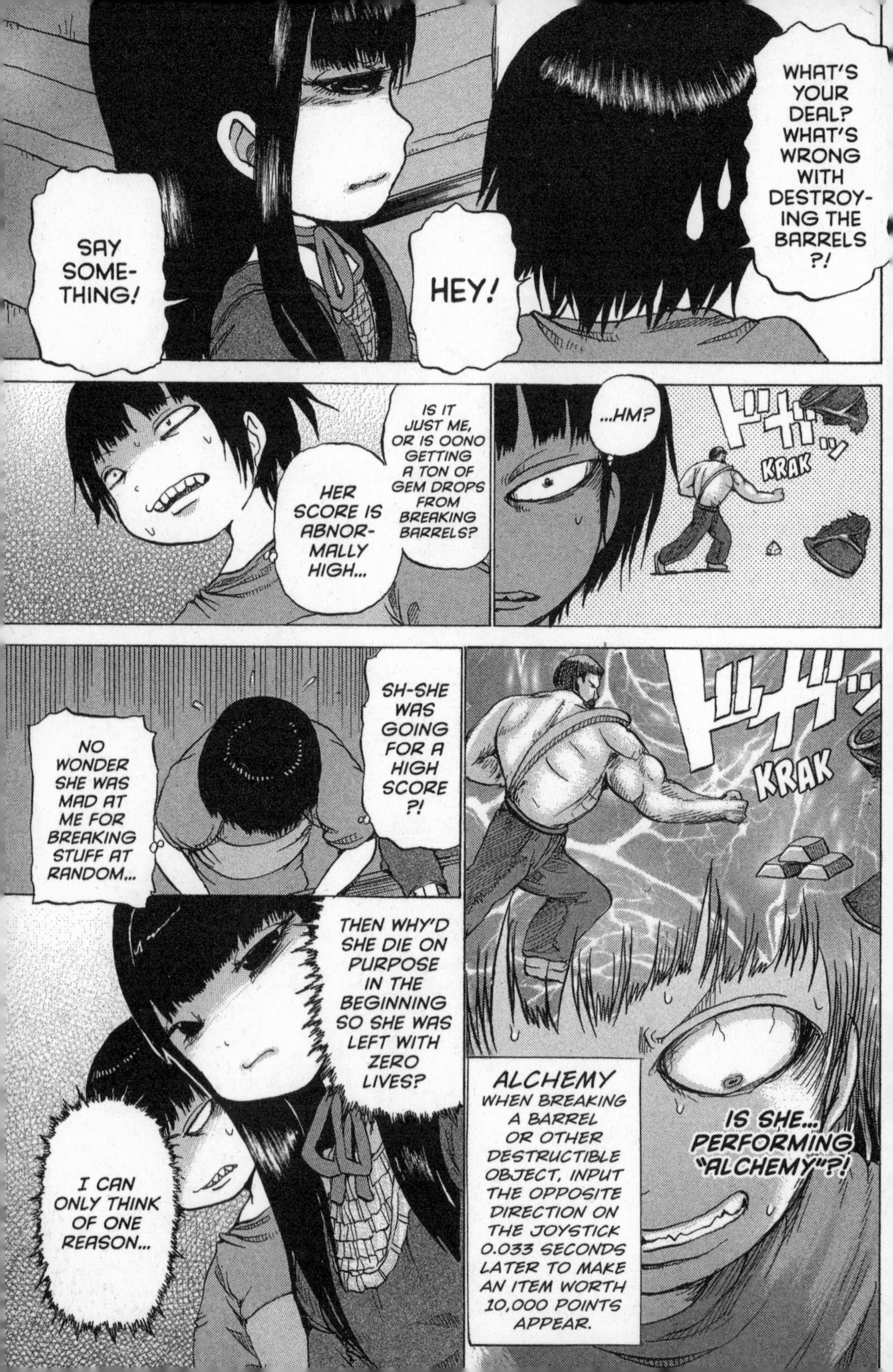
WHAT'S YOUR DEAL? WHAT'S WRONG WITH DESTROYING THE BARRELS?!
HEY!
SAY SOMETHING!
...HM?
KRAK
IS IT JUST ME, OR IS OONO GETTING A TON OF GEM DROPS FROM BREAKING BARRELS?
HER SCORE IS ABNORMALLY HIGH...
KRAK
IS SHE... PERFORMING "ALCHEMY"?!
ALCHEMY
WHEN BREAKING A BARREL OR OTHER DESTRUCTIBLE OBJECT, INPUT THE OPPOSITE DIRECTION ON THE JOYSTICK 0.033 SECONDS LATER TO MAKE AN ITEM WORTH 10,000 POINTS APPEAR.
SH-SHE WAS GOING FOR A HIGH SCORE?!
NO WONDER SHE WAS MAD AT ME FOR BREAKING STUFF AT RANDOM...
THEN WHY'D SHE DIE ON PURPOSE IN THE BEGINNING SO SHE WAS LEFT WITH ZERO LIVES?
I CAN ONLY THINK OF ONE REASON...

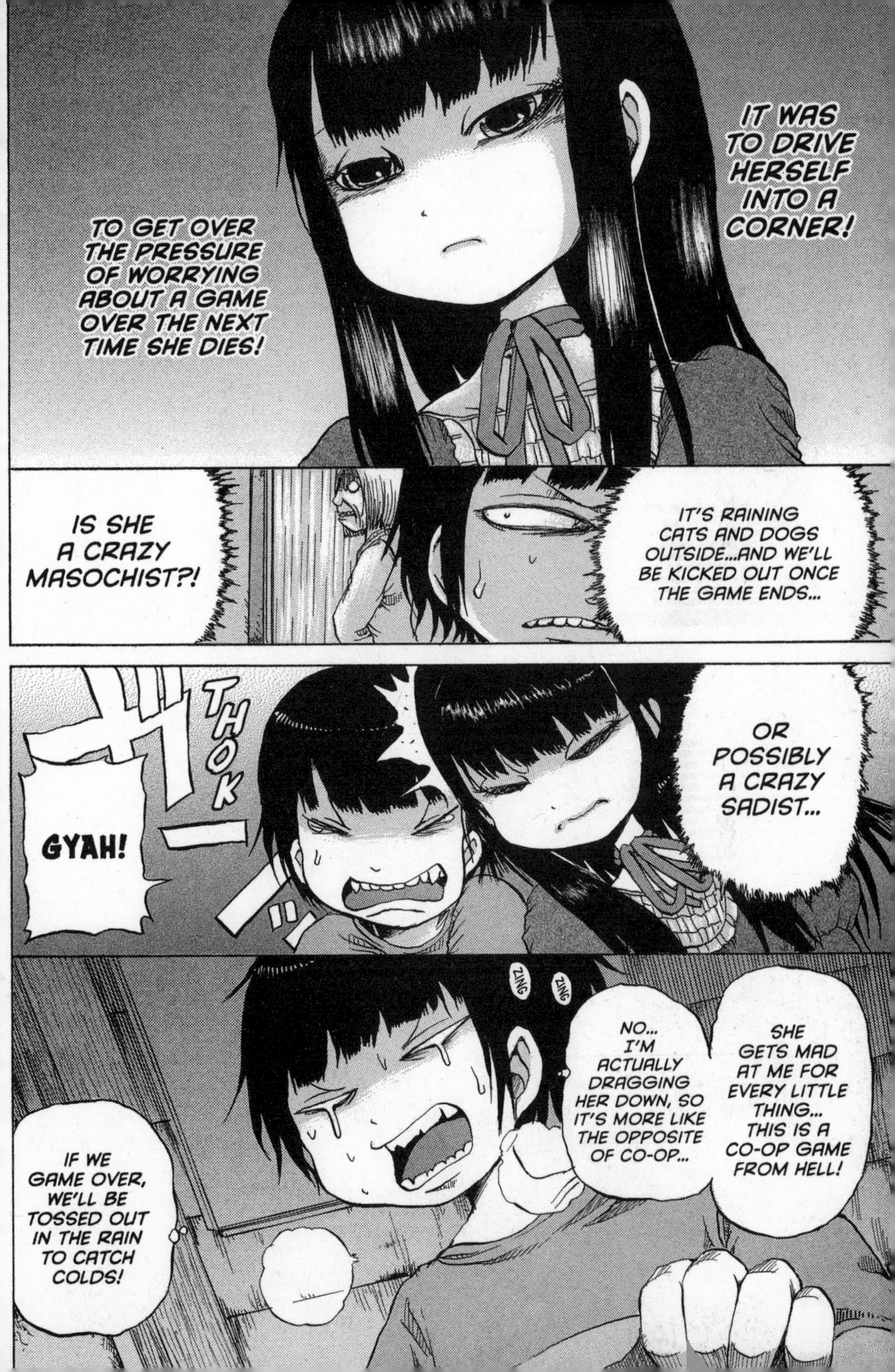
IT WAS TO DRIVE HERSELF INTO A CORNER!
TO GET OVER THE PRESSURE OF WORRYING ABOUT A GAME OVER THE NEXT TIME SHE DIES!
IT'S RAINING CATS AND DOGS OUTSIDE...AND WE'LL BE KICKED OUT ONCE THE GAME ENDS...
IS SHE A CRAZY MASOCHIST?!
OR POSSIBLY A CRAZY SADIST...
THOK
GYAH!
SHE GETS MAD AT ME FOR EVERY LITTLE THING... THIS IS A CO-OP GAME FROM HELL!
NO... I'M ACTUALLY DRAGGING HER DOWN, SO IT'S MORE LIKE THE OPPOSITE OF CO-OP...
ZING
ZING
IF WE GAME OVER, WE'LL BE TOSSED OUT IN THE RAIN TO CATCH COLDS!

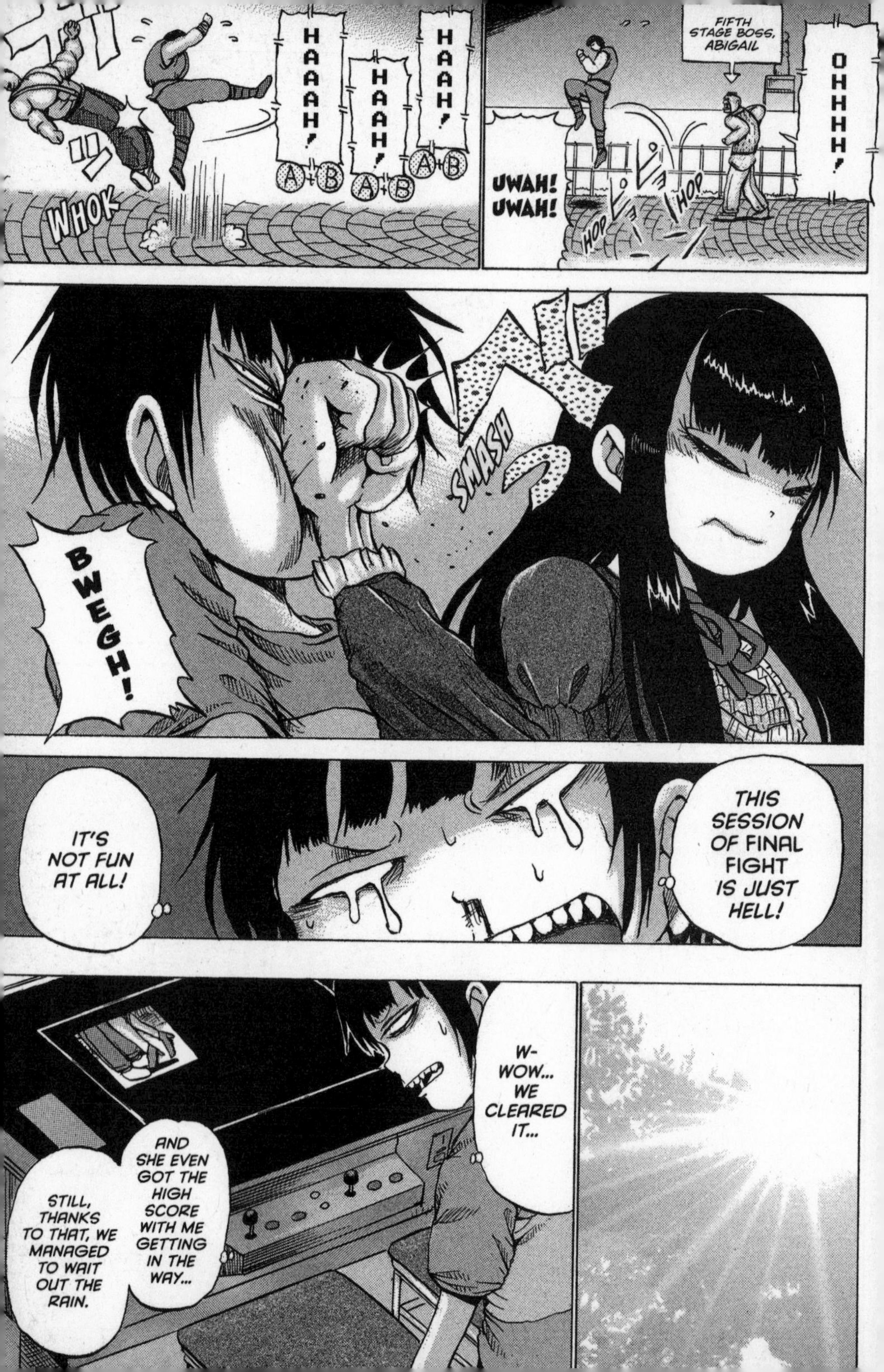
OHHHH!
FIFTH STAGE BOSS, ABIGAIL
HOP
HOP
UWAH! UWAH!
HAAAH!
HAAAH!
HAAAH!
A B A B A B
WHOK
SMASH
BWEGH!
THIS SESSION OF FINAL FIGHT IS JUST HELL!
IT'S NOT FUN AT ALL!
W-WOW... WE CLEARED IT...
AND SHE EVEN GOT THE HIGH SCORE WITH ME GETTING IN THE WAY...
STILL, THANKS TO THAT, WE MANAGED TO WAIT OUT THE RAIN.

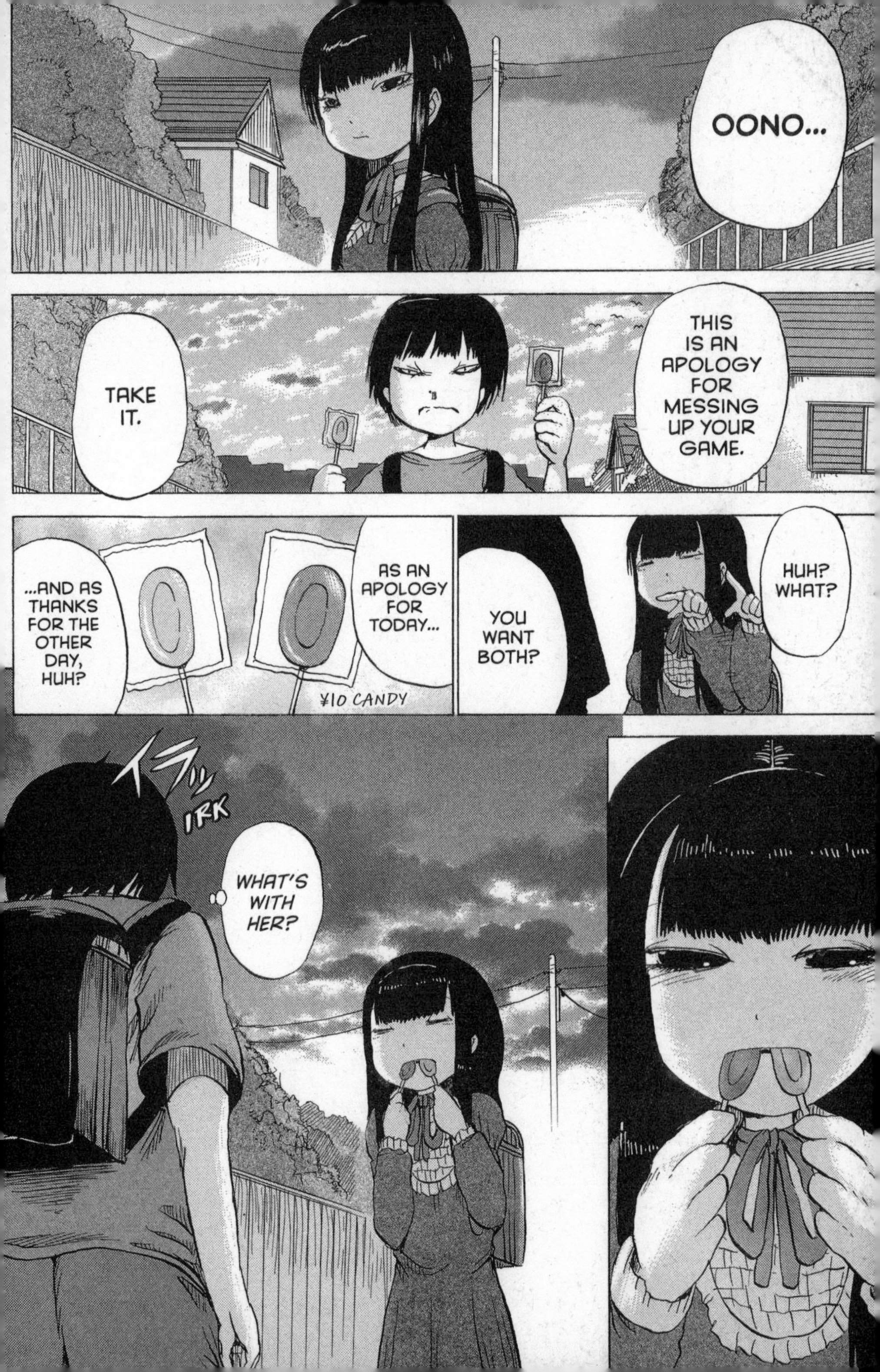
OONO...
THIS IS AN APOLOGY FOR MESSING UP YOUR GAME.
TAKE IT.
HUH? WHAT?
YOU WANT BOTH?
AS AN APOLOGY FOR TODAY...
...AND AS THANKS FOR THE OTHER DAY, HUH?
¥10 CANDY
イラッ
IRK
WHAT'S WITH HER?

HI SCORE GIRL

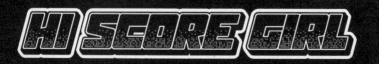

HI SCORE GIRL

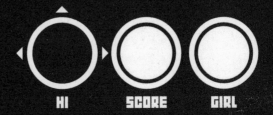

6-CREDIT

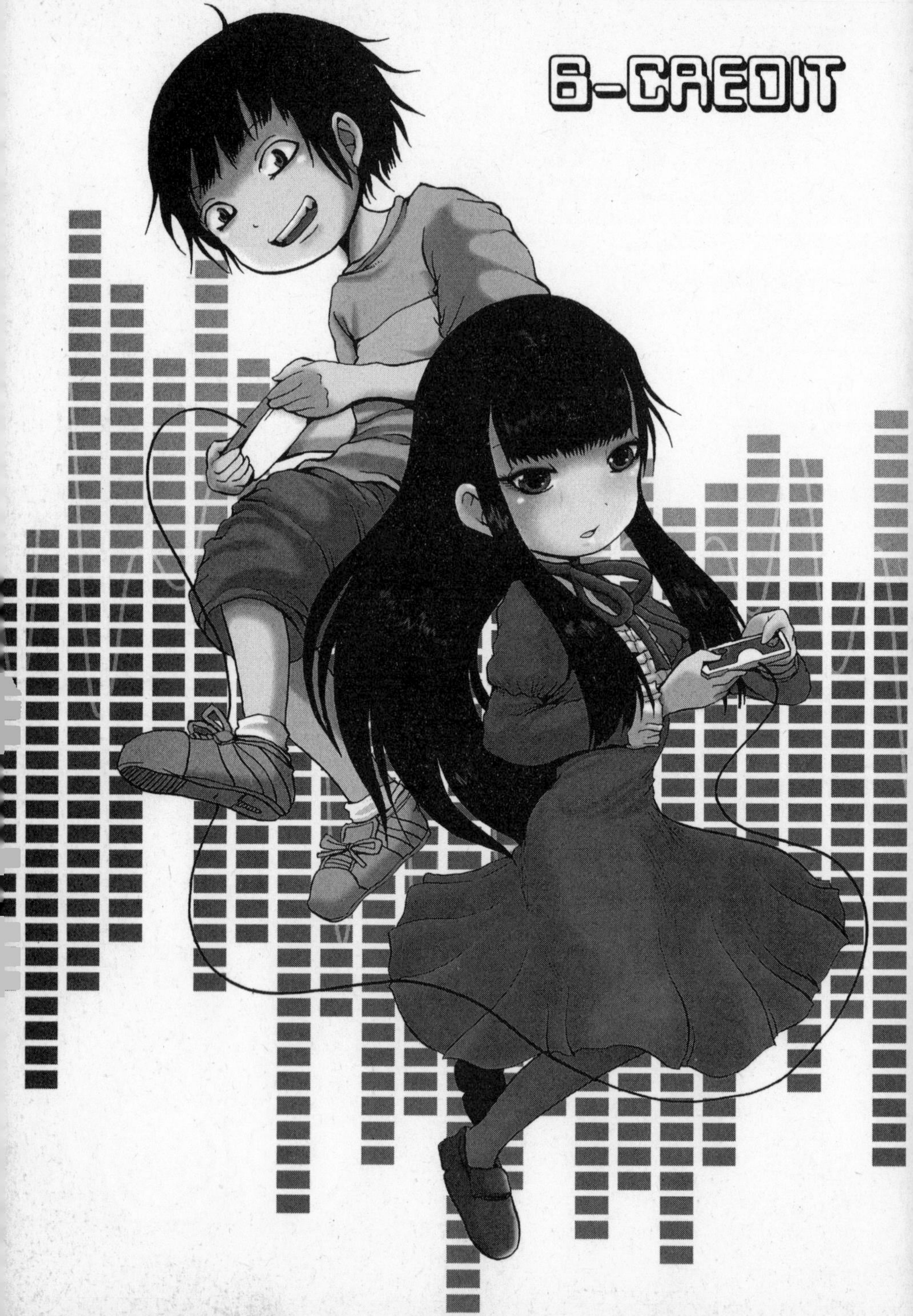

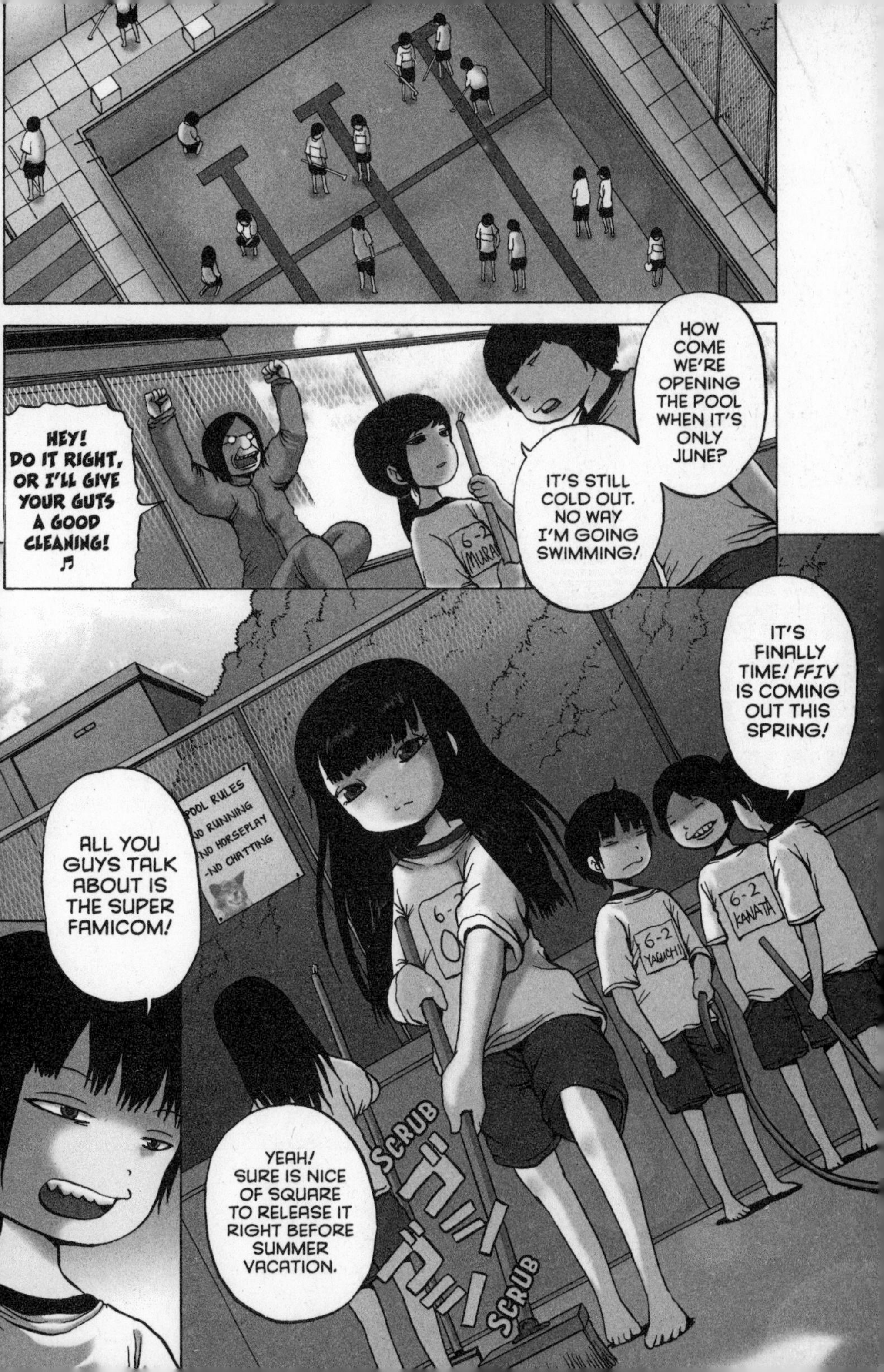

HOW COME WE'RE OPENING THE POOL WHEN IT'S ONLY JUNE?
IT'S STILL COLD OUT. NO WAY I'M GOING SWIMMING!
6-2 MURA
HEY! DO IT RIGHT, OR I'LL GIVE YOUR GUTS A GOOD CLEANING! ♬
IT'S FINALLY TIME! *FFIV* IS COMING OUT THIS SPRING!
6-2 KANATA
6-2 YAGUCHI
POOL RULES
-NO RUNNING
-NO HORSEPLAY
-NO CHATTING
ALL YOU GUYS TALK ABOUT IS THE SUPER FAMICOM!
YEAH! SURE IS NICE OF SQUARE TO RELEASE IT RIGHT BEFORE SUMMER VACATION.
SCRUB
SCRUB
SCRUB

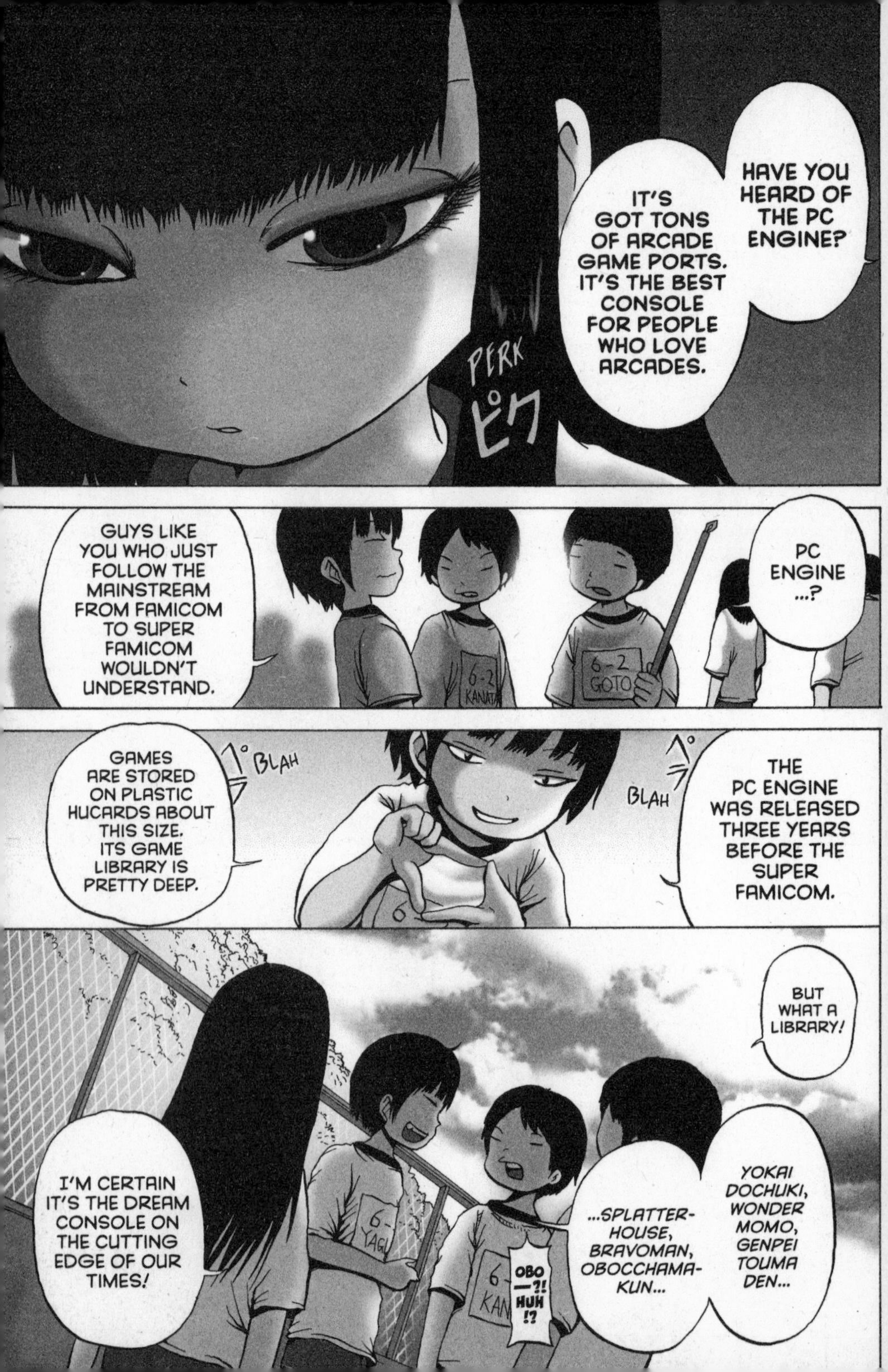
HAVE YOU HEARD OF THE PC ENGINE?
IT'S GOT TONS OF ARCADE GAME PORTS. IT'S THE BEST CONSOLE FOR PEOPLE WHO LOVE ARCADES.
PERK
ピク
PC ENGINE ...?
6-2 GOTO
6-2 KANATA
GUYS LIKE YOU WHO JUST FOLLOW THE MAINSTREAM FROM FAMICOM TO SUPER FAMICOM WOULDN'T UNDERSTAND.
THE PC ENGINE WAS RELEASED THREE YEARS BEFORE THE SUPER FAMICOM.
BLAH
BLAH
GAMES ARE STORED ON PLASTIC HUCARDS ABOUT THIS SIZE. ITS GAME LIBRARY IS PRETTY DEEP.
BUT WHAT A LIBRARY!
YOKAI DOCHUKI, WONDER MOMO, GENPEI TOUMA DEN...
...SPLATTER-HOUSE, BRAVOMAN, OBOCCHAMA-KUN...
OBO—?! HUH!?
I'M CERTAIN IT'S THE DREAM CONSOLE ON THE CUTTING EDGE OF OUR TIMES!

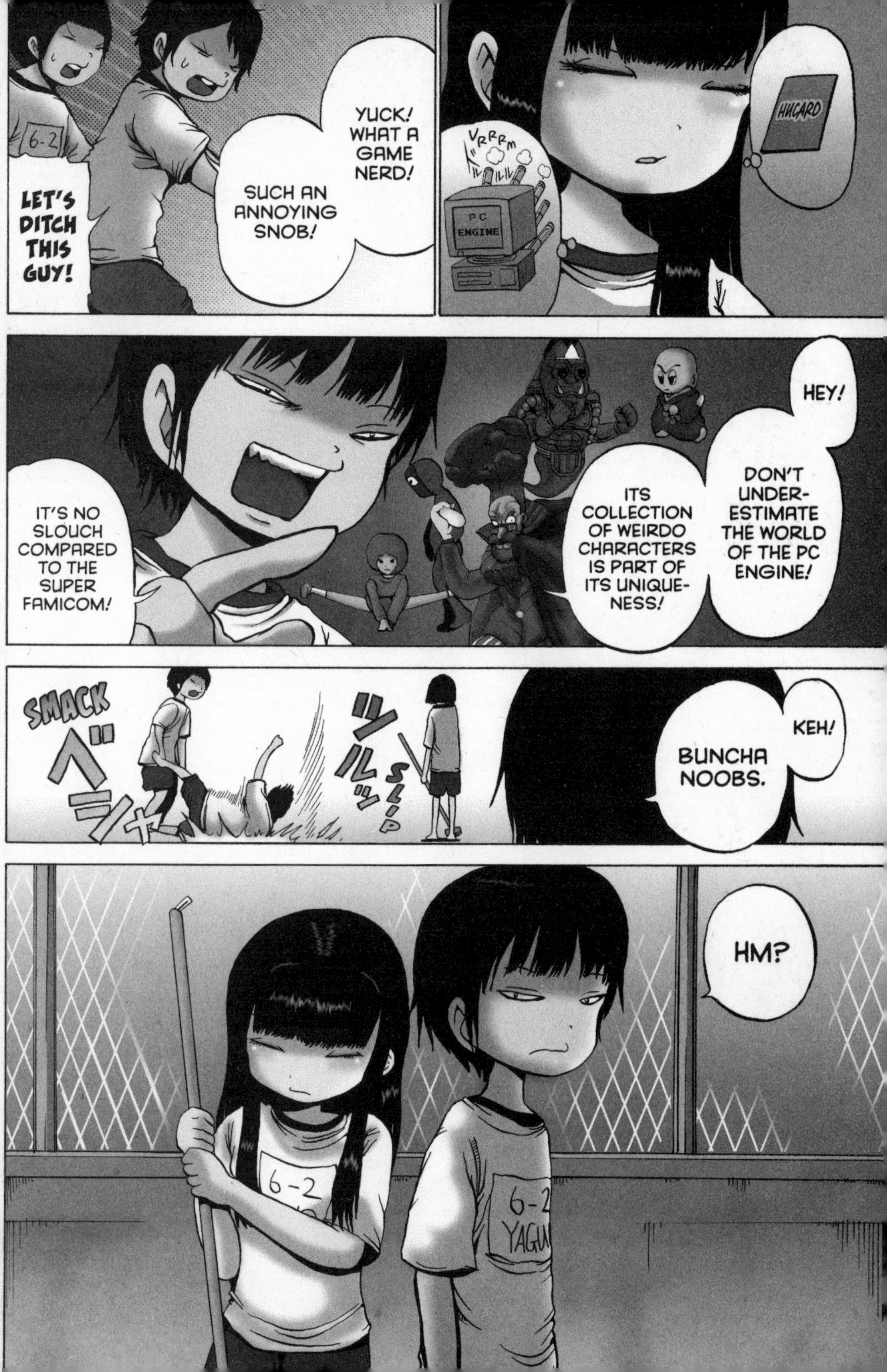
HUCARD
VRRRM
PC ENGINE
YUCK! WHAT A GAME NERD!
SUCH AN ANNOYING SNOB!
6-2
LET'S DITCH THIS GUY!
HEY!
DON'T UNDER-ESTIMATE THE WORLD OF THE PC ENGINE!
ITS COLLECTION OF WEIRDO CHARACTERS IS PART OF ITS UNIQUE-NESS!
IT'S NO SLOUCH COMPARED TO THE SUPER FAMICOM!
KEH!
BUNCHA NOOBS.
SLIP
ツルッ
SMACK
ベシャ
HM?
6-2
YAGU
6-2

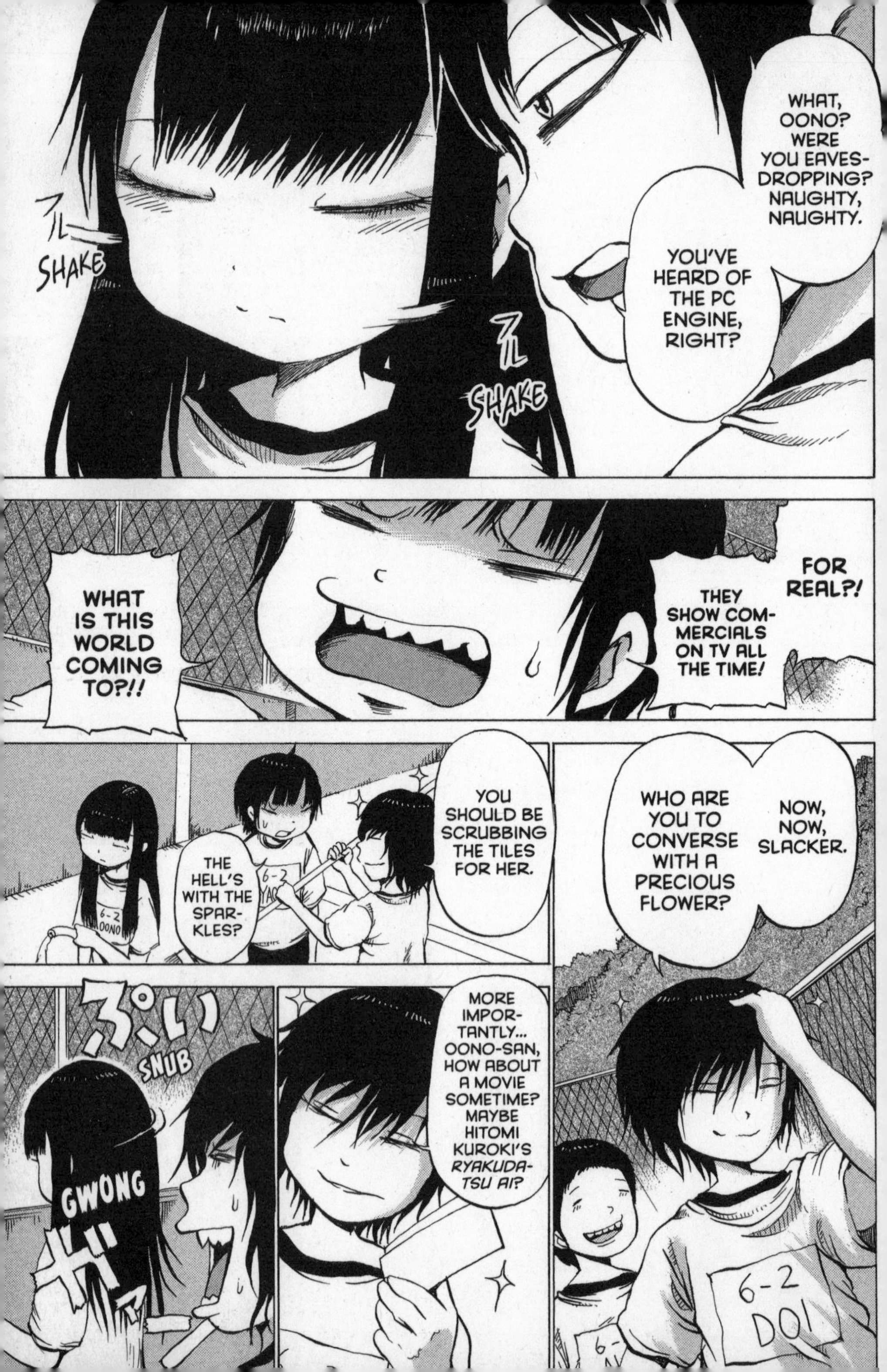
WHAT, OONO? WERE YOU EAVES-DROPPING? NAUGHTY, NAUGHTY.
YOU'VE HEARD OF THE PC ENGINE, RIGHT?
フル SHAKE
フル SHAKE
FOR REAL?!
THEY SHOW COM-MERCIALS ON TV ALL THE TIME!
WHAT IS THIS WORLD COMING TO?!!
NOW, NOW, SLACKER.
WHO ARE YOU TO CONVERSE WITH A PRECIOUS FLOWER?
6-2 DOI
YOU SHOULD BE SCRUBBING THE TILES FOR HER.
THE HELL'S WITH THE SPAR-KLES?
6-2 OONO
MORE IMPOR-TANTLY... OONO-SAN, HOW ABOUT A MOVIE SOMETIME? MAYBE HITOMI KUROKI'S *RYAKUDA-TSU AI*?
ぷいっ SNUB
GWONG
ガッ

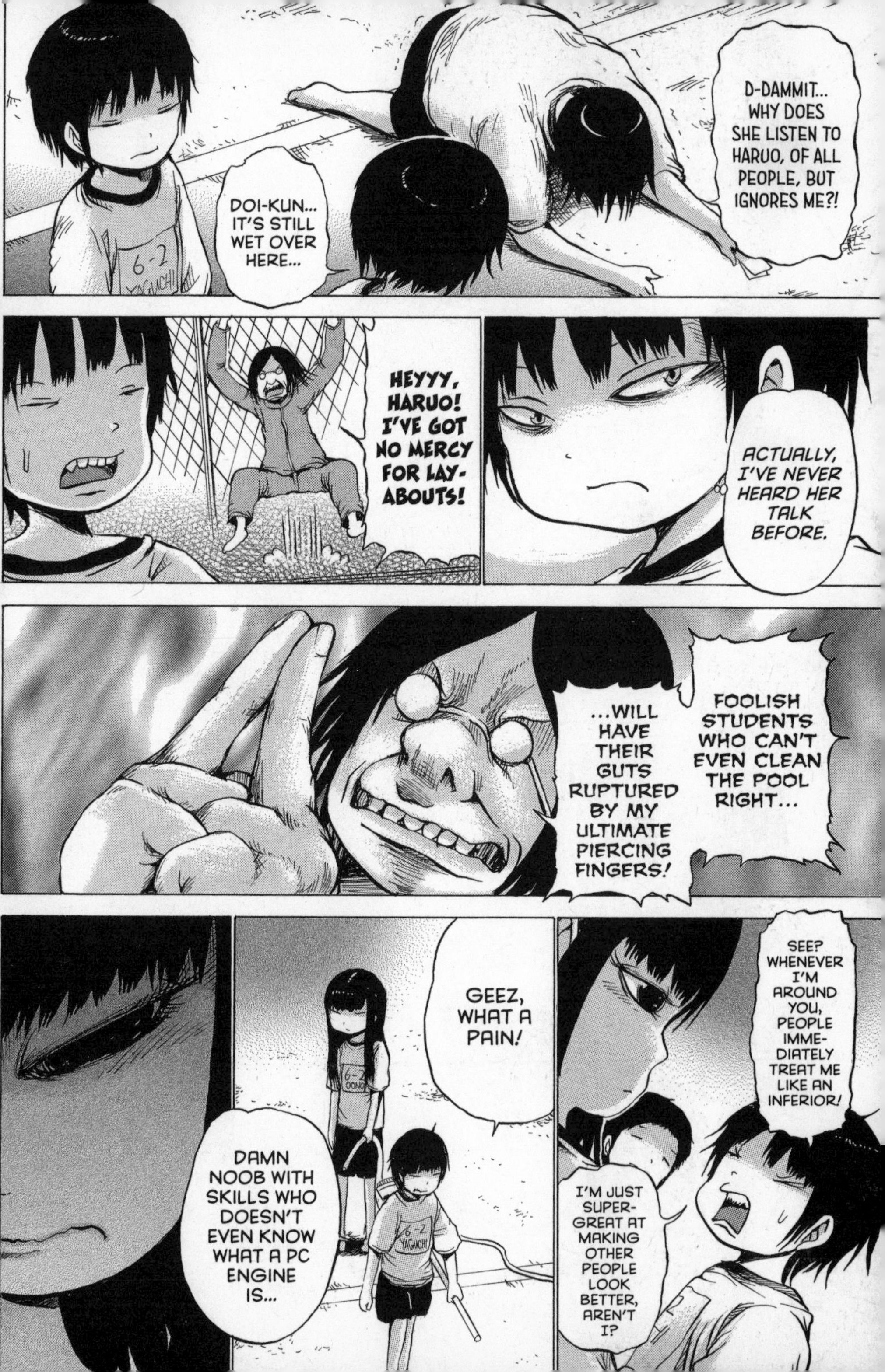
D-DAMMIT... WHY DOES SHE LISTEN TO HARUO, OF ALL PEOPLE, BUT IGNORES ME?!
DOI-KUN... IT'S STILL WET OVER HERE...
ACTUALLY, I'VE NEVER HEARD HER TALK BEFORE.
HEYYY, HARUO! I'VE GOT NO MERCY FOR LAY-ABOUTS!
FOOLISH STUDENTS WHO CAN'T EVEN CLEAN THE POOL RIGHT...
...WILL HAVE THEIR GUTS RUPTURED BY MY ULTIMATE PIERCING FINGERS!
SEE? WHENEVER I'M AROUND YOU, PEOPLE IMME-DIATELY TREAT ME LIKE AN INFERIOR!
I'M JUST SUPER-GREAT AT MAKING OTHER PEOPLE LOOK BETTER, AREN'T I?
GEEZ, WHAT A PAIN!
DAMN NOOB WITH SKILLS WHO DOESN'T EVEN KNOW WHAT A PC ENGINE IS...

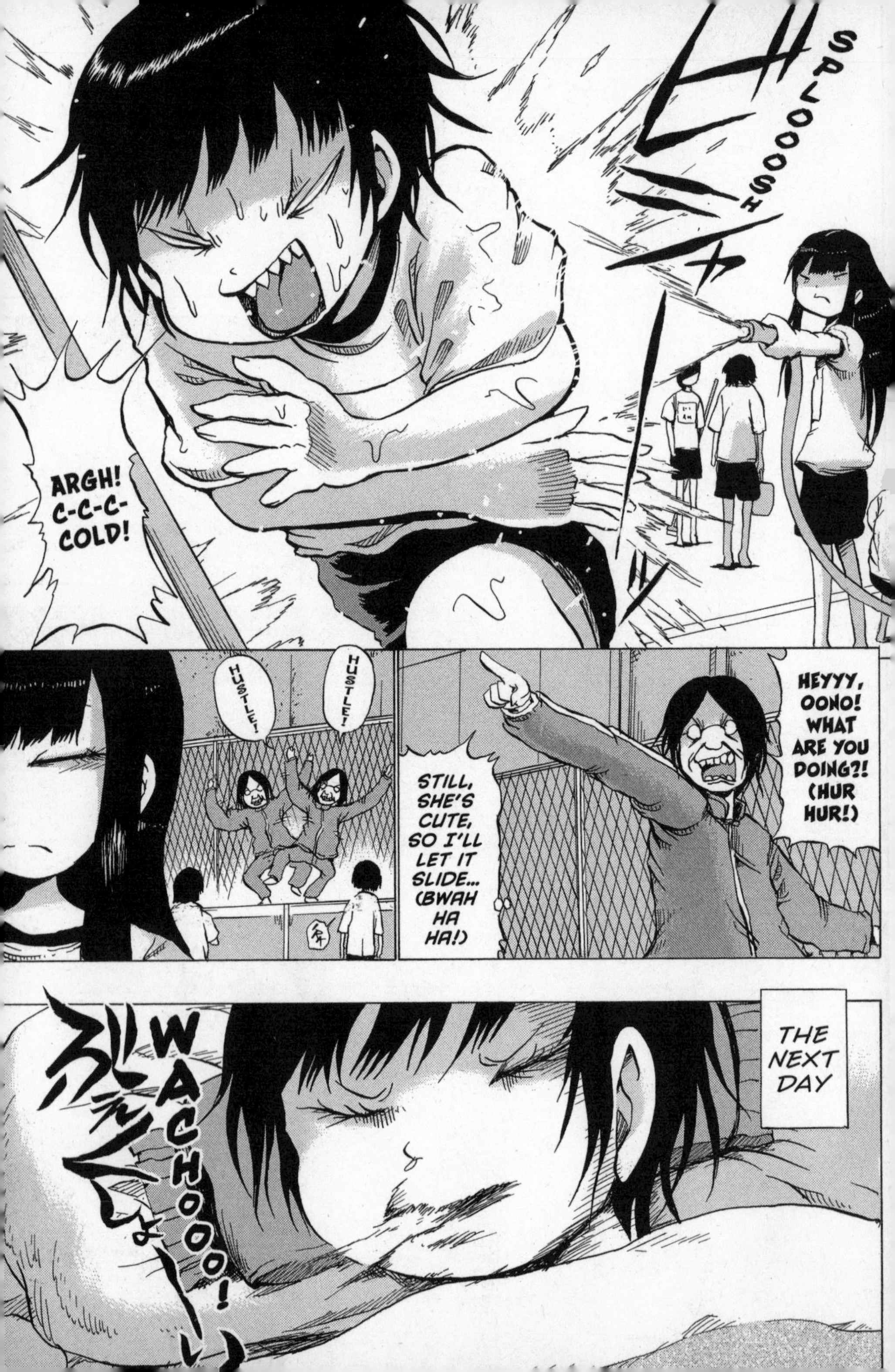
SPLOOOOSH
ARGH! C-C-C-COLD!
HEYYY, OONO! WHAT ARE YOU DOING?! (HUR HUR!)
STILL, SHE'S CUTE, SO I'LL LET IT SLIDE... (BWAH HA HA!)
HUSTLE!
HUSTLE!
THE NEXT DAY
WACHOOOO!

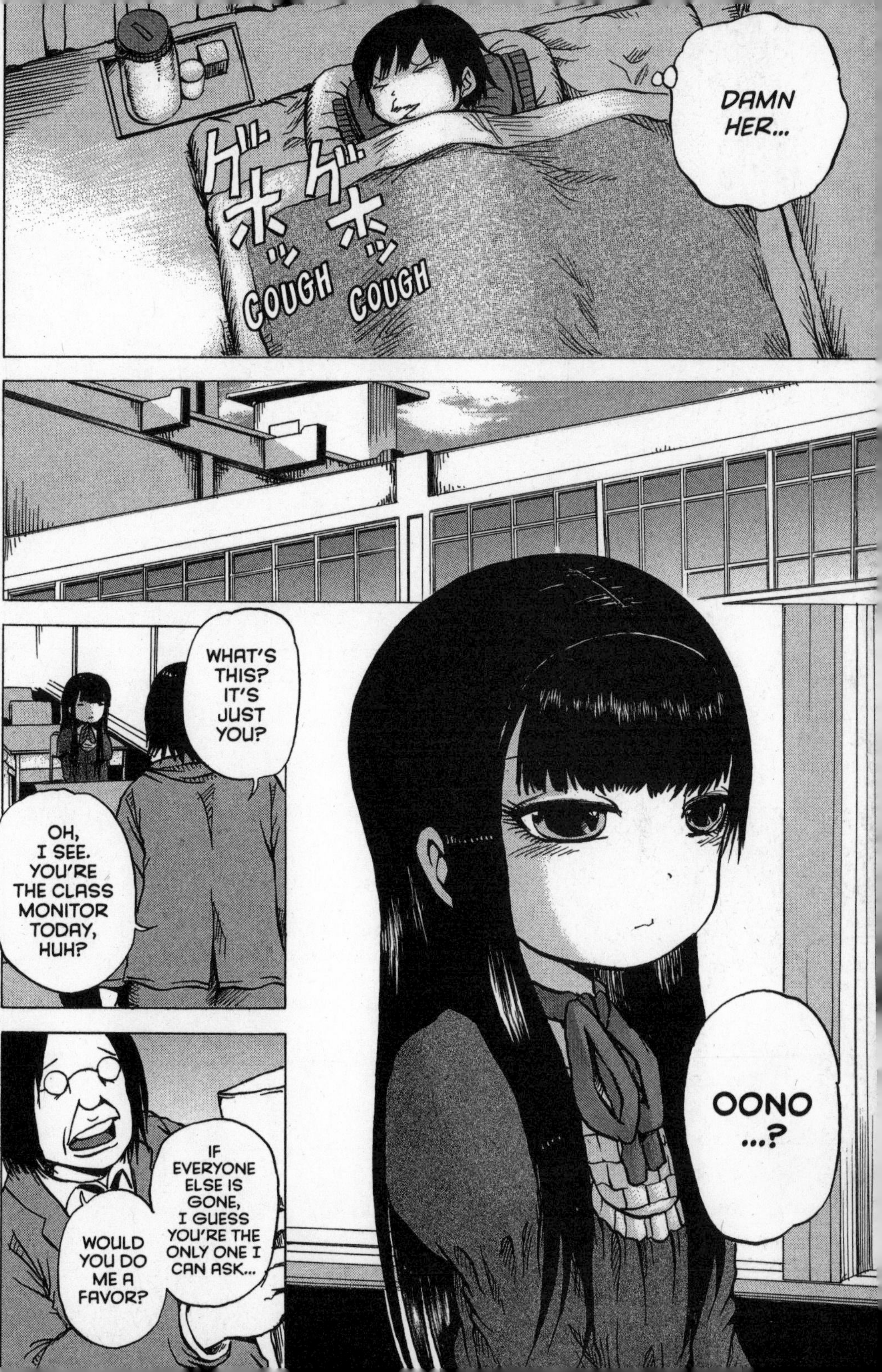
DAMN HER...
ゲホッ
COUGH
ゲホッ
COUGH
OONO ...?
WHAT'S THIS? IT'S JUST YOU?
OH, I SEE. YOU'RE THE CLASS MONITOR TODAY, HUH?
IF EVERYONE ELSE IS GONE, I GUESS YOU'RE THE ONLY ONE I CAN ASK...
WOULD YOU DO ME A FAVOR?

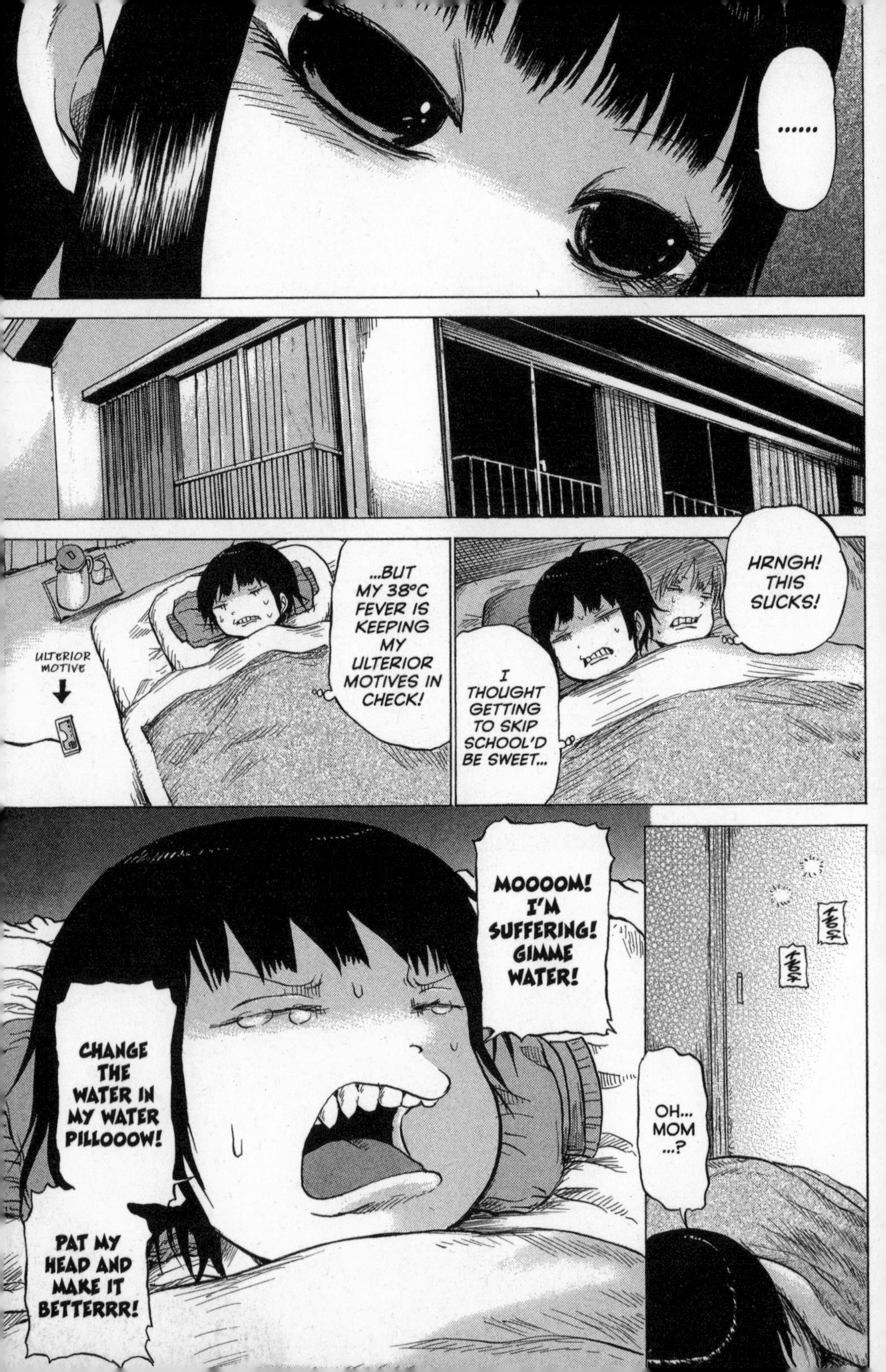
......
HRNGH! THIS SUCKS!
I THOUGHT GETTING TO SKIP SCHOOL'D BE SWEET...
...BUT MY 38°C FEVER IS KEEPING MY ULTERIOR MOTIVES IN CHECK!
ULTERIOR MOTIVE
OH... MOM ...?
MOOOOM! I'M SUFFERING! GIMME WATER!
CHANGE THE WATER IN MY WATER PILLOOOW!
PAT MY HEAD AND MAKE IT BETTERRR!

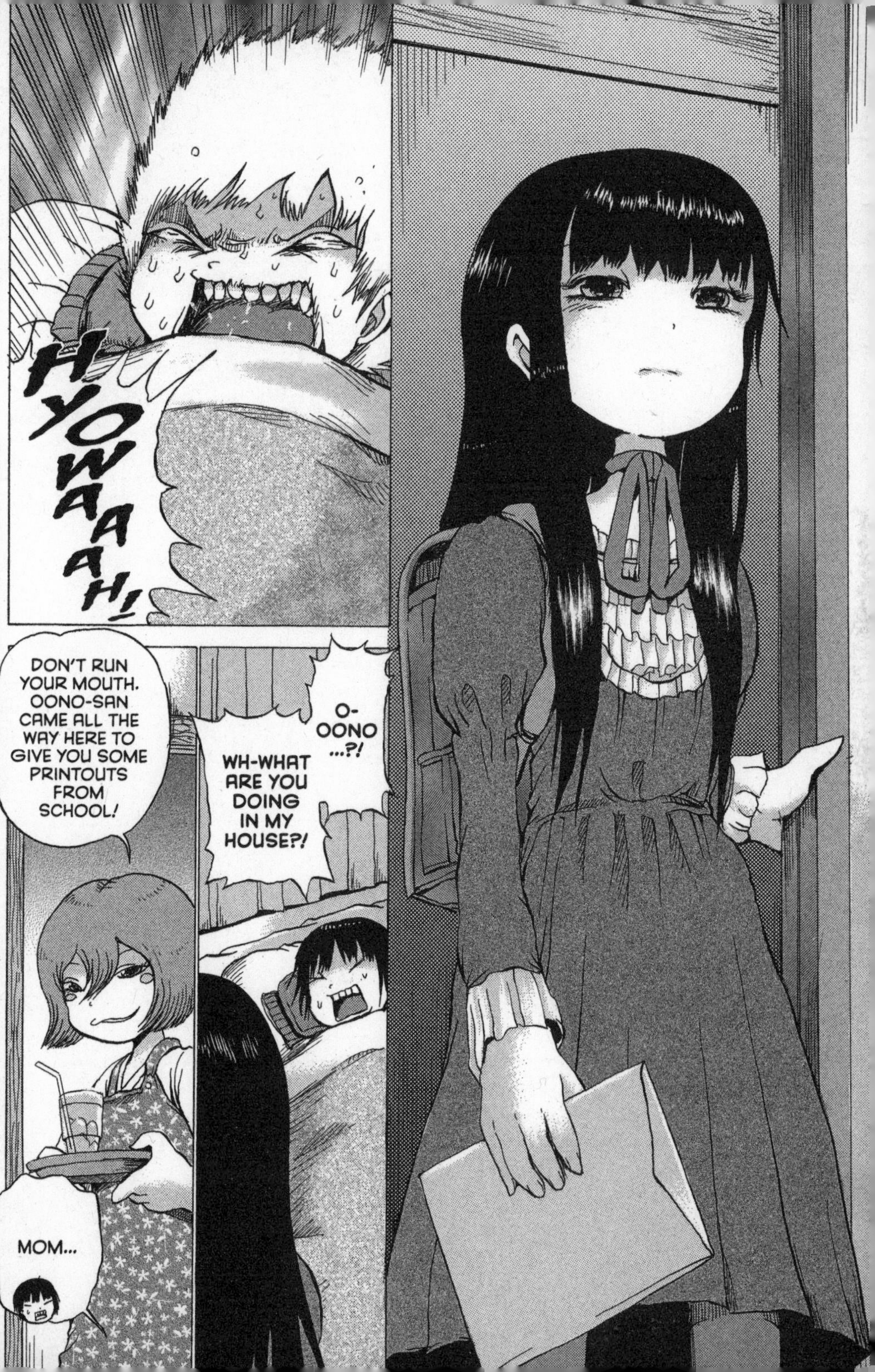
HYOWAAAH!
O-OONO ...?!
WH-WHAT ARE YOU DOING IN MY HOUSE?!
DON'T RUN YOUR MOUTH. OONO-SAN CAME ALL THE WAY HERE TO GIVE YOU SOME PRINTOUTS FROM SCHOOL!
MOM...

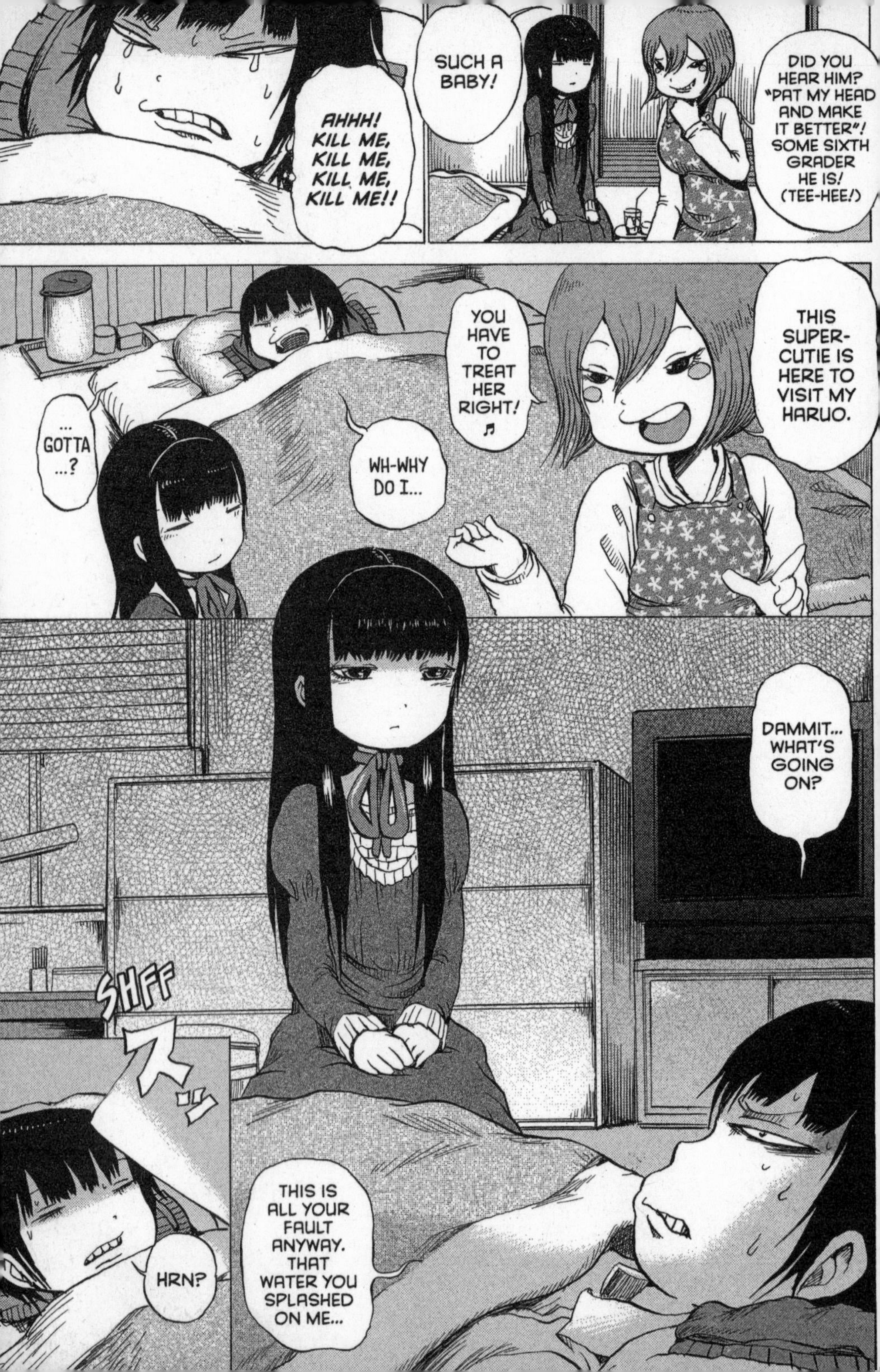
DID YOU HEAR HIM? "PAT MY HEAD AND MAKE IT BETTER"! SOME SIXTH GRADER HE IS! (TEE-HEE!)
SUCH A BABY!
AHHH! KILL ME, KILL ME, KILL ME, KILL ME!!
THIS SUPER-CUTIE IS HERE TO VISIT MY HARUO.
YOU HAVE TO TREAT HER RIGHT! ♪
WH-WHY DO I...
... GOTTA ...?
DAMMIT... WHAT'S GOING ON?
SHFF
スッ
THIS IS ALL YOUR FAULT ANYWAY. THAT WATER YOU SPLASHED ON ME...
HRN?

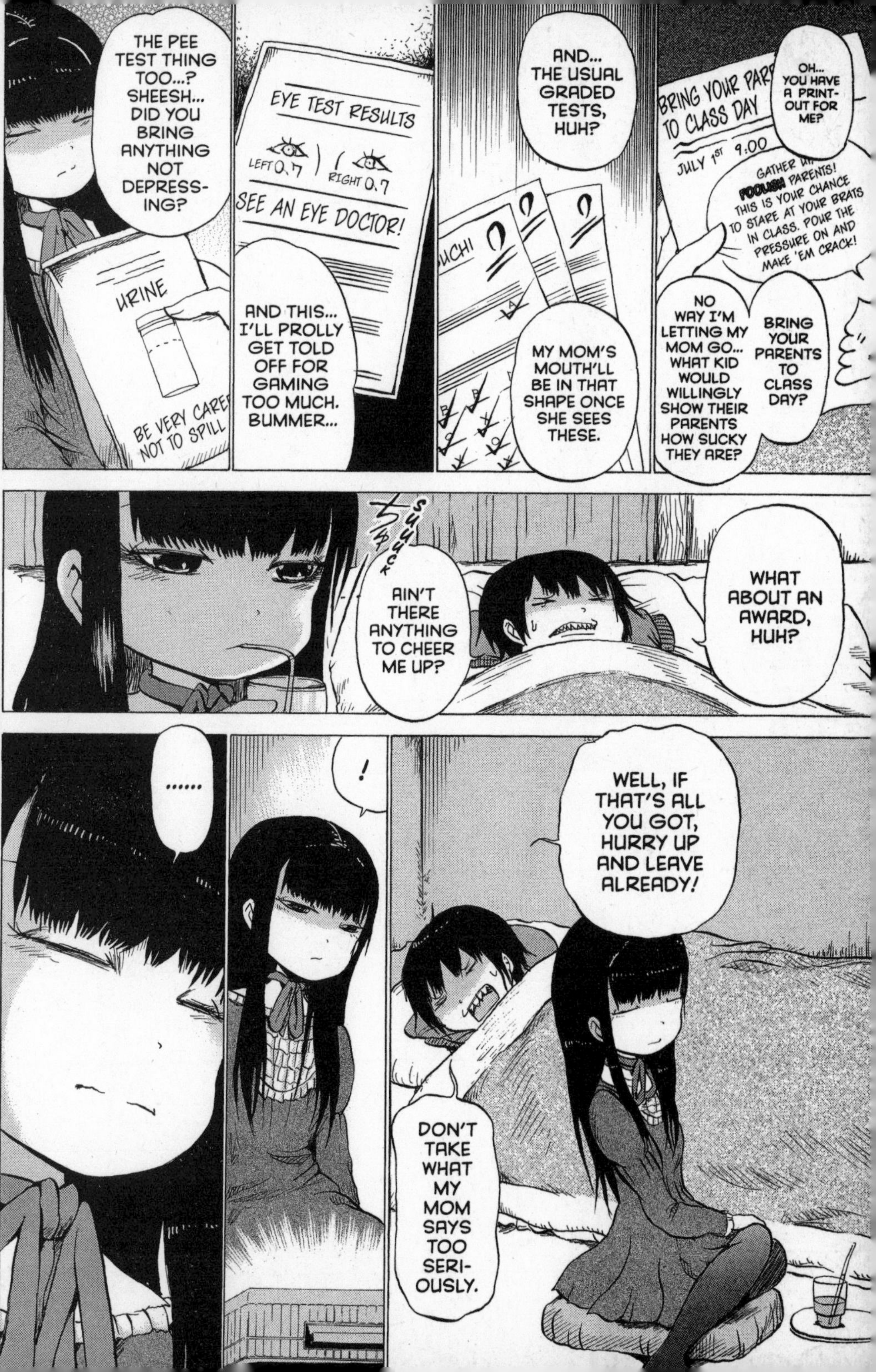
OH... YOU HAVE A PRINT-OUT FOR ME?
BRING YOUR PARE
TO CLASS DAY
JULY 1ST 9:00
GATHER U FOOLISH PARENTS! THIS IS YOUR CHANCE TO STARE AT YOUR BRATS IN CLASS. POUR THE PRESSURE ON AND MAKE 'EM CRACK!
BRING YOUR PARENTS TO CLASS DAY?
NO WAY I'M LETTING MY MOM GO... WHAT KID WOULD WILLINGLY SHOW THEIR PARENTS HOW SUCKY THEY ARE?
AND... THE USUAL GRADED TESTS, HUH?
MY MOM'S MOUTH'LL BE IN THAT SHAPE ONCE SHE SEES THESE.
EYE TEST RESULTS
LEFT 0.7
RIGHT 0.7
SEE AN EYE DOCTOR!
AND THIS... I'LL PROLLY GET TOLD OFF FOR GAMING TOO MUCH. BUMMER...
THE PEE TEST THING TOO...? SHEESH... DID YOU BRING ANYTHING NOT DEPRESS-ING?
URINE
BE VERY CARE
NOT TO SPILL
WHAT ABOUT AN AWARD, HUH?
SUUUCK
AIN'T THERE ANYTHING TO CHEER ME UP?
WELL, IF THAT'S ALL YOU GOT, HURRY UP AND LEAVE ALREADY!
DON'T TAKE WHAT MY MOM SAYS TOO SERI-OUSLY.
!
......

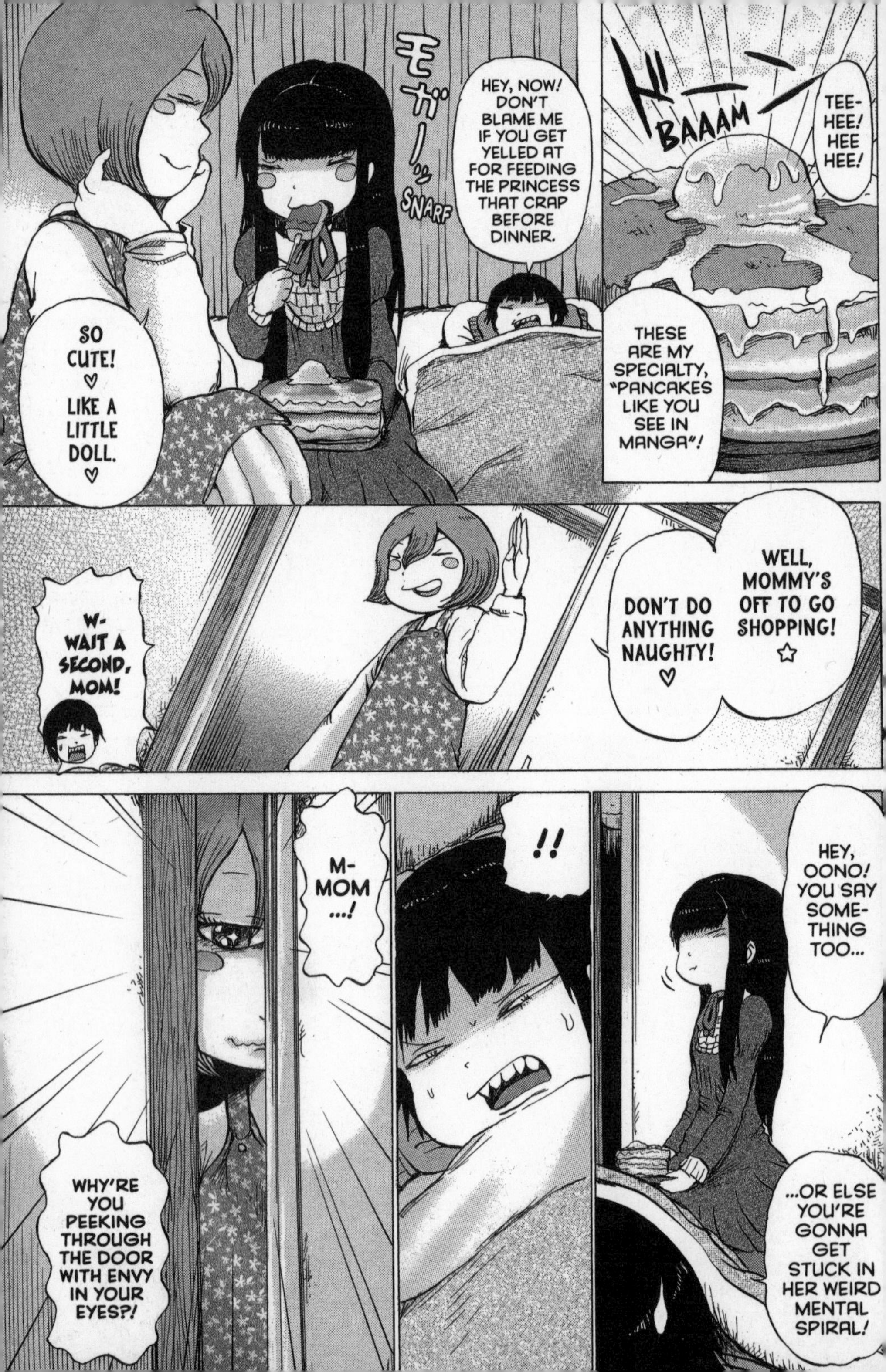
TEE-HEE! HEE HEE!
ドーン
BAAAM
THESE ARE MY SPECIALTY, "PANCAKES LIKE YOU SEE IN MANGA"!
HEY, NOW! DON'T BLAME ME IF YOU GET YELLED AT FOR FEEDING THE PRINCESS THAT CRAP BEFORE DINNER.
モガー
SNARF
SO CUTE! ♡ LIKE A LITTLE DOLL. ♡
WELL, MOMMY'S OFF TO GO SHOPPING! ☆
DON'T DO ANYTHING NAUGHTY! ♡
W-WAIT A SECOND, MOM!
HEY, OONO! YOU SAY SOME-THING TOO...
...OR ELSE YOU'RE GONNA GET STUCK IN HER WEIRD MENTAL SPIRAL!
!!
M-MOM...!
WHY'RE YOU PEEKING THROUGH THE DOOR WITH ENVY IN YOUR EYES?!

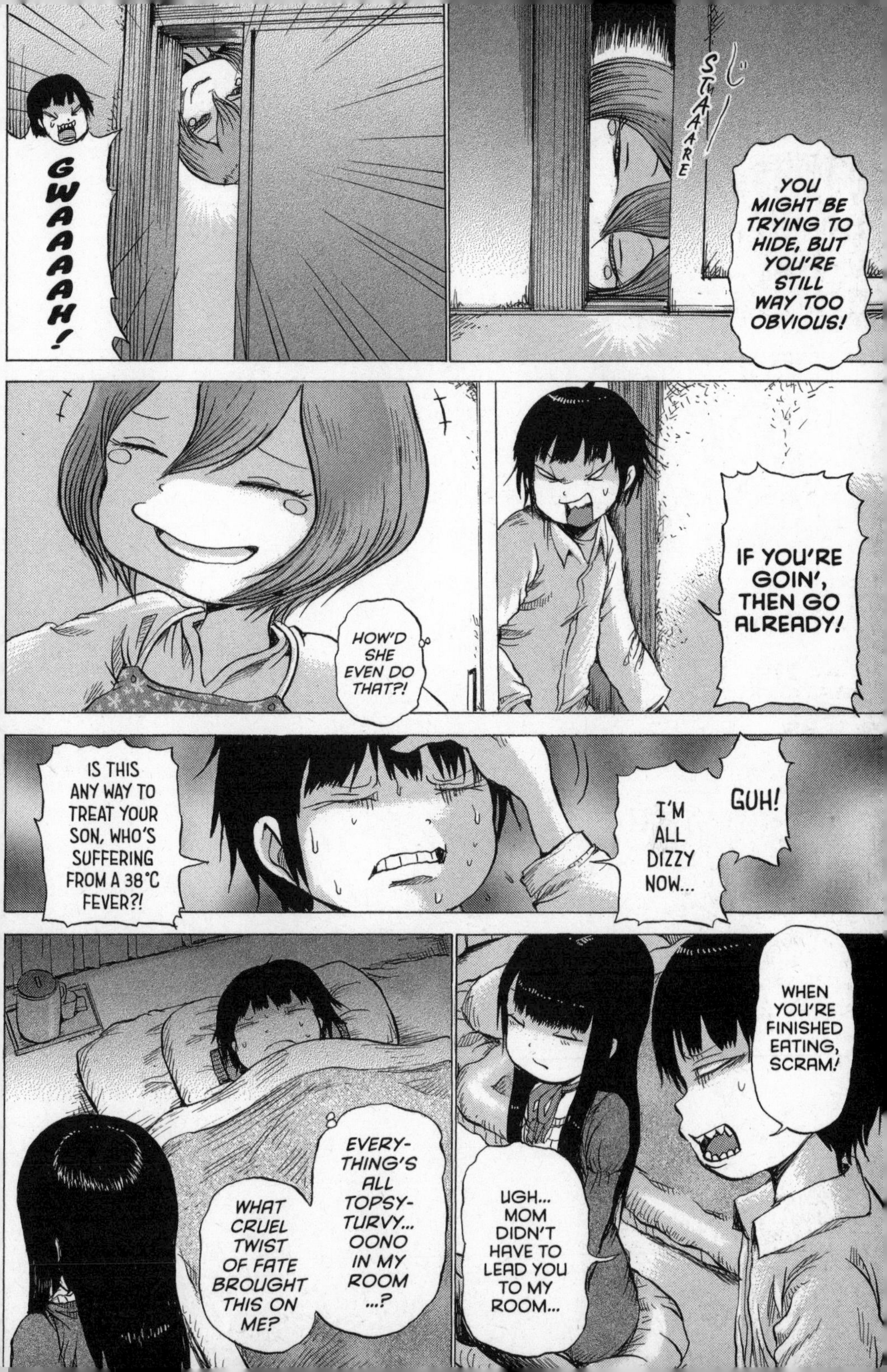
STAAAARE
YOU MIGHT BE TRYING TO HIDE, BUT YOU'RE STILL WAY TOO OBVIOUS!
GWAAAAAH!
IF YOU'RE GOIN', THEN GO ALREADY!
HOW'D SHE EVEN DO THAT?!
GUH!
I'M ALL DIZZY NOW...
IS THIS ANY WAY TO TREAT YOUR SON, WHO'S SUFFERING FROM A 38°C FEVER?!
WHEN YOU'RE FINISHED EATING, SCRAM!
UGH... MOM DIDN'T HAVE TO LEAD YOU TO MY ROOM...
EVERY-THING'S ALL TOPSY-TURVY... OONO IN MY ROOM ...?
WHAT CRUEL TWIST OF FATE BROUGHT THIS ON ME?

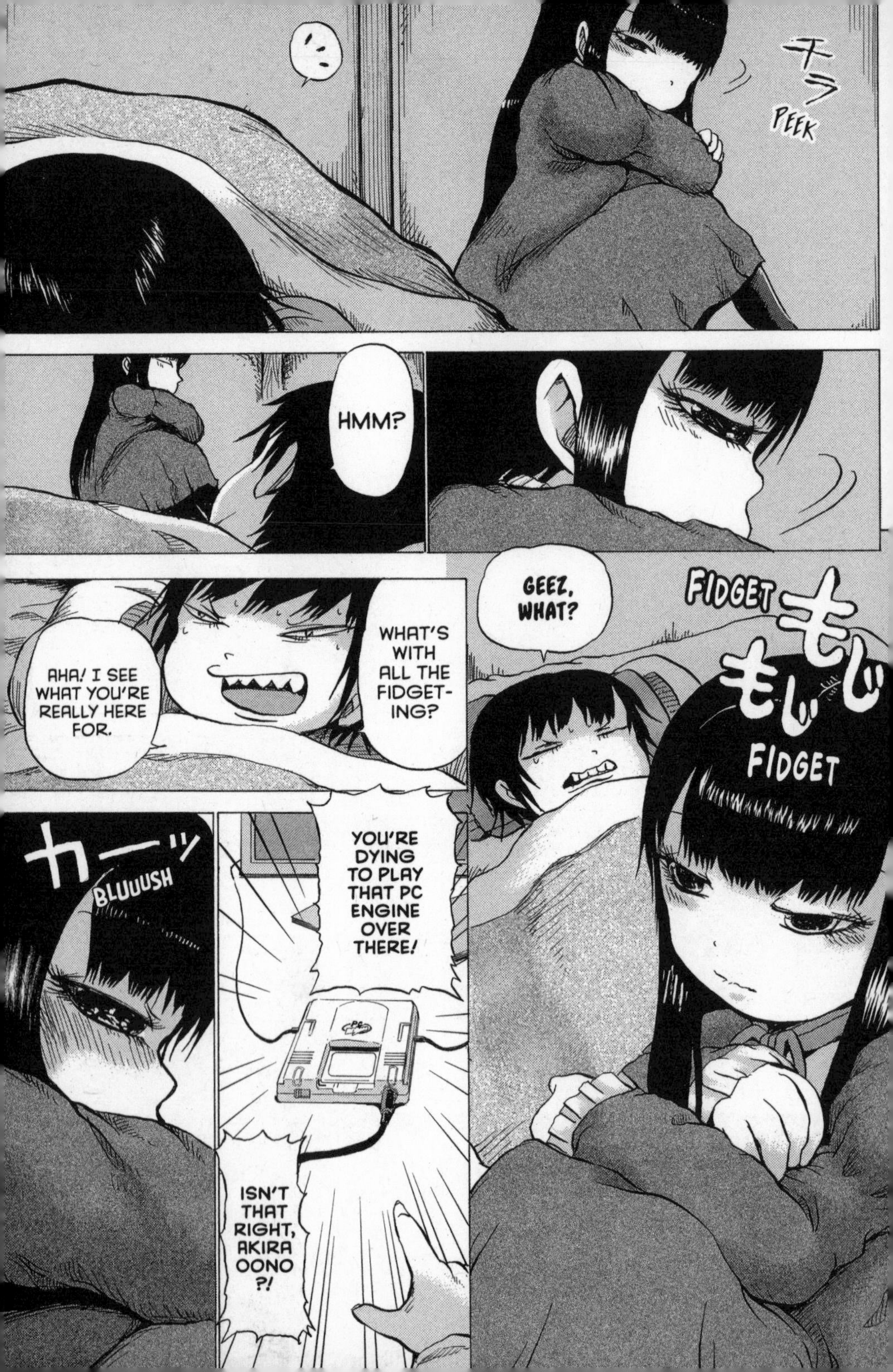
チラ
PEEK
HMM?
GEEZ, WHAT?
FIDGET もじもじ FIDGET
WHAT'S WITH ALL THE FIDGET-ING?
AHA! I SEE WHAT YOU'RE REALLY HERE FOR.
YOU'RE DYING TO PLAY THAT PC ENGINE OVER THERE!
ISN'T THAT RIGHT, AKIRA OONO?!
カーッ
BLUUUSH

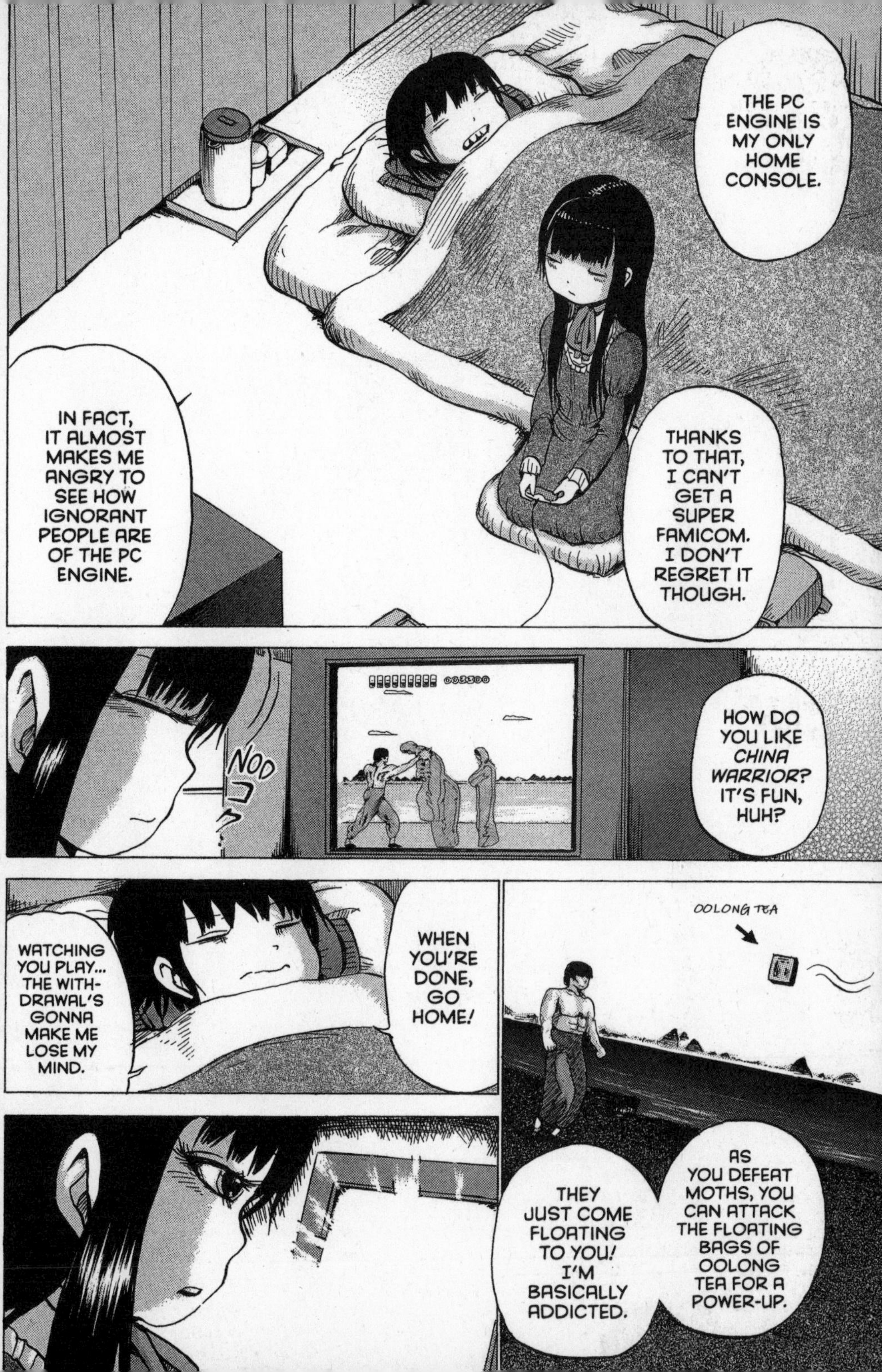
THE PC ENGINE IS MY ONLY HOME CONSOLE.
THANKS TO THAT, I CAN'T GET A SUPER FAMICOM. I DON'T REGRET IT THOUGH.
IN FACT, IT ALMOST MAKES ME ANGRY TO SEE HOW IGNORANT PEOPLE ARE OF THE PC ENGINE.
HOW DO YOU LIKE *CHINA WARRIOR*? IT'S FUN, HUH?
NOD
OOLONG TEA
AS YOU DEFEAT MOTHS, YOU CAN ATTACK THE FLOATING BAGS OF OOLONG TEA FOR A POWER-UP.
THEY JUST COME FLOATING TO YOU! I'M BASICALLY ADDICTED.
WHEN YOU'RE DONE, GO HOME!
WATCHING YOU PLAY... THE WITH-DRAWAL'S GONNA MAKE ME LOSE MY MIND.

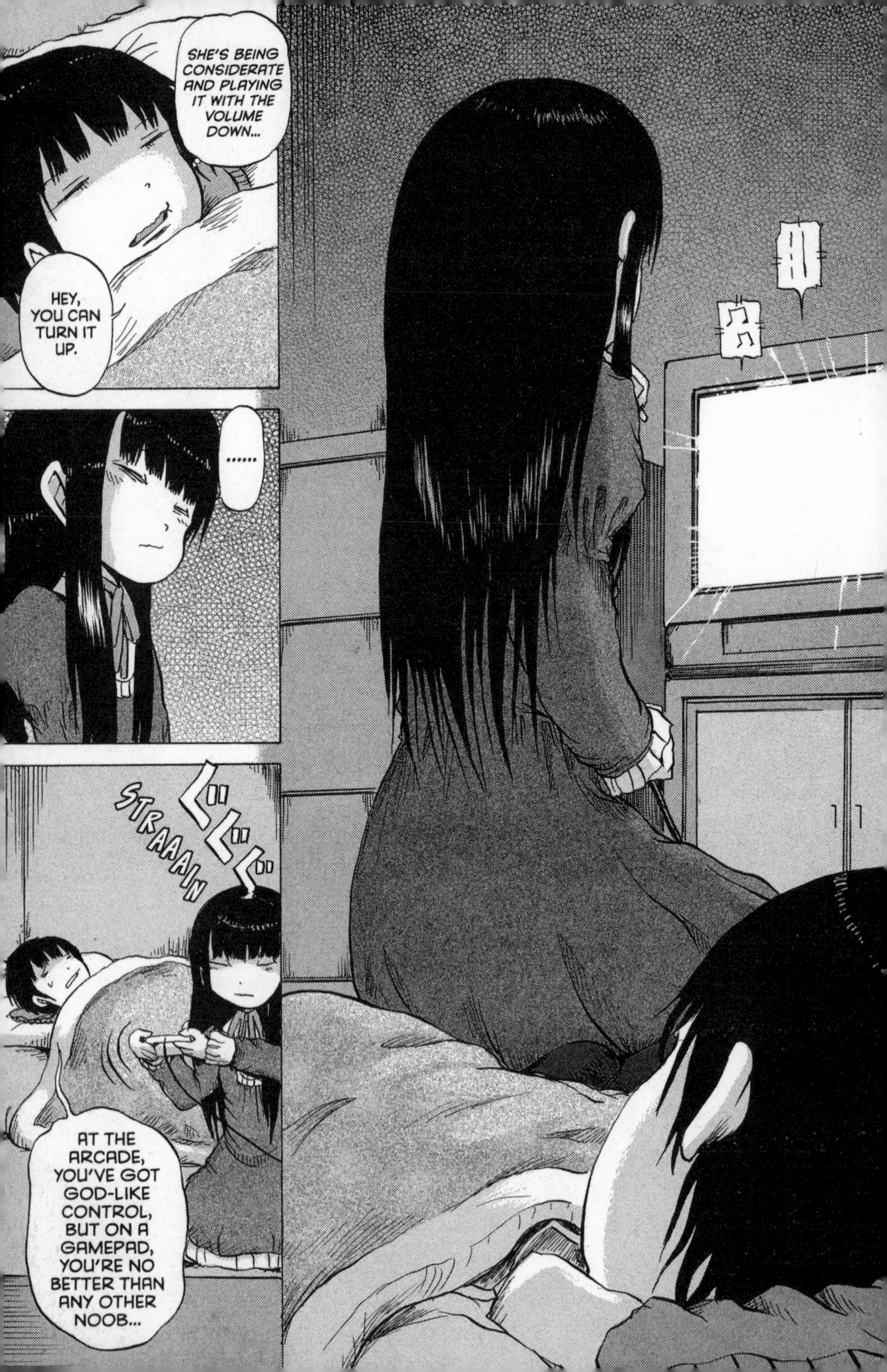
SHE'S BEING CONSIDERATE AND PLAYING IT WITH THE VOLUME DOWN...
HEY, YOU CAN TURN IT UP.
......
STRAAAIN
AT THE ARCADE, YOU'VE GOT GOD-LIKE CONTROL, BUT ON A GAMEPAD, YOU'RE NO BETTER THAN ANY OTHER NOOB...

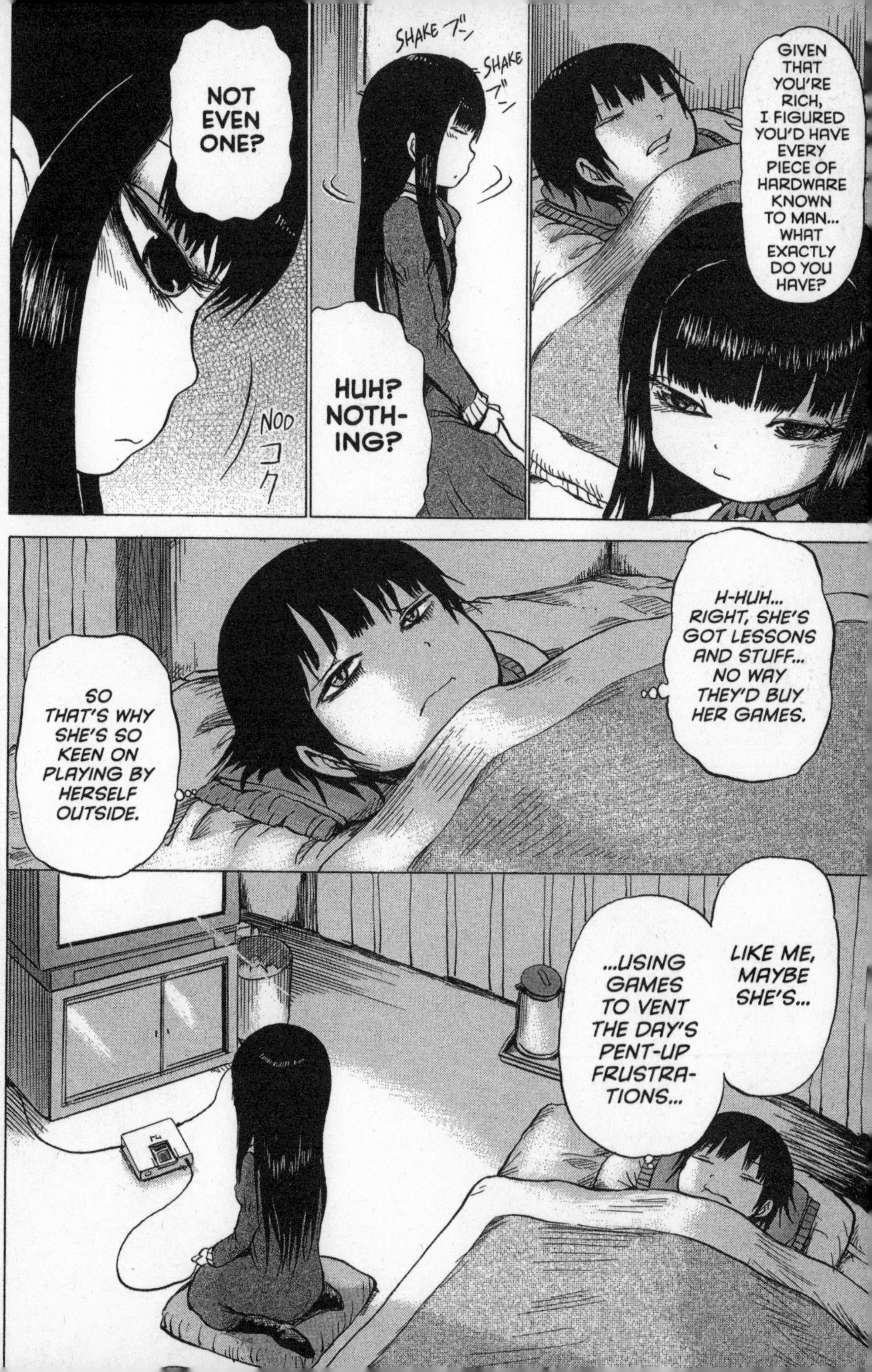

GIVEN THAT YOU'RE RICH, I FIGURED YOU'D HAVE EVERY PIECE OF HARDWARE KNOWN TO MAN... WHAT EXACTLY DO YOU HAVE?
SHAKE ブン
SHAKE ブン
HUH? NOTHING-ING?
NOT EVEN ONE?
NOD コク
H-HUH... RIGHT, SHE'S GOT LESSONS AND STUFF... NO WAY THEY'D BUY HER GAMES.
SO THAT'S WHY SHE'S SO KEEN ON PLAYING BY HERSELF OUTSIDE.
LIKE ME, MAYBE SHE'S...
...USING GAMES TO VENT THE DAY'S PENT-UP FRUSTRA-TIONS...

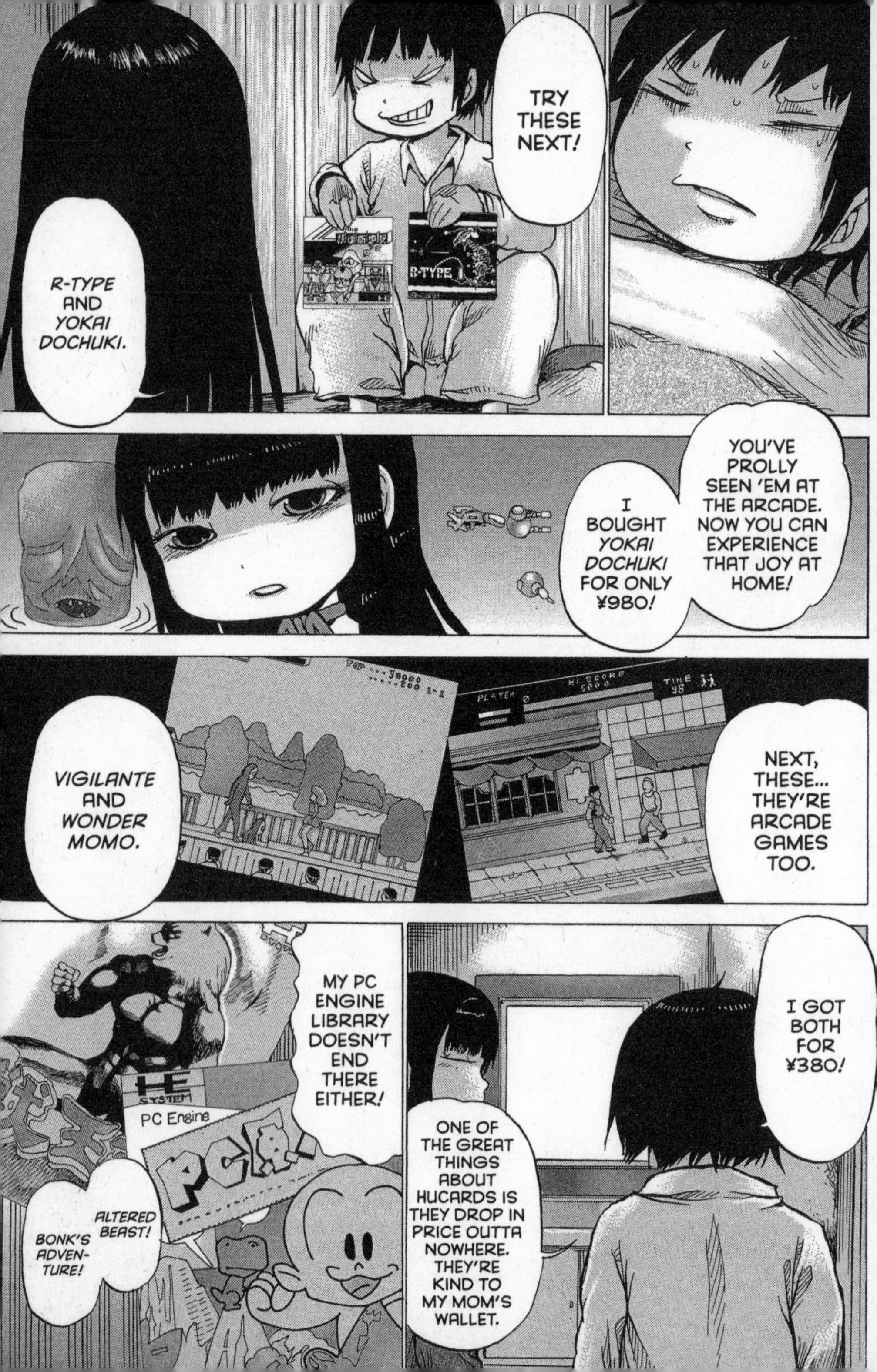
TRY THESE NEXT!
R-TYPE
R-TYPE AND YOKAI DOCHUKI.
YOU'VE PROLLY SEEN 'EM AT THE ARCADE. NOW YOU CAN EXPERIENCE THAT JOY AT HOME!
I BOUGHT YOKAI DOCHUKI FOR ONLY ¥980!
NEXT, THESE... THEY'RE ARCADE GAMES TOO.
PLAYER
HI SCORE
TIME
VIGILANTE AND WONDER MOMO.
I GOT BOTH FOR ¥380!
ONE OF THE GREAT THINGS ABOUT HUCARDS IS THEY DROP IN PRICE OUTTA NOWHERE. THEY'RE KIND TO MY MOM'S WALLET.
MY PC ENGINE LIBRARY DOESN'T END THERE EITHER!
PC Engine
ALTERED BEAST!
BONK'S ADVEN-TURE!

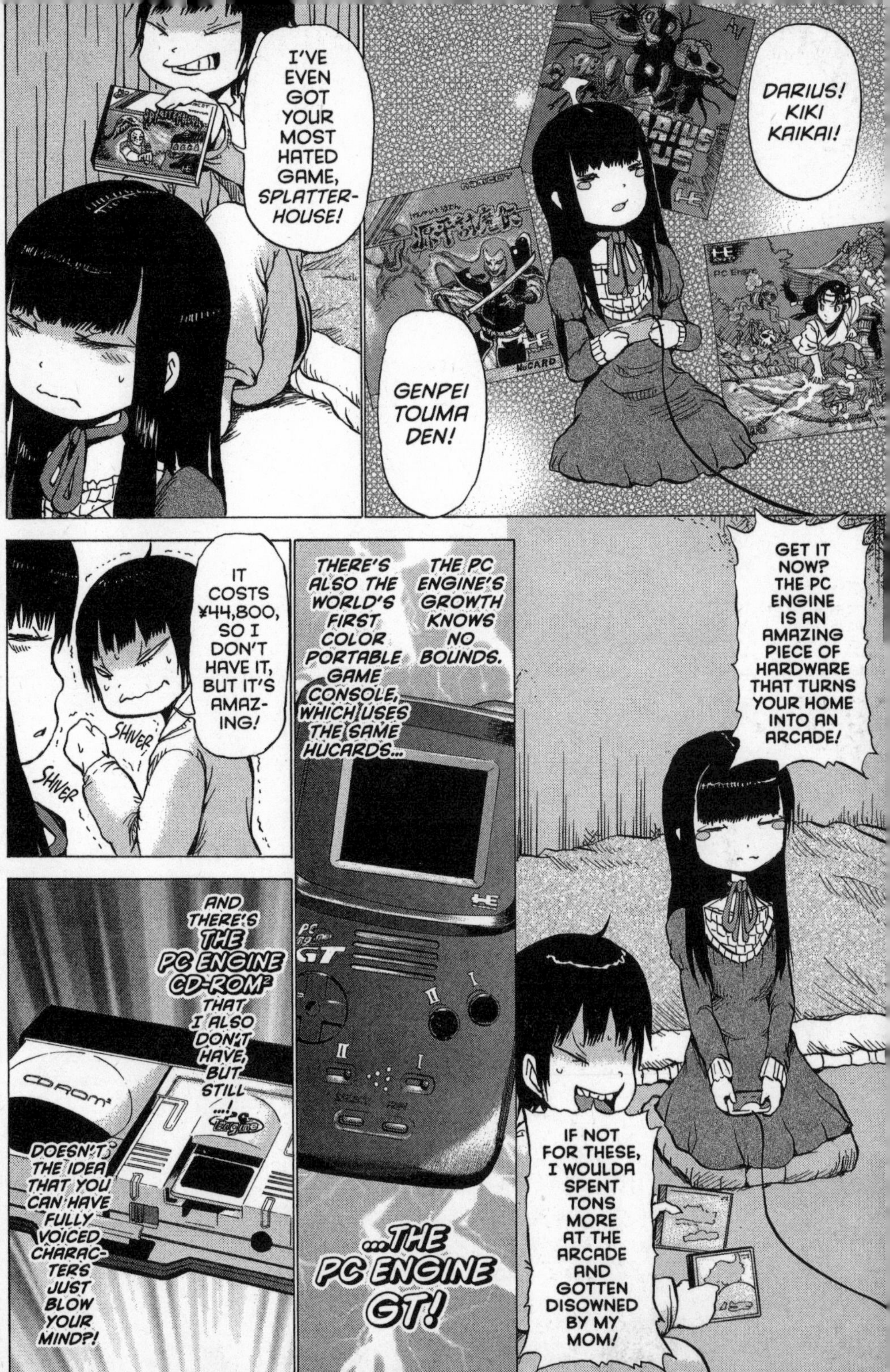
DARIUS! KIKI KAIKAI!
GENPEI TOUMA DEN!
I'VE EVEN GOT YOUR MOST HATED GAME, SPLATTER-HOUSE!
GET IT NOW? THE PC ENGINE IS AN AMAZING PIECE OF HARDWARE THAT TURNS YOUR HOME INTO AN ARCADE!
IF NOT FOR THESE, I WOULDA SPENT TONS MORE AT THE ARCADE AND GOTTEN DISOWNED BY MY MOM!
THE PC ENGINE'S GROWTH KNOWS NO BOUNDS.
THERE'S ALSO THE WORLD'S FIRST COLOR PORTABLE GAME CONSOLE, WHICH USES THE SAME HUCARDS...
...THE PC ENGINE GT!
IT COSTS ¥44,800, SO I DON'T HAVE IT, BUT IT'S AMAZ-ING!
SHIVER
SHIVER
AND THERE'S THE PC ENGINE CD-ROM^2 THAT I ALSO DON'T HAVE, BUT STILL...!
DOESN'T THE IDEA THAT YOU CAN HAVE FULLY VOICED CHARAC-TERS JUST BLOW YOUR MIND?!

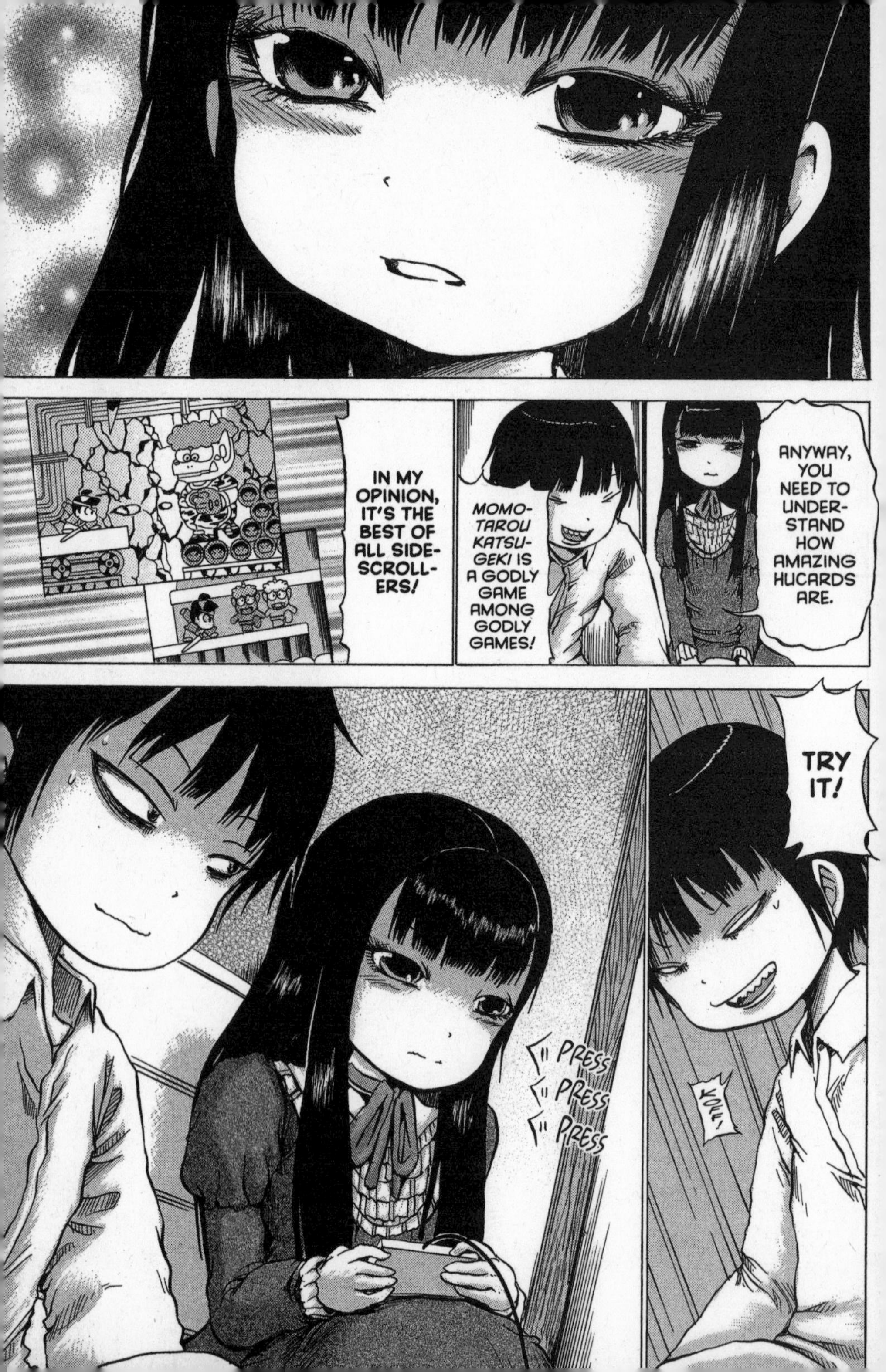
ANYWAY, YOU NEED TO UNDERSTAND HOW AMAZING HUCARDS ARE.
MOMOTAROU KATSUGEKI IS A GODLY GAME AMONG GODLY GAMES!
IN MY OPINION, IT'S THE BEST OF ALL SIDE-SCROLLERS!
TRY IT!
PRESS
PRESS
PRESS

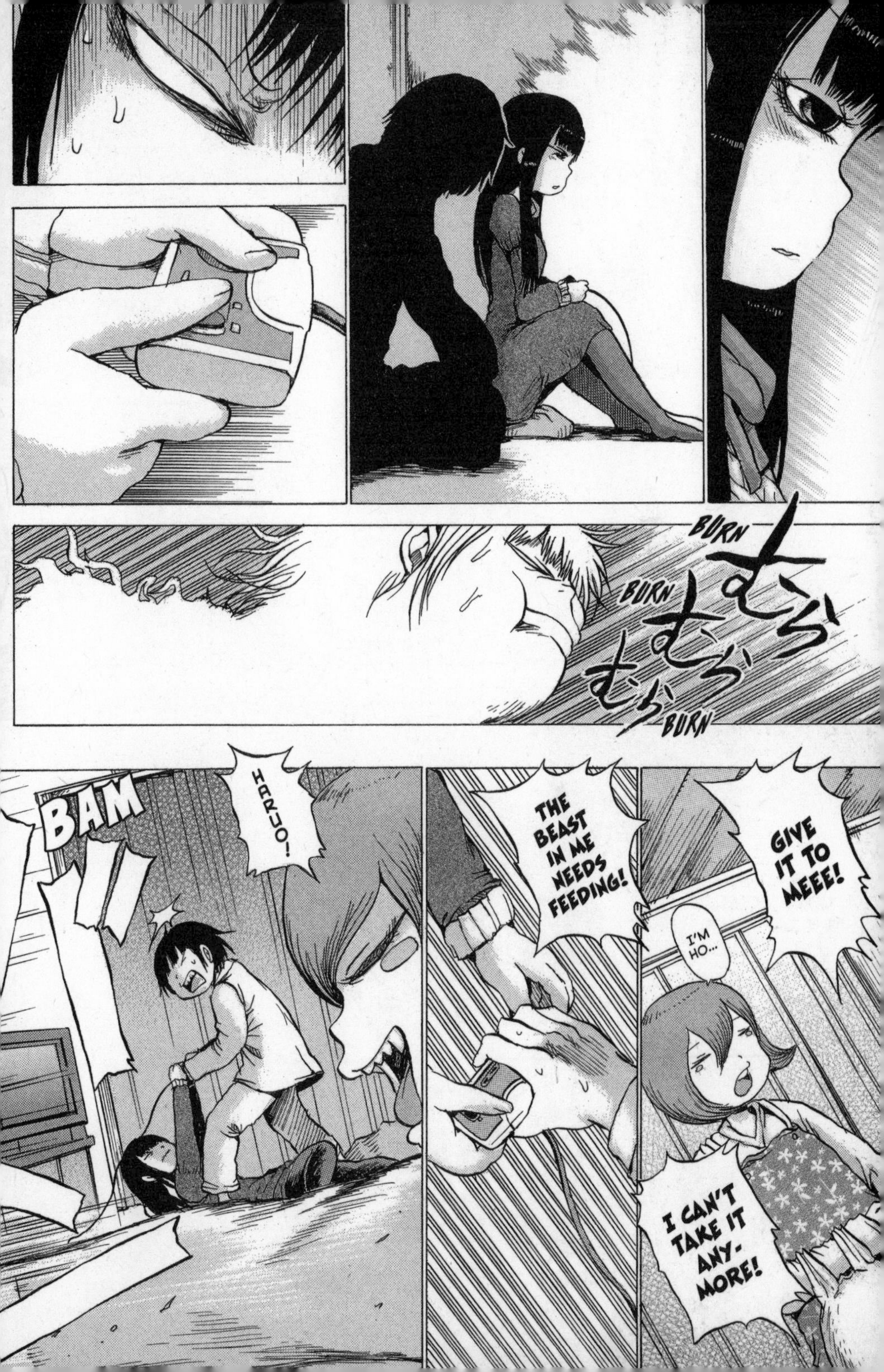
むら
BURN
むら
BURN
むら
BURN
GIVE IT TO MEEE!
I'M HO...
I CAN'T TAKE IT ANY-MORE!
THE BEAST IN ME NEEDS FEEDING!
HARUO!
BAM

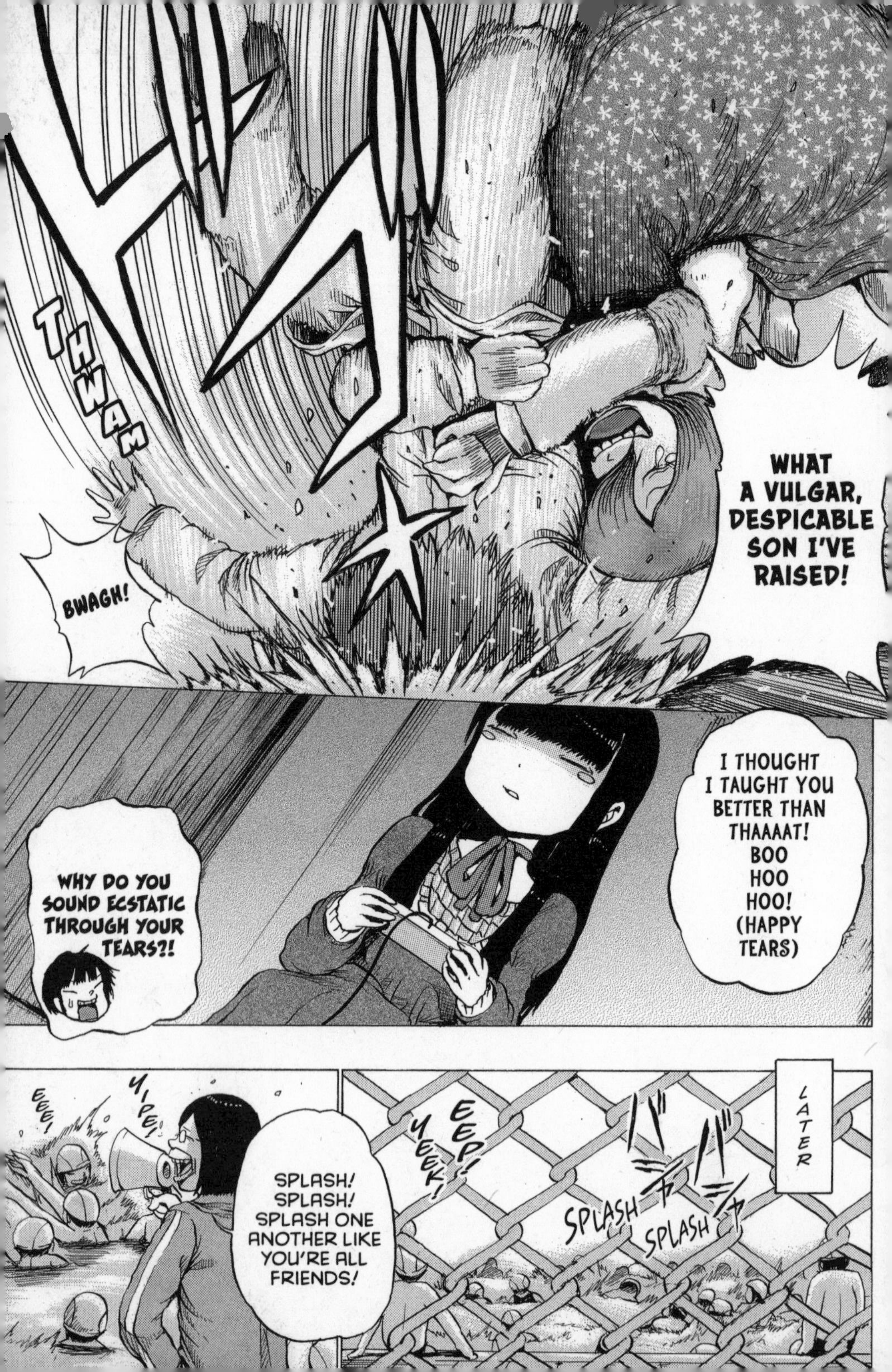
WHAT A VULGAR, DESPICABLE SON I'VE RAISED!
THWAM
BWAGH!
I THOUGHT I TAUGHT YOU BETTER THAN THAAAAT! BOO HOO HOO! (HAPPY TEARS)
WHY DO YOU SOUND ECSTATIC THROUGH YOUR TEARS?!
LATER
SPLASH
SPLASH
EEP!
YEEK!
SPLASH! SPLASH! SPLASH ONE ANOTHER LIKE YOU'RE ALL FRIENDS!
YIPE!
EEE!

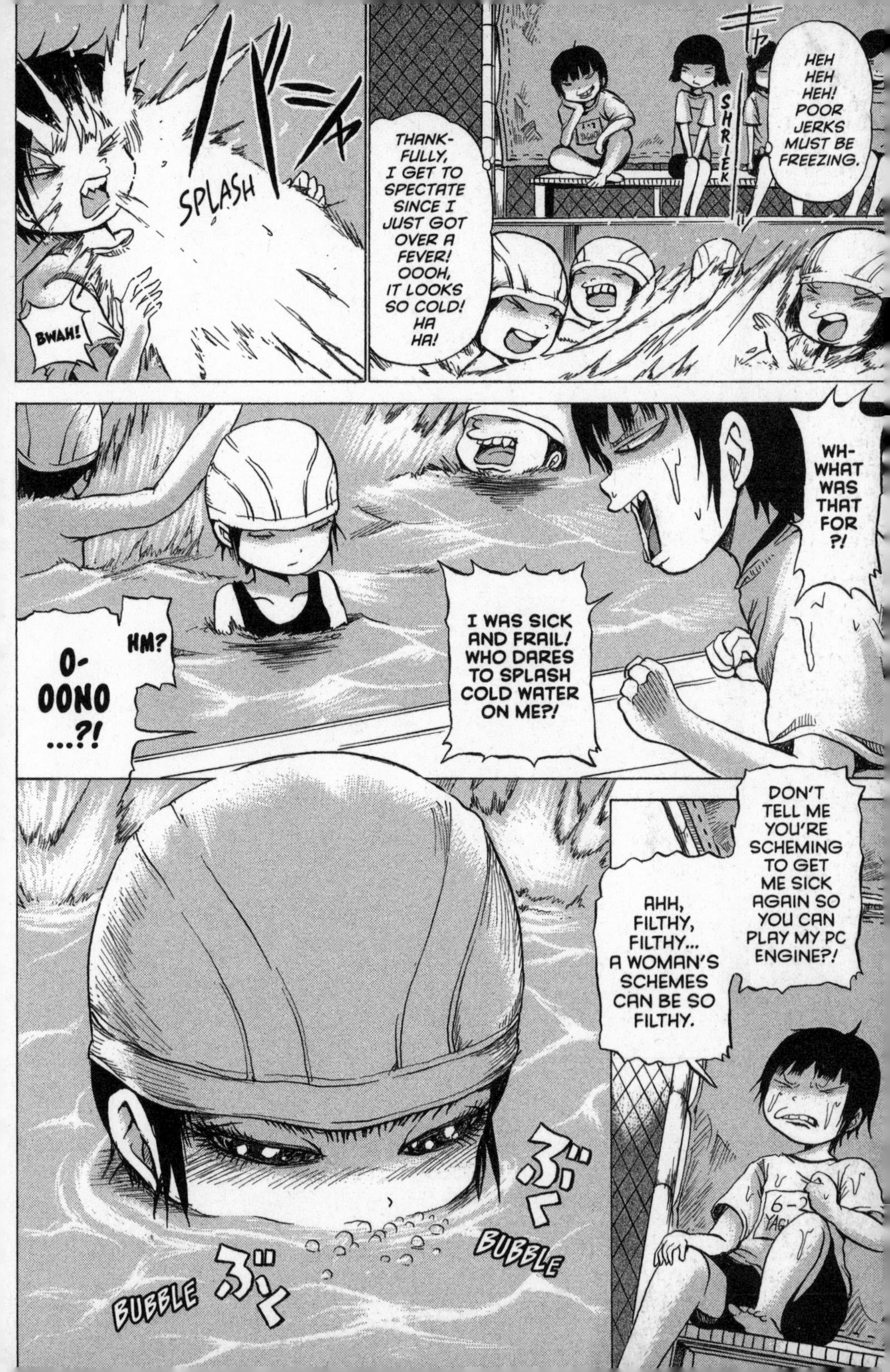
HEH HEH HEH! POOR JERKS MUST BE FREEZING.
SHRIEK
THANK-FULLY, I GET TO SPECTATE SINCE I JUST GOT OVER A FEVER! OOOH, IT LOOKS SO COLD! HA HA!
SPLASH
BWAH!
WH-WHAT WAS THAT FOR?!
I WAS SICK AND FRAIL! WHO DARES TO SPLASH COLD WATER ON ME?!
HM?
O-OONO ...?!
DON'T TELL ME YOU'RE SCHEMING TO GET ME SICK AGAIN SO YOU CAN PLAY MY PC ENGINE?!
AHH, FILTHY, FILTHY... A WOMAN'S SCHEMES CAN BE SO FILTHY.
BUBBLE
BUBBLE

HI SCORE GIRL

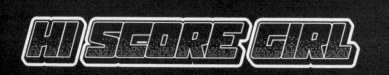

HI   SCORE   GIRL

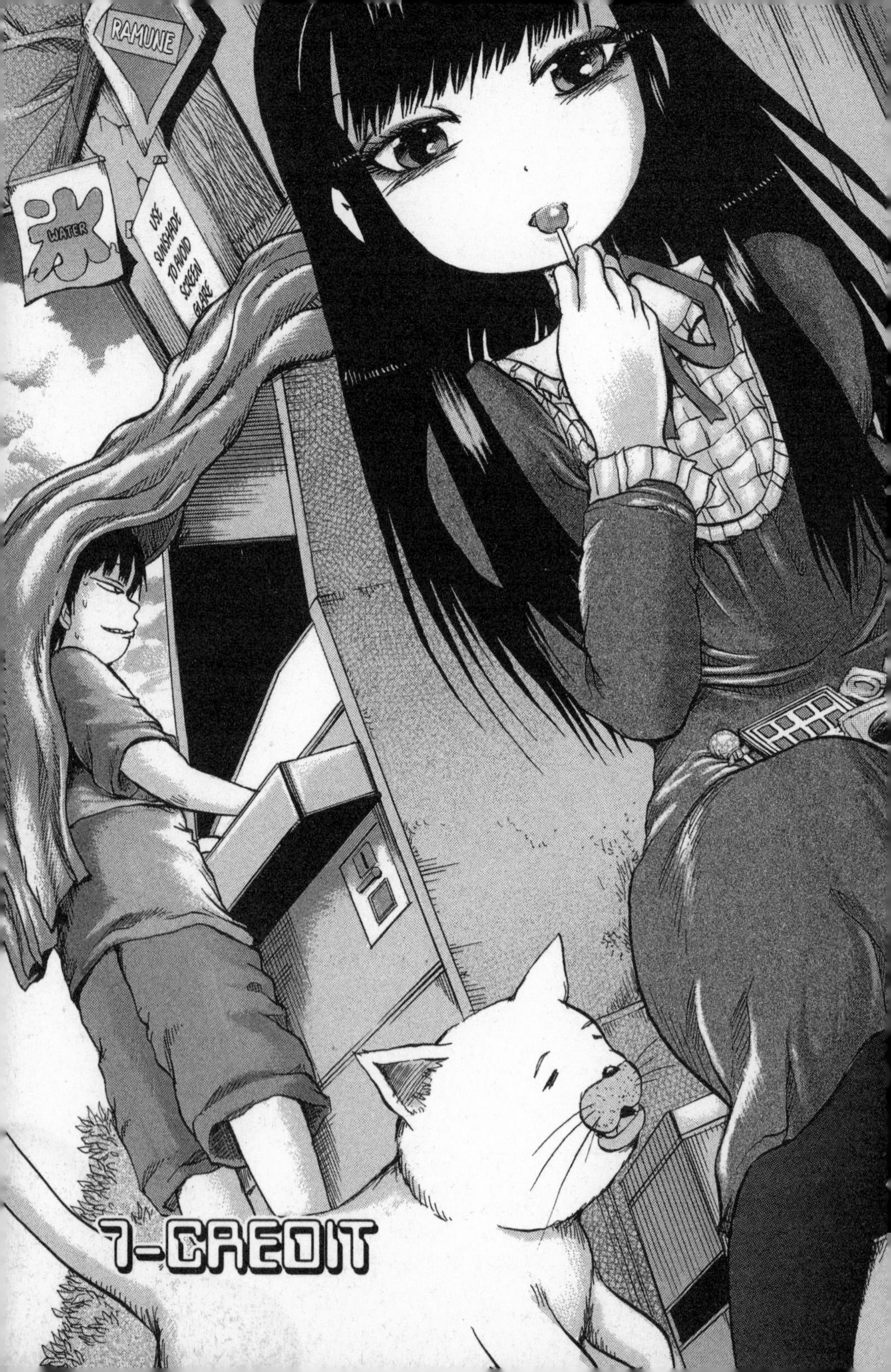
RAMUNE
WATER
USE SUNSHADE TO AVOID SCREEN GLARE
7-CREDIT

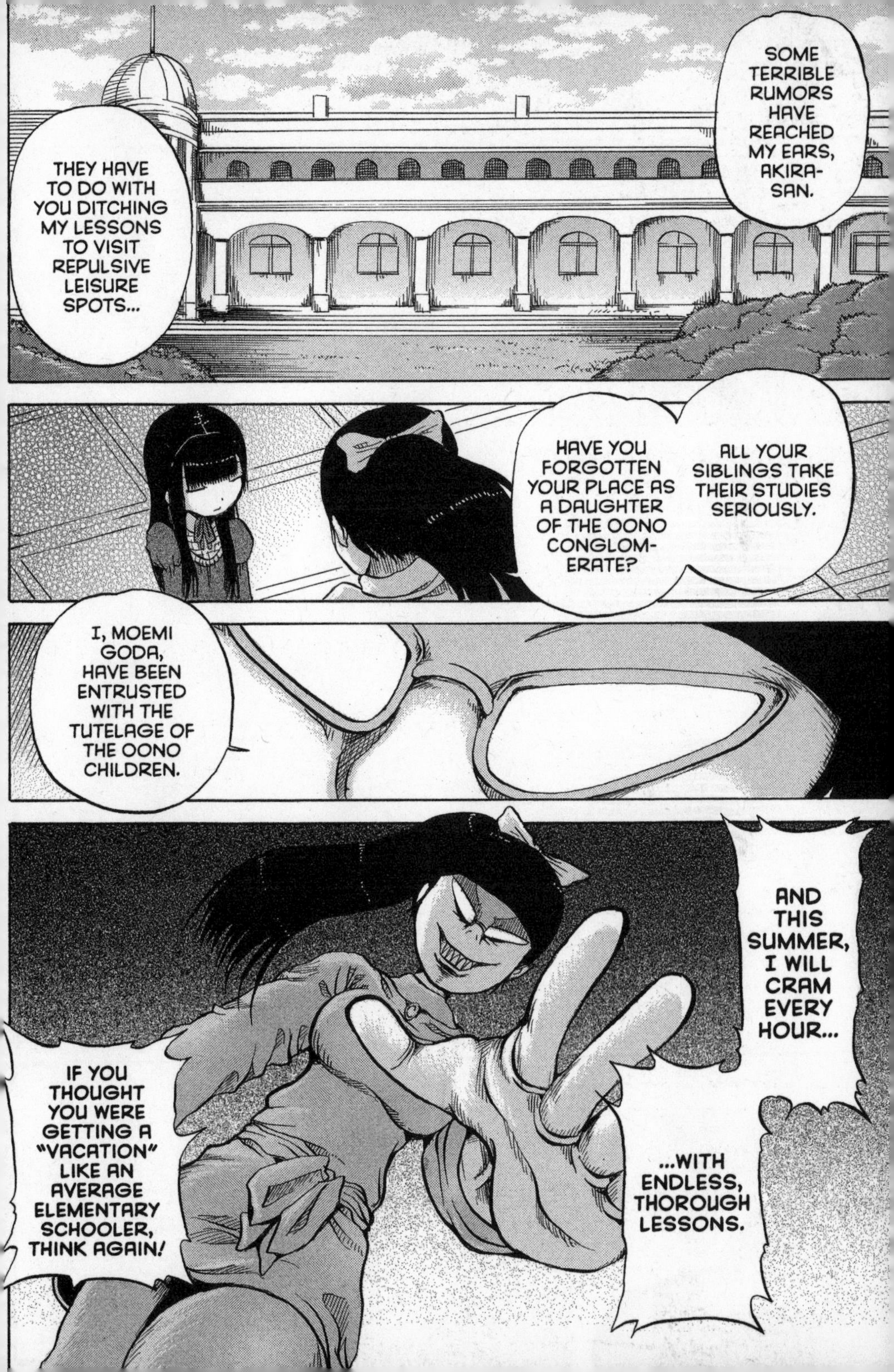
SOME TERRIBLE RUMORS HAVE REACHED MY EARS, AKIRA-SAN.
THEY HAVE TO DO WITH YOU DITCHING MY LESSONS TO VISIT REPULSIVE LEISURE SPOTS...
ALL YOUR SIBLINGS TAKE THEIR STUDIES SERIOUSLY.
HAVE YOU FORGOTTEN YOUR PLACE AS A DAUGHTER OF THE OONO CONGLOM-ERATE?
I, MOEMI GODA, HAVE BEEN ENTRUSTED WITH THE TUTELAGE OF THE OONO CHILDREN.
AND THIS SUMMER, I WILL CRAM EVERY HOUR...
...WITH ENDLESS, THOROUGH LESSONS.
IF YOU THOUGHT YOU WERE GETTING A "VACATION" LIKE AN AVERAGE ELEMENTARY SCHOOLER, THINK AGAIN!

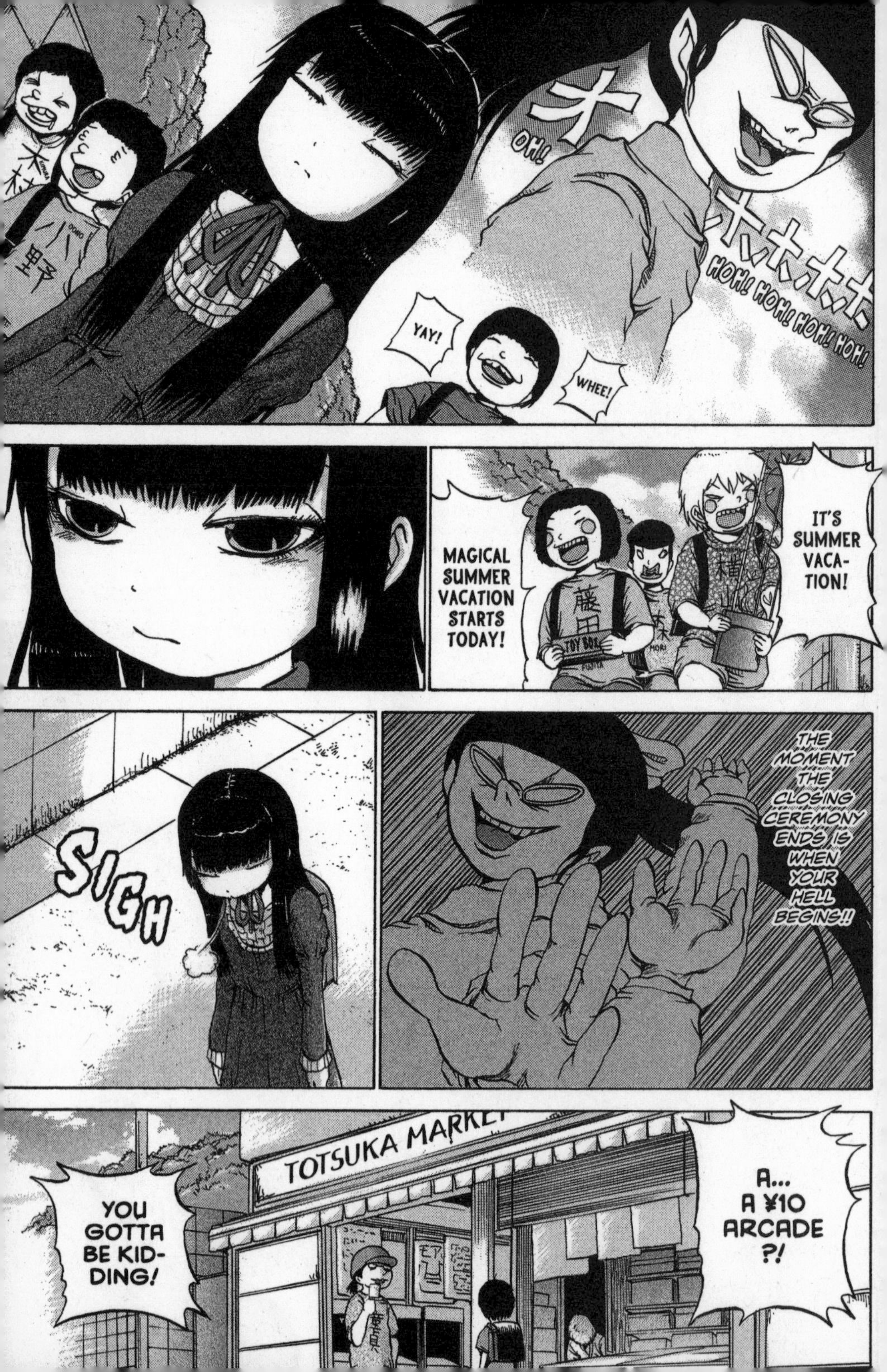
OH!
HOH! HOH! HOH! HOH!
WHEE!
YAY!
IT'S SUMMER VACA-TION!
MAGICAL SUMMER VACATION STARTS TODAY!
TOY BOX
THE MOMENT THE CLOSING CEREMONY ENDS IS WHEN YOUR HELL BEGINS!!
SIGH
A... A ¥10 ARCADE ?!
TOTSUKA MARKE
YOU GOTTA BE KID-DING!

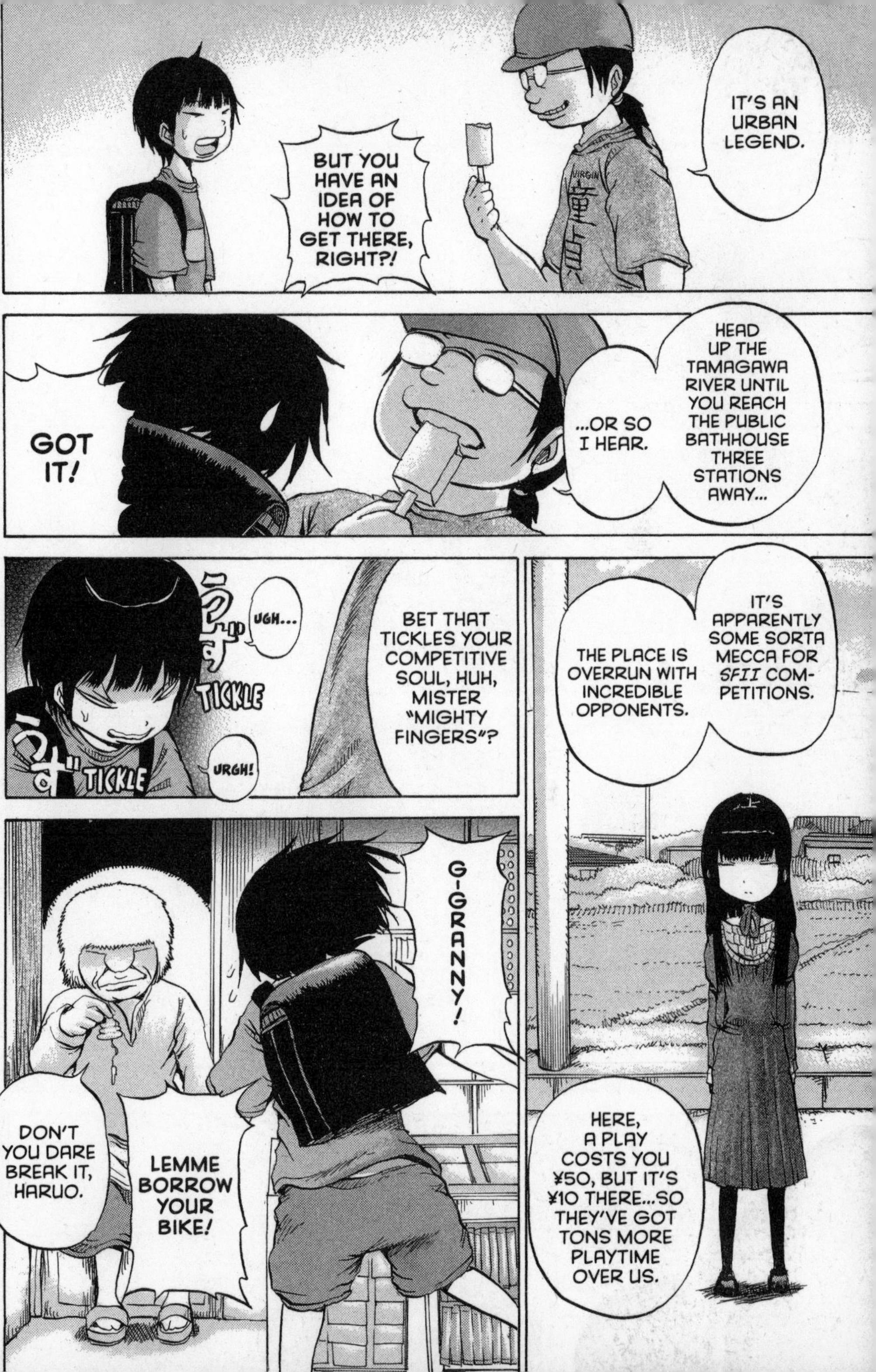
IT'S AN URBAN LEGEND.
BUT YOU HAVE AN IDEA OF HOW TO GET THERE, RIGHT?!
HEAD UP THE TAMAGAWA RIVER UNTIL YOU REACH THE PUBLIC BATHHOUSE THREE STATIONS AWAY...
...OR SO I HEAR.
GOT IT!
IT'S APPARENTLY SOME SORTA MECCA FOR *SFII* COMPETITIONS.
THE PLACE IS OVERRUN WITH INCREDIBLE OPPONENTS.
HERE, A PLAY COSTS YOU ¥50, BUT IT'S ¥10 THERE...SO THEY'VE GOT TONS MORE PLAYTIME OVER US.
BET THAT TICKLES YOUR COMPETITIVE SOUL, HUH, MISTER "MIGHTY FINGERS"?
UGH...
うずうず TICKLE
うずうず TICKLE
URGH!
G-GRANNY!
LEMME BORROW YOUR BIKE!
DON'T YOU DARE BREAK IT, HARUO.

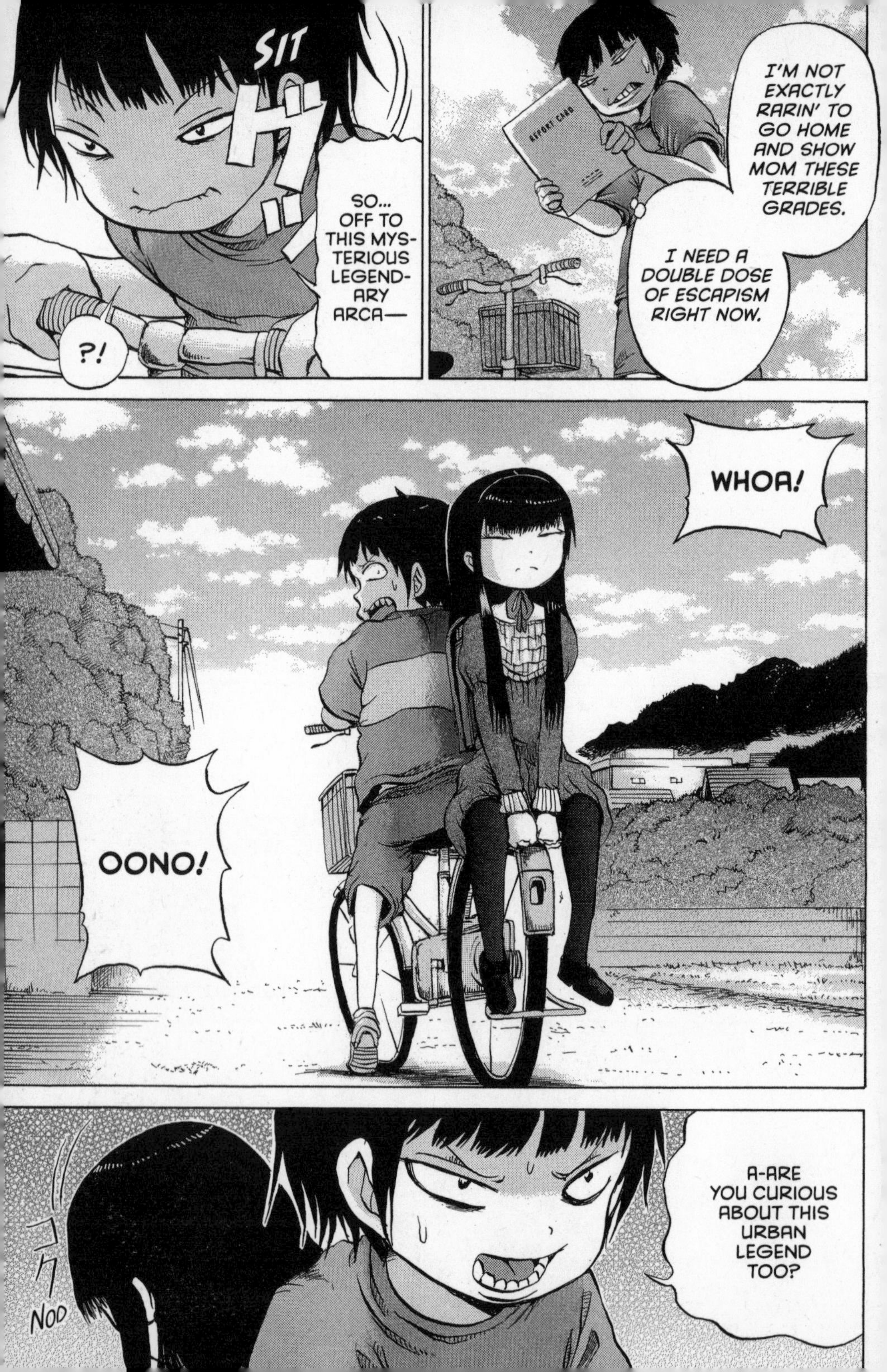
I'M NOT EXACTLY RARIN' TO GO HOME AND SHOW MOM THESE TERRIBLE GRADES.
I NEED A DOUBLE DOSE OF ESCAPISM RIGHT NOW.
REPORT CARD
SIT
SO... OFF TO THIS MYS-TERIOUS LEGEND-ARY ARCA—
?!
WHOA!
OONO!
A-ARE YOU CURIOUS ABOUT THIS URBAN LEGEND TOO?
NOD

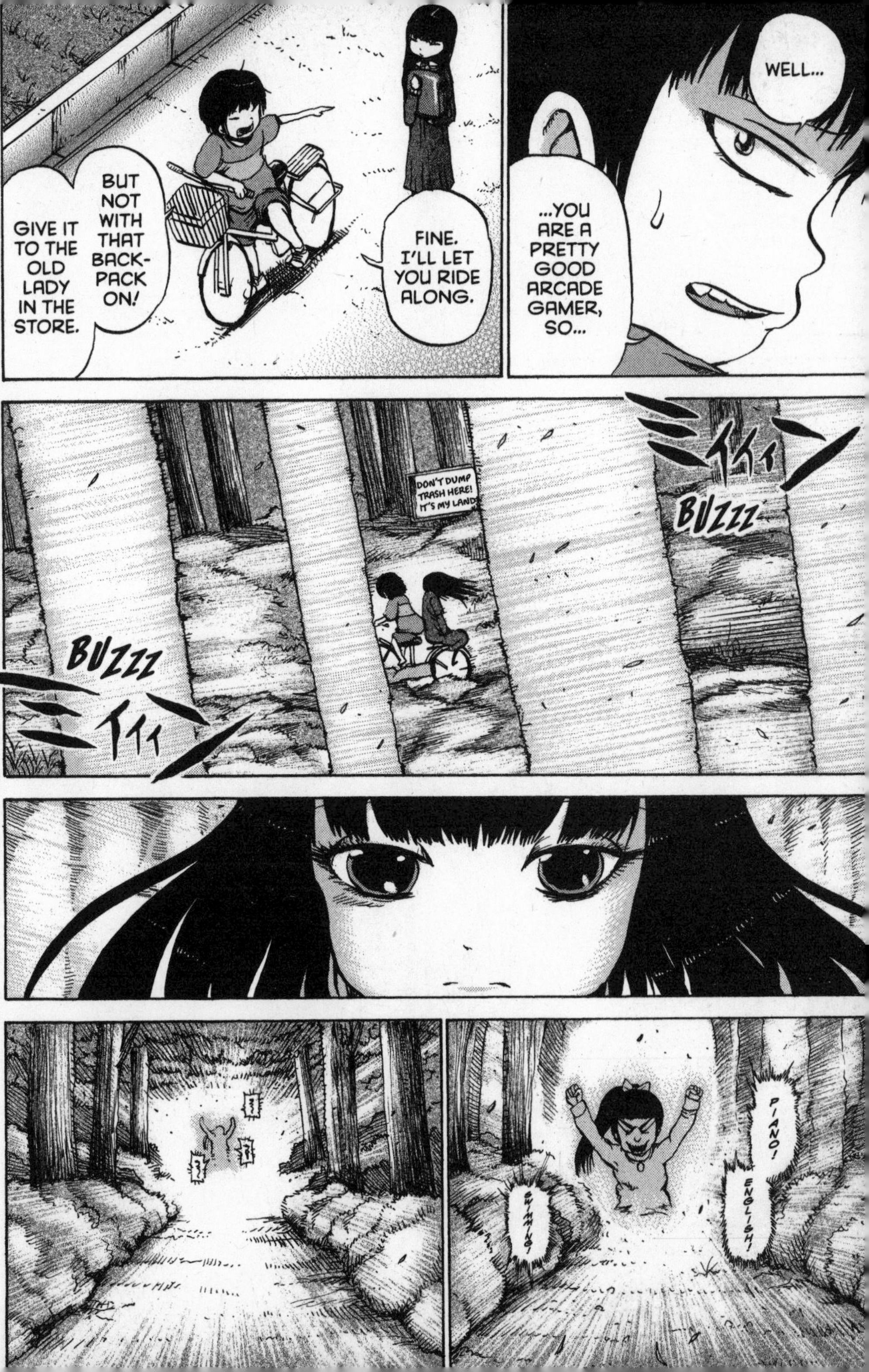
WELL...
...YOU ARE A PRETTY GOOD ARCADE GAMER, SO...
FINE. I'LL LET YOU RIDE ALONG.
BUT NOT WITH THAT BACKPACK ON!
GIVE IT TO THE OLD LADY IN THE STORE.
BUZZZ
DON'T DUMP TRASH HERE! IT'S MY LAND
BUZZZ
PIANO!
ENGLISH!
SWIMMING!

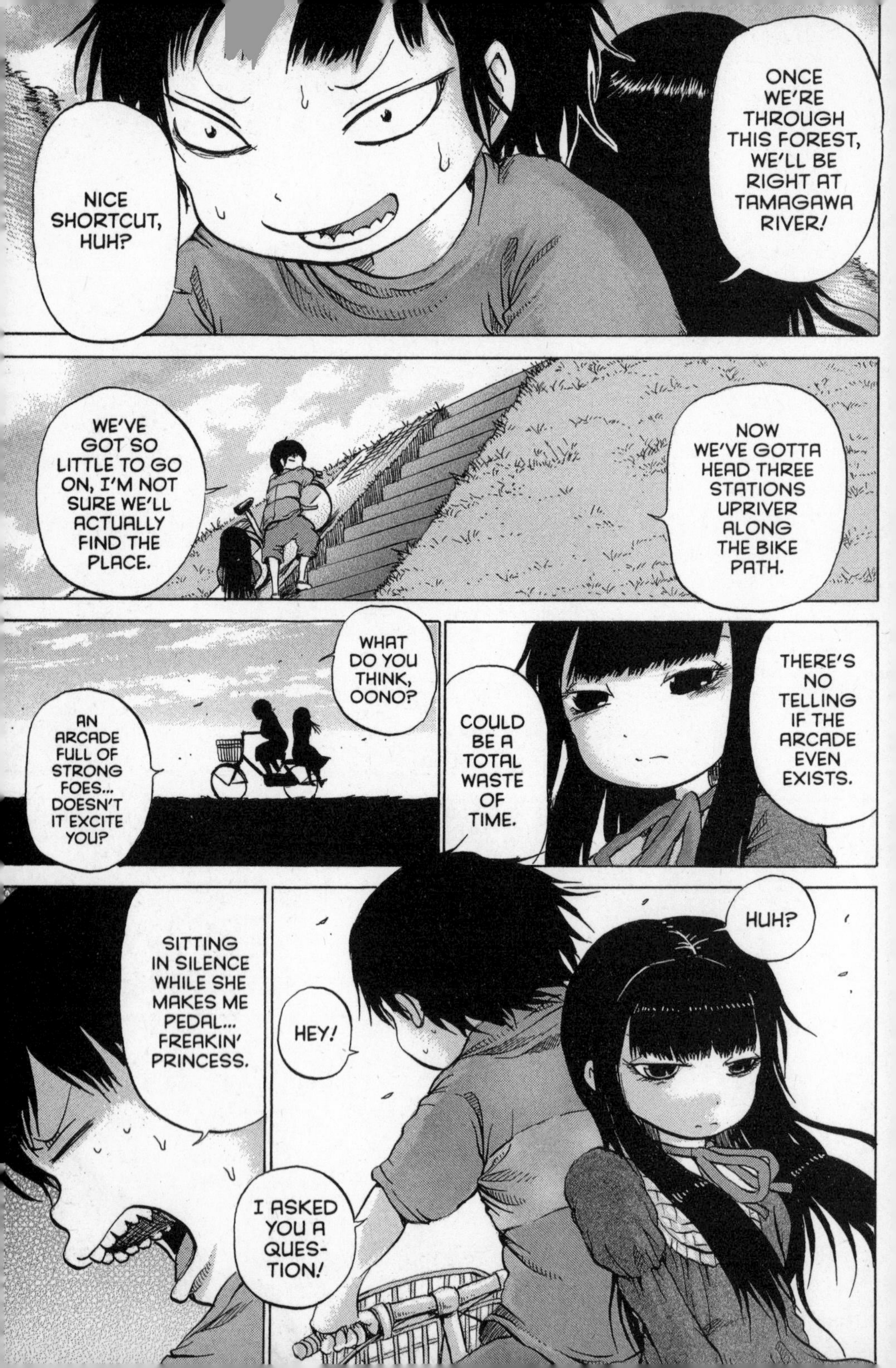
ONCE WE'RE THROUGH THIS FOREST, WE'LL BE RIGHT AT TAMAGAWA RIVER!
NICE SHORTCUT, HUH?
NOW WE'VE GOTTA HEAD THREE STATIONS UPRIVER ALONG THE BIKE PATH.
WE'VE GOT SO LITTLE TO GO ON, I'M NOT SURE WE'LL ACTUALLY FIND THE PLACE.
THERE'S NO TELLING IF THE ARCADE EVEN EXISTS.
COULD BE A TOTAL WASTE OF TIME.
WHAT DO YOU THINK, OONO?
AN ARCADE FULL OF STRONG FOES... DOESN'T IT EXCITE YOU?
HUH?
HEY!
I ASKED YOU A QUES-TION!
SITTING IN SILENCE WHILE SHE MAKES ME PEDAL... FREAKIN' PRINCESS.

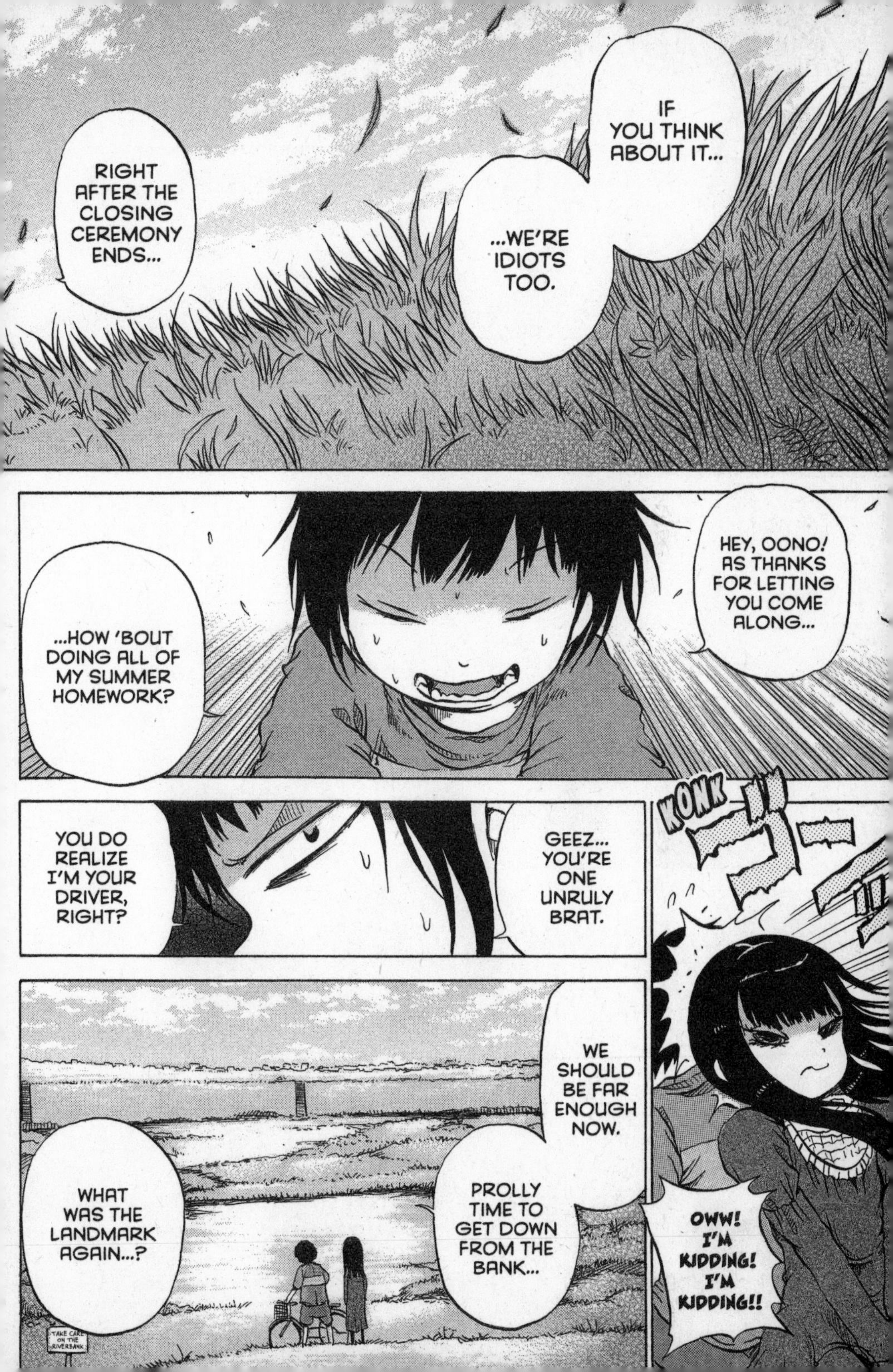
IF YOU THINK ABOUT IT...
...WE'RE IDIOTS TOO.
RIGHT AFTER THE CLOSING CEREMONY ENDS...
HEY, OONO! AS THANKS FOR LETTING YOU COME ALONG...
...HOW 'BOUT DOING ALL OF MY SUMMER HOMEWORK?
KONK
OWW! I'M KIDDING! I'M KIDDING!!
GEEZ... YOU'RE ONE UNRULY BRAT.
YOU DO REALIZE I'M YOUR DRIVER, RIGHT?
WE SHOULD BE FAR ENOUGH NOW.
PROLLY TIME TO GET DOWN FROM THE BANK...
WHAT WAS THE LANDMARK AGAIN...?
TAKE CARE ON THE RIVERBANK

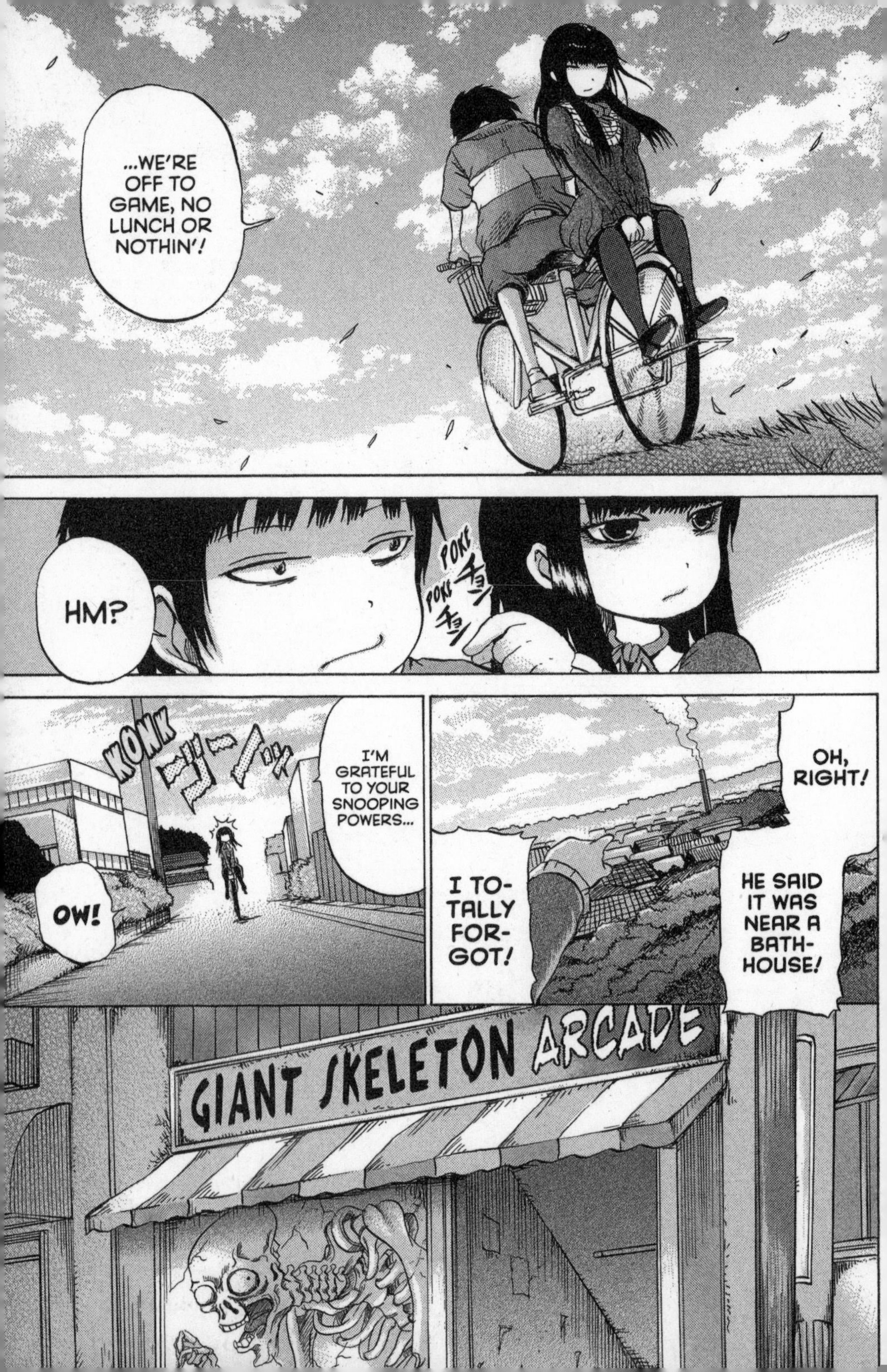
...WE'RE OFF TO GAME, NO LUNCH OR NOTHIN'!
POKE
POKE
HM?
OH, RIGHT!
HE SAID IT WAS NEAR A BATH-HOUSE!
I TO-TALLY FOR-GOT!
I'M GRATEFUL TO YOUR SNOOPING POWERS...
KONK
OW!
GIANT SKELETON ARCADE

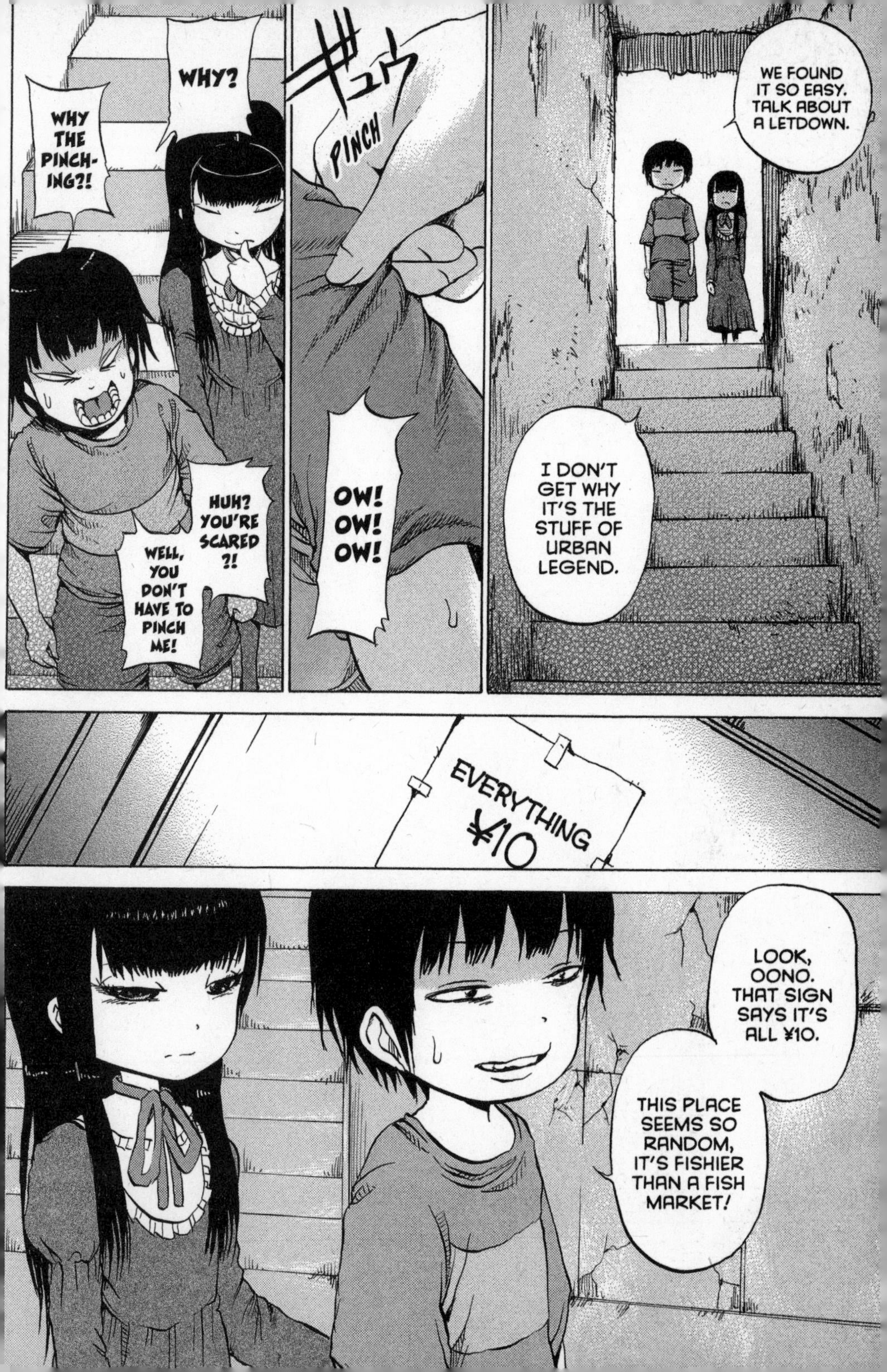

WE FOUND IT SO EASY. TALK ABOUT A LETDOWN.
I DON'T GET WHY IT'S THE STUFF OF URBAN LEGEND.
PINCH
OW! OW! OW!
WHY?
WHY THE PINCH-ING?!
HUH? YOU'RE SCARED?!
WELL, YOU DON'T HAVE TO PINCH ME!
EVERYTHING ¥10
LOOK, OONO. THAT SIGN SAYS IT'S ALL ¥10.
THIS PLACE SEEMS SO RANDOM, IT'S FISHIER THAN A FISH MARKET!

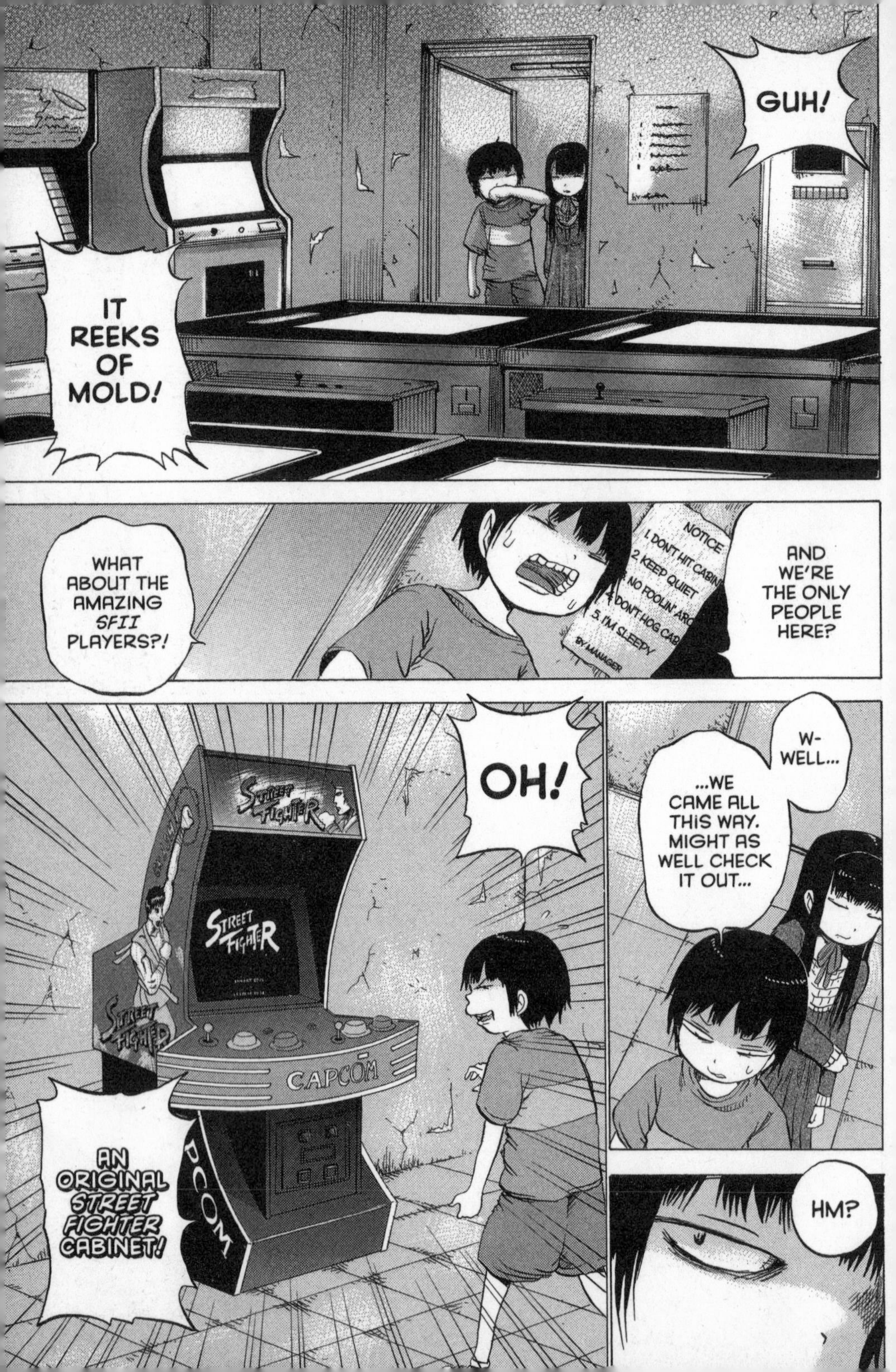
GUH!
IT REEKS OF MOLD!
AND WE'RE THE ONLY PEOPLE HERE?
NOTICE
1. DON'T HIT CABIN
2. KEEP QUIET
3. NO FOOLIN' ARO
4. DON'T HOG CAB
5. I'M SLEEPY
BY MANAGER
WHAT ABOUT THE AMAZING SFII PLAYERS?!
W-WELL...
...WE CAME ALL THIS WAY. MIGHT AS WELL CHECK IT OUT...
HM?
OH!
STREET FIGHTER
STREET FIGHTER
STREET FIGHTER
CAPCOM
AN ORIGINAL STREET FIGHTER CABINET!

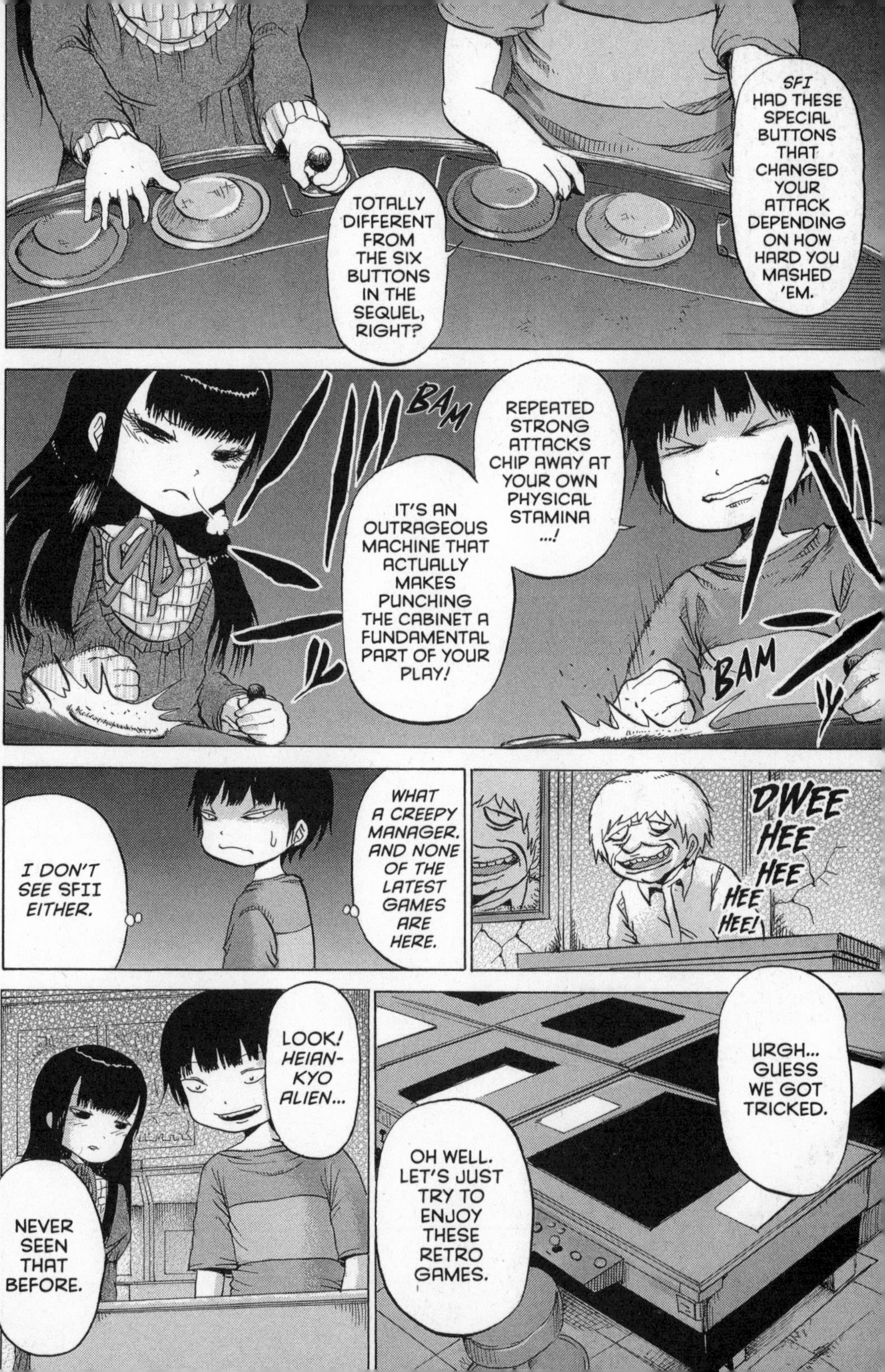
SFI HAD THESE SPECIAL BUTTONS THAT CHANGED YOUR ATTACK DEPENDING ON HOW HARD YOU MASHED 'EM.
TOTALLY DIFFERENT FROM THE SIX BUTTONS IN THE SEQUEL, RIGHT?
REPEATED STRONG ATTACKS CHIP AWAY AT YOUR OWN PHYSICAL STAMINA ...!
BAM
IT'S AN OUTRAGEOUS MACHINE THAT ACTUALLY MAKES PUNCHING THE CABINET A FUNDAMENTAL PART OF YOUR PLAY!
BAM
DWEE HEE HEE HEE HEE!
WHAT A CREEPY MANAGER. AND NONE OF THE LATEST GAMES ARE HERE.
I DON'T SEE SFII EITHER.
URGH... GUESS WE GOT TRICKED.
OH WELL. LET'S JUST TRY TO ENJOY THESE RETRO GAMES.
LOOK! HEIAN-KYO ALIEN...
NEVER SEEN THAT BEFORE.

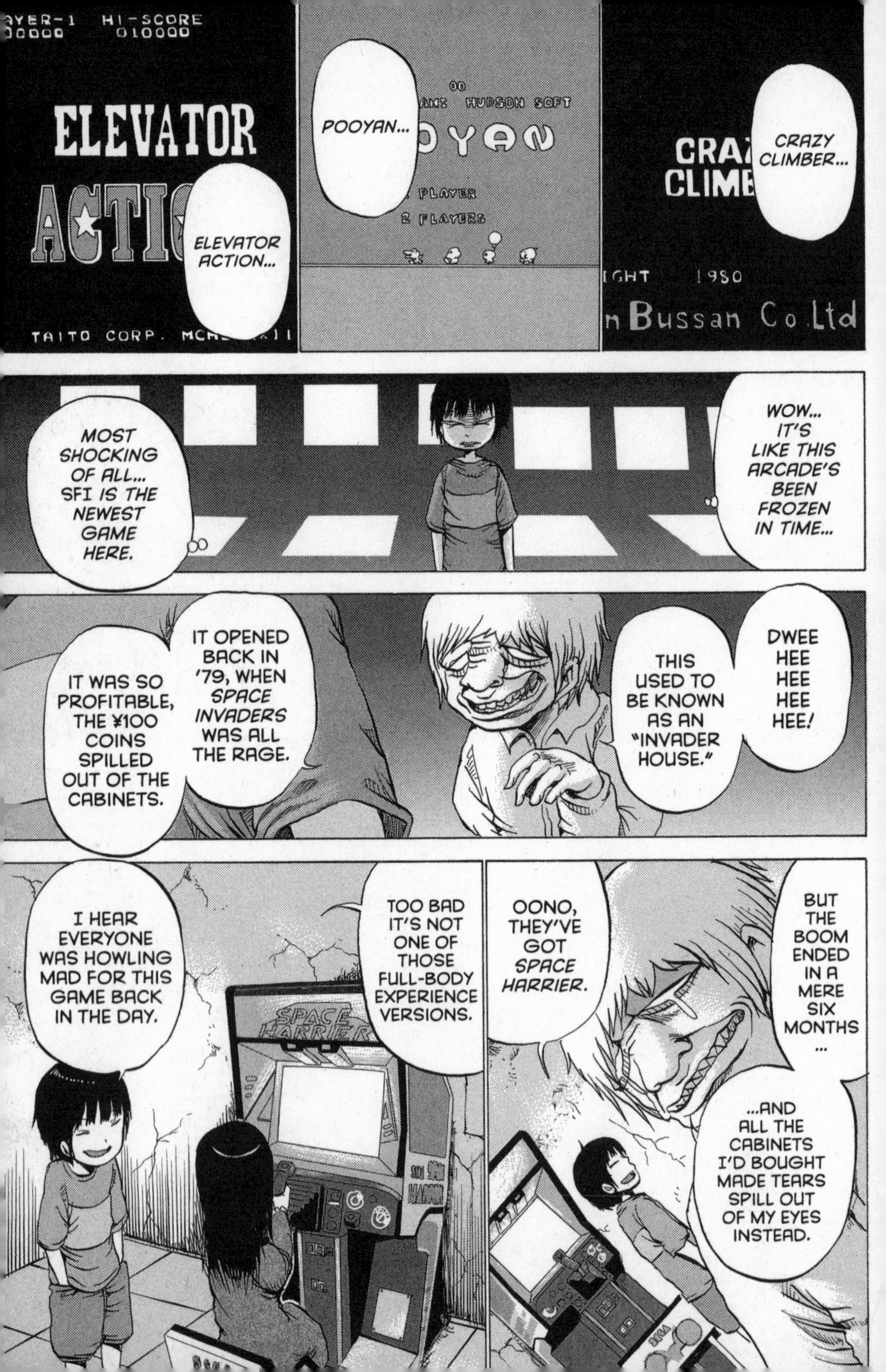
CRAZY CLIMBER...
1980
HUDSON SOFT
2 PLAYERS
POOYAN...
HI-SCORE
010000
ELEVATOR
TAITO CORP.
ELEVATOR ACTION...
WOW... IT'S LIKE THIS ARCADE'S BEEN FROZEN IN TIME...
MOST SHOCKING OF ALL... SFI IS THE NEWEST GAME HERE.
DWEE HEE HEE HEE HEE!
THIS USED TO BE KNOWN AS AN "INVADER HOUSE."
IT OPENED BACK IN '79, WHEN *SPACE INVADERS* WAS ALL THE RAGE.
IT WAS SO PROFITABLE, THE ¥100 COINS SPILLED OUT OF THE CABINETS.
BUT THE BOOM ENDED IN A MERE SIX MONTHS...
...AND ALL THE CABINETS I'D BOUGHT MADE TEARS SPILL OUT OF MY EYES INSTEAD.
OONO, THEY'VE GOT *SPACE HARRIER.*
TOO BAD IT'S NOT ONE OF THOSE FULL-BODY EXPERIENCE VERSIONS.
SPACE HARRIER
I HEAR EVERYONE WAS HOWLING MAD FOR THIS GAME BACK IN THE DAY.

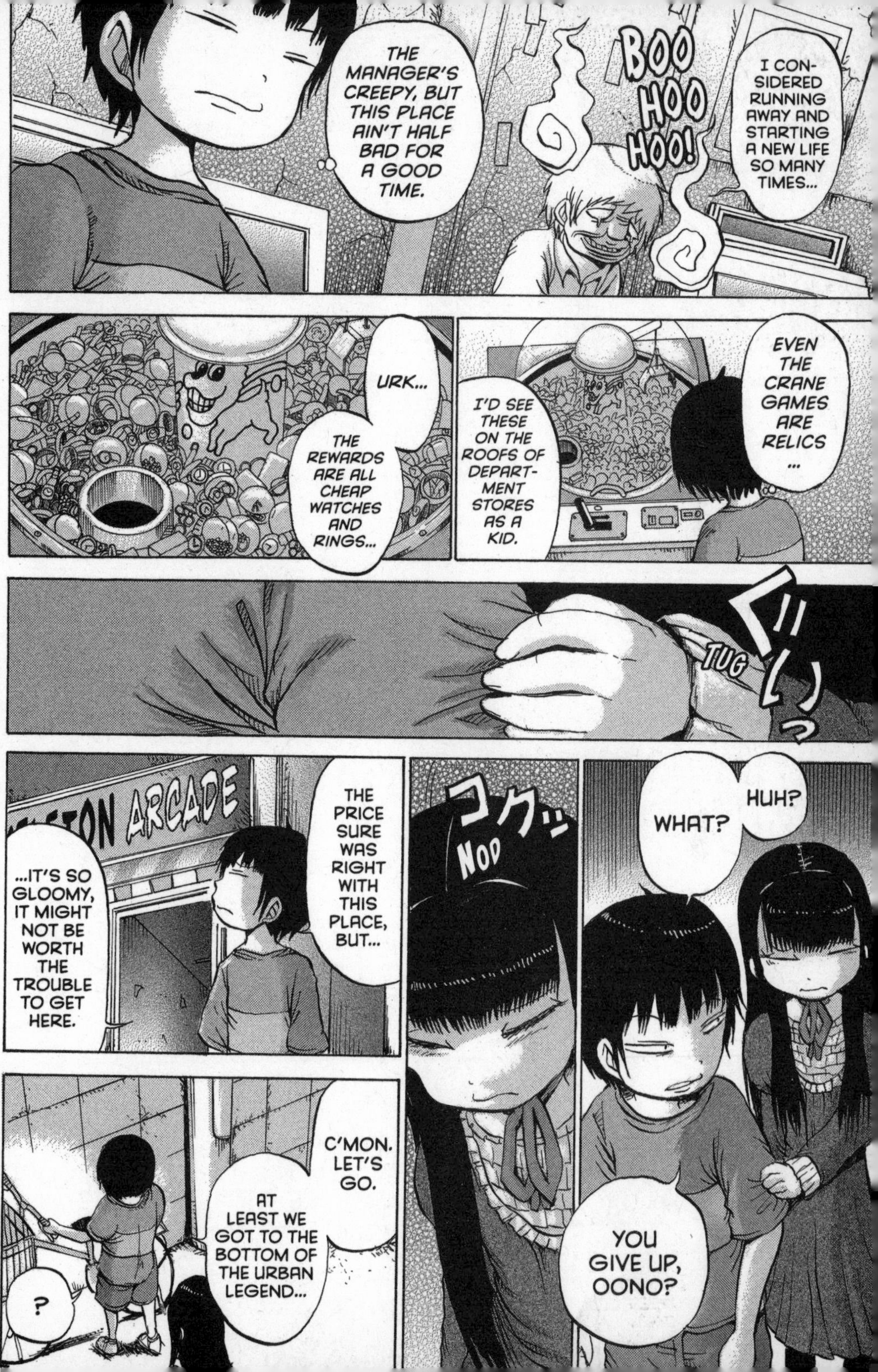
I CONSIDERED RUNNING AWAY AND STARTING A NEW LIFE SO MANY TIMES...
BOO HOO HOO!
THE MANAGER'S CREEPY, BUT THIS PLACE AIN'T HALF BAD FOR A GOOD TIME.
EVEN THE CRANE GAMES ARE RELICS ...
I'D SEE THESE ON THE ROOFS OF DEPARTMENT STORES AS A KID.
URK...
THE REWARDS ARE ALL CHEAP WATCHES AND RINGS...
くいっ
TUG
HUH?
WHAT?
コクッ
NOD
YOU GIVE UP, OONO?
ARCADE
THE PRICE SURE WAS RIGHT WITH THIS PLACE, BUT...
...IT'S SO GLOOMY, IT MIGHT NOT BE WORTH THE TROUBLE TO GET HERE.
C'MON. LET'S GO.
AT LEAST WE GOT TO THE BOTTOM OF THE URBAN LEGEND...
?

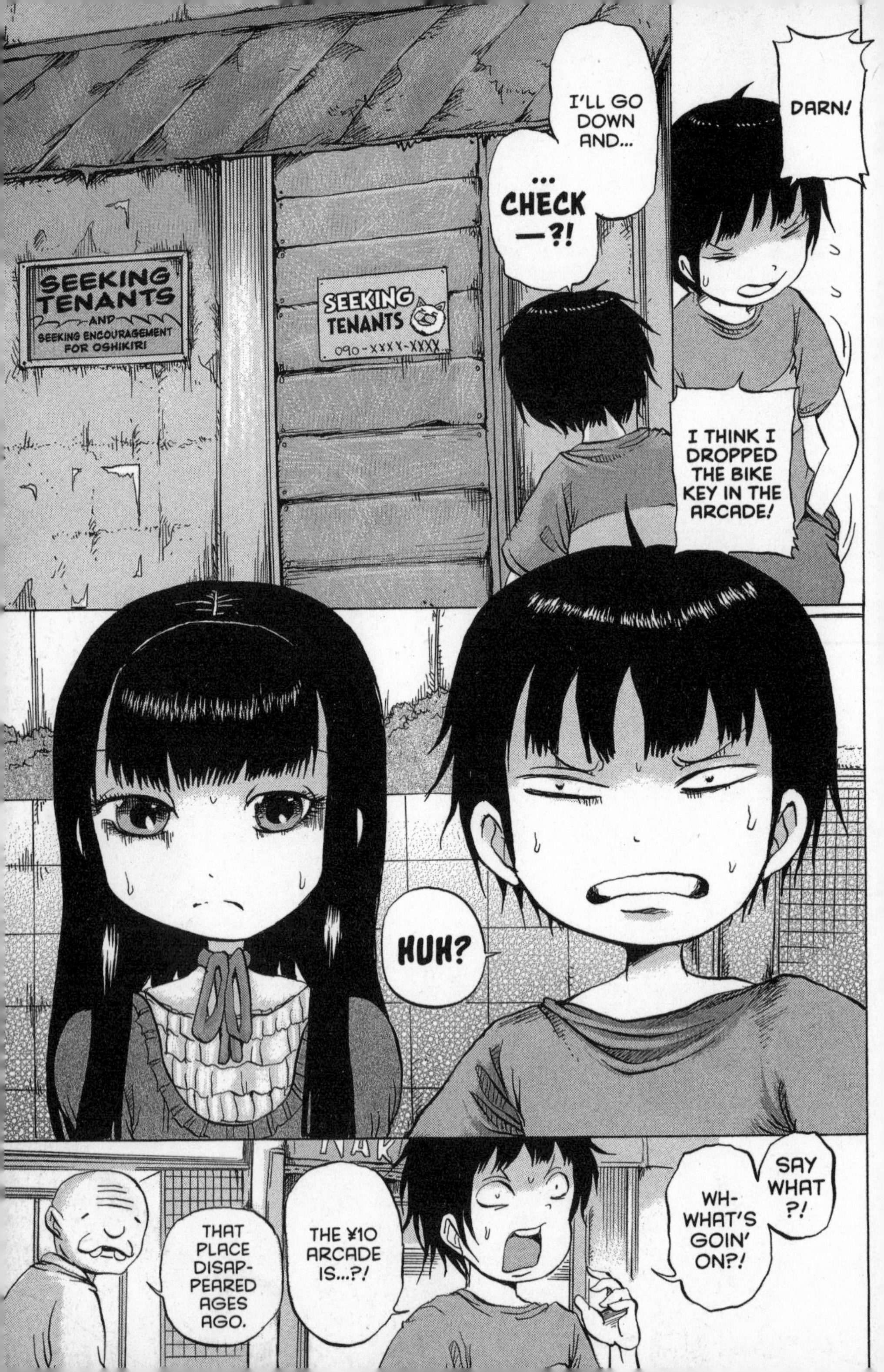
DARN!
I THINK I DROPPED THE BIKE KEY IN THE ARCADE!
I'LL GO DOWN AND...
... CHECK —?!
SEEKING TENANTS 090-XXXX-XXXX
SEEKING TENANTS AND SEEKING ENCOURAGEMENT FOR OSHIKIRI
HUH?
SAY WHAT?!
WH-WHAT'S GOIN' ON?!
THE ¥10 ARCADE IS...?!
THAT PLACE DISAP-PEARED AGES AGO.

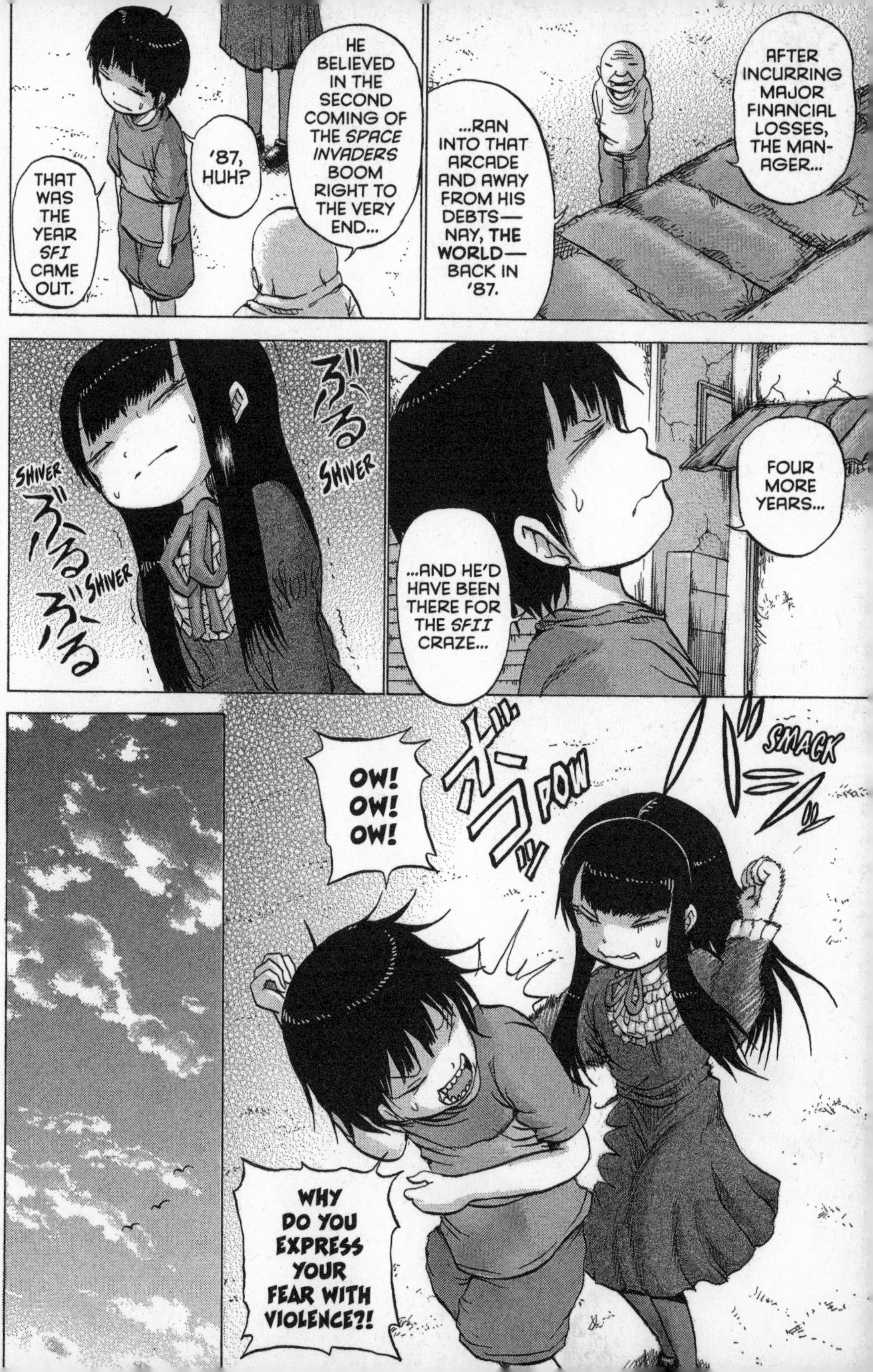
AFTER INCURRING MAJOR FINANCIAL LOSSES, THE MANAGER...
...RAN INTO THAT ARCADE AND AWAY FROM HIS DEBTS—NAY, THE WORLD—BACK IN '87.
HE BELIEVED IN THE SECOND COMING OF THE *SPACE INVADERS* BOOM RIGHT TO THE VERY END...
'87, HUH?
THAT WAS THE YEAR *SFI* CAME OUT.
FOUR MORE YEARS...
...AND HE'D HAVE BEEN THERE FOR THE *SFII* CRAZE...
ぶる
SHIVER
ぶるぶる
SHIVER
SHIVER
SMACK
POW
OW! OW! OW!
WHY DO YOU EXPRESS YOUR FEAR WITH VIOLENCE?!

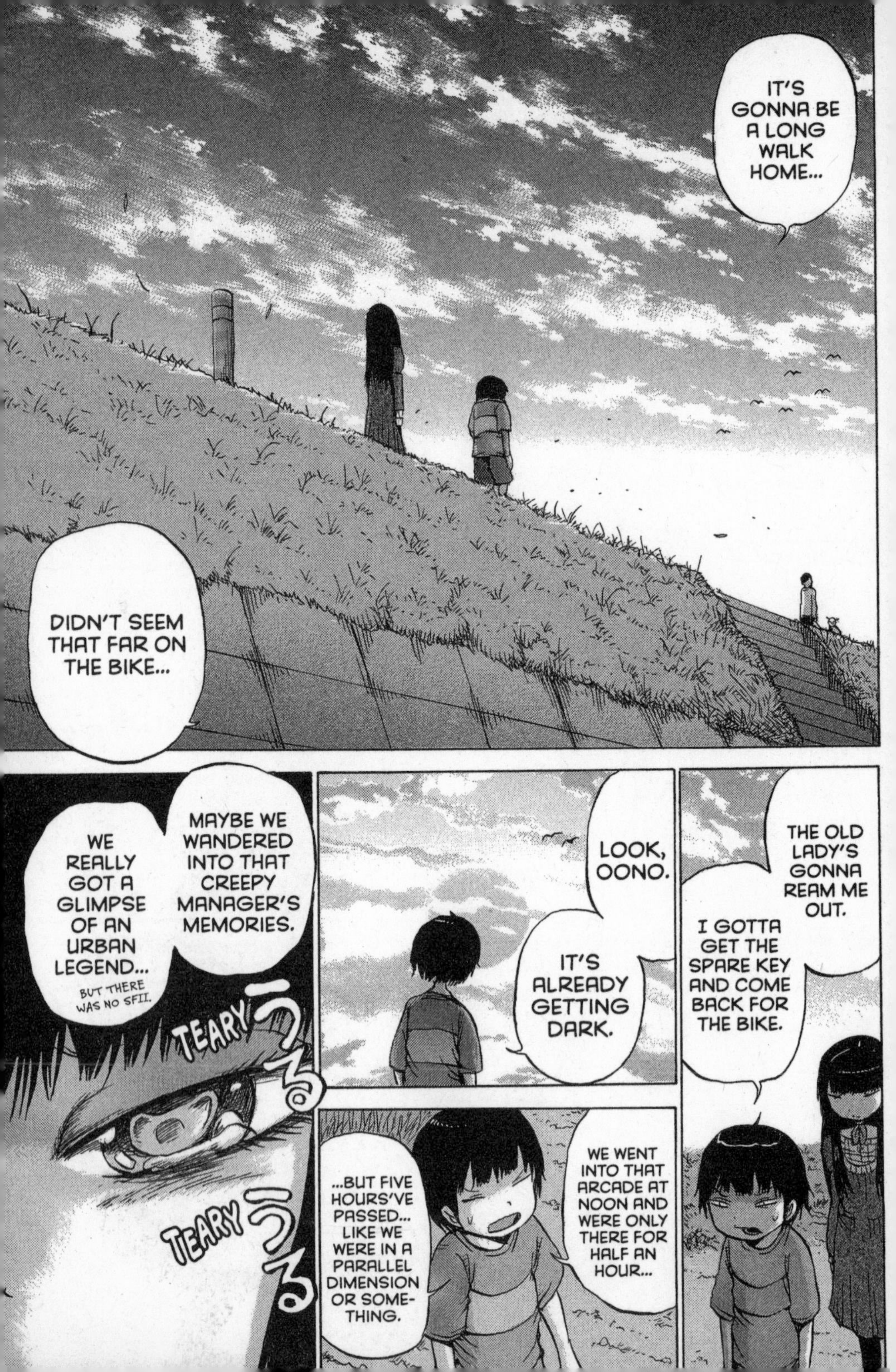

IT'S GONNA BE A LONG WALK HOME...
DIDN'T SEEM THAT FAR ON THE BIKE...
THE OLD LADY'S GONNA REAM ME OUT.
I GOTTA GET THE SPARE KEY AND COME BACK FOR THE BIKE.
LOOK, OONO.
IT'S ALREADY GETTING DARK.
WE WENT INTO THAT ARCADE AT NOON AND WERE ONLY THERE FOR HALF AN HOUR...
...BUT FIVE HOURS'VE PASSED... LIKE WE WERE IN A PARALLEL DIMENSION OR SOME-THING.
MAYBE WE WANDERED INTO THAT CREEPY MANAGER'S MEMORIES.
WE REALLY GOT A GLIMPSE OF AN URBAN LEGEND...
BUT THERE WAS NO SFII.
TEARY うる
TEARY うる

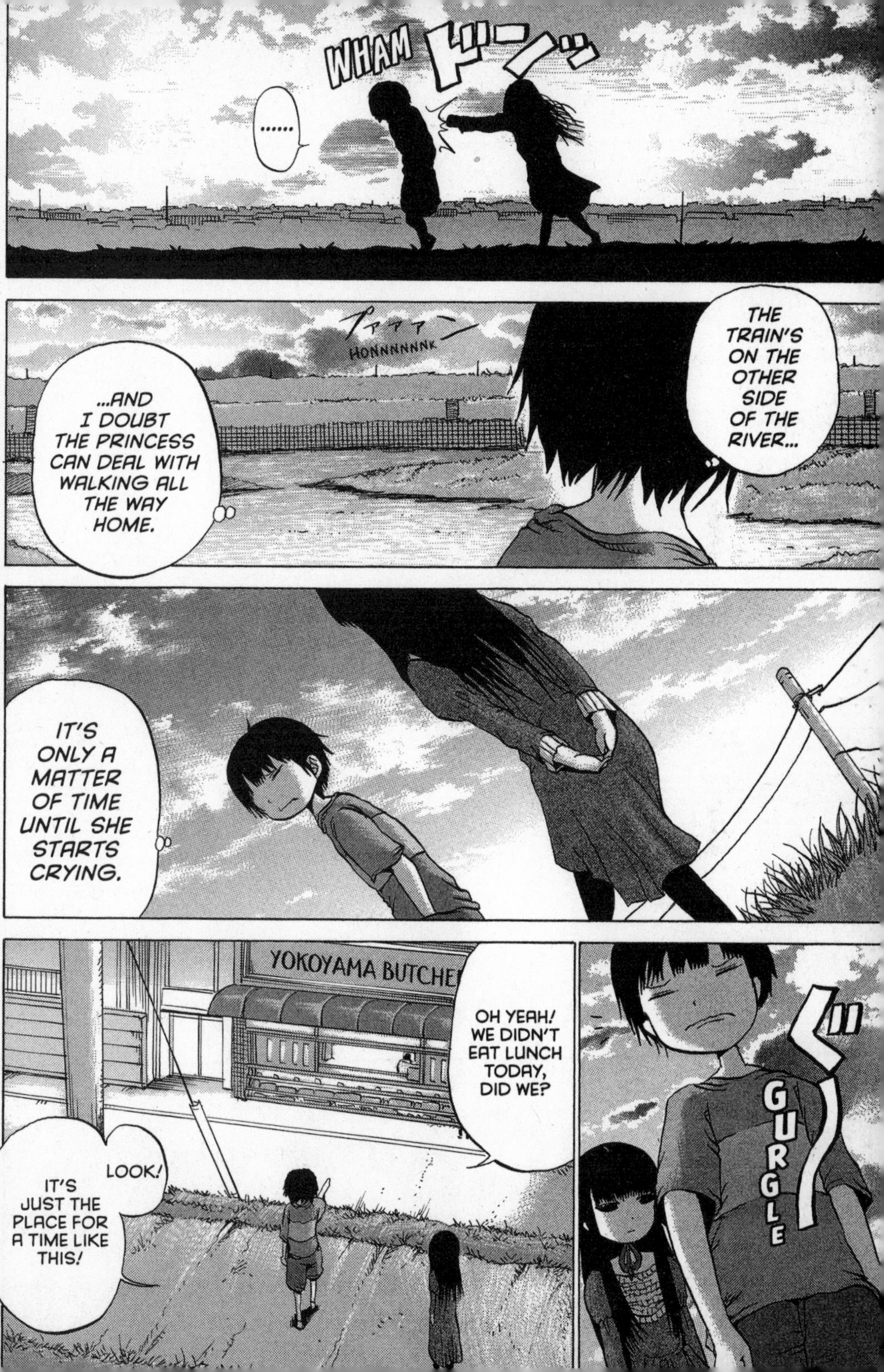
WHAM
......
THE TRAIN'S ON THE OTHER SIDE OF THE RIVER...
...AND I DOUBT THE PRINCESS CAN DEAL WITH WALKING ALL THE WAY HOME.
HONNNNNNK
IT'S ONLY A MATTER OF TIME UNTIL SHE STARTS CRYING.
GURGLE
YOKOYAMA BUTCHE
OH YEAH! WE DIDN'T EAT LUNCH TODAY, DID WE?
LOOK!
IT'S JUST THE PLACE FOR A TIME LIKE THIS!

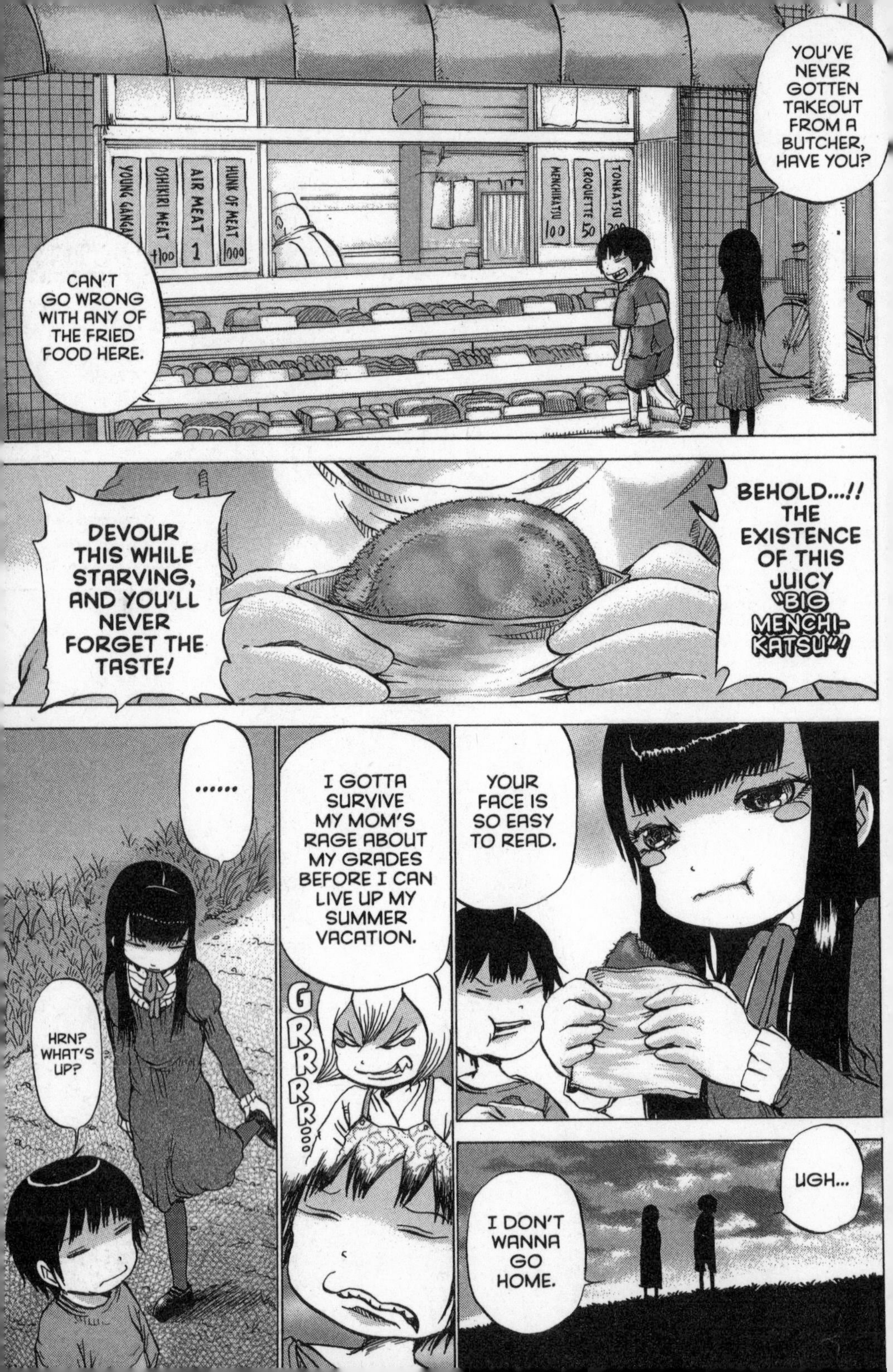
YOU'VE NEVER GOTTEN TAKEOUT FROM A BUTCHER, HAVE YOU?
TONKATSU
CROQUETTE 50
MENCHIKATSU 100
HUNK OF MEAT 1000
AIR MEAT 1
OSHIKIRI MEAT +100
CAN'T GO WRONG WITH ANY OF THE FRIED FOOD HERE.
BEHOLD...!! THE EXISTENCE OF THIS JUICY "BIG MENCHI-KATSU"!
DEVOUR THIS WHILE STARVING, AND YOU'LL NEVER FORGET THE TASTE!
YOUR FACE IS SO EASY TO READ.
UGH...
I DON'T WANNA GO HOME.
I GOTTA SURVIVE MY MOM'S RAGE ABOUT MY GRADES BEFORE I CAN LIVE UP MY SUMMER VACATION.
GRRRR...
......
HRN? WHAT'S UP?

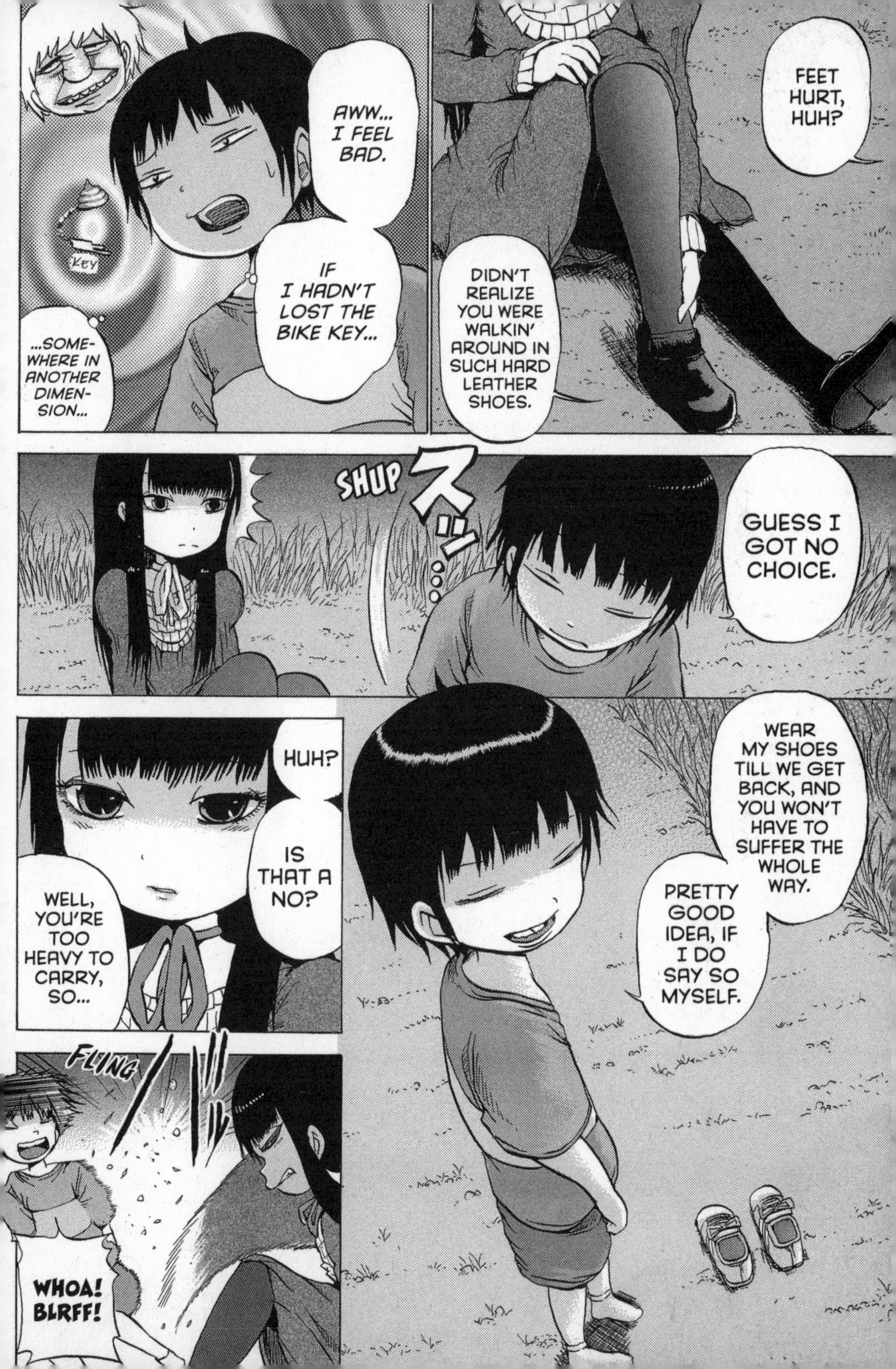
FEET HURT, HUH?
DIDN'T REALIZE YOU WERE WALKIN' AROUND IN SUCH HARD LEATHER SHOES.
AWW... I FEEL BAD.
IF I HADN'T LOST THE BIKE KEY...
KEY
...SOME-WHERE IN ANOTHER DIMEN-SION...
GUESS I GOT NO CHOICE.
SHUP
WEAR MY SHOES TILL WE GET BACK, AND YOU WON'T HAVE TO SUFFER THE WHOLE WAY.
PRETTY GOOD IDEA, IF I DO SAY SO MYSELF.
HUH?
IS THAT A NO?
WELL, YOU'RE TOO HEAVY TO CARRY, SO...
FLING
WHOA! BLRFF!

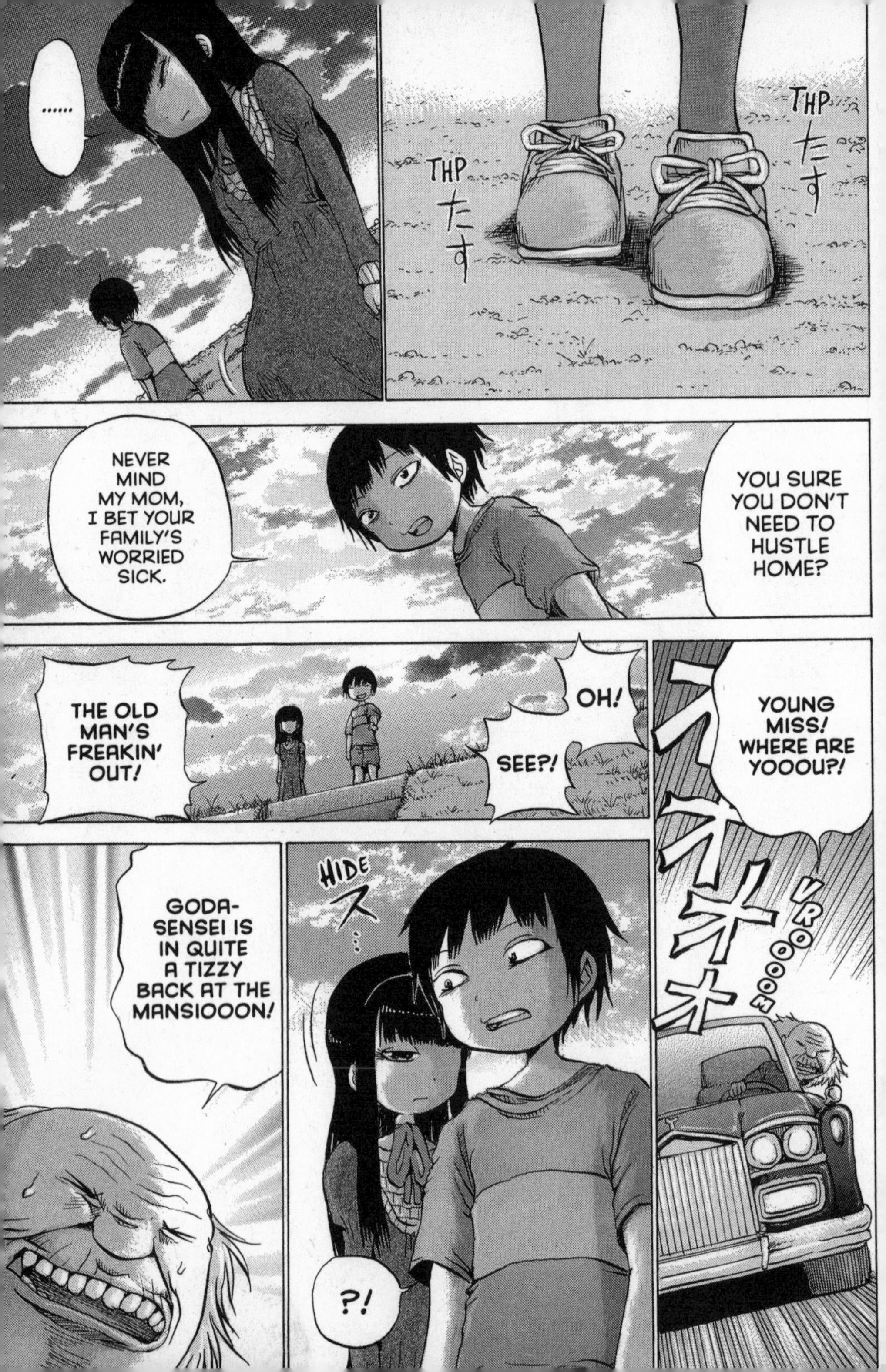
THP
たす
THP
たす
......
YOU SURE YOU DON'T NEED TO HUSTLE HOME?
NEVER MIND MY MOM, I BET YOUR FAMILY'S WORRIED SICK.
YOUNG MISS! WHERE ARE YOOOU?!
VROOOOM
OH!
SEE?!
THE OLD MAN'S FREAKIN' OUT!
HIDE
ス...
?!
GODA-SENSEI IS IN QUITE A TIZZY BACK AT THE MANSIOOON!

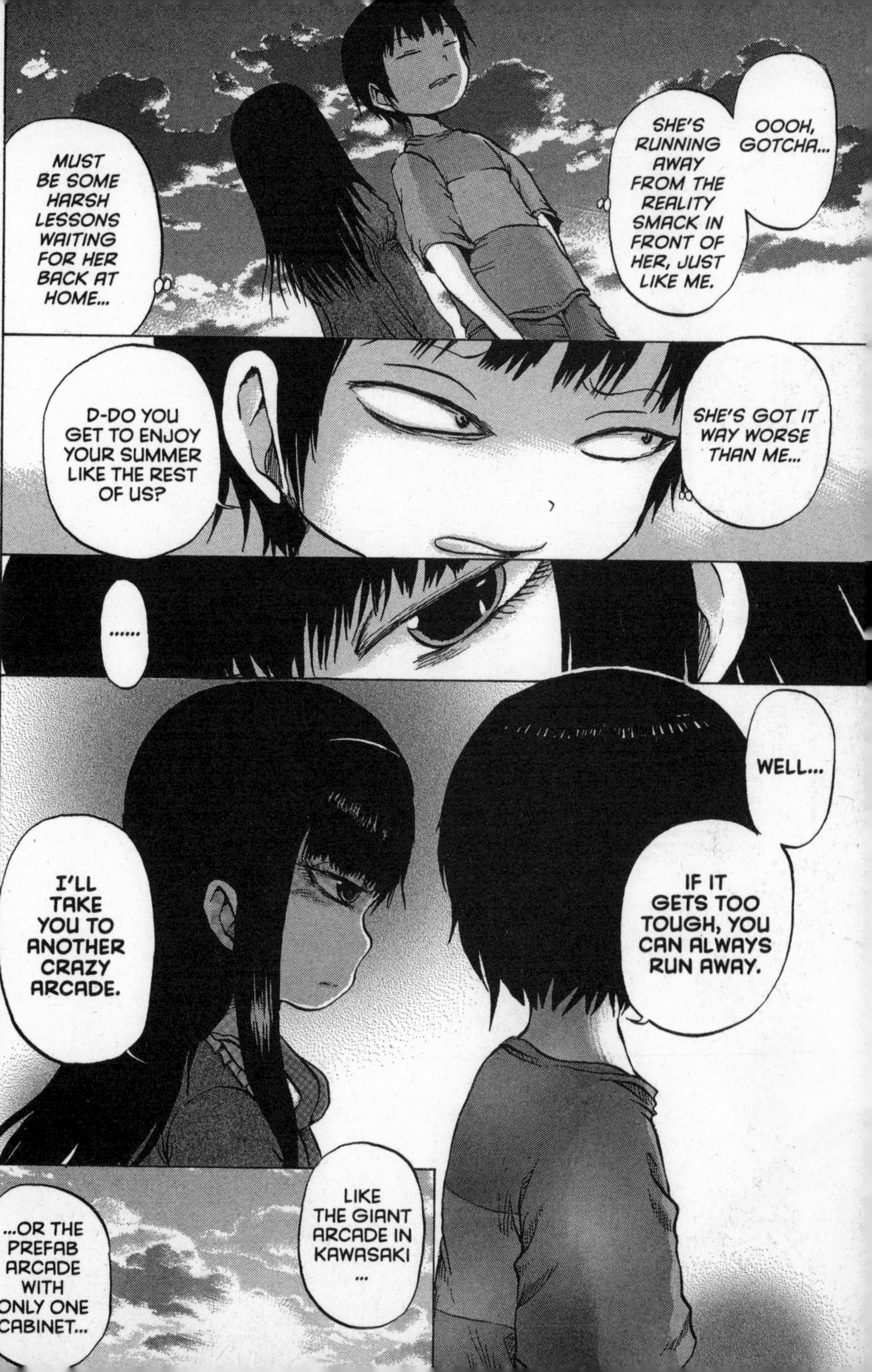
OOOH, GOTCHA...
SHE'S RUNNING AWAY FROM THE REALITY SMACK IN FRONT OF HER, JUST LIKE ME.
MUST BE SOME HARSH LESSONS WAITING FOR HER BACK AT HOME...
SHE'S GOT IT WAY WORSE THAN ME...
D-DO YOU GET TO ENJOY YOUR SUMMER LIKE THE REST OF US?
......
WELL...
IF IT GETS TOO TOUGH, YOU CAN ALWAYS RUN AWAY.
I'LL TAKE YOU TO ANOTHER CRAZY ARCADE.
LIKE THE GIANT ARCADE IN KAWASAKI ...
...OR THE PREFAB ARCADE WITH ONLY ONE CABINET...

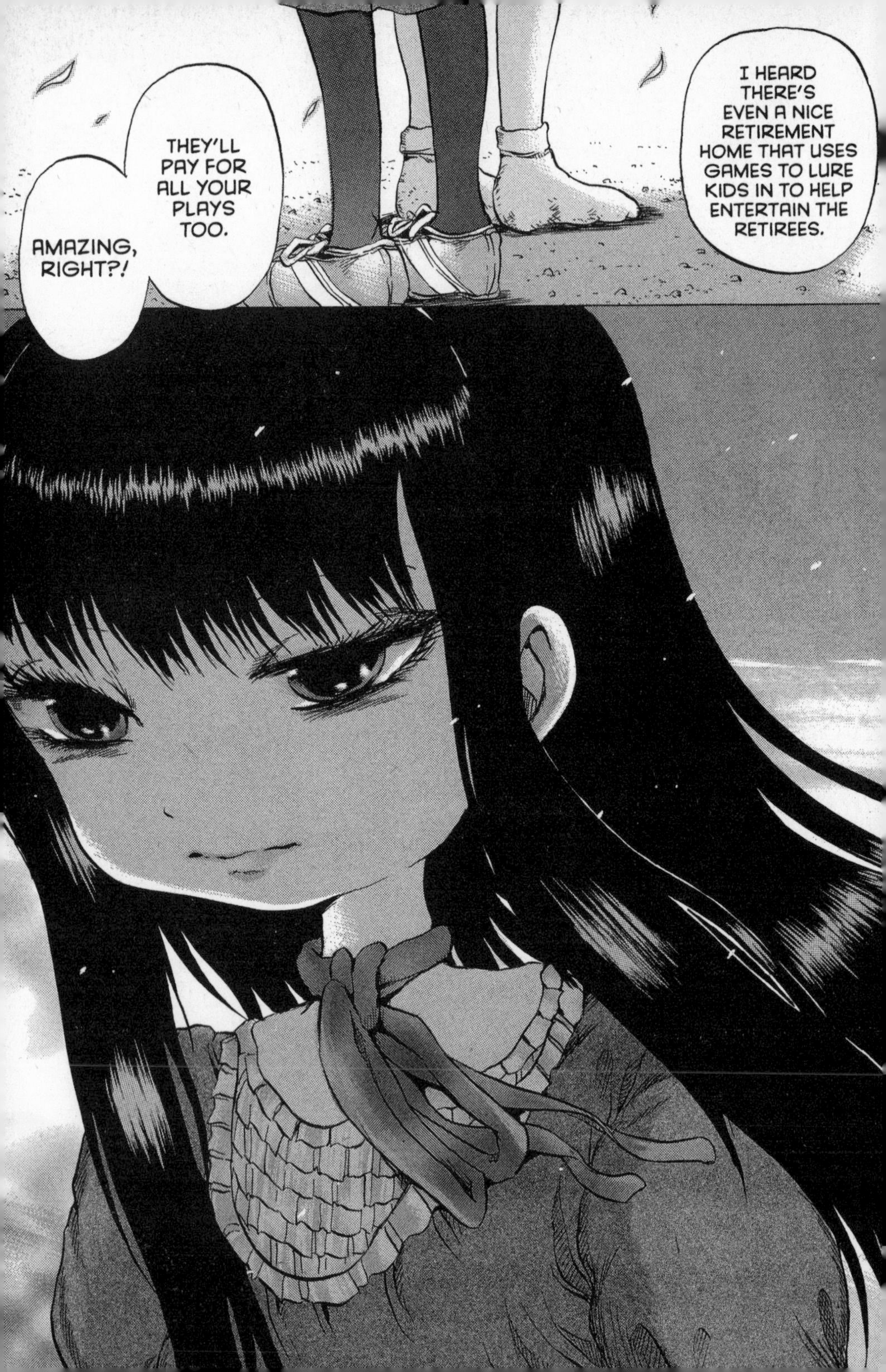
I HEARD THERE'S EVEN A NICE RETIREMENT HOME THAT USES GAMES TO LURE KIDS IN TO HELP ENTERTAIN THE RETIREES.
THEY'LL PAY FOR ALL YOUR PLAYS TOO.
AMAZING, RIGHT?!

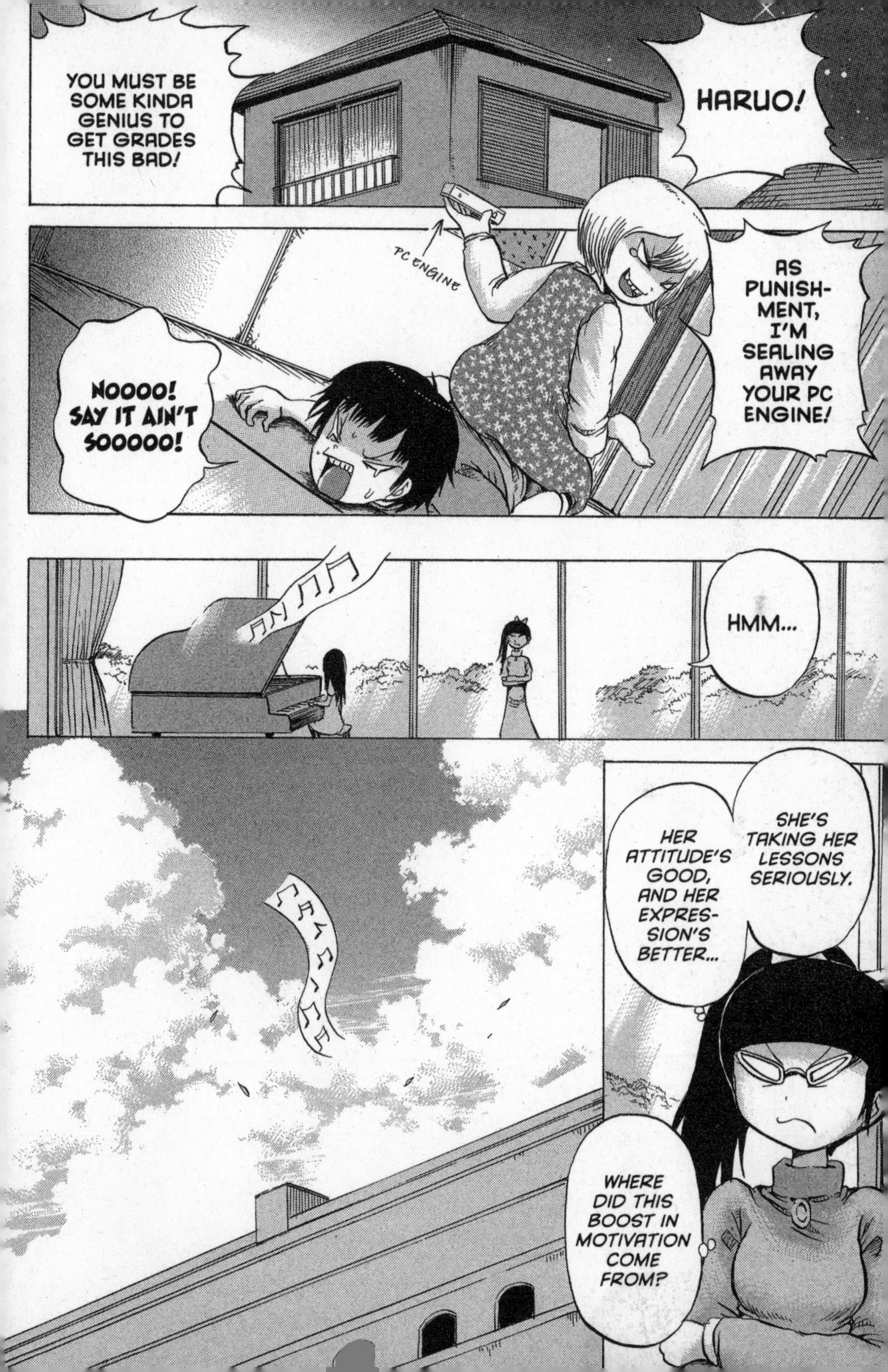
HARUO!
YOU MUST BE SOME KINDA GENIUS TO GET GRADES THIS BAD!
AS PUNISHMENT, I'M SEALING AWAY YOUR PC ENGINE!
PC ENGINE
NOOOO! SAY IT AIN'T SOOOOO!
HMM...
SHE'S TAKING HER LESSONS SERIOUSLY.
HER ATTITUDE'S GOOD, AND HER EXPRESSION'S BETTER...
WHERE DID THIS BOOST IN MOTIVATION COME FROM?

HI SCORE GIRL

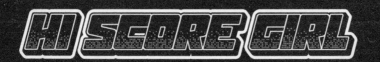

HI SCORE GIRL

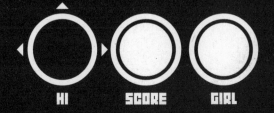

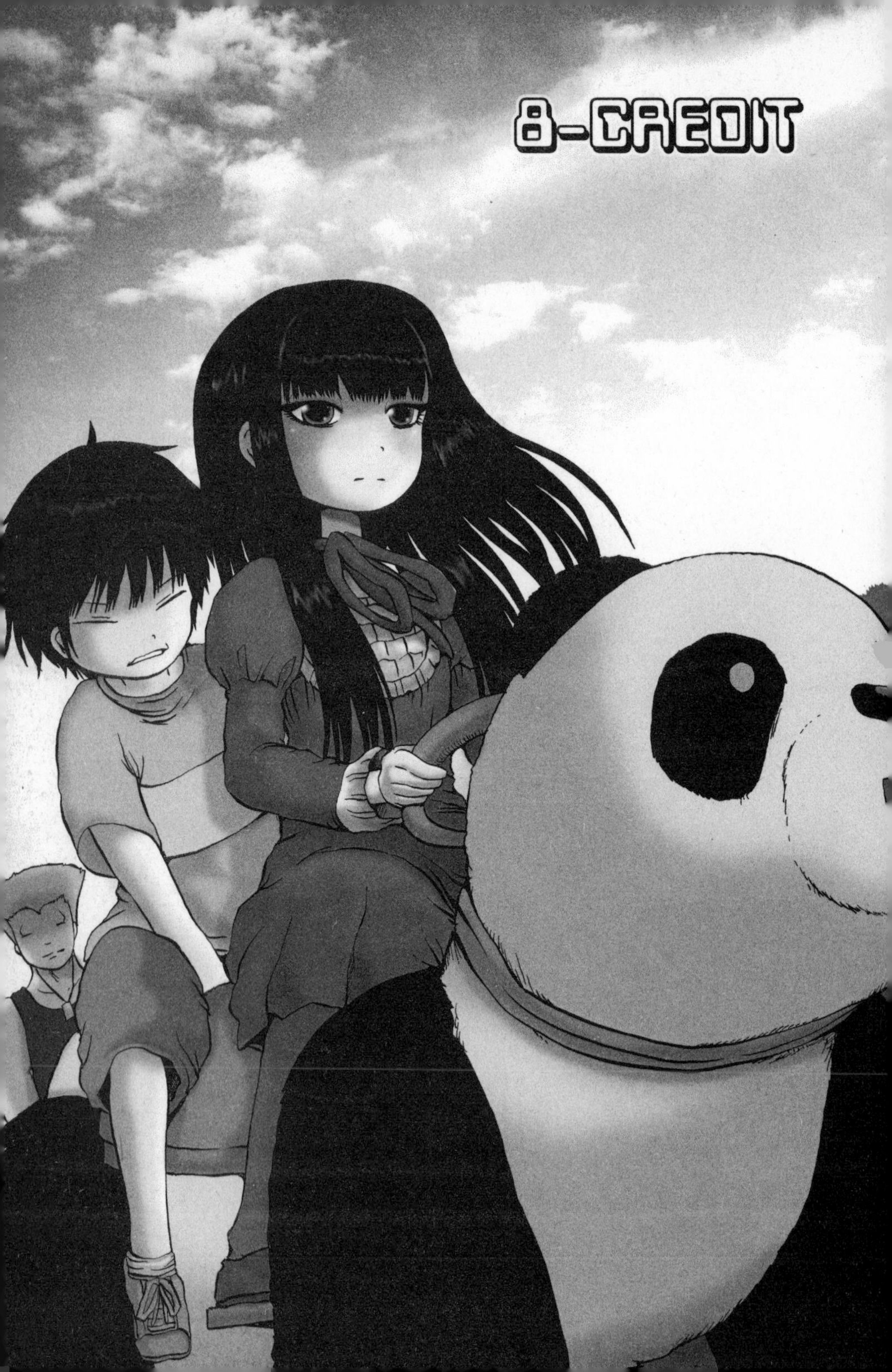
8-CREDIT

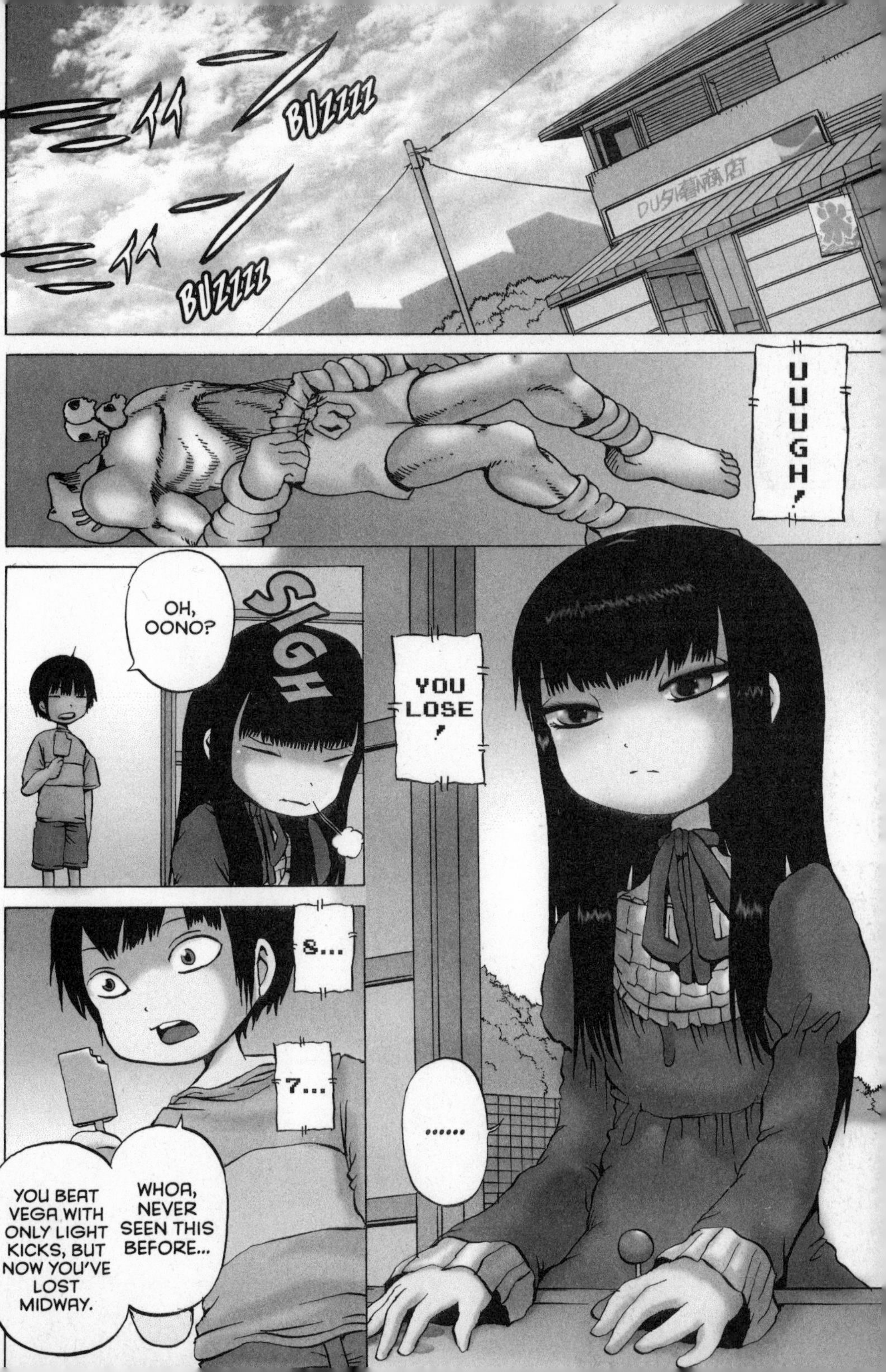

BUZZZZ
BUZZZZ
UUUGH!
YOU LOSE!
......
OH, OONO?
SIGH
8...
7...
WHOA, NEVER SEEN THIS BEFORE...
YOU BEAT VEGA WITH ONLY LIGHT KICKS, BUT NOW YOU'VE LOST MIDWAY.

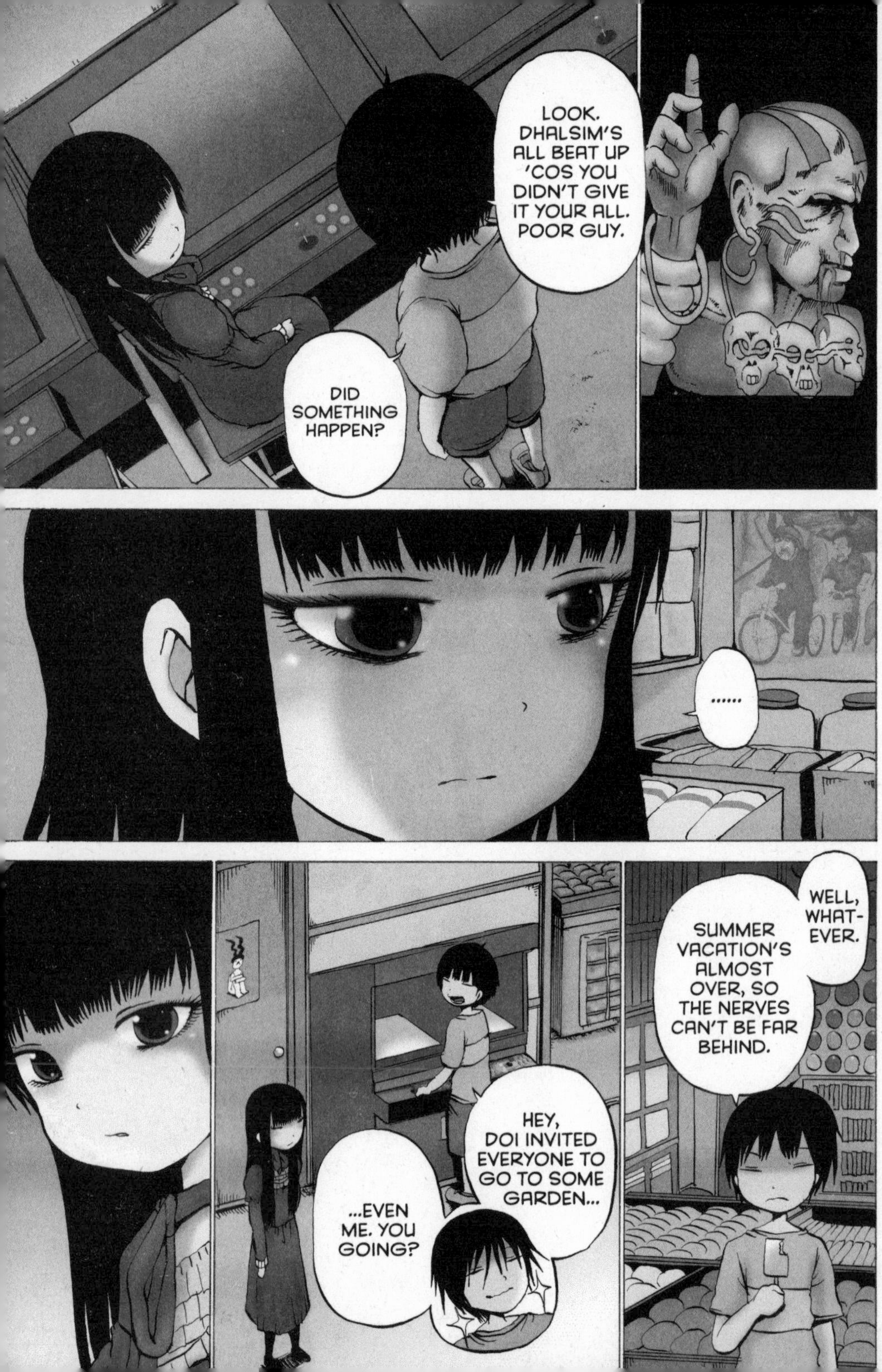

LOOK. DHALSIM'S ALL BEAT UP 'COS YOU DIDN'T GIVE IT YOUR ALL. POOR GUY.
DID SOMETHING HAPPEN?
......
WELL, WHATEVER.
SUMMER VACATION'S ALMOST OVER, SO THE NERVES CAN'T BE FAR BEHIND.
HEY, DOI INVITED EVERYONE TO GO TO SOME GARDEN...
...EVEN ME. YOU GOING?

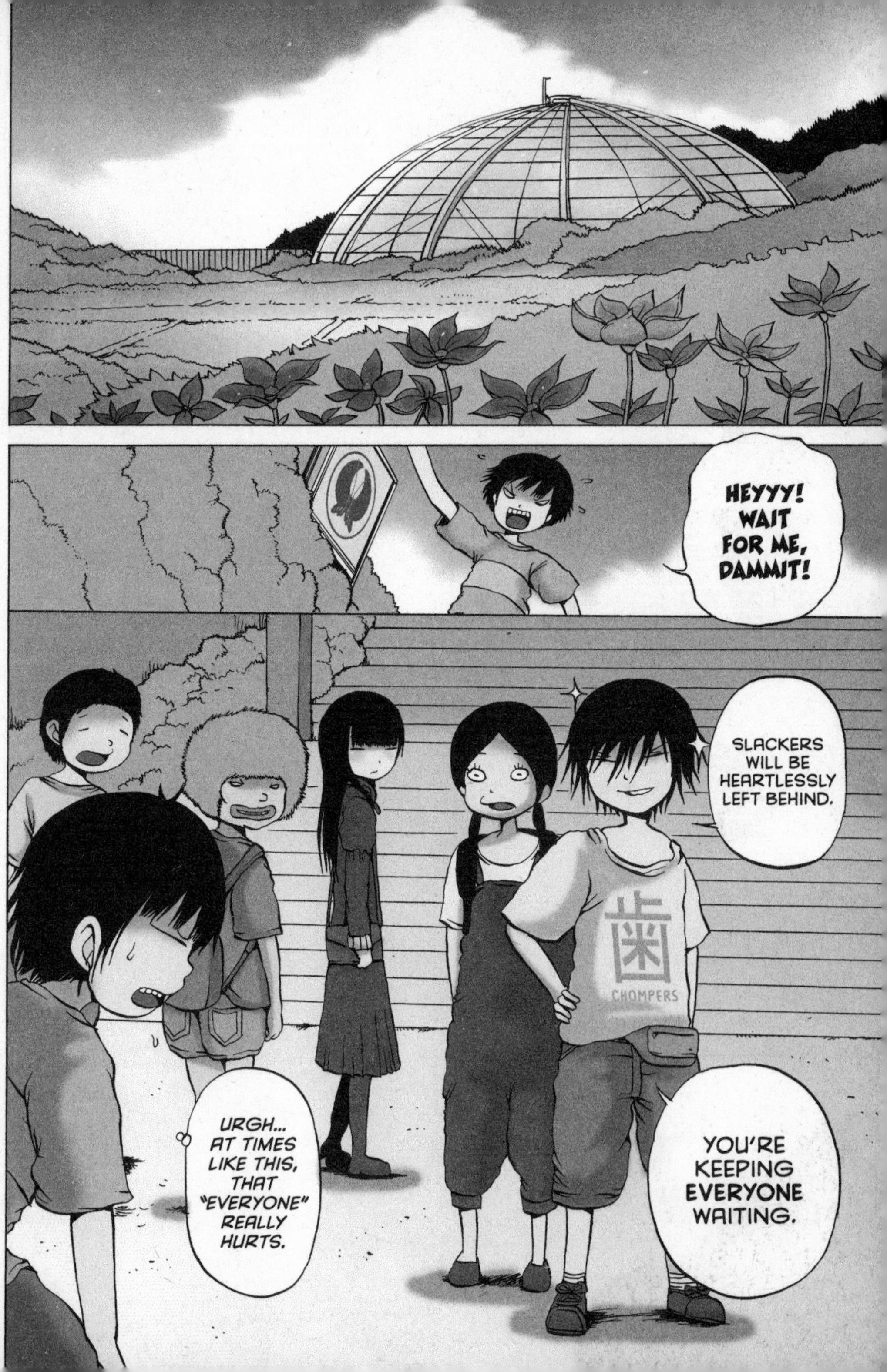
HEYYY! WAIT FOR ME, DAMMIT!
SLACKERS WILL BE HEARTLESSLY LEFT BEHIND.
歯
CHOMPERS
YOU'RE KEEPING EVERYONE WAITING.
URGH... AT TIMES LIKE THIS, THAT "EVERYONE" REALLY HURTS.

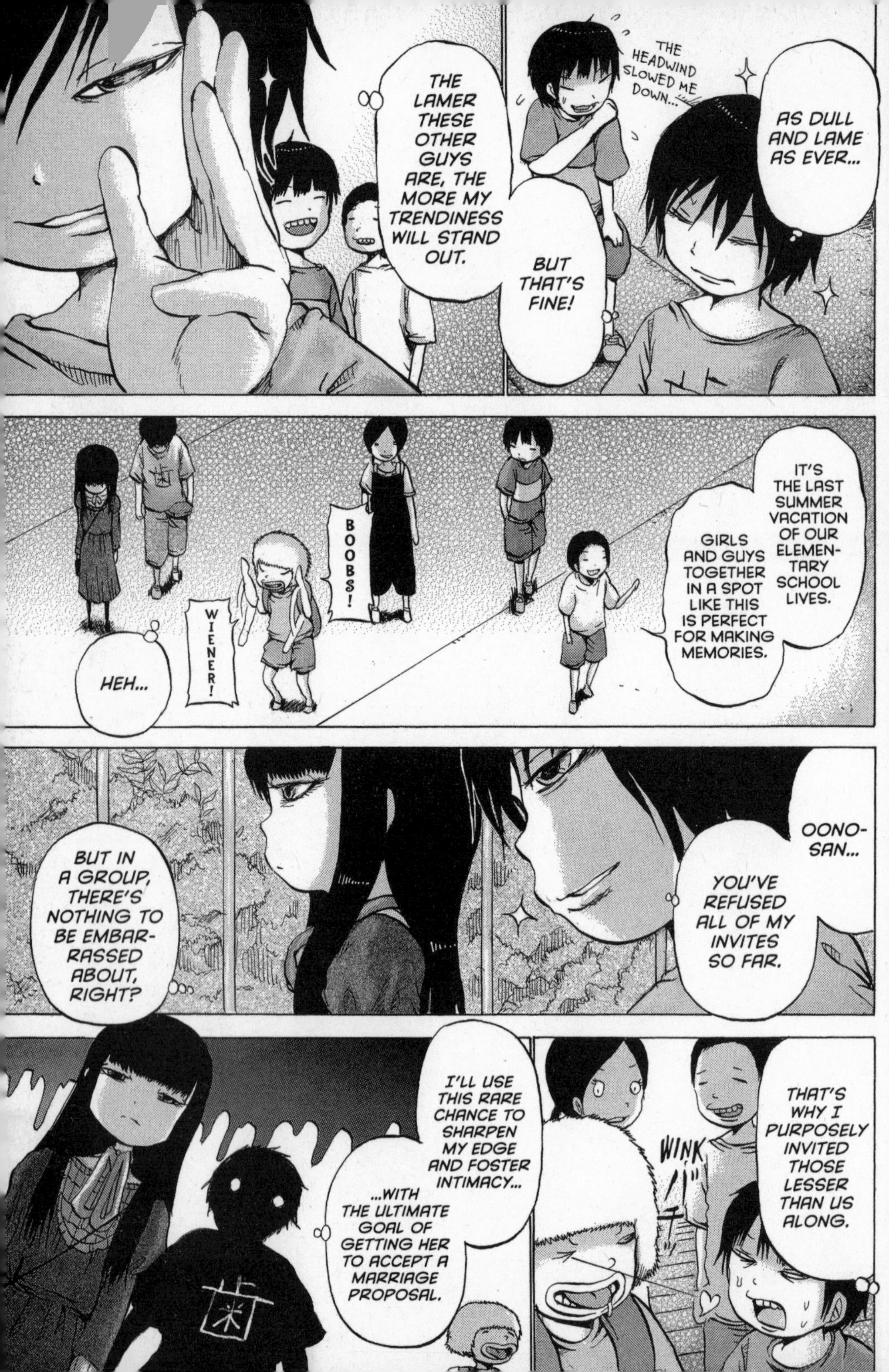
AS DULL AND LAME AS EVER...
THE HEADWIND SLOWED ME DOWN...
BUT THAT'S FINE!
THE LAMER THESE OTHER GUYS ARE, THE MORE MY TRENDINESS WILL STAND OUT.
IT'S THE LAST SUMMER VACATION OF OUR ELEMENTARY SCHOOL LIVES.
GIRLS AND GUYS TOGETHER IN A SPOT LIKE THIS IS PERFECT FOR MAKING MEMORIES.
BOOBS!
WIENER!
HEH...
OONO-SAN...
YOU'VE REFUSED ALL OF MY INVITES SO FAR.
BUT IN A GROUP, THERE'S NOTHING TO BE EMBARRASSED ABOUT, RIGHT?
THAT'S WHY I PURPOSELY INVITED THOSE LESSER THAN US ALONG.
WINK
I'LL USE THIS RARE CHANCE TO SHARPEN MY EDGE AND FOSTER INTIMACY...
...WITH THE ULTIMATE GOAL OF GETTING HER TO ACCEPT A MARRIAGE PROPOSAL.

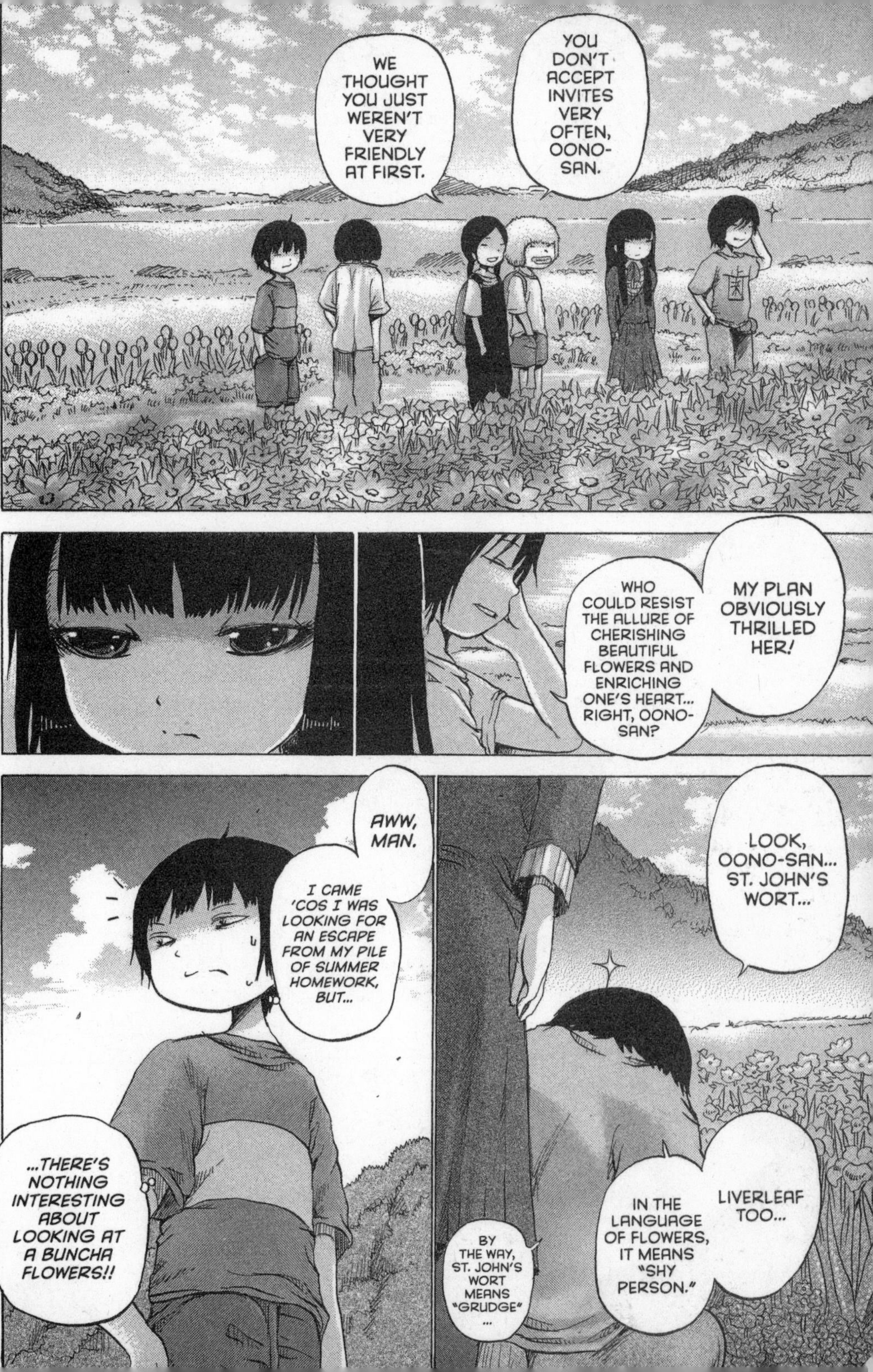
YOU DON'T ACCEPT INVITES VERY OFTEN, OONO-SAN.
WE THOUGHT YOU JUST WEREN'T VERY FRIENDLY AT FIRST.
MY PLAN OBVIOUSLY THRILLED HER!
WHO COULD RESIST THE ALLURE OF CHERISHING BEAUTIFUL FLOWERS AND ENRICHING ONE'S HEART... RIGHT, OONO-SAN?
LOOK, OONO-SAN... ST. JOHN'S WORT...
LIVERLEAF TOO...
IN THE LANGUAGE OF FLOWERS, IT MEANS "SHY PERSON."
BY THE WAY, ST. JOHN'S WORT MEANS "GRUDGE"...
AWW, MAN.
I CAME 'COS I WAS LOOKING FOR AN ESCAPE FROM MY PILE OF SUMMER HOMEWORK, BUT...
...THERE'S NOTHING INTERESTING ABOUT LOOKING AT A BUNCHA FLOWERS!!

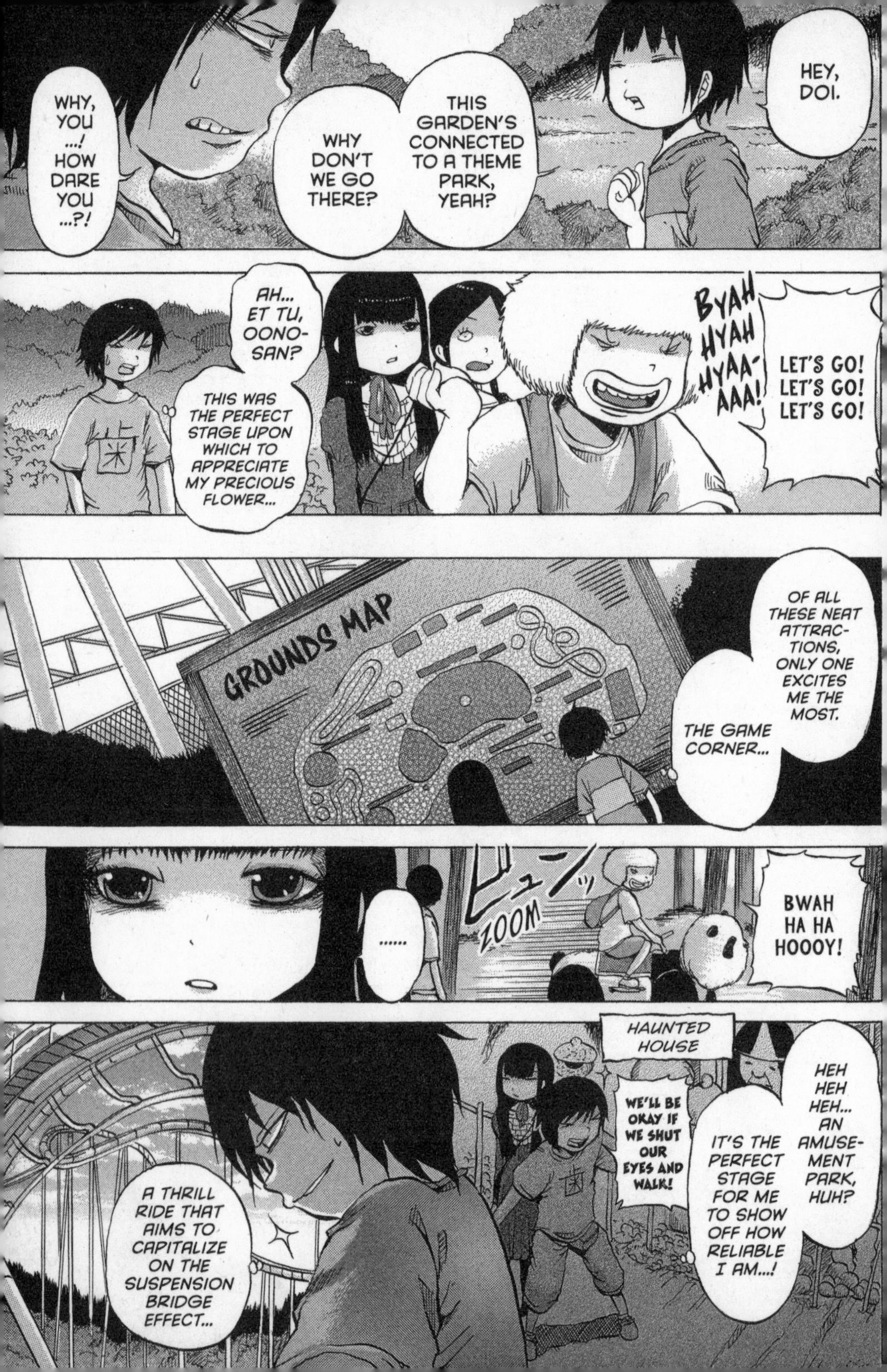
HEY, DOI.
THIS GARDEN'S CONNECTED TO A THEME PARK, YEAH?
WHY DON'T WE GO THERE?
WHY, YOU ...! HOW DARE YOU ...?!
LET'S GO! LET'S GO! LET'S GO!
BYAH HYAH HYAA-AAA!
AH... ET TU, OONO-SAN?
THIS WAS THE PERFECT STAGE UPON WHICH TO APPRECIATE MY PRECIOUS FLOWER...
OF ALL THESE NEAT ATTRACTIONS, ONLY ONE EXCITES ME THE MOST.
THE GAME CORNER...
GROUNDS MAP
BWAH HA HA HOOOY!
ZOOM
......
HEH HEH HEH... AN AMUSEMENT PARK, HUH?
IT'S THE PERFECT STAGE FOR ME TO SHOW OFF HOW RELIABLE I AM...!
HAUNTED HOUSE
WE'LL BE OKAY IF WE SHUT OUR EYES AND WALK!
A THRILL RIDE THAT AIMS TO CAPITALIZE ON THE SUSPENSION BRIDGE EFFECT...

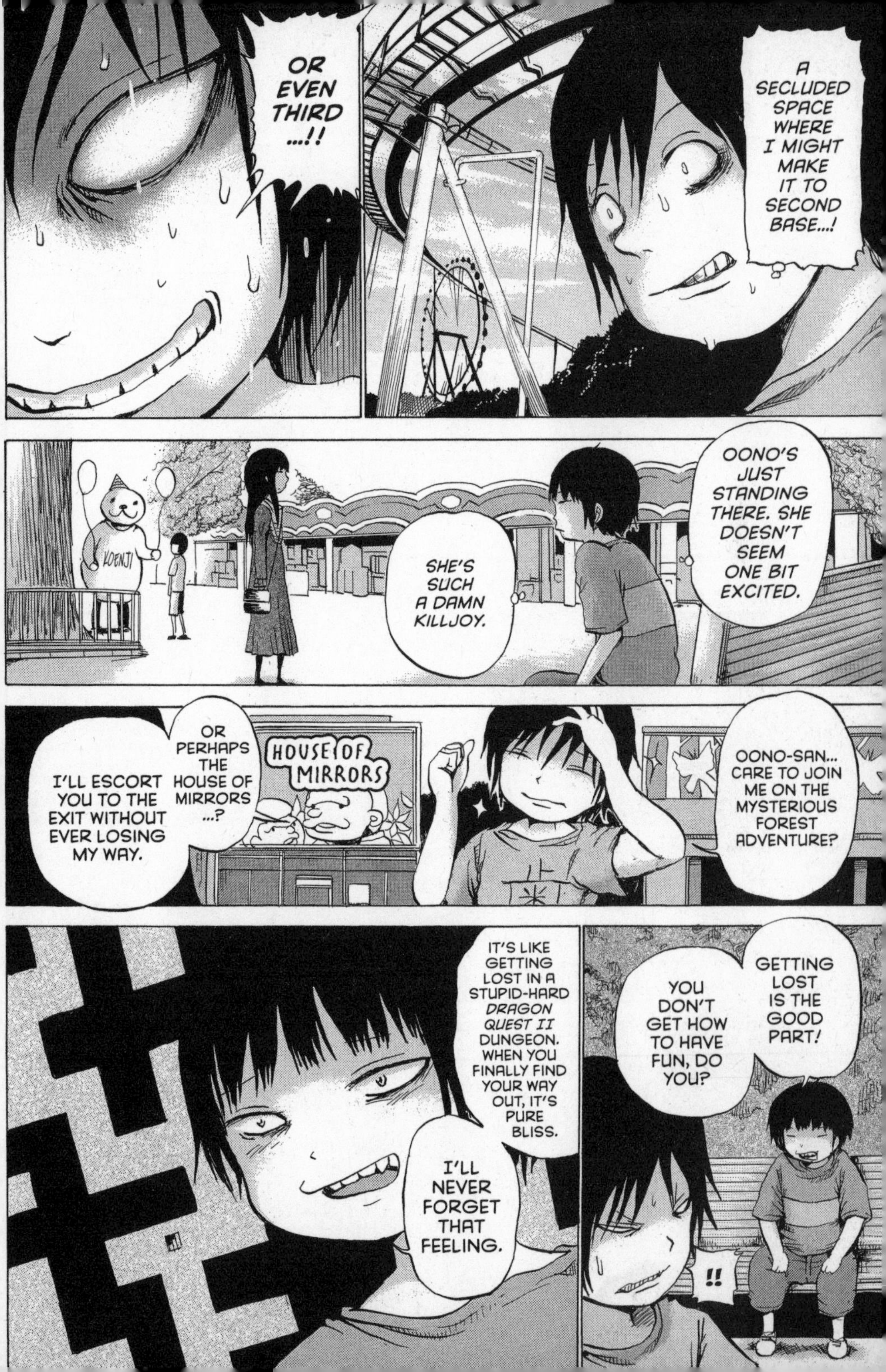
A SECLUDED SPACE WHERE I MIGHT MAKE IT TO SECOND BASE...!
OR EVEN THIRD ...!!
OONO'S JUST STANDING THERE. SHE DOESN'T SEEM ONE BIT EXCITED.
SHE'S SUCH A DAMN KILLJOY.
KOENJI
OONO-SAN... CARE TO JOIN ME ON THE MYSTERIOUS FOREST ADVENTURE?
HOUSE OF MIRRORS
OR PERHAPS THE HOUSE OF MIRRORS ...?
I'LL ESCORT YOU TO THE EXIT WITHOUT EVER LOSING MY WAY.
GETTING LOST IS THE GOOD PART!
YOU DON'T GET HOW TO HAVE FUN, DO YOU?
!!
IT'S LIKE GETTING LOST IN A STUPID-HARD *DRAGON QUEST II* DUNGEON. WHEN YOU FINALLY FIND YOUR WAY OUT, IT'S PURE BLISS.
I'LL NEVER FORGET THAT FEELING.

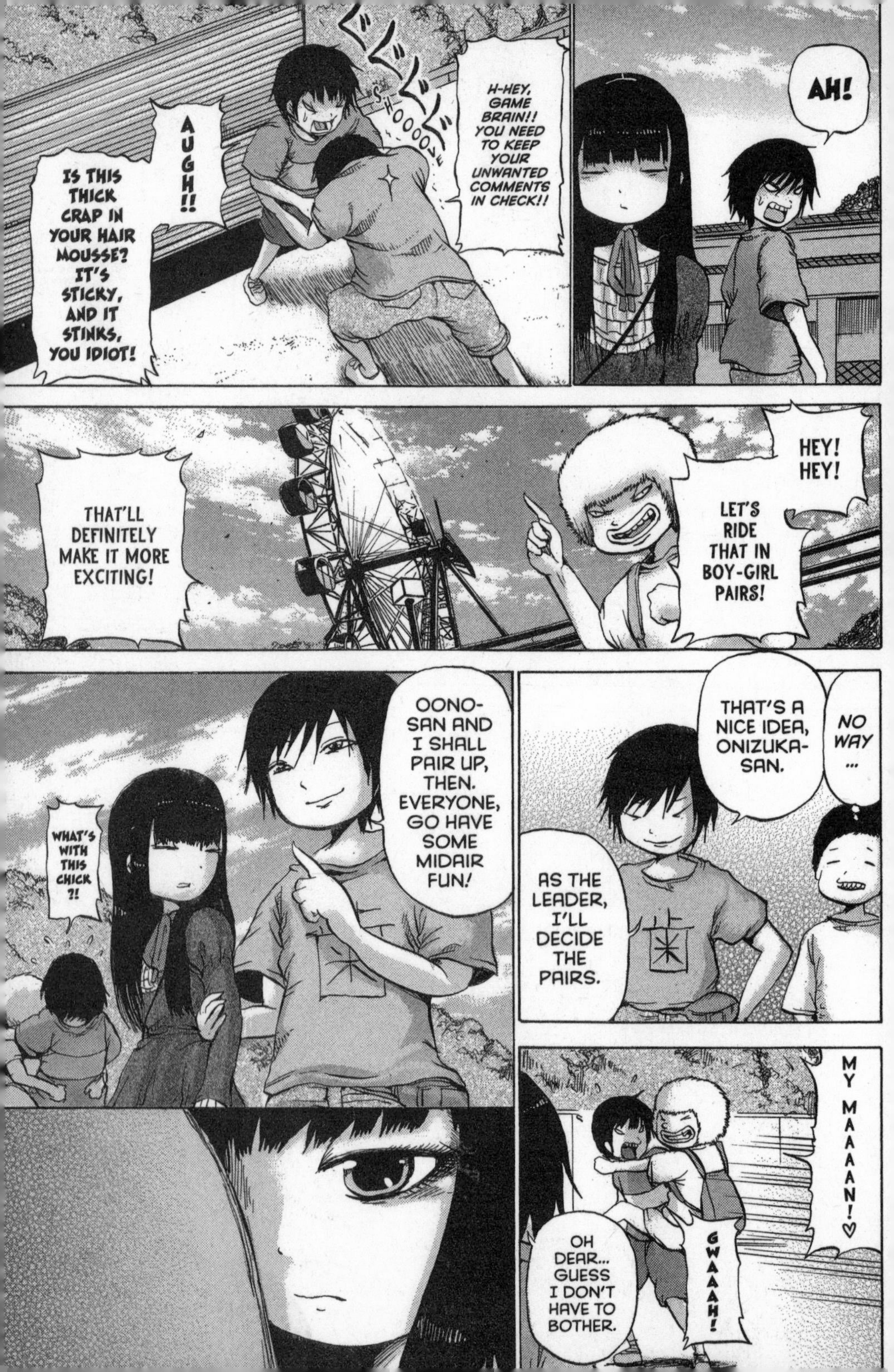
AH!
H-HEY, GAME BRAIN!! YOU NEED TO KEEP YOUR UNWANTED COMMENTS IN CHECK!!
SHOOOOVE
AUGH!!
IS THIS THICK CRAP IN YOUR HAIR MOUSSE? IT'S STICKY, AND IT STINKS, YOU IDIOT!
HEY! HEY!
LET'S RIDE THAT IN BOY-GIRL PAIRS!
THAT'LL DEFINITELY MAKE IT MORE EXCITING!
NO WAY...
THAT'S A NICE IDEA, ONIZUKA-SAN.
AS THE LEADER, I'LL DECIDE THE PAIRS.
OONO-SAN AND I SHALL PAIR UP, THEN. EVERYONE, GO HAVE SOME MIDAIR FUN!
WHAT'S WITH THIS CHICK?!
MY MAAAAN!♡
GWAAAH!
OH DEAR... GUESS I DON'T HAVE TO BOTHER.

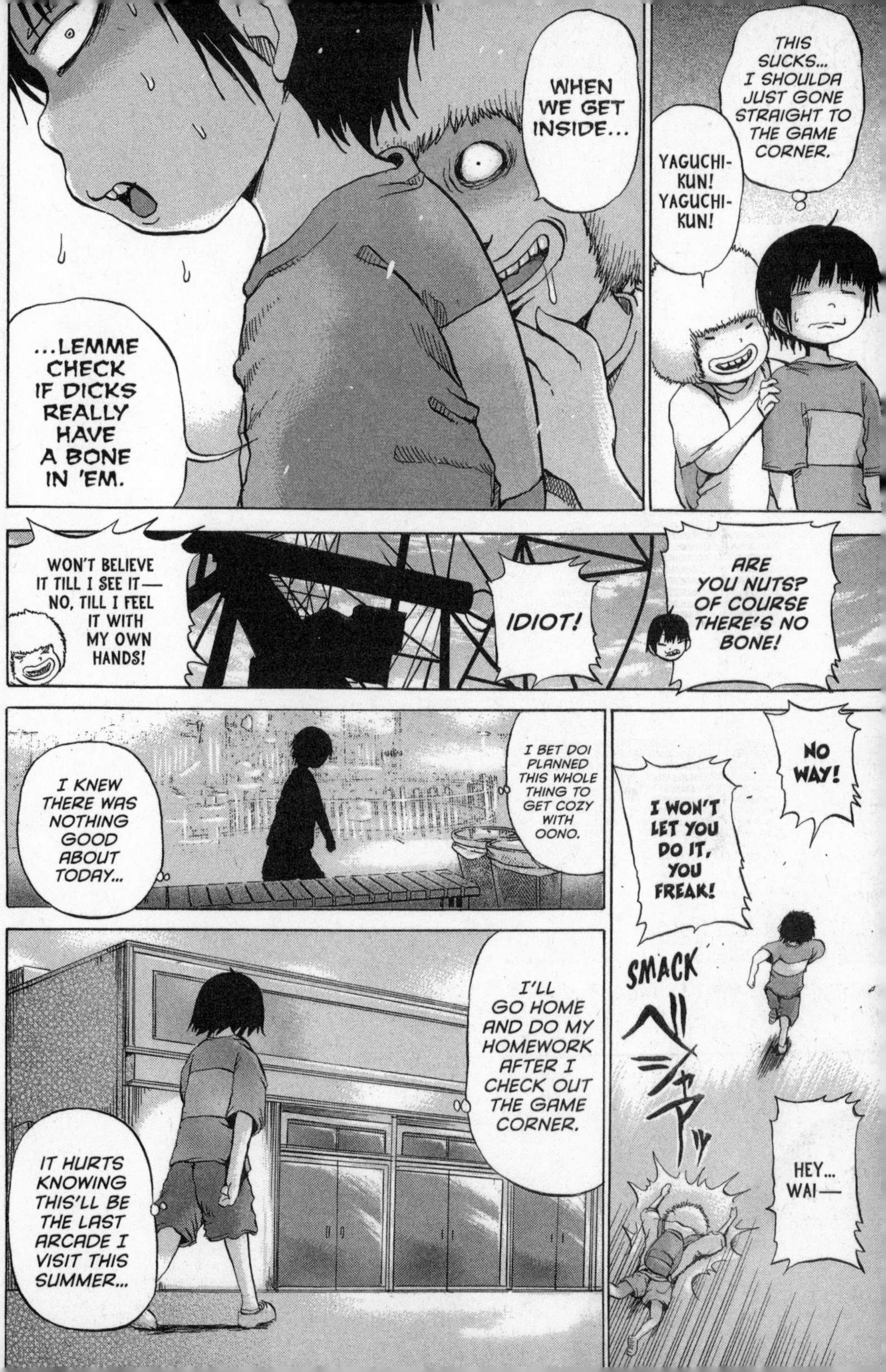
THIS SUCKS... I SHOULDA JUST GONE STRAIGHT TO THE GAME CORNER.
YAGUCHI-KUN! YAGUCHI-KUN!
WHEN WE GET INSIDE...
...LEMME CHECK IF DICKS REALLY HAVE A BONE IN 'EM.
ARE YOU NUTS? OF COURSE THERE'S NO BONE!
IDIOT!
WON'T BELIEVE IT TILL I SEE IT—NO, TILL I FEEL IT WITH MY OWN HANDS!
NO WAY!
I WON'T LET YOU DO IT, YOU FREAK!
SMACK
ベシャアッ
HEY... WAI—
I BET DOI PLANNED THIS WHOLE THING TO GET COZY WITH OONO.
I KNEW THERE WAS NOTHING GOOD ABOUT TODAY...
I'LL GO HOME AND DO MY HOMEWORK AFTER I CHECK OUT THE GAME CORNER.
IT HURTS KNOWING THIS'LL BE THE LAST ARCADE I VISIT THIS SUMMER...

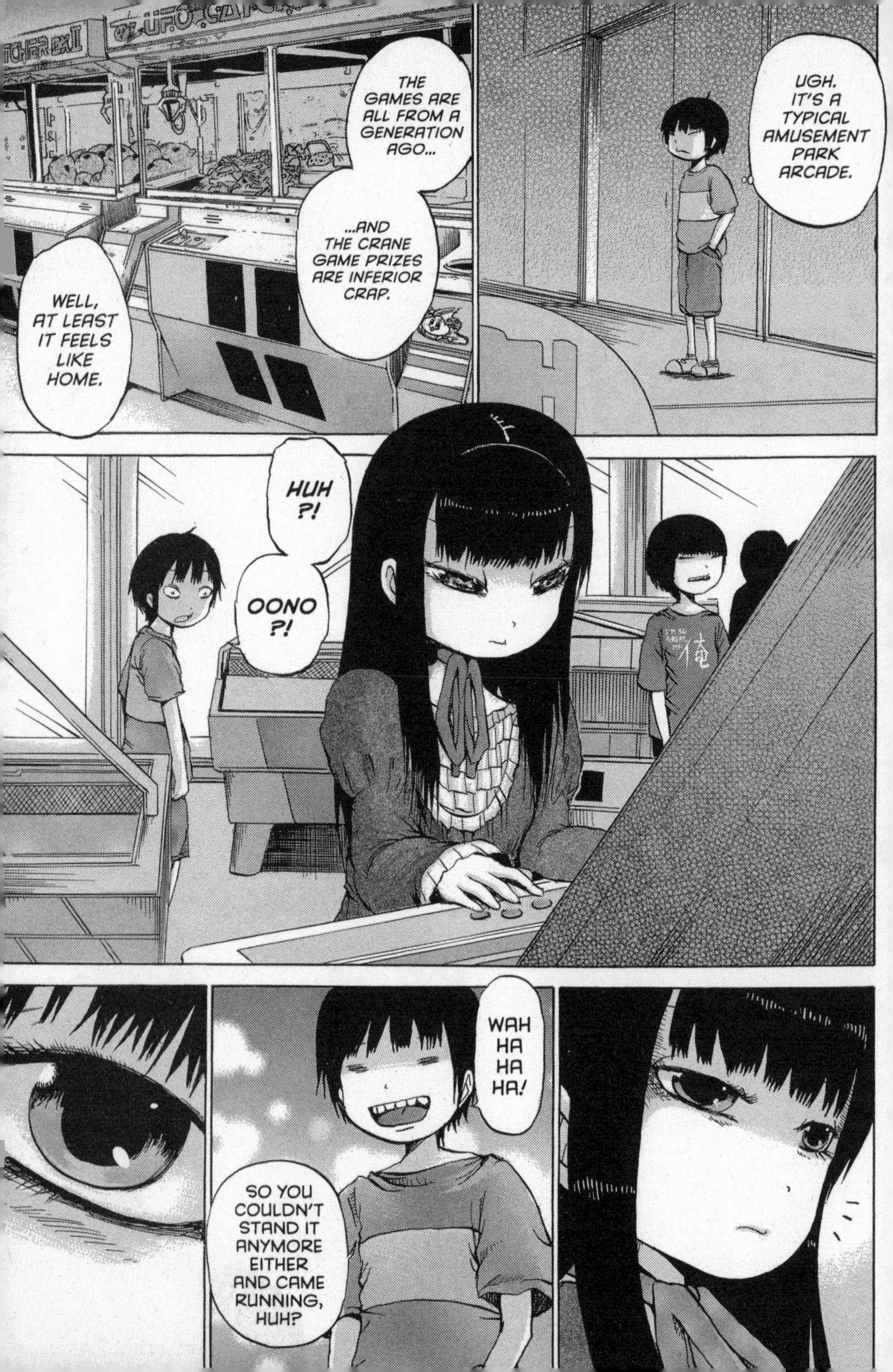
UGH. IT'S A TYPICAL AMUSEMENT PARK ARCADE.
THE GAMES ARE ALL FROM A GENERATION AGO...
...AND THE CRANE GAME PRIZES ARE INFERIOR CRAP.
WELL, AT LEAST IT FEELS LIKE HOME.
HUH?!
OONO?!
WAH HA HA HA!
SO YOU COULDN'T STAND IT ANYMORE EITHER AND CAME RUNNING, HUH?

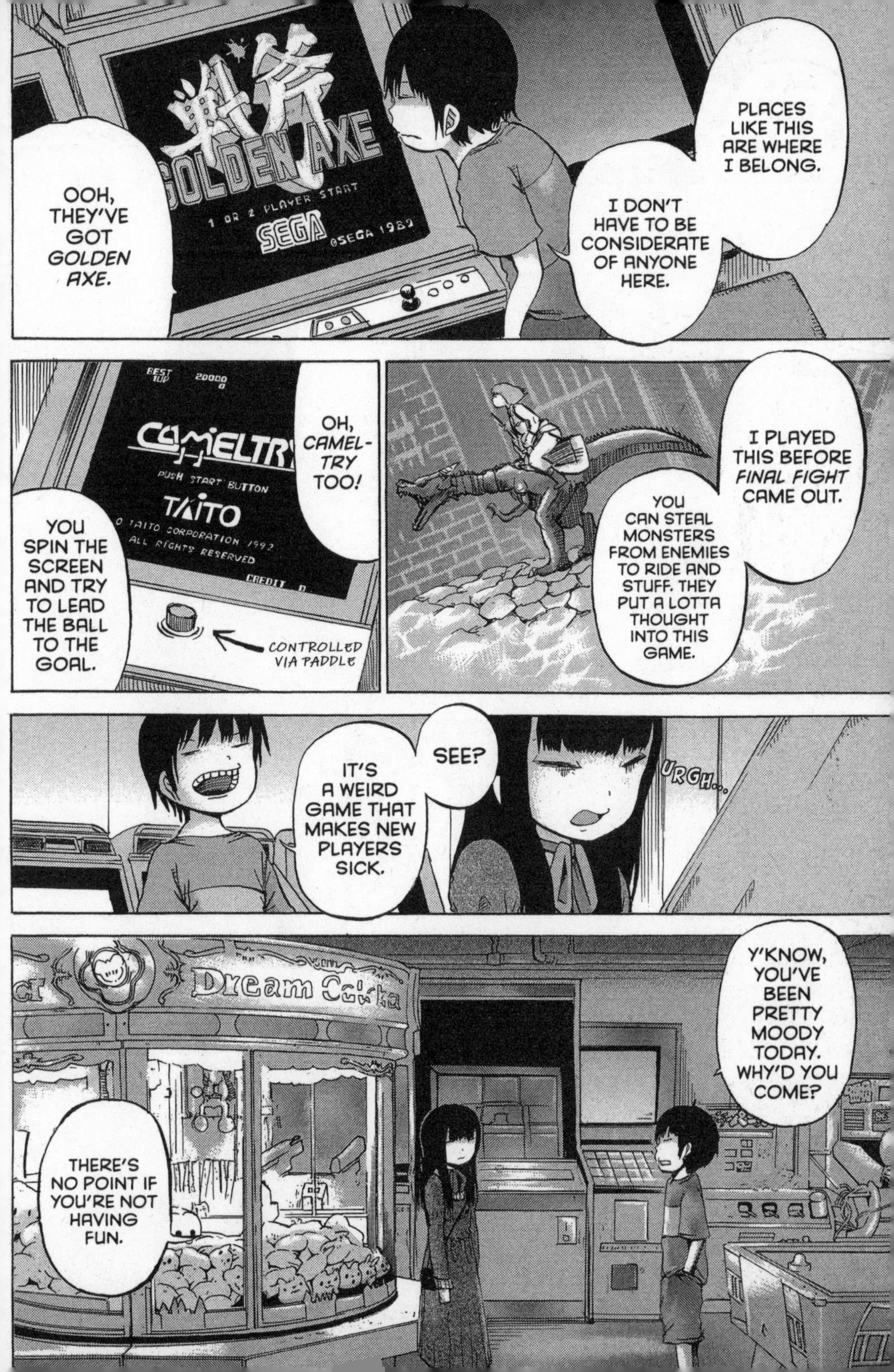
PLACES LIKE THIS ARE WHERE I BELONG.
I DON'T HAVE TO BE CONSIDERATE OF ANYONE HERE.
GOLDEN AXE
1 OR 2 PLAYER START
SEGA
©SEGA 1989
OOH, THEY'VE GOT *GOLDEN AXE*.
I PLAYED THIS BEFORE *FINAL FIGHT* CAME OUT.
YOU CAN STEAL MONSTERS FROM ENEMIES TO RIDE AND STUFF. THEY PUT A LOTTA THOUGHT INTO THIS GAME.
BEST 1UP 20000 0
CAMELTRY
PUSH START BUTTON
TAITO
© TAITO CORPORATION 1992
ALL RIGHTS RESERVED
CREDIT 0
OH, *CAMELTRY* TOO!
YOU SPIN THE SCREEN AND TRY TO LEAD THE BALL TO THE GOAL.
CONTROLLED VIA PADDLE
URGH...
SEE?
IT'S A WEIRD GAME THAT MAKES NEW PLAYERS SICK.
Y'KNOW, YOU'VE BEEN PRETTY MOODY TODAY. WHY'D YOU COME?
THERE'S NO POINT IF YOU'RE NOT HAVING FUN.

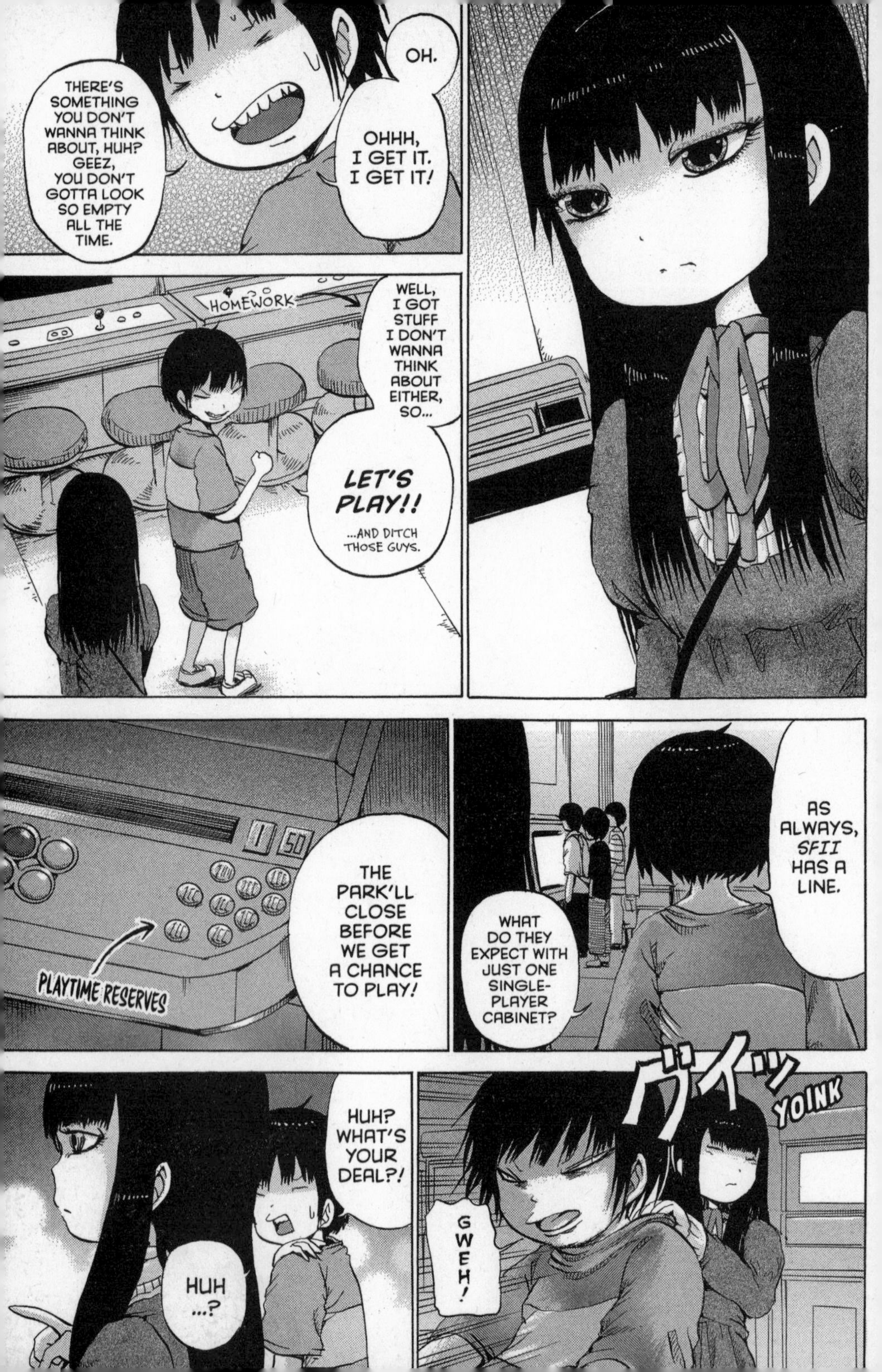
OH.
OHHH, I GET IT. I GET IT!
THERE'S SOMETHING YOU DON'T WANNA THINK ABOUT, HUH? GEEZ, YOU DON'T GOTTA LOOK SO EMPTY ALL THE TIME.
WELL, I GOT STUFF I DON'T WANNA THINK ABOUT EITHER, SO...
LET'S PLAY!! ...AND DITCH THOSE GUYS.
HOMEWORK
AS ALWAYS, SFII HAS A LINE.
WHAT DO THEY EXPECT WITH JUST ONE SINGLE-PLAYER CABINET?
THE PARK'LL CLOSE BEFORE WE GET A CHANCE TO PLAY!
PLAYTIME RESERVES
ヴイッ
YOINK
GWEH!
HUH? WHAT'S YOUR DEAL?!
HUH ...?

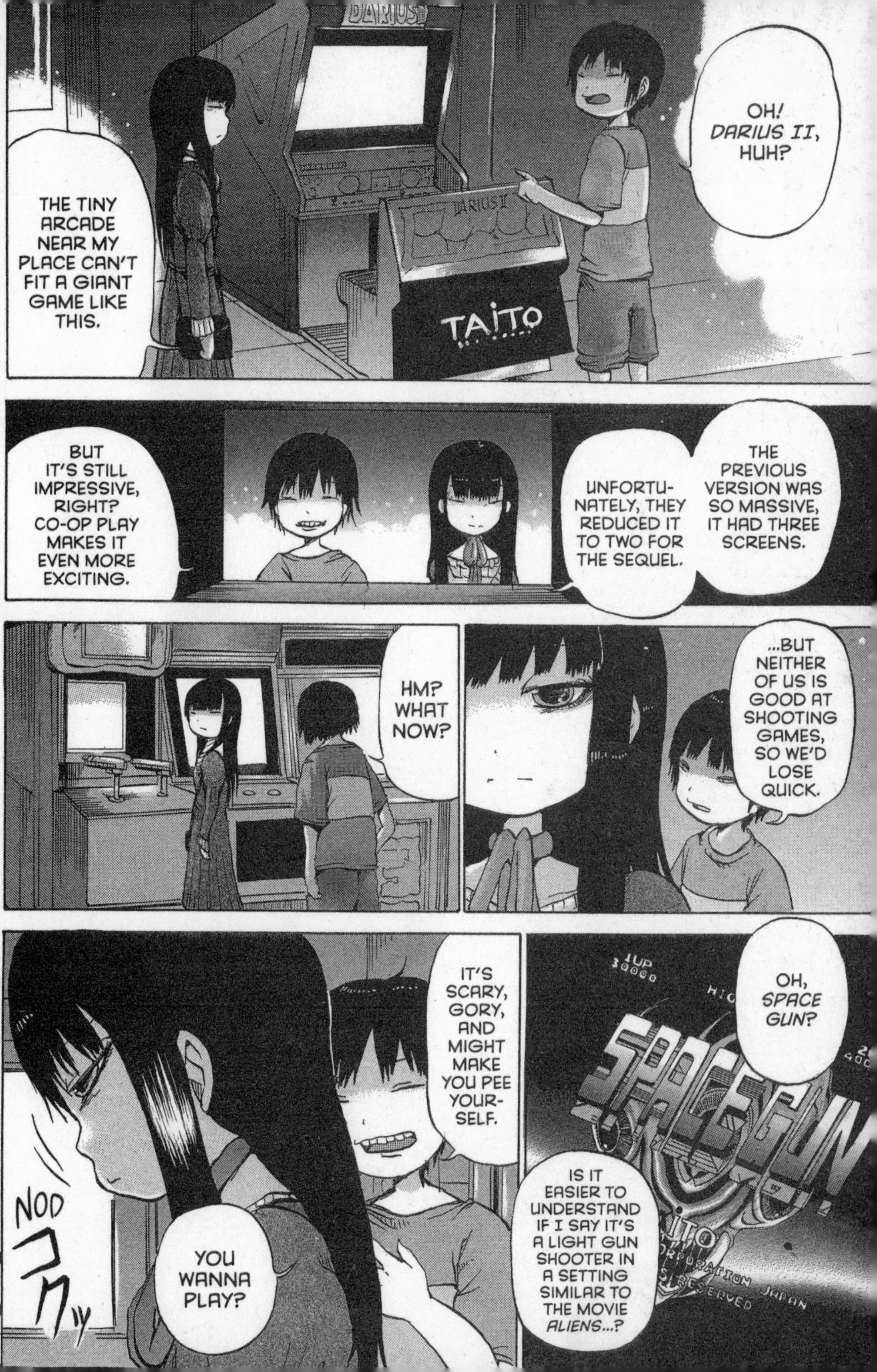
OH! *DARIUS II*, HUH?
THE TINY ARCADE NEAR MY PLACE CAN'T FIT A GIANT GAME LIKE THIS.
TAITO
THE PREVIOUS VERSION WAS SO MASSIVE, IT HAD THREE SCREENS.
UNFORTU-NATELY, THEY REDUCED IT TO TWO FOR THE SEQUEL.
BUT IT'S STILL IMPRESSIVE, RIGHT? CO-OP PLAY MAKES IT EVEN MORE EXCITING.
...BUT NEITHER OF US IS GOOD AT SHOOTING GAMES, SO WE'D LOSE QUICK.
HM? WHAT NOW?
OH, *SPACE GUN*?
SPACE GUN
IS IT EASIER TO UNDERSTAND IF I SAY IT'S A LIGHT GUN SHOOTER IN A SETTING SIMILAR TO THE MOVIE *ALIENS*...?
IT'S SCARY, GORY, AND MIGHT MAKE YOU PEE YOUR-SELF.
YOU WANNA PLAY?
NOD

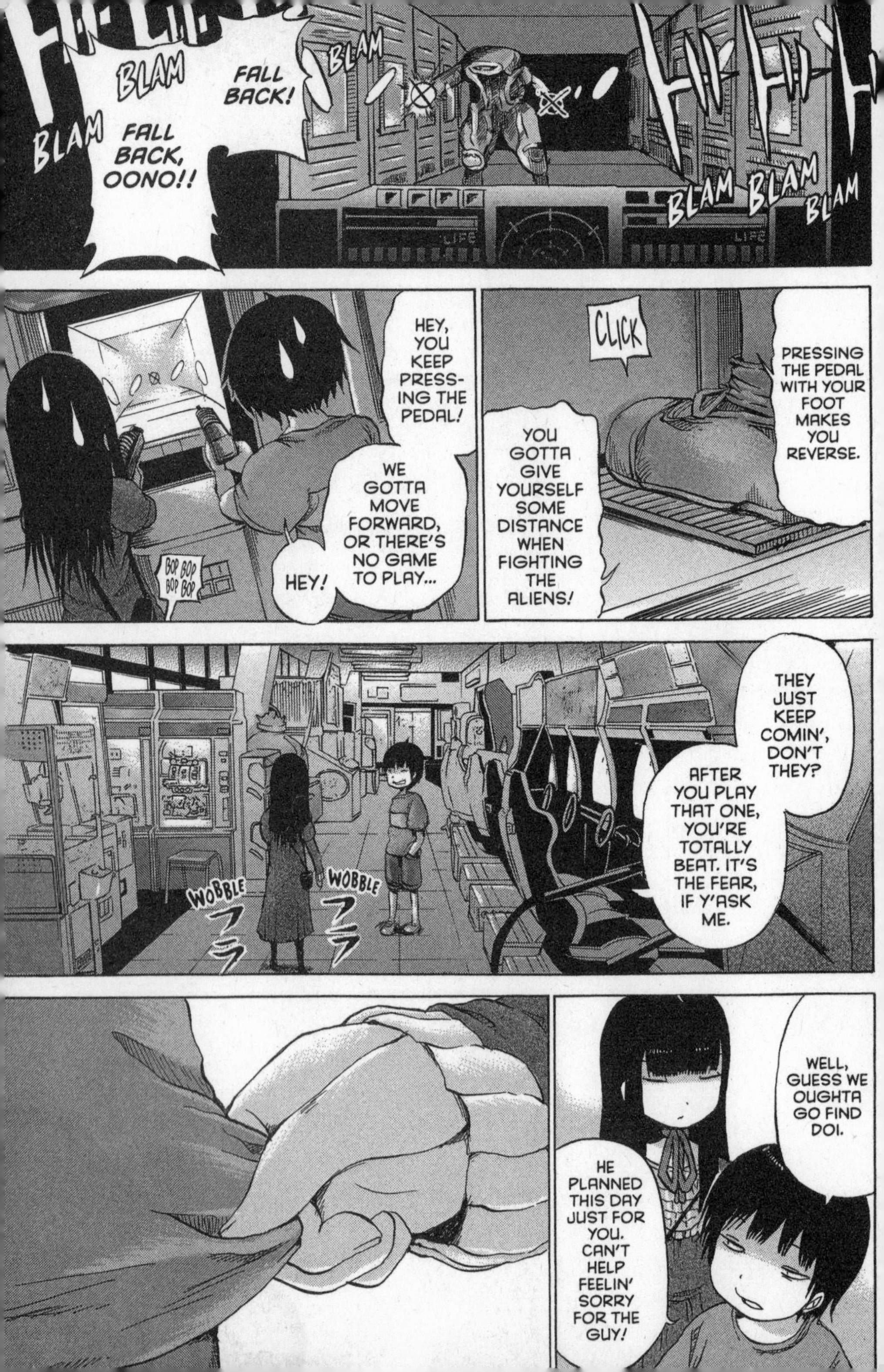
BLAM
BLAM
BLAM
BLAM
BLAM
FALL BACK!
BLAM
FALL BACK, OONO!!
CLICK
PRESSING THE PEDAL WITH YOUR FOOT MAKES YOU REVERSE.
YOU GOTTA GIVE YOURSELF SOME DISTANCE WHEN FIGHTING THE ALIENS!
HEY, YOU KEEP PRESS-ING THE PEDAL!
WE GOTTA MOVE FORWARD, OR THERE'S NO GAME TO PLAY...
HEY!
BOP BOP BOP BOP
THEY JUST KEEP COMIN', DON'T THEY?
AFTER YOU PLAY THAT ONE, YOU'RE TOTALLY BEAT. IT'S THE FEAR, IF Y'ASK ME.
WOBBLE
WOBBLE
WELL, GUESS WE OUGHTA GO FIND DOI.
HE PLANNED THIS DAY JUST FOR YOU. CAN'T HELP FEELIN' SORRY FOR THE GUY!

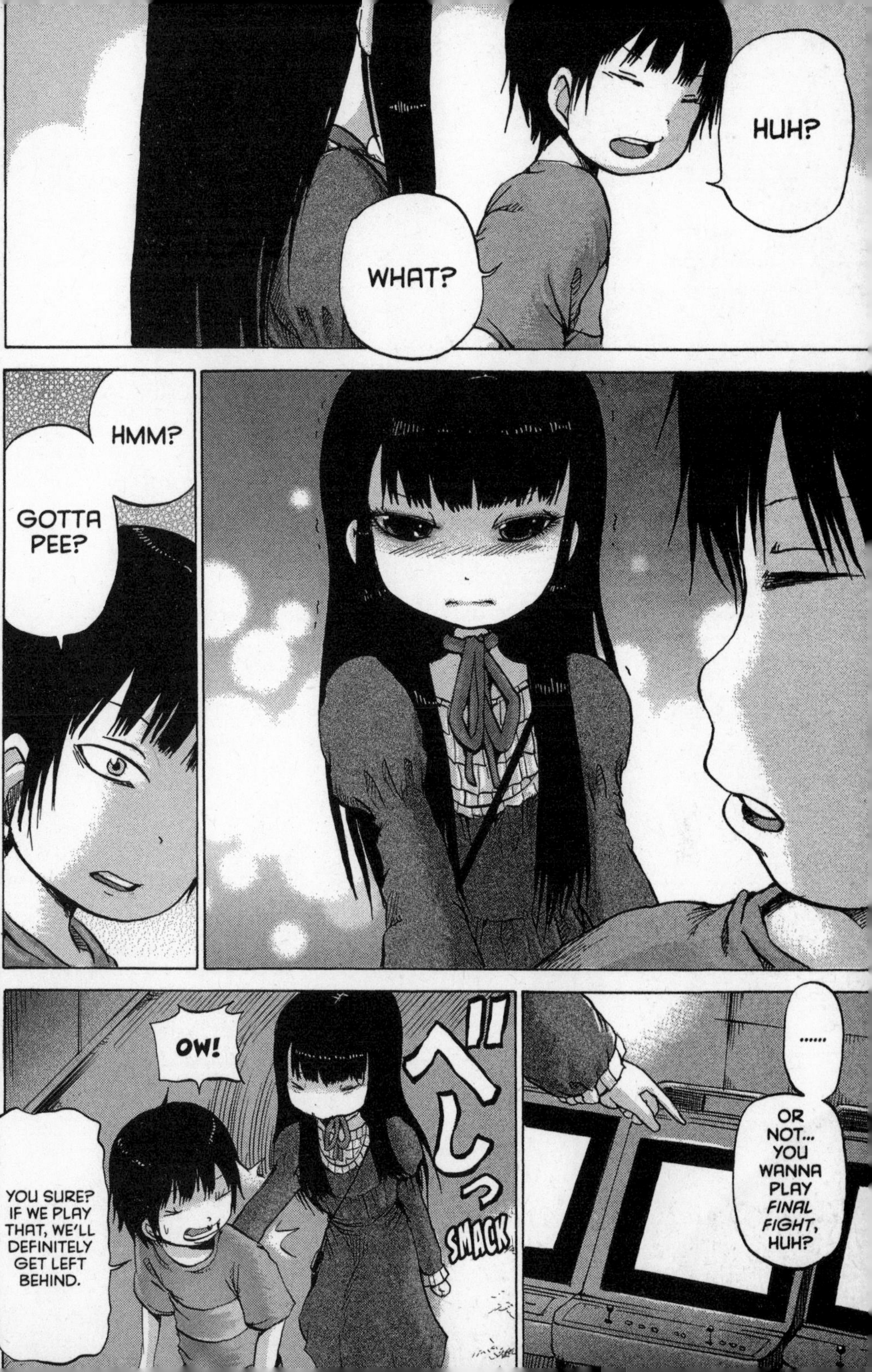
HUH?
WHAT?
HMM?
GOTTA PEE?
......
OR NOT... YOU WANNA PLAY *FINAL FIGHT*, HUH?
へしっ
SMACK
OW!
YOU SURE? IF WE PLAY THAT, WE'LL DEFINITELY GET LEFT BEHIND.

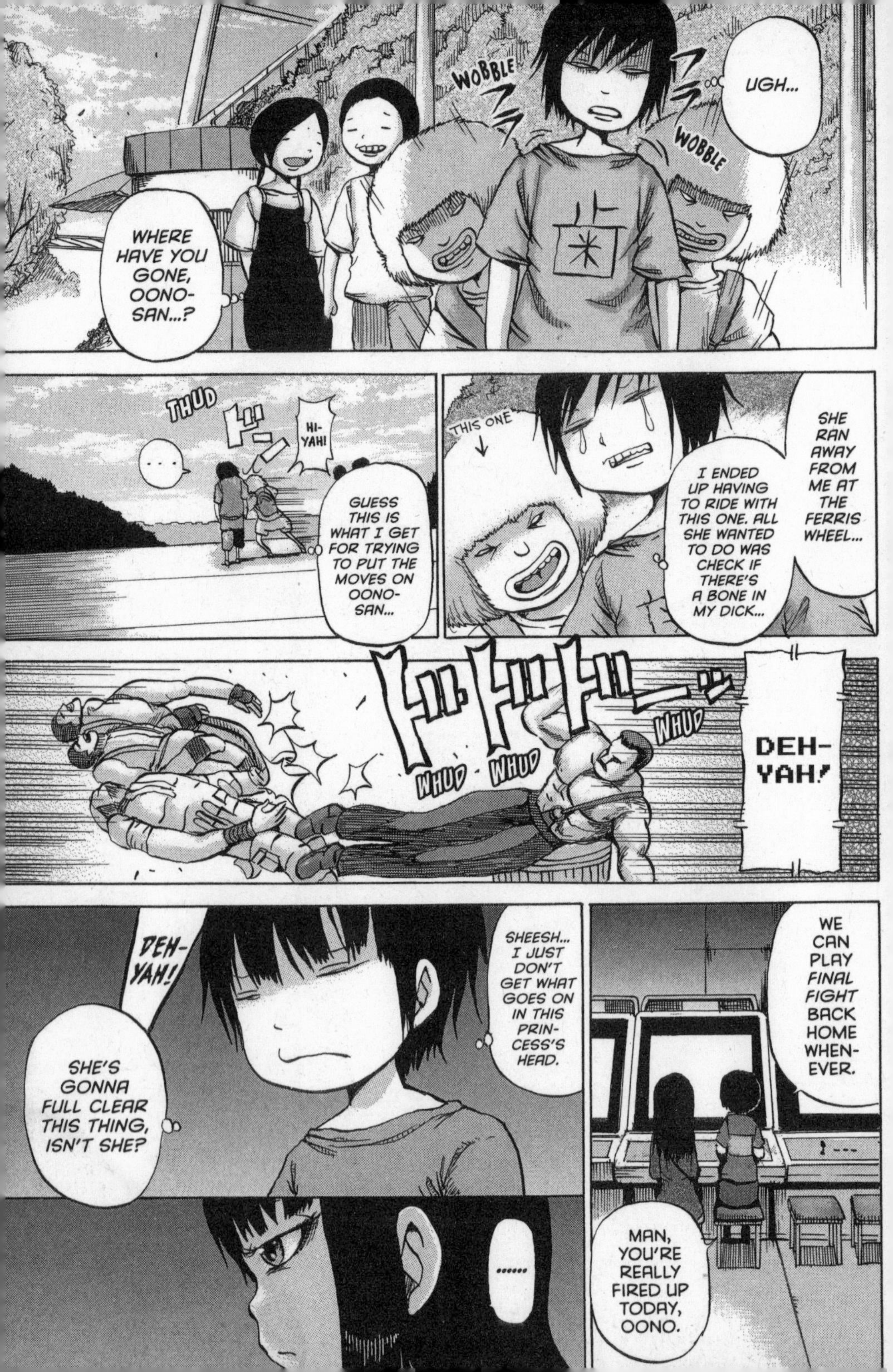
UGH...
WOBBLE
WOBBLE
WHERE HAVE YOU GONE, OONO-SAN...?
SHE RAN AWAY FROM ME AT THE FERRIS WHEEL...
I ENDED UP HAVING TO RIDE WITH THIS ONE. ALL SHE WANTED TO DO WAS CHECK IF THERE'S A BONE IN MY DICK...
THIS ONE
HI-YAH!
THUD
...
GUESS THIS IS WHAT I GET FOR TRYING TO PUT THE MOVES ON OONO-SAN...
DEH-YAH!
WHUD
WHUD
WHUD
WE CAN PLAY FINAL FIGHT BACK HOME WHENEVER.
MAN, YOU'RE REALLY FIRED UP TODAY, OONO.
SHEESH... I JUST DON'T GET WHAT GOES ON IN THIS PRINCESS'S HEAD.
DEH-YAH!
SHE'S GONNA FULL CLEAR THIS THING, ISN'T SHE?
......

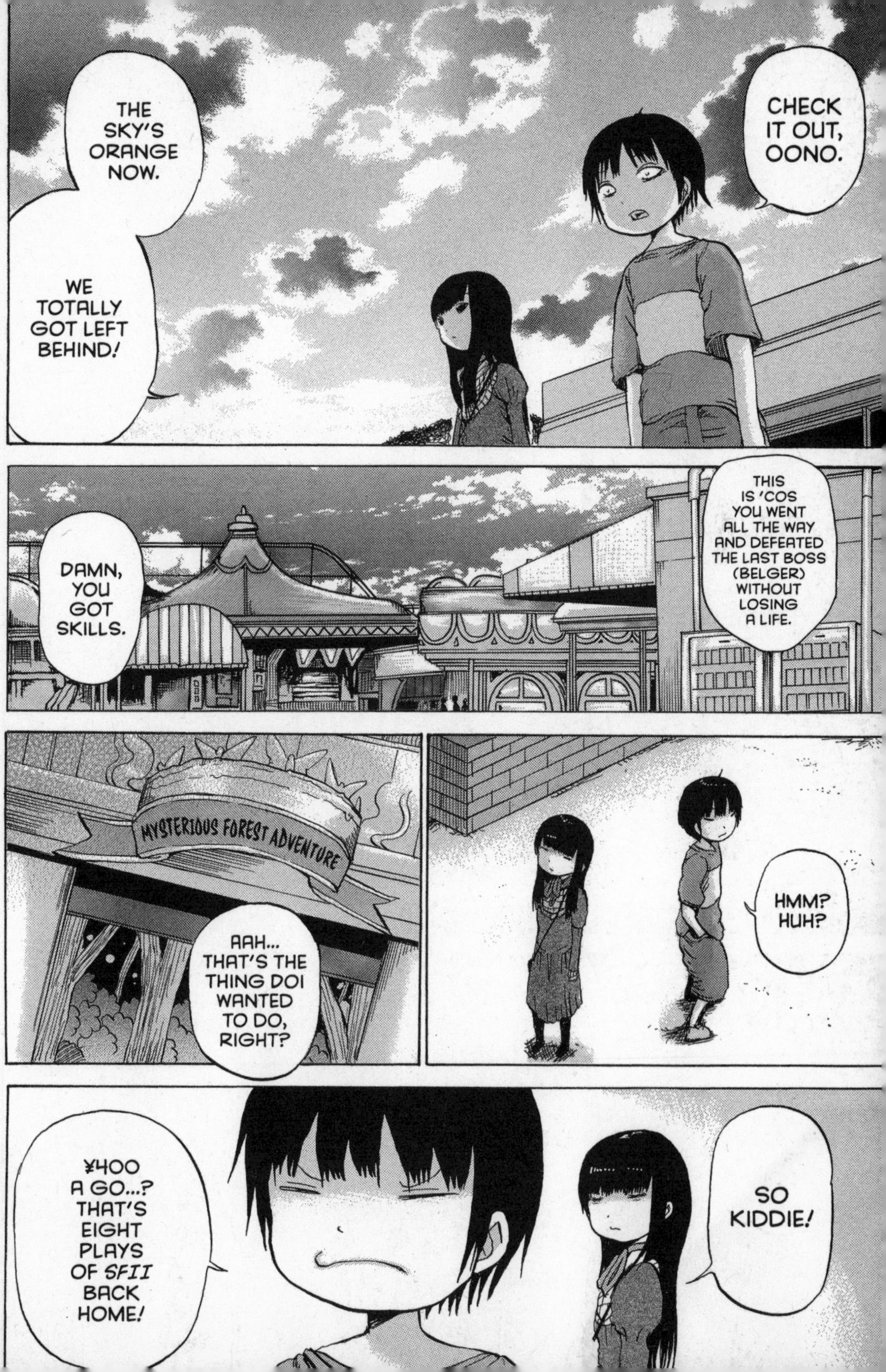
CHECK IT OUT, OONO.
THE SKY'S ORANGE NOW.
WE TOTALLY GOT LEFT BEHIND!
THIS IS 'COS YOU WENT ALL THE WAY AND DEFEATED THE LAST BOSS (BELGER) WITHOUT LOSING A LIFE.
DAMN, YOU GOT SKILLS.
HMM? HUH?
MYSTERIOUS FOREST ADVENTURE
AAH... THAT'S THE THING DOI WANTED TO DO, RIGHT?
SO KIDDIE!
¥400 A GO...? THAT'S EIGHT PLAYS OF *SFII* BACK HOME!

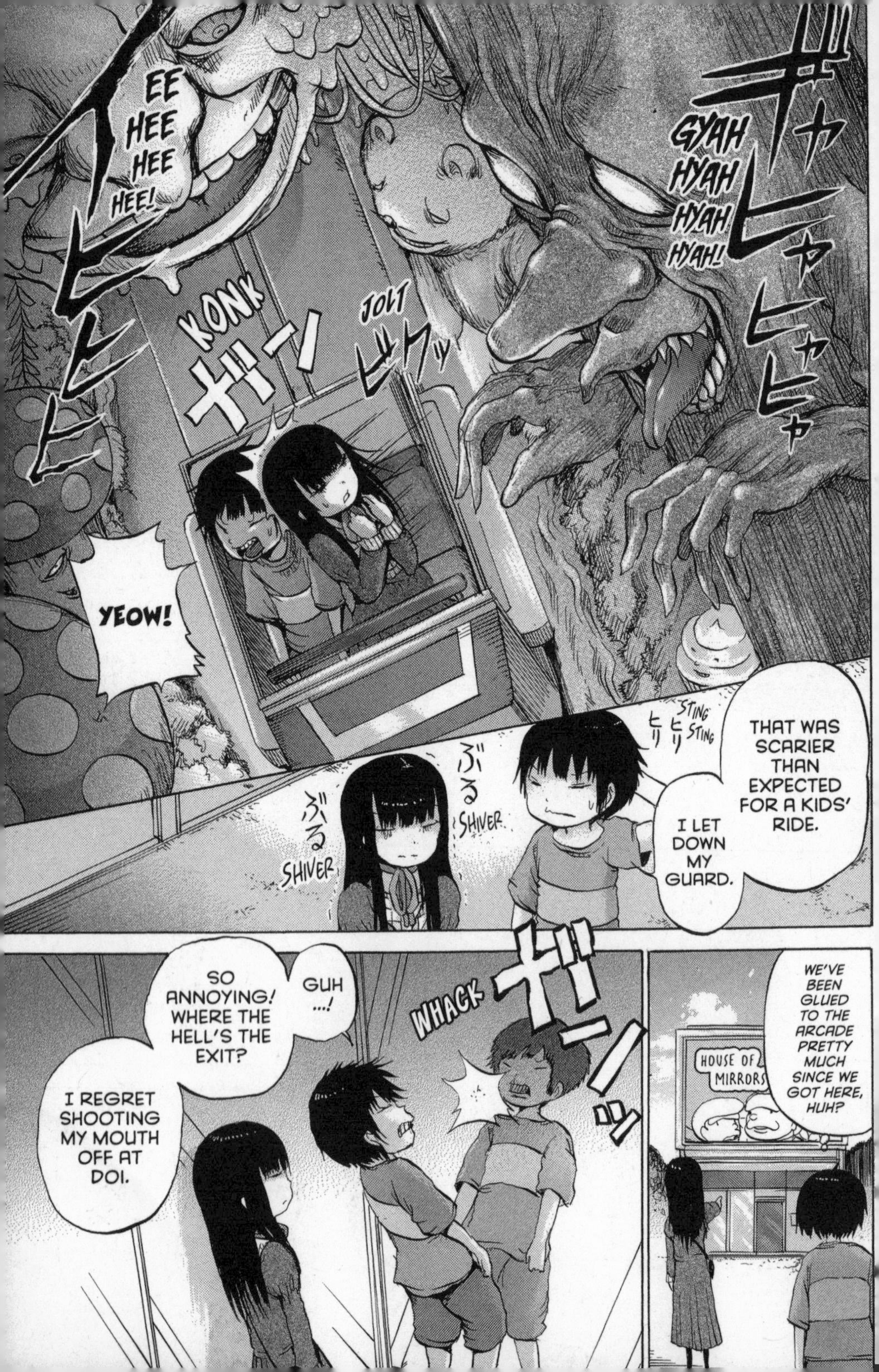
GYAH HYAH HYAH HYAH!
ギャヒャヒャヒャ
JOLT
ビクッ
KONK
ゴーン
EE HEE HEE HEE!
イヒヒヒ
YEOW!
THAT WAS SCARIER THAN EXPECTED FOR A KIDS' RIDE.
STING STING
ヒリヒリ
I LET DOWN MY GUARD.
ぶる
SHIVER
ぶる
SHIVER
WE'VE BEEN GLUED TO THE ARCADE PRETTY MUCH SINCE WE GOT HERE, HUH?
HOUSE OF MIRRORS
WHACK
ゴーン
GUH ...!
SO ANNOYING! WHERE THE HELL'S THE EXIT?
I REGRET SHOOTING MY MOUTH OFF AT DOI.

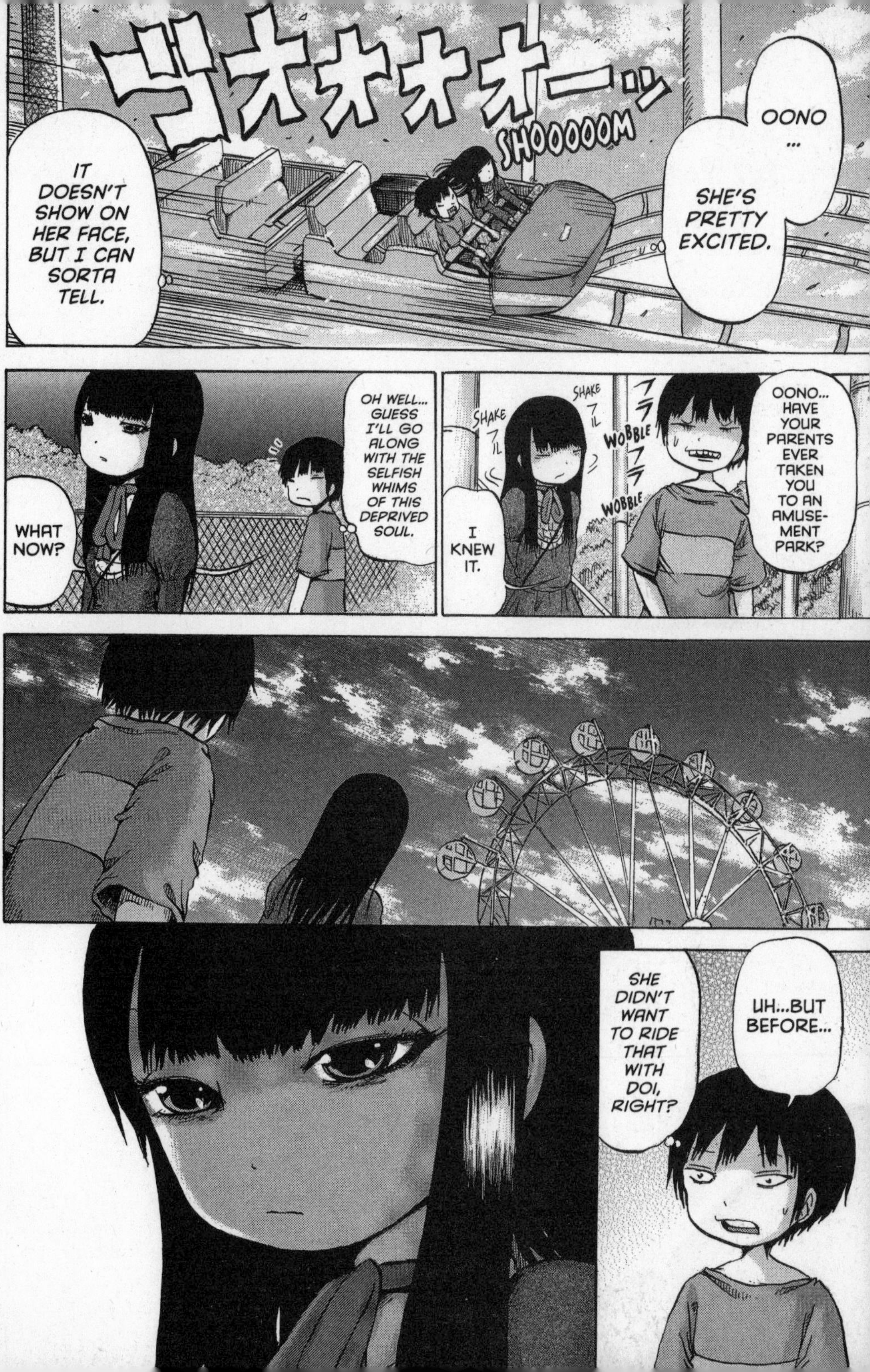
ゴオオオオーッ
SHOOOOOM
OONO ... SHE'S PRETTY EXCITED.
IT DOESN'T SHOW ON HER FACE, BUT I CAN SORTA TELL.
OONO... HAVE YOUR PARENTS EVER TAKEN YOU TO AN AMUSEMENT PARK?
フラ WOBBLE
フラ WOBBLE
SHAKE フル
SHAKE フル
I KNEW IT.
OH WELL... GUESS I'LL GO ALONG WITH THE SELFISH WHIMS OF THIS DEPRIVED SOUL.
WHAT NOW?
UH...BUT BEFORE...
SHE DIDN'T WANT TO RIDE THAT WITH DOI, RIGHT?

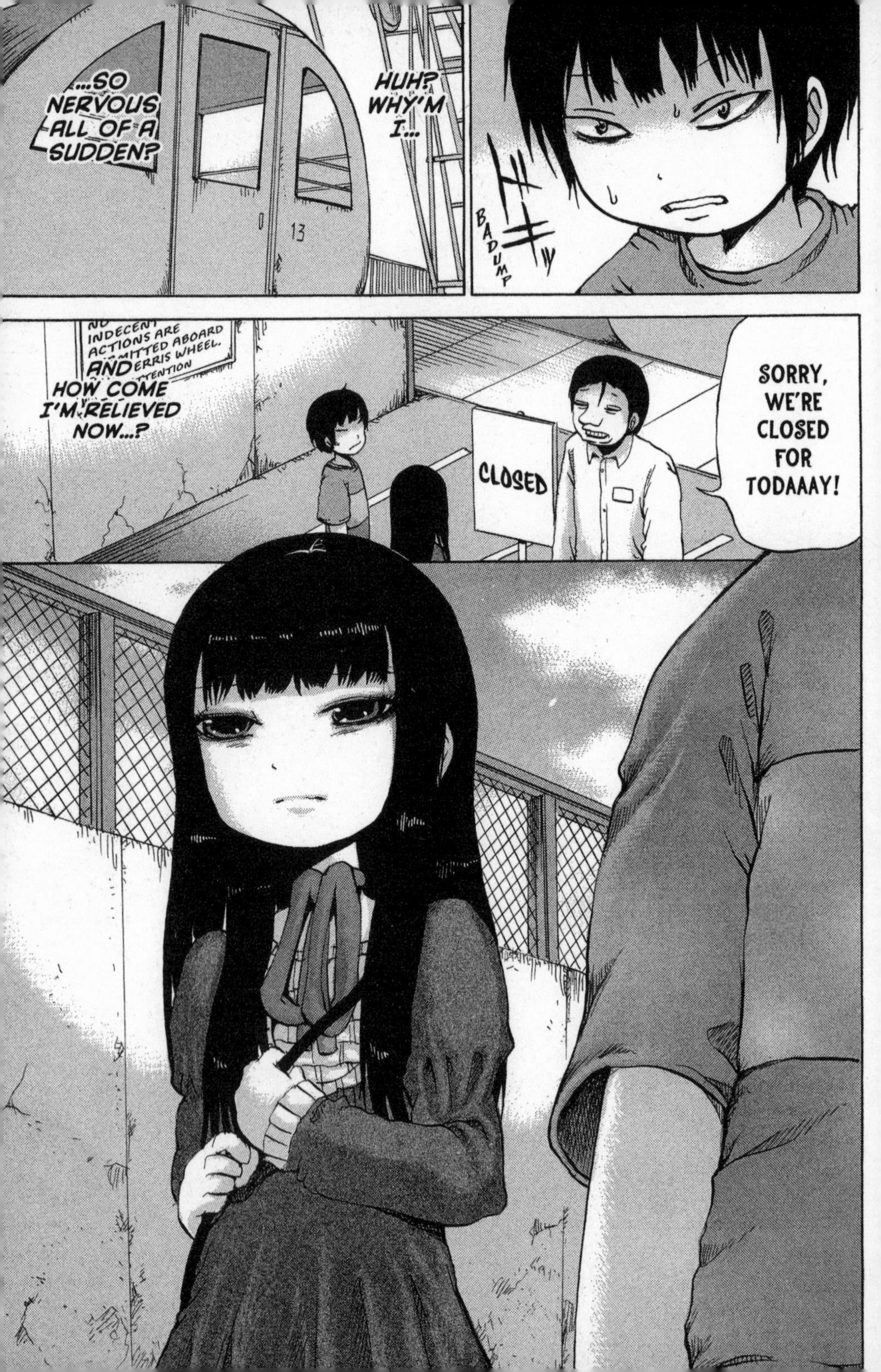
BADUMP
HUH? WHY'M I...
...SO NERVOUS ALL OF A SUDDEN?
SORRY, WE'RE CLOSED FOR TODAAAY!
CLOSED
AND HOW COME I'M RELIEVED NOW...?

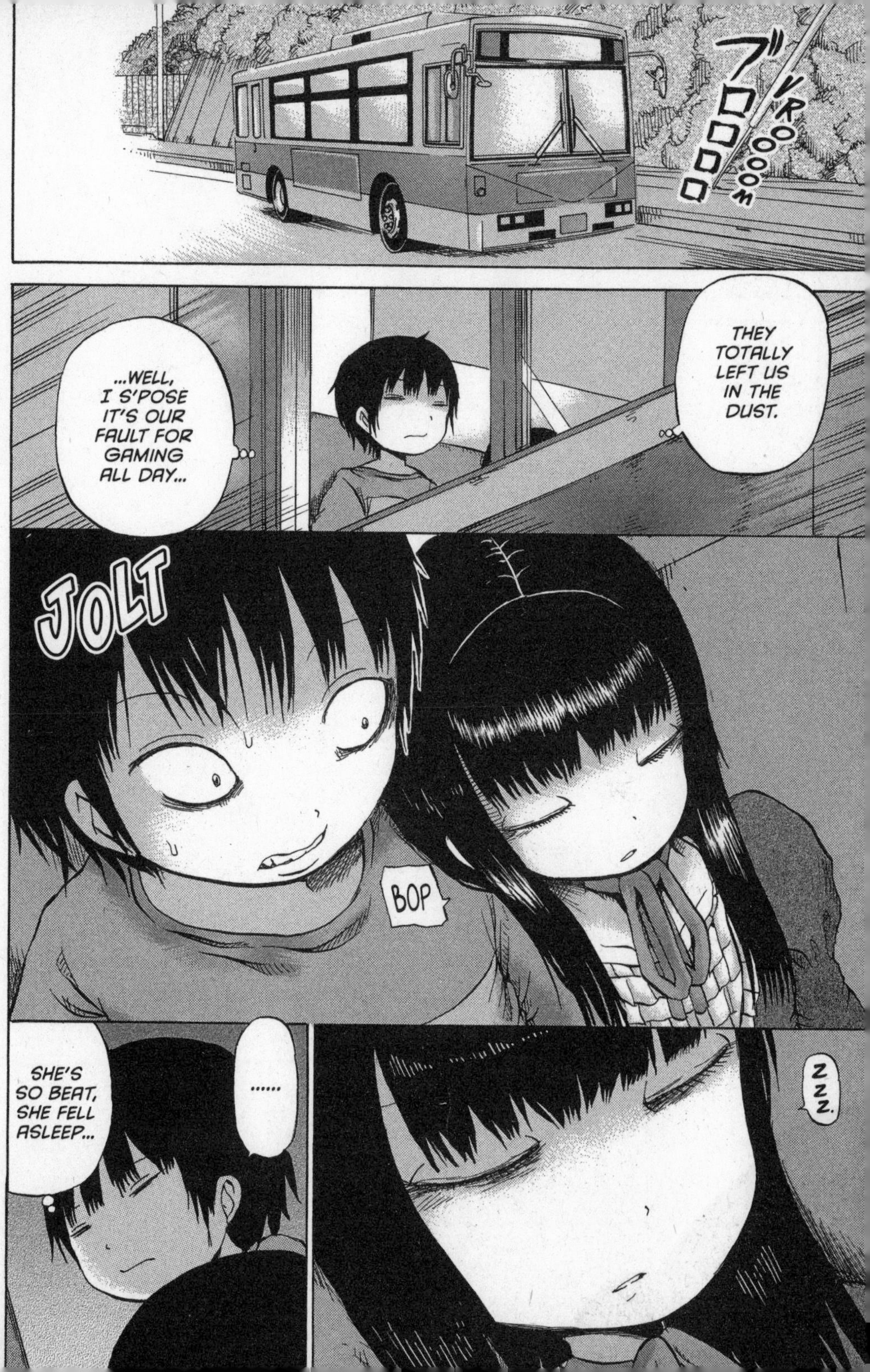
ブロロロロ
VROOOOM
THEY TOTALLY LEFT US IN THE DUST.
...WELL, I S'POSE IT'S OUR FAULT FOR GAMING ALL DAY...
JOLT
BOP
ZZZ.
......
SHE'S SO BEAT, SHE FELL ASLEEP...

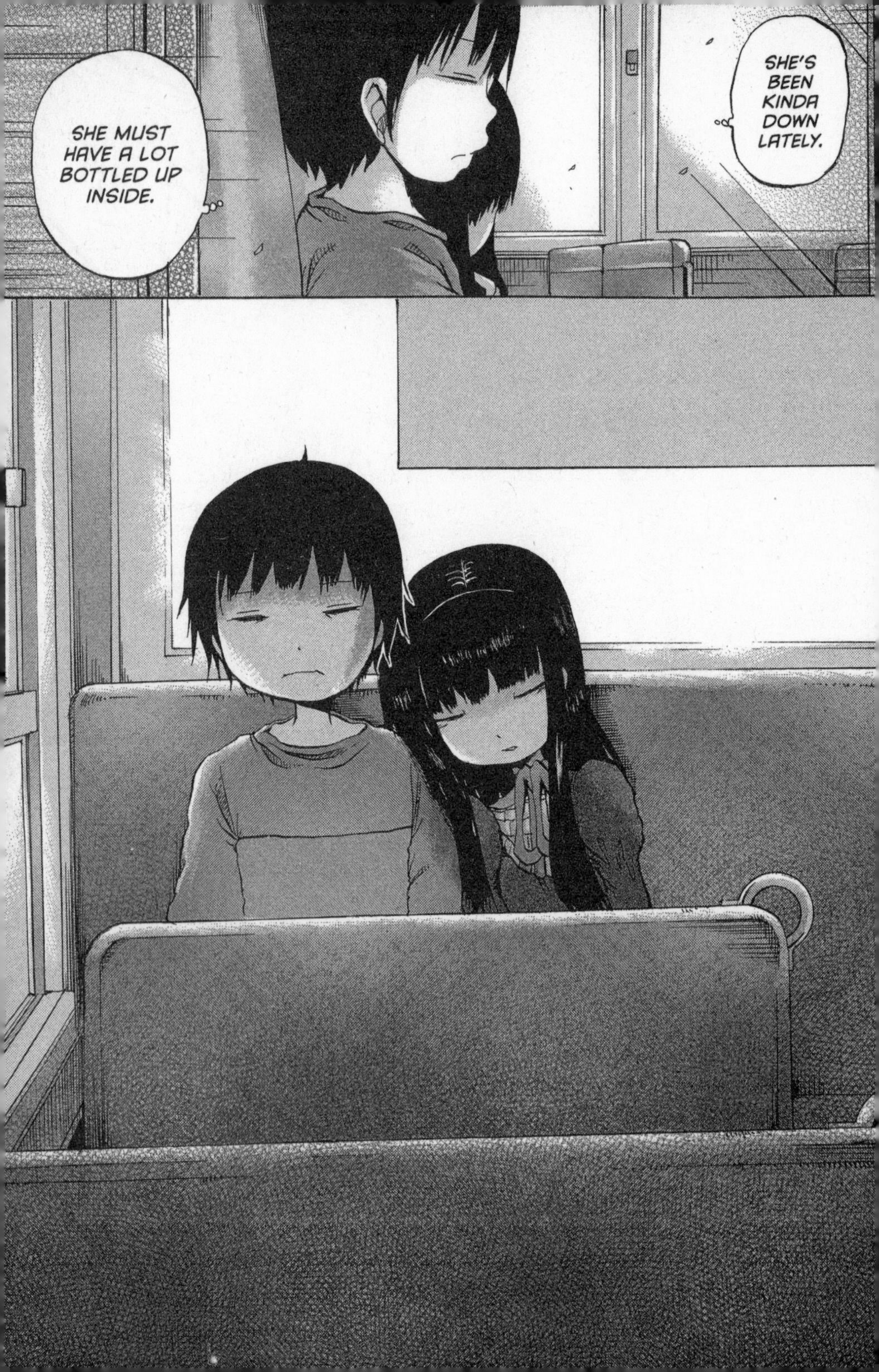
SHE'S BEEN KINDA DOWN LATELY.
SHE MUST HAVE A LOT BOTTLED UP INSIDE.

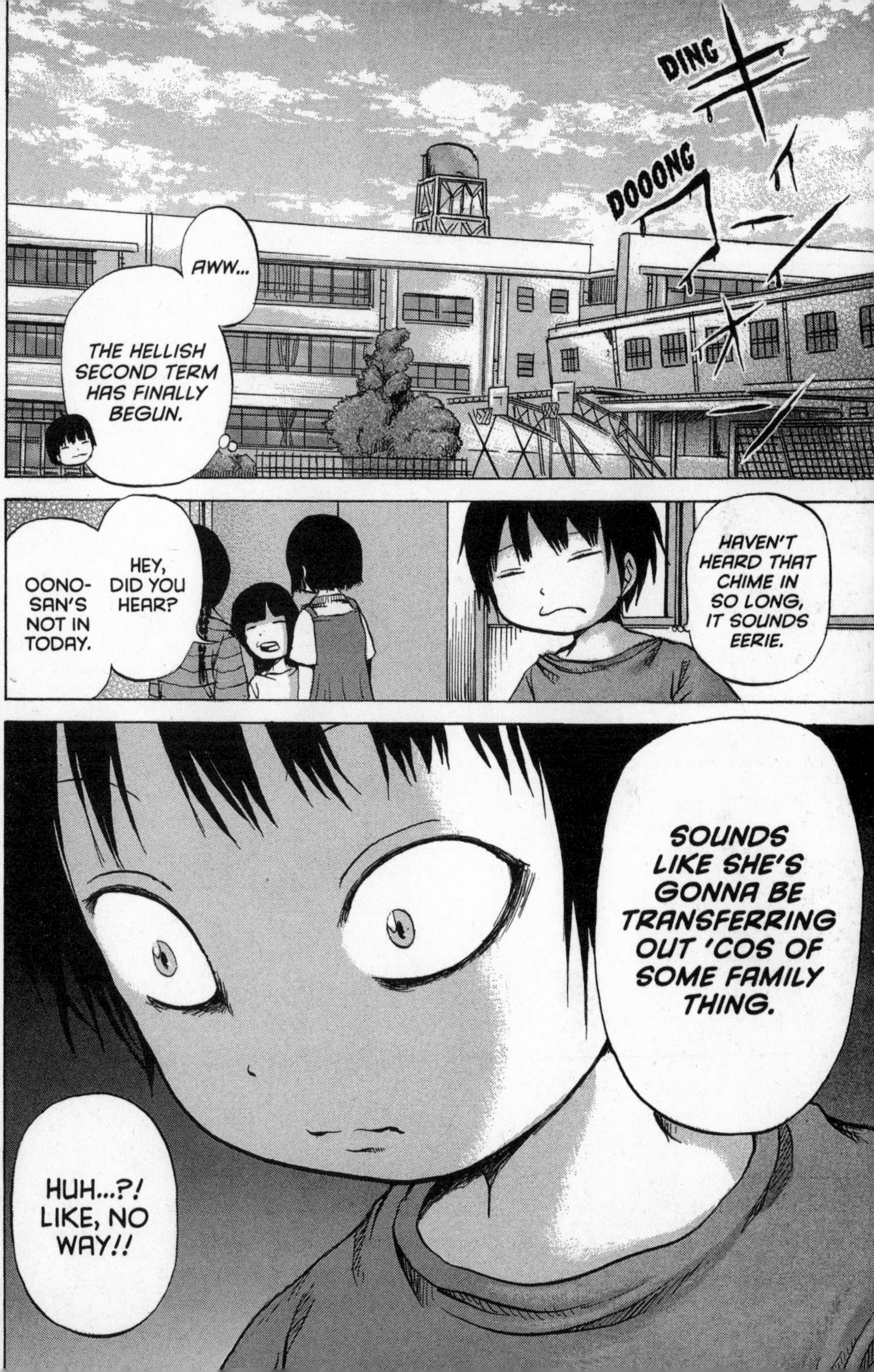
DING
DOOONG
AWW...
THE HELLISH SECOND TERM HAS FINALLY BEGUN.
HAVEN'T HEARD THAT CHIME IN SO LONG, IT SOUNDS EERIE.
HEY, DID YOU HEAR?
OONO-SAN'S NOT IN TODAY.
SOUNDS LIKE SHE'S GONNA BE TRANSFERRING OUT 'COS OF SOME FAMILY THING.
HUH...?! LIKE, NO WAY!!

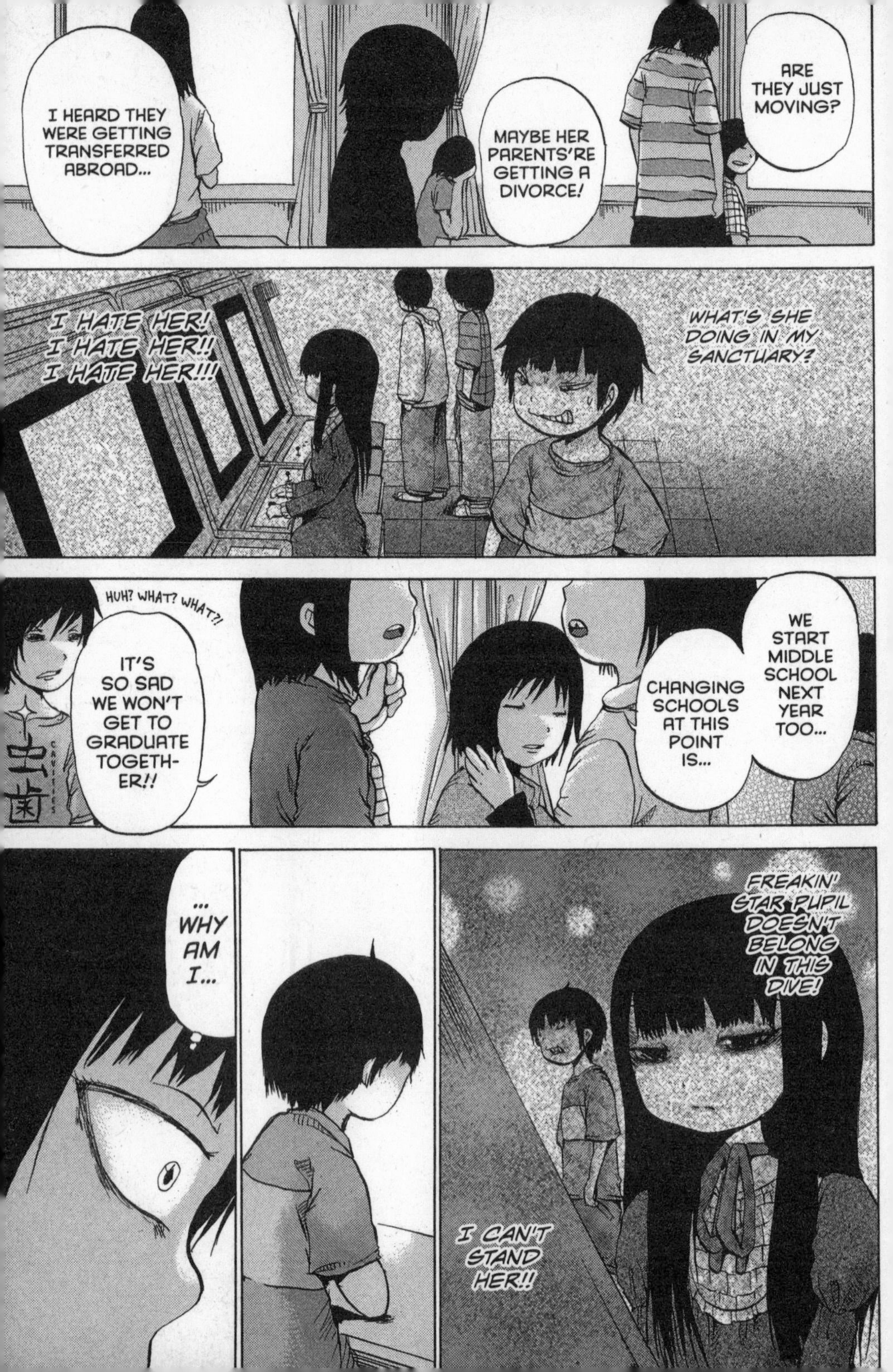
ARE THEY JUST MOVING?
MAYBE HER PARENTS'RE GETTING A DIVORCE!
I HEARD THEY WERE GETTING TRANSFERRED ABROAD...
WHAT'S SHE DOING IN MY SANCTUARY?
I HATE HER! I HATE HER!! I HATE HER!!!
WE START MIDDLE SCHOOL NEXT YEAR TOO...
CHANGING SCHOOLS AT THIS POINT IS...
HUH? WHAT? WHAT?!
IT'S SO SAD WE WON'T GET TO GRADUATE TOGETH-ER!!
CAVITIES
FREAKIN' STAR PUPIL DOESN'T BELONG IN THIS DIVE!
I CAN'T STAND HER!!
... WHY AM I...

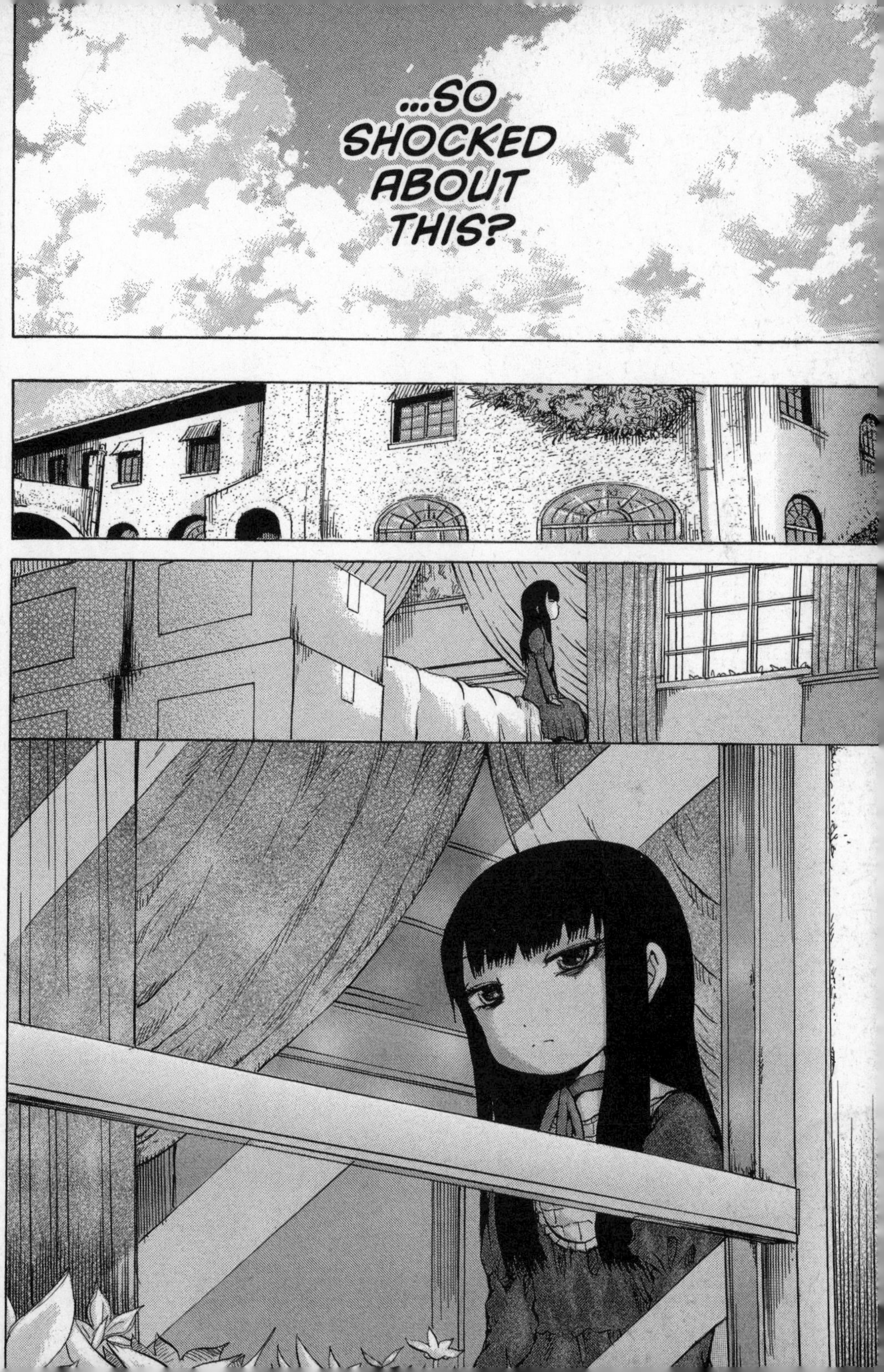
...SO SHOCKED ABOUT THIS?

HI SCORE GIRL

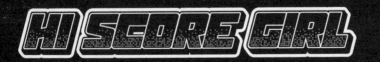

HI SCORE GIRL

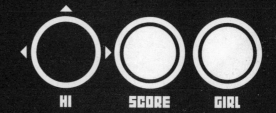

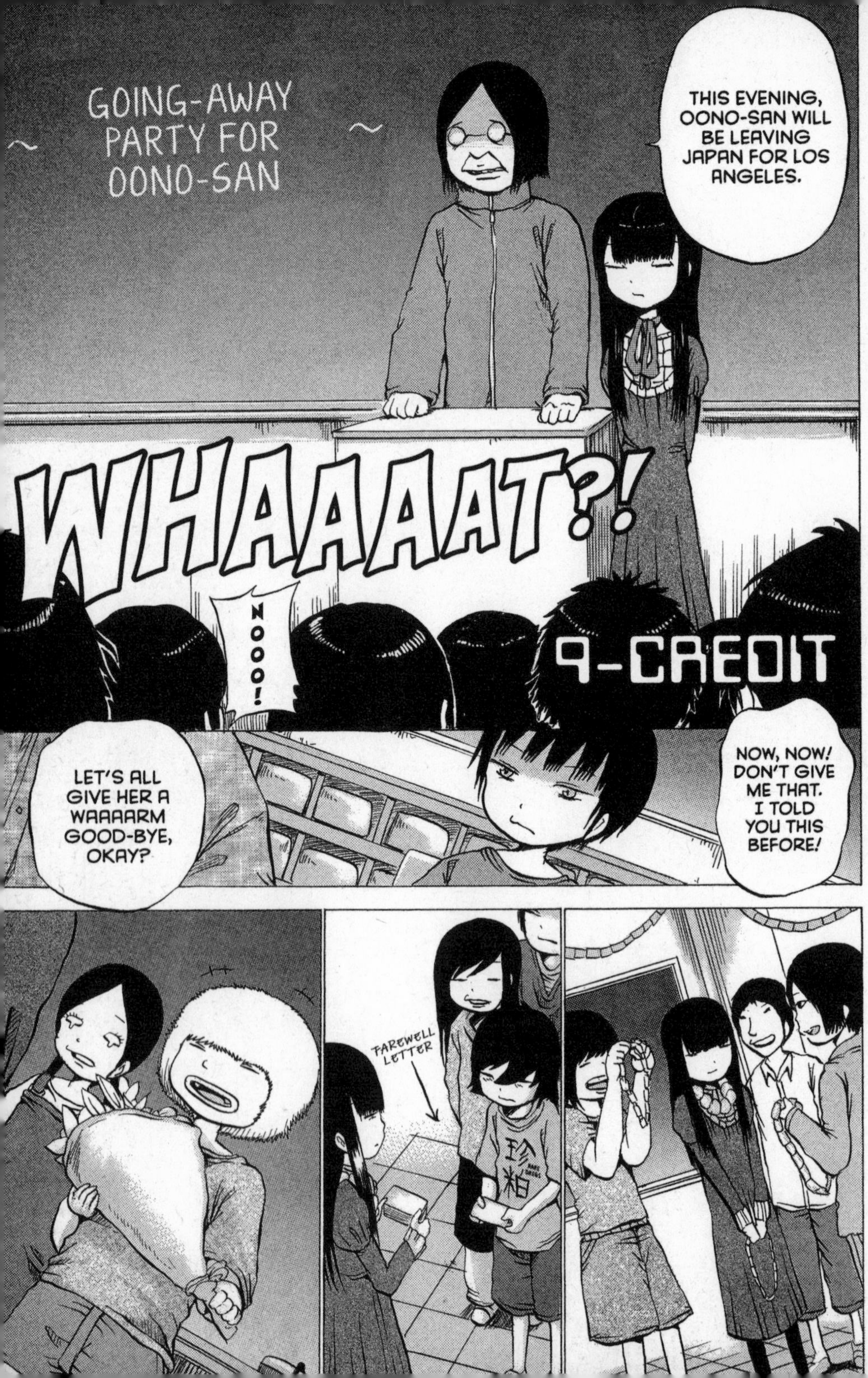
THIS EVENING, OONO-SAN WILL BE LEAVING JAPAN FOR LOS ANGELES.
~ GOING-AWAY PARTY FOR OONO-SAN ~
WHAAAAT?!
NOOOO!
9-CREDIT
NOW, NOW! DON'T GIVE ME THAT. I TOLD YOU THIS BEFORE!
LET'S ALL GIVE HER A WAAAARM GOOD-BYE, OKAY?
FAREWELL LETTER

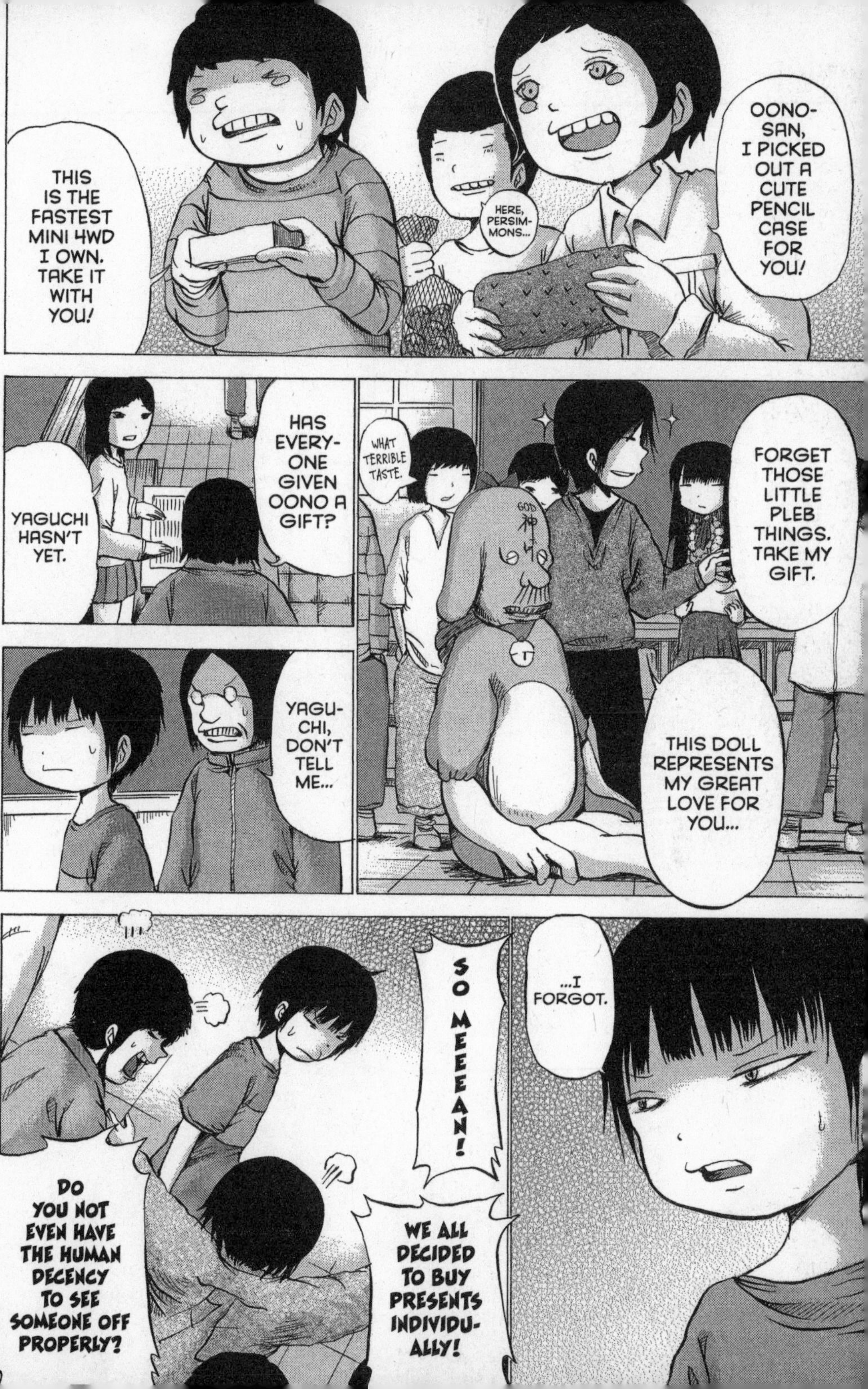
OONO-SAN, I PICKED OUT A CUTE PENCIL CASE FOR YOU!
HERE, PERSIMMONS...
THIS IS THE FASTEST MINI 4WD I OWN. TAKE IT WITH YOU!
FORGET THOSE LITTLE PLEB THINGS. TAKE MY GIFT.
WHAT TERRIBLE TASTE.
GOD
THIS DOLL REPRESENTS MY GREAT LOVE FOR YOU...
HAS EVERYONE GIVEN OONO A GIFT?
YAGUCHI HASN'T YET.
YAGUCHI, DON'T TELL ME...
...I FORGOT.
SO MEEEEAN!
WE ALL DECIDED TO BUY PRESENTS INDIVIDUALLY!
DO YOU NOT EVEN HAVE THE HUMAN DECENCY TO SEE SOMEONE OFF PROPERLY?

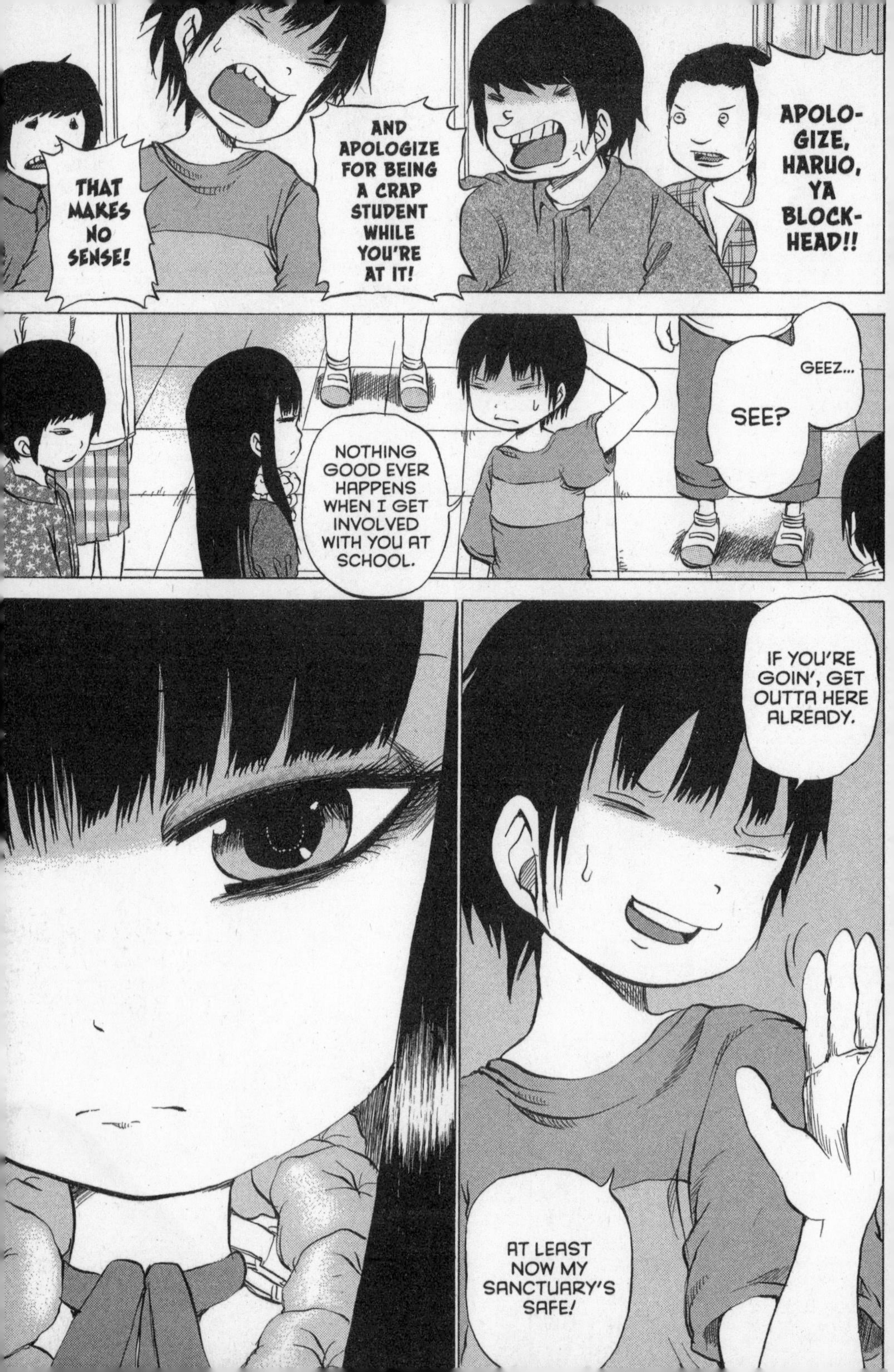
APOLOGIZE, HARUO, YA BLOCKHEAD!!
AND APOLOGIZE FOR BEING A CRAP STUDENT WHILE YOU'RE AT IT!
THAT MAKES NO SENSE!
GEEZ... SEE?
NOTHING GOOD EVER HAPPENS WHEN I GET INVOLVED WITH YOU AT SCHOOL.
IF YOU'RE GOIN', GET OUTTA HERE ALREADY.
AT LEAST NOW MY SANCTUARY'S SAFE!

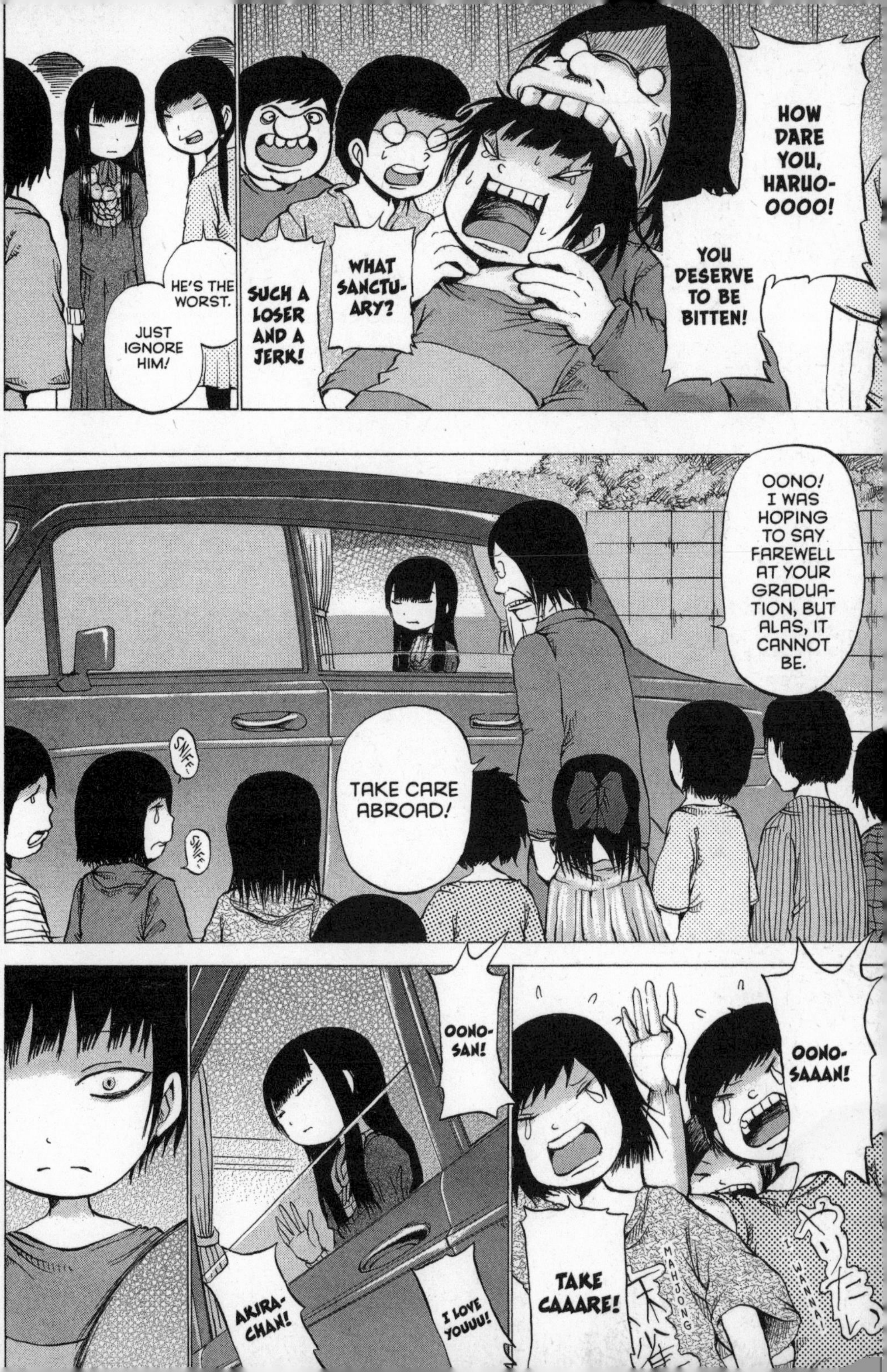
HOW DARE YOU, HARUO-OOOO!
YOU DESERVE TO BE BITTEN!
WHAT SANCTUARY?
SUCH A LOSER AND A JERK!
HE'S THE WORST.
JUST IGNORE HIM!
OONO! I WAS HOPING TO SAY FAREWELL AT YOUR GRADUATION, BUT ALAS, IT CANNOT BE.
TAKE CARE ABROAD!
SNIFF...
SNIFF...
OONO-SAAAN!
I WANNA...
TAKE CAAARE!
MAHJONG
OONO-SAN!
I LOVE YOUUU!
AKIRA-CHAN!

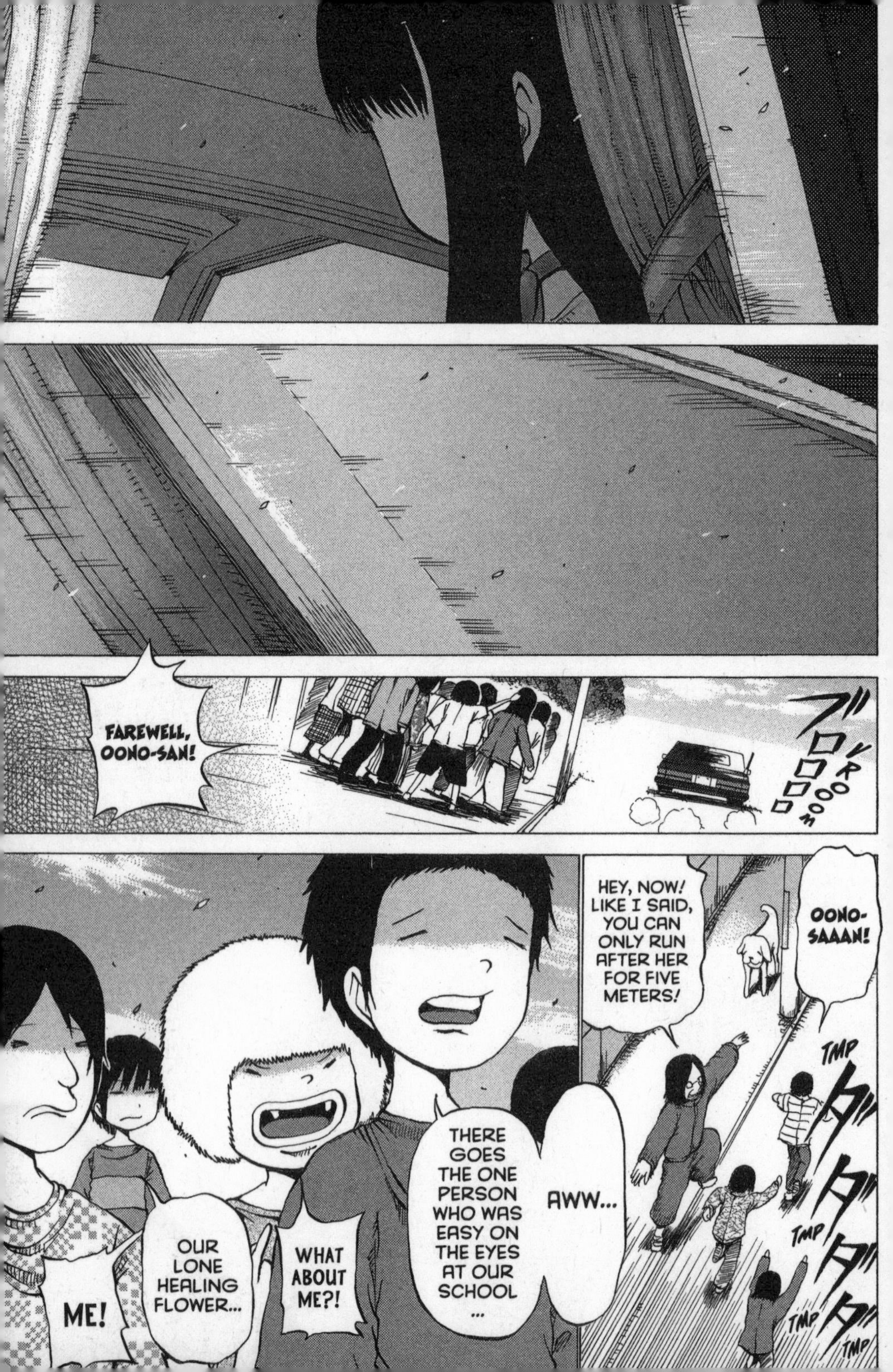

VROOOOM
FAREWELL, OONO-SAN!
OONO-SAAAN!
HEY, NOW! LIKE I SAID, YOU CAN ONLY RUN AFTER HER FOR FIVE METERS!
TMP
TMP
TMP
TMP
AWW...
THERE GOES THE ONE PERSON WHO WAS EASY ON THE EYES AT OUR SCHOOL ...
WHAT ABOUT ME?!
OUR LONE HEALING FLOWER...
ME!

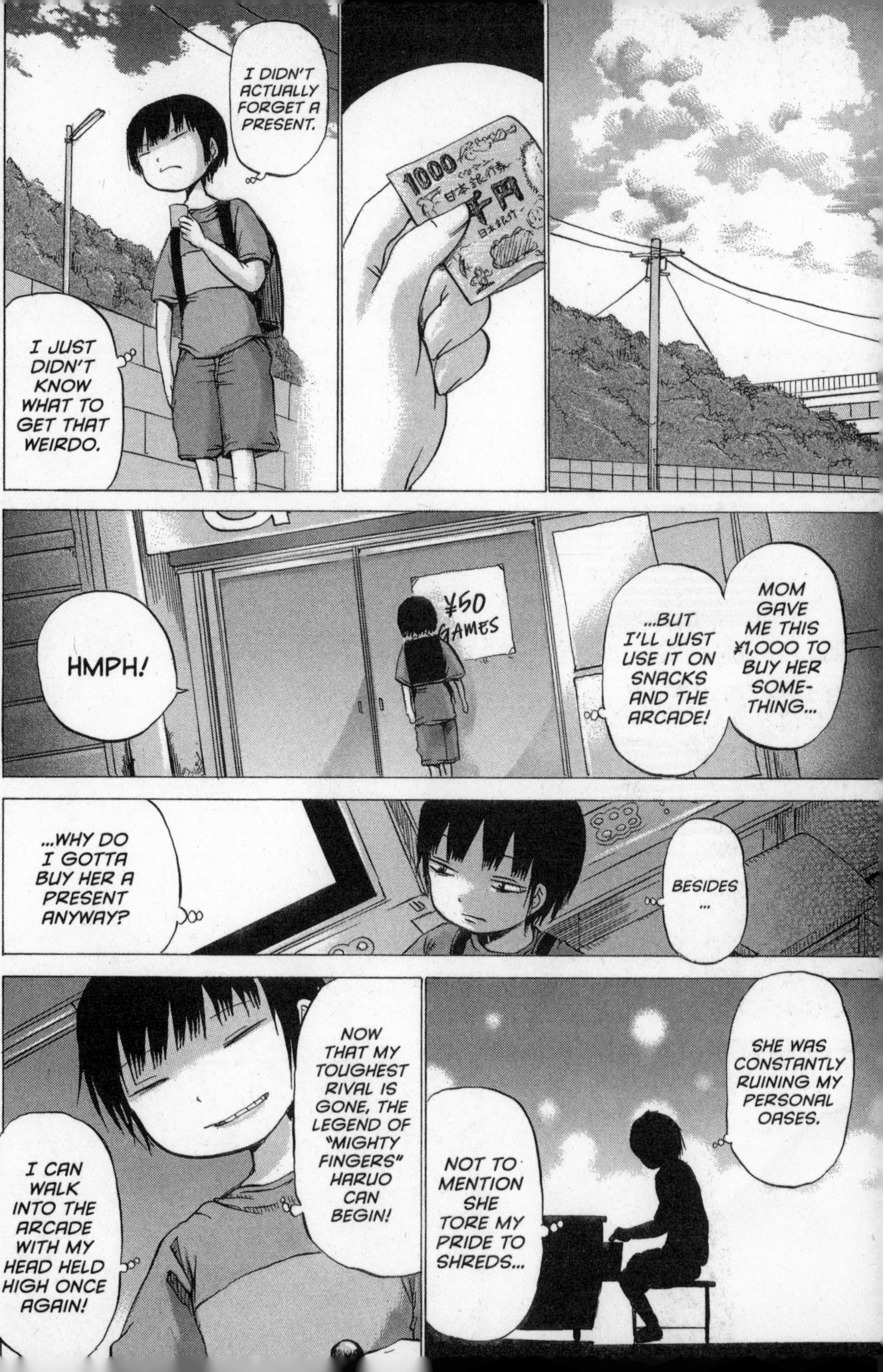

I DIDN'T ACTUALLY FORGET A PRESENT.
I JUST DIDN'T KNOW WHAT TO GET THAT WEIRDO.
MOM GAVE ME THIS ¥1,000 TO BUY HER SOME-THING...
...BUT I'LL JUST USE IT ON SNACKS AND THE ARCADE!
¥50 GAMES
HMPH!
BESIDES...
...WHY DO I GOTTA BUY HER A PRESENT ANYWAY?
SHE WAS CONSTANTLY RUINING MY PERSONAL OASES.
NOT TO MENTION SHE TORE MY PRIDE TO SHREDS...
NOW THAT MY TOUGHEST RIVAL IS GONE, THE LEGEND OF "MIGHTY FINGERS" HARUO CAN BEGIN!
I CAN WALK INTO THE ARCADE WITH MY HEAD HELD HIGH ONCE AGAIN!

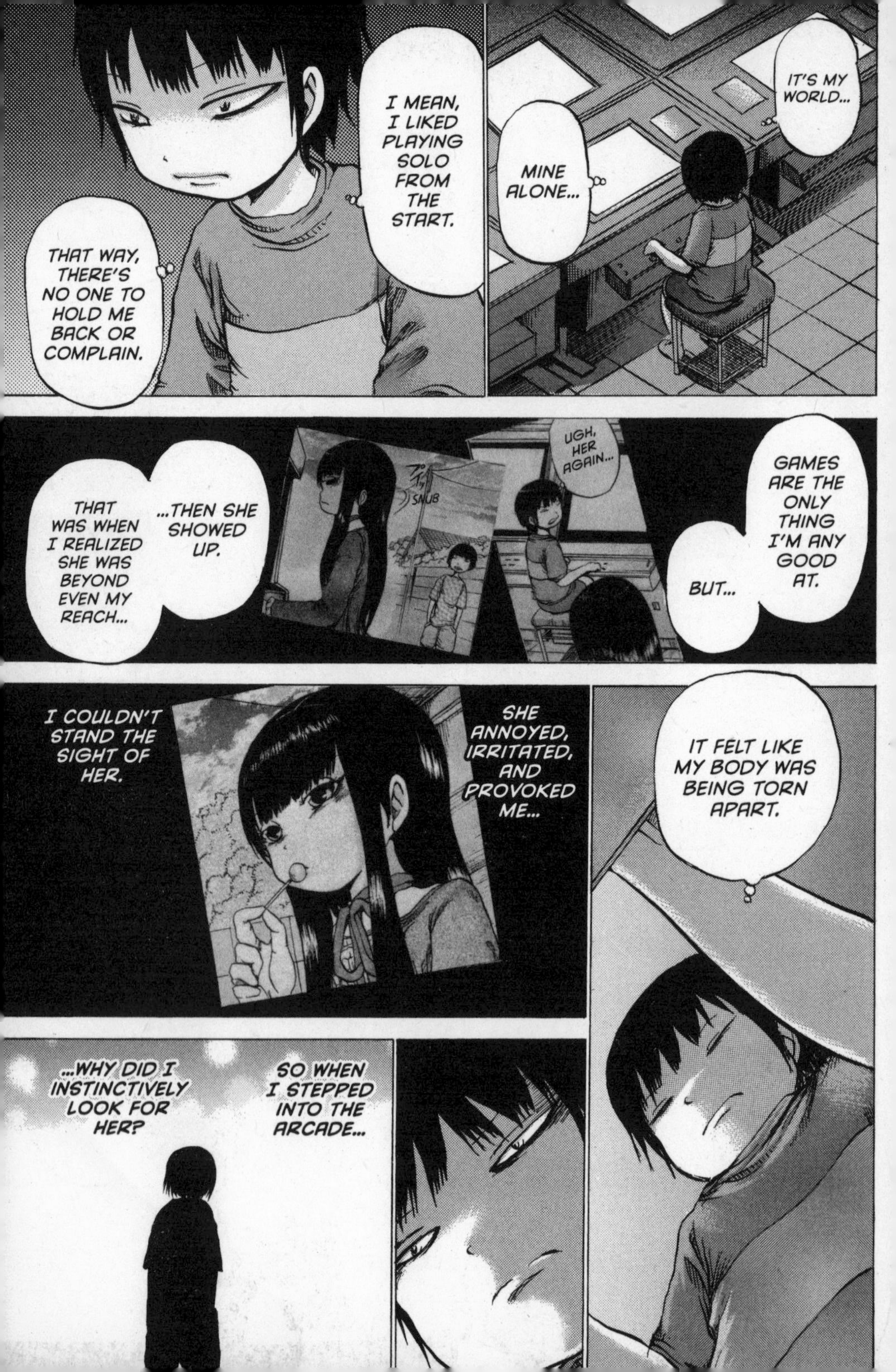
IT'S MY WORLD...
MINE ALONE...
I MEAN, I LIKED PLAYING SOLO FROM THE START.
THAT WAY, THERE'S NO ONE TO HOLD ME BACK OR COMPLAIN.
GAMES ARE THE ONLY THING I'M ANY GOOD AT.
BUT...
UGH, HER AGAIN...
...THEN SHE SHOWED UP.
SNUB
THAT WAS WHEN I REALIZED SHE WAS BEYOND EVEN MY REACH...
IT FELT LIKE MY BODY WAS BEING TORN APART.
SHE ANNOYED, IRRITATED, AND PROVOKED ME...
I COULDN'T STAND THE SIGHT OF HER.
SO WHEN I STEPPED INTO THE ARCADE...
...WHY DID I INSTINCTIVELY LOOK FOR HER?

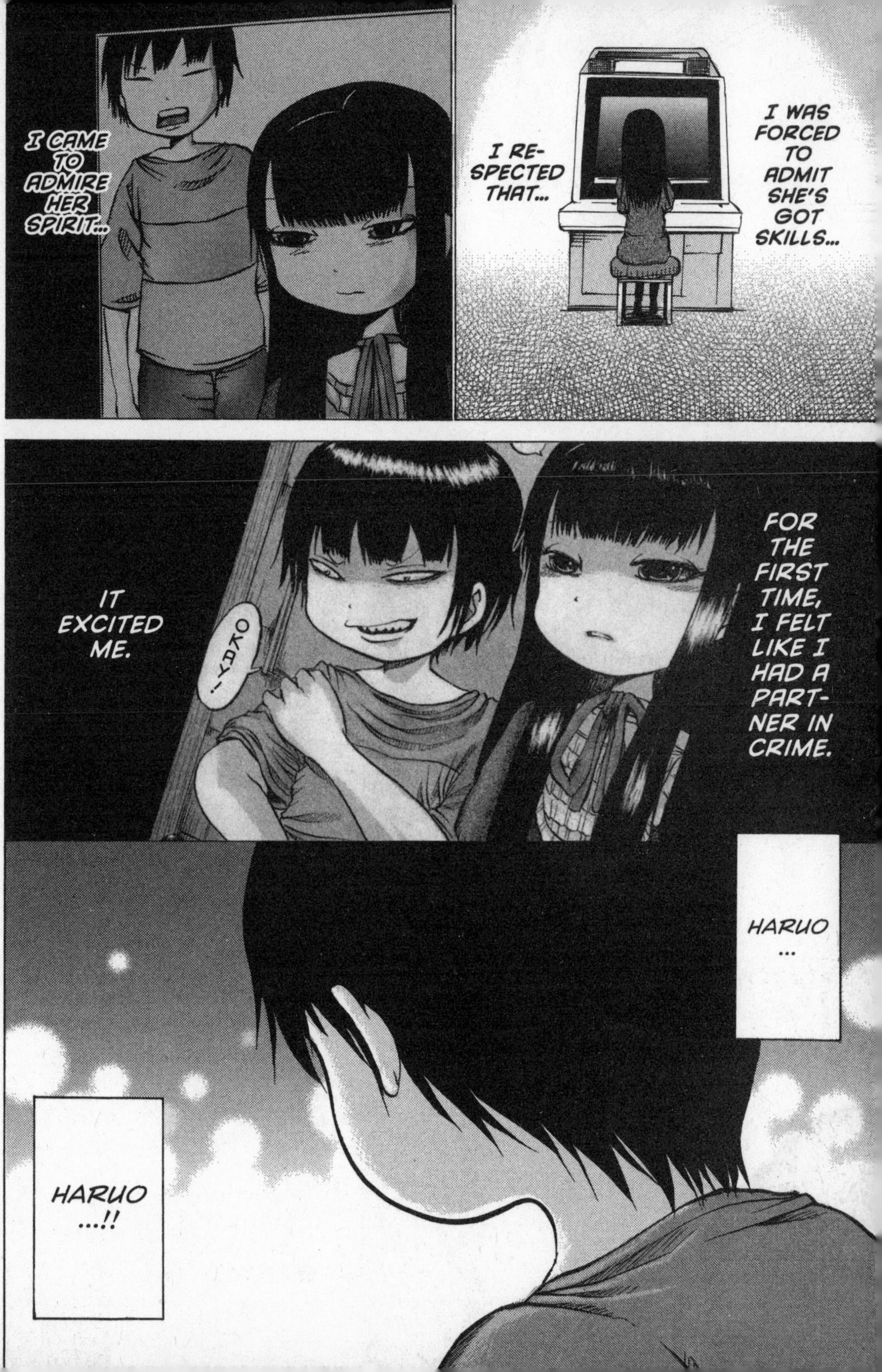
I WAS FORCED TO ADMIT SHE'S GOT SKILLS...
I RE-SPECTED THAT...
I CAME TO ADMIRE HER SPIRIT...
FOR THE FIRST TIME, I FELT LIKE I HAD A PART-NER IN CRIME.
OKAY!
IT EXCITED ME.
HARUO...
HARUO...!!

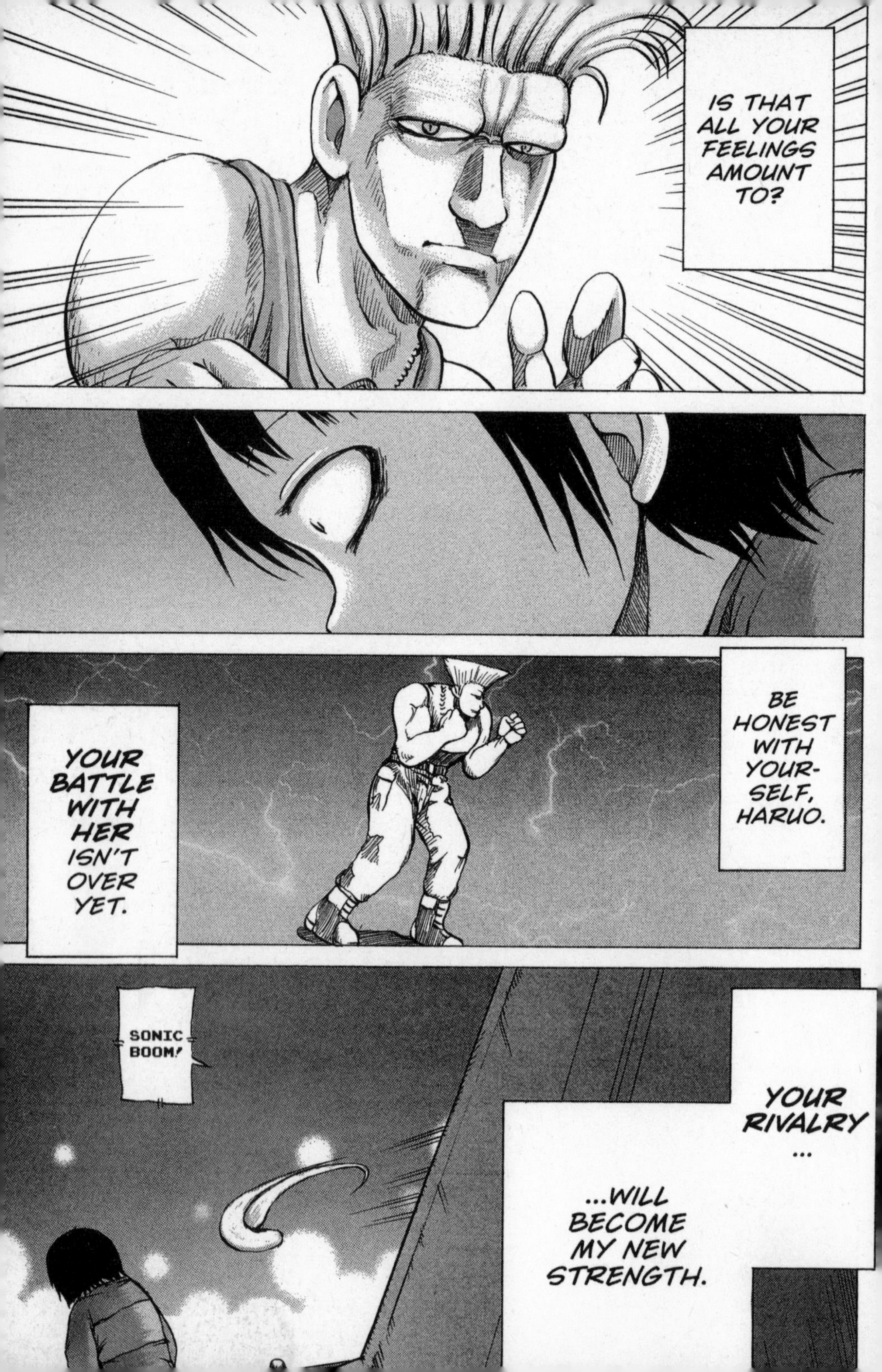
IS THAT ALL YOUR FEELINGS AMOUNT TO?
BE HONEST WITH YOURSELF, HARUO.
YOUR BATTLE WITH HER ISN'T OVER YET.
YOUR RIVALRY ...
...WILL BECOME MY NEW STRENGTH.
SONIC BOOM!

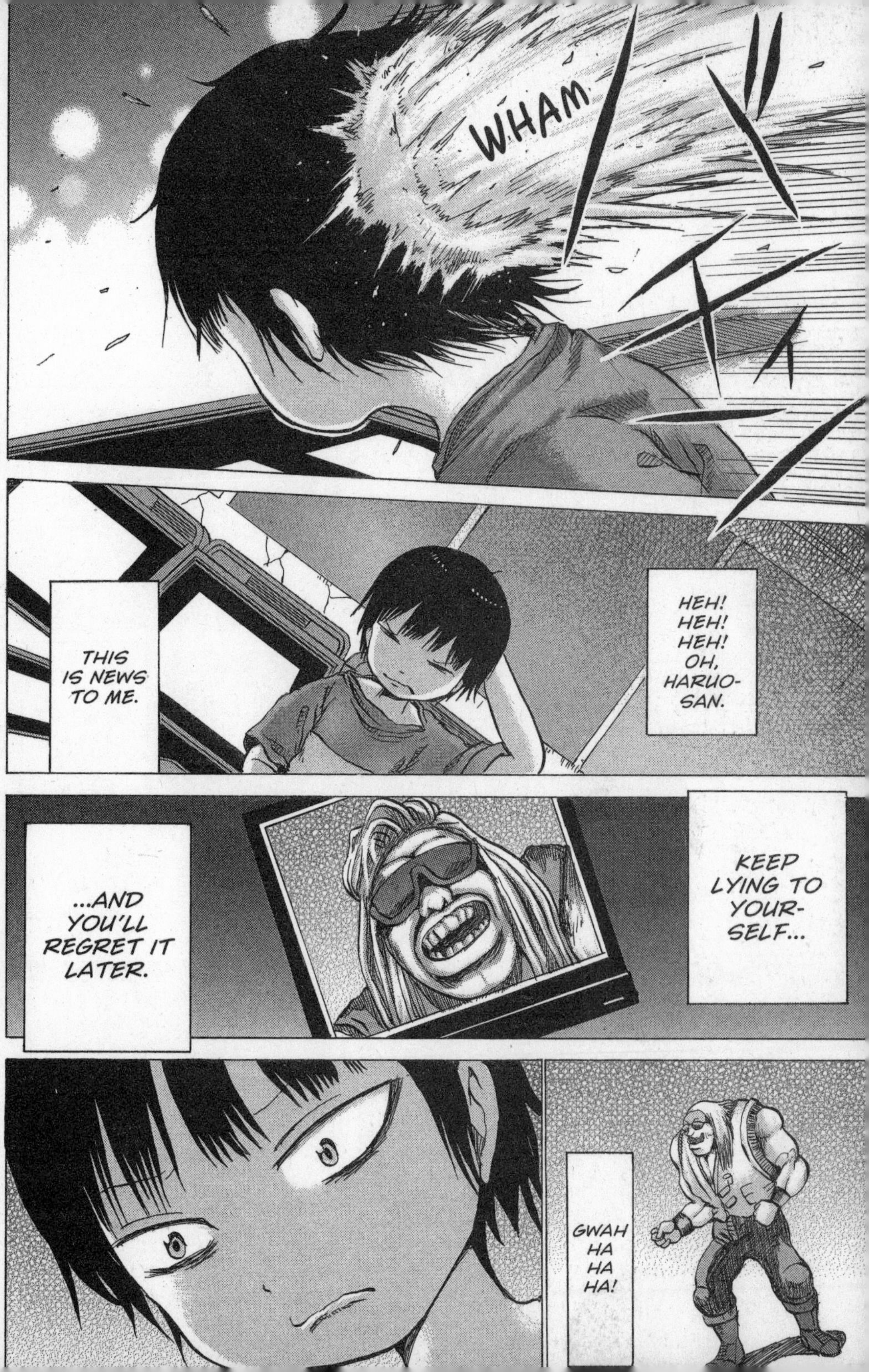
WHAM
HEH! HEH! HEH! OH, HARUO-SAN.
THIS IS NEWS TO ME.
KEEP LYING TO YOURSELF...
...AND YOU'LL REGRET IT LATER.
GWAH HA HA HA!

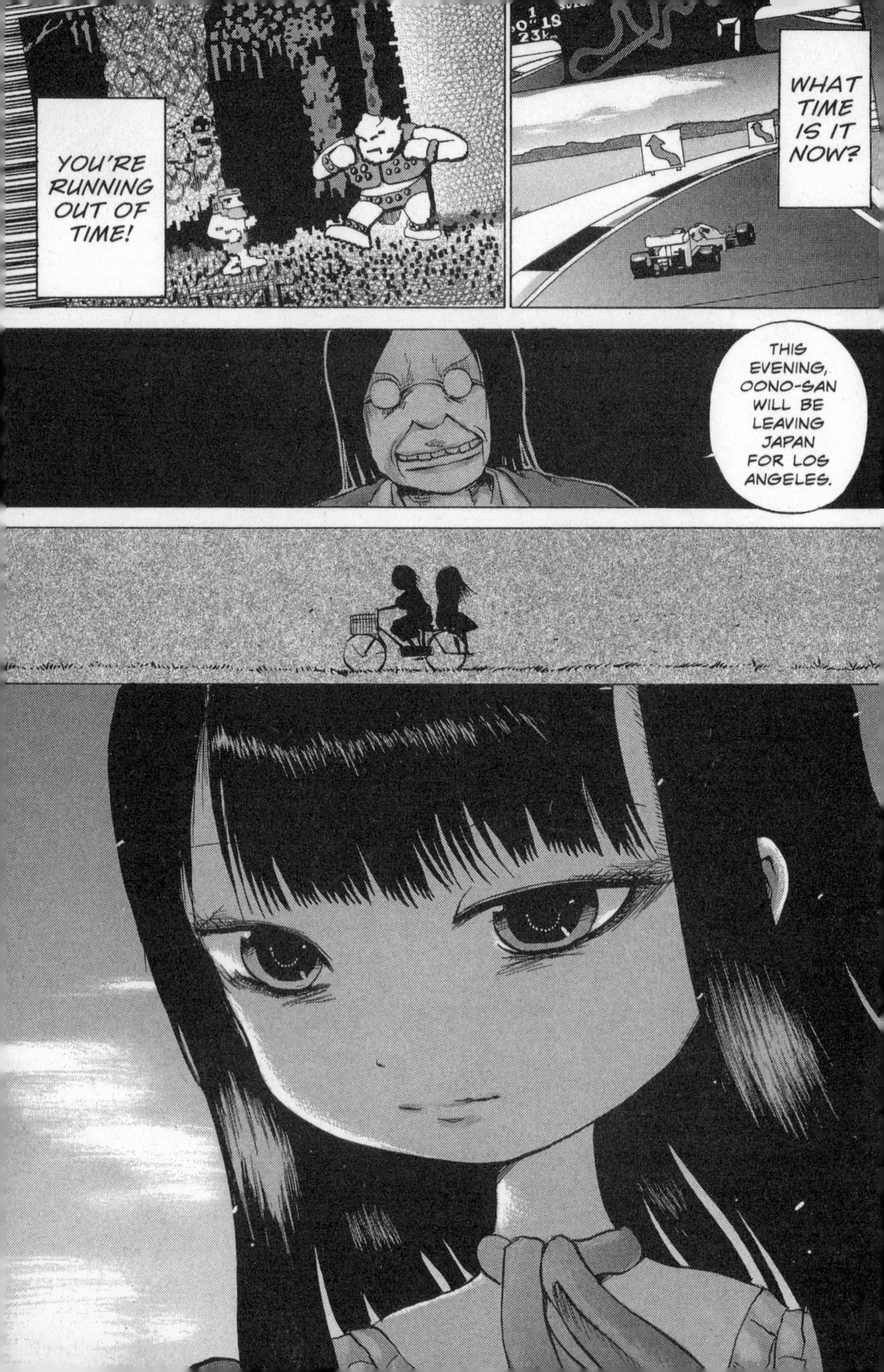
WHAT TIME IS IT NOW?
YOU'RE RUNNING OUT OF TIME!
THIS EVENING, OONO-SAN WILL BE LEAVING JAPAN FOR LOS ANGELES.

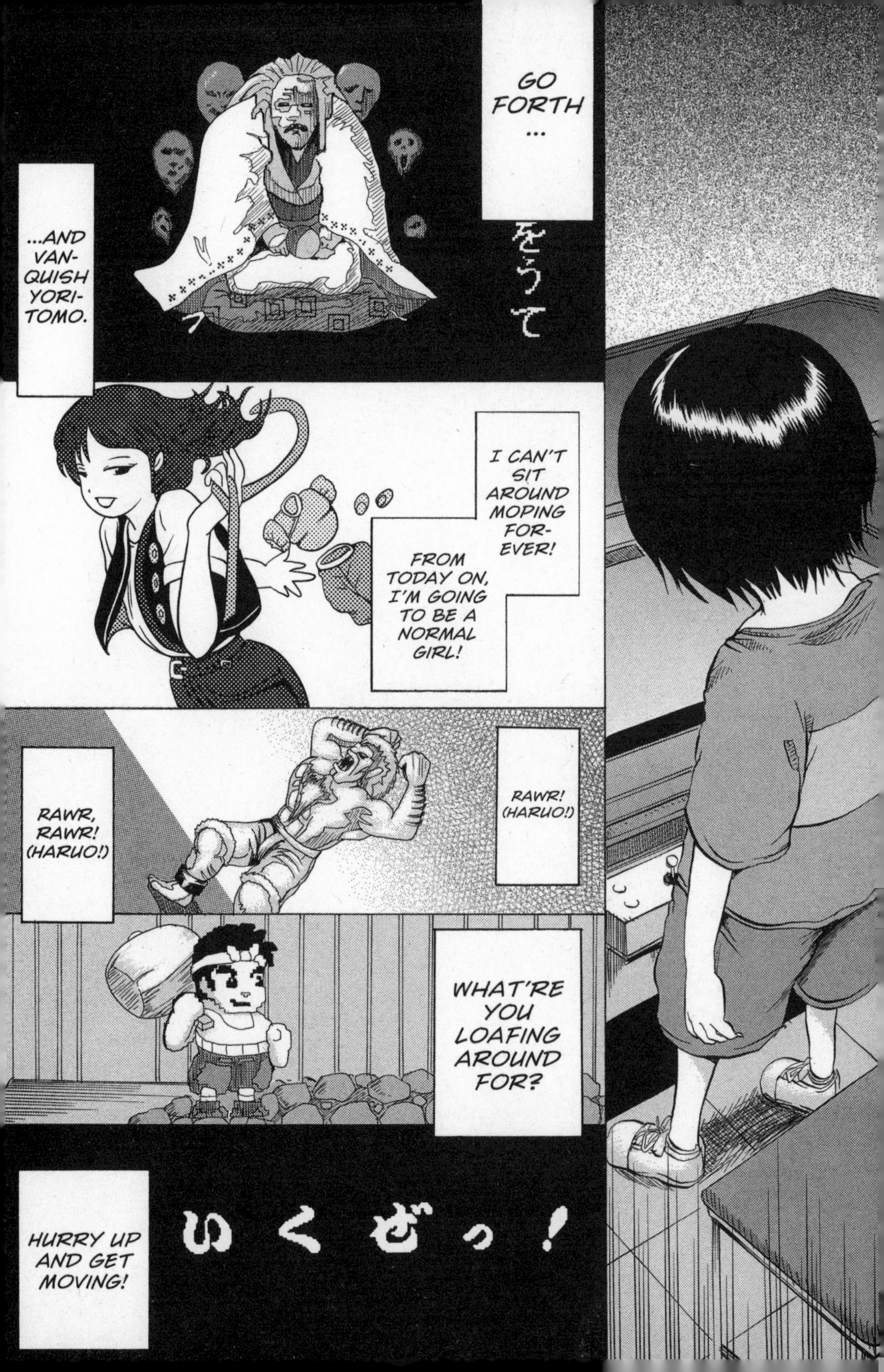
GO FORTH ...
...AND VAN-QUISH YORI-TOMO.
をうて
I CAN'T SIT AROUND MOPING FOR-EVER!
FROM TODAY ON, I'M GOING TO BE A NORMAL GIRL!
RAWR! (HARUO!)
RAWR, RAWR! (HARUO!)
WHAT'RE YOU LOAFING AROUND FOR?
いくぞっ!
HURRY UP AND GET MOVING!

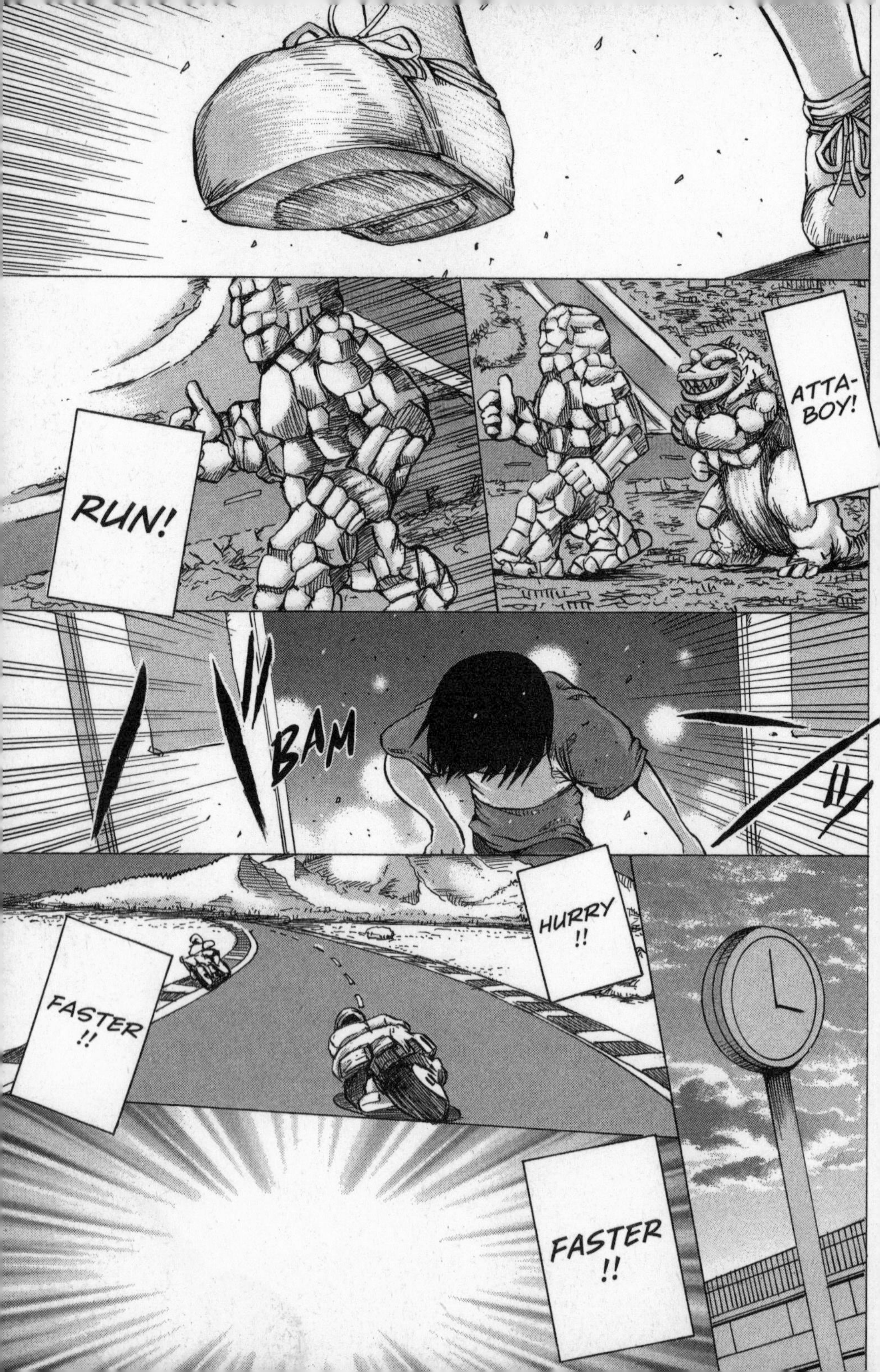
ATTA-BOY!
RUN!
BAM
HURRY !!
FASTER !!
FASTER !!

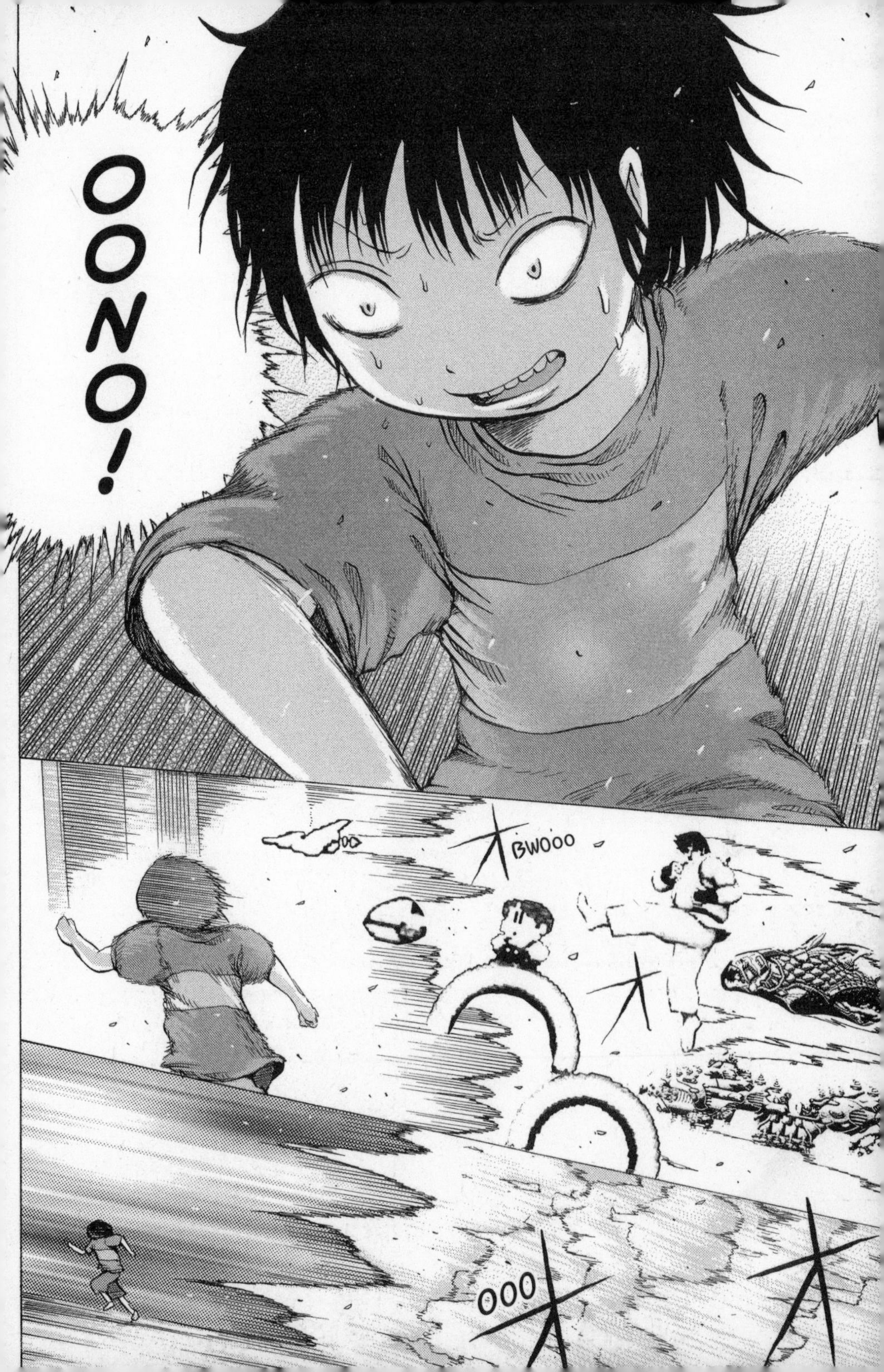
OONO!
BWOOO
OOO

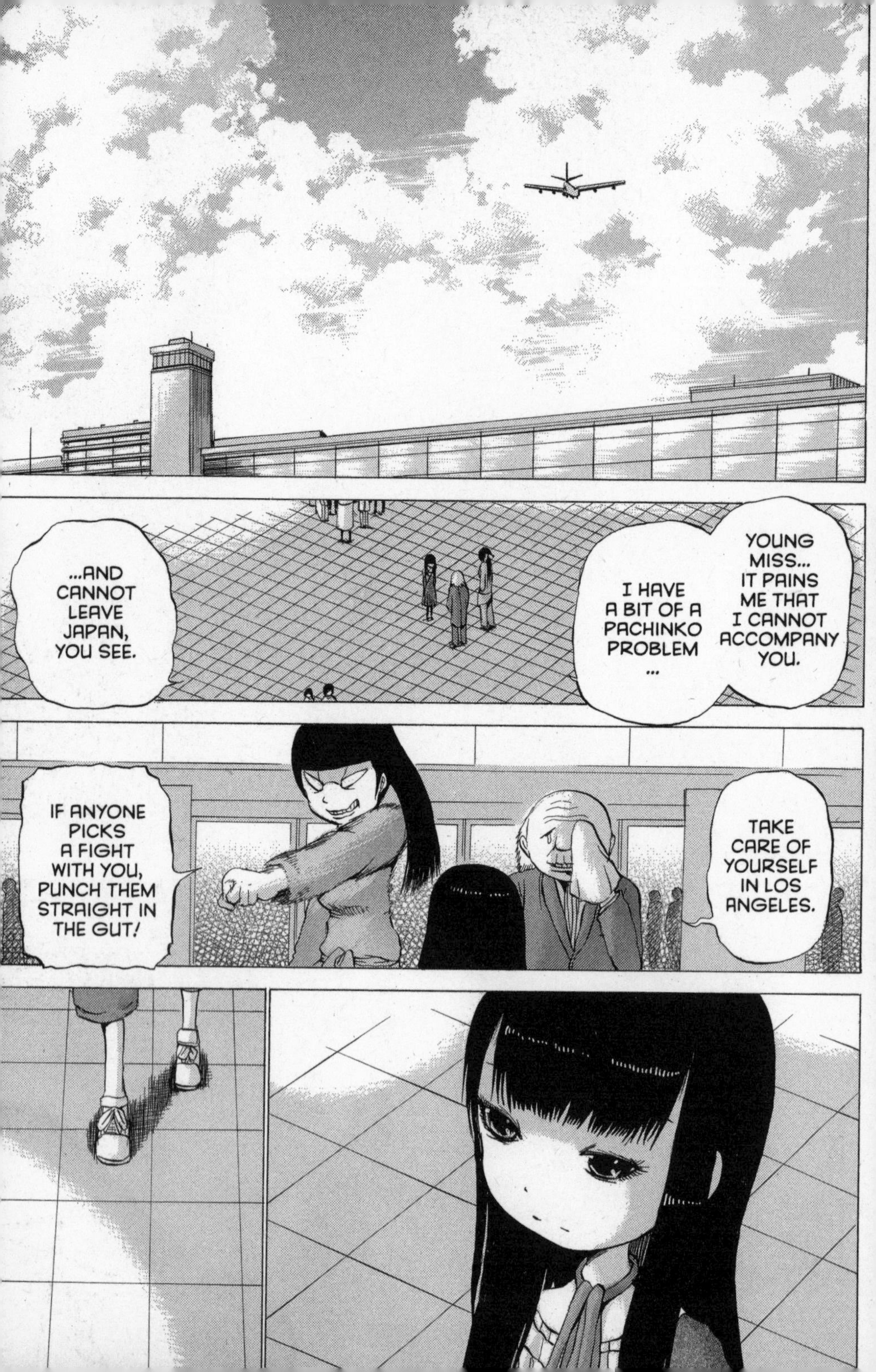
YOUNG MISS... IT PAINS ME THAT I CANNOT ACCOMPANY YOU.
I HAVE A BIT OF A PACHINKO PROBLEM ...
...AND CANNOT LEAVE JAPAN, YOU SEE.
TAKE CARE OF YOURSELF IN LOS ANGELES.
IF ANYONE PICKS A FIGHT WITH YOU, PUNCH THEM STRAIGHT IN THE GUT!

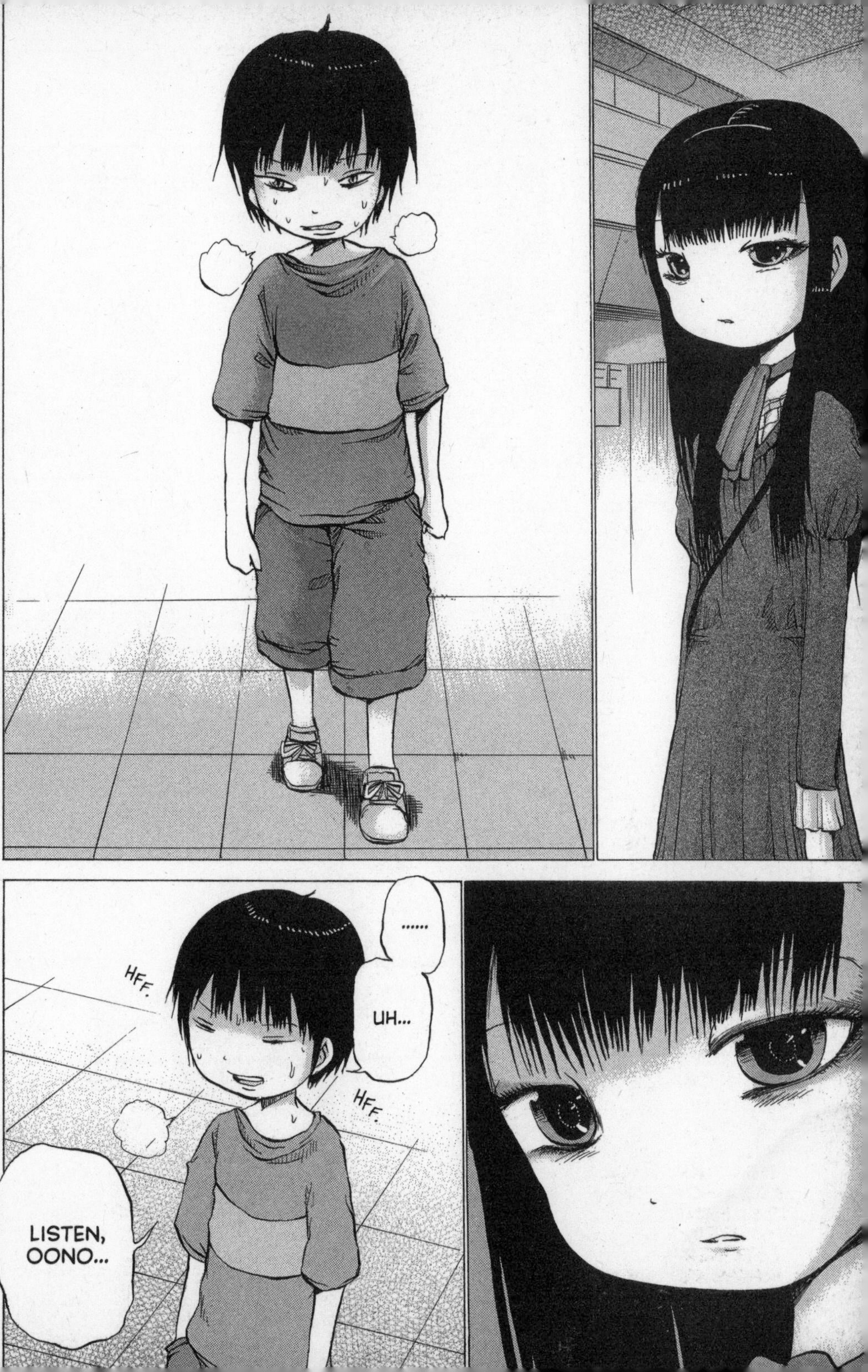
......
UH...
HFF.
HFF.
LISTEN, OONO...

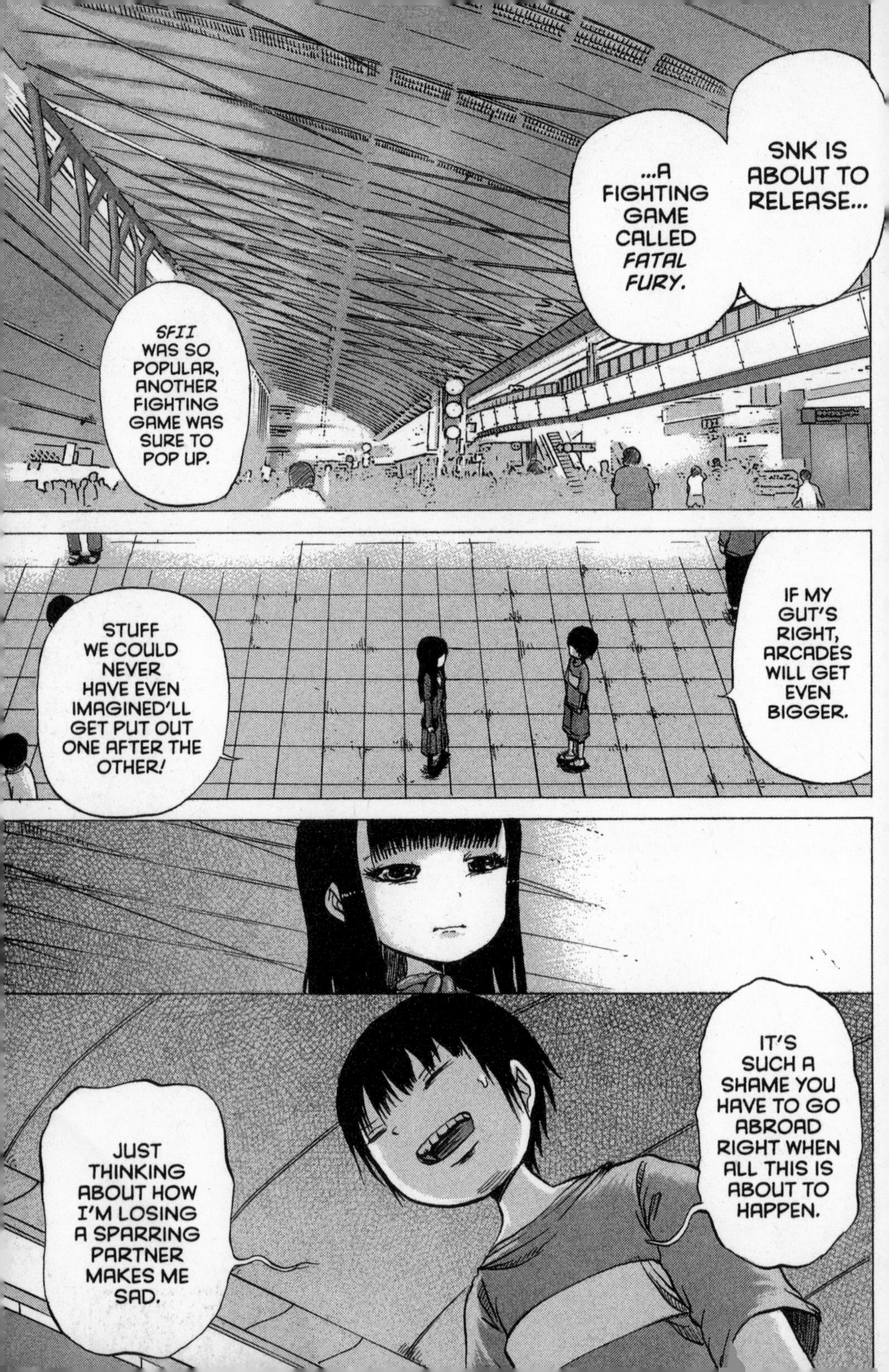
SNK IS ABOUT TO RELEASE...
...A FIGHTING GAME CALLED *FATAL FURY*.
SFII WAS SO POPULAR, ANOTHER FIGHTING GAME WAS SURE TO POP UP.
IF MY GUT'S RIGHT, ARCADES WILL GET EVEN BIGGER.
STUFF WE COULD NEVER HAVE EVEN IMAGINED'LL GET PUT OUT ONE AFTER THE OTHER!
IT'S SUCH A SHAME YOU HAVE TO GO ABROAD RIGHT WHEN ALL THIS IS ABOUT TO HAPPEN.
JUST THINKING ABOUT HOW I'M LOSING A SPARRING PARTNER MAKES ME SAD.

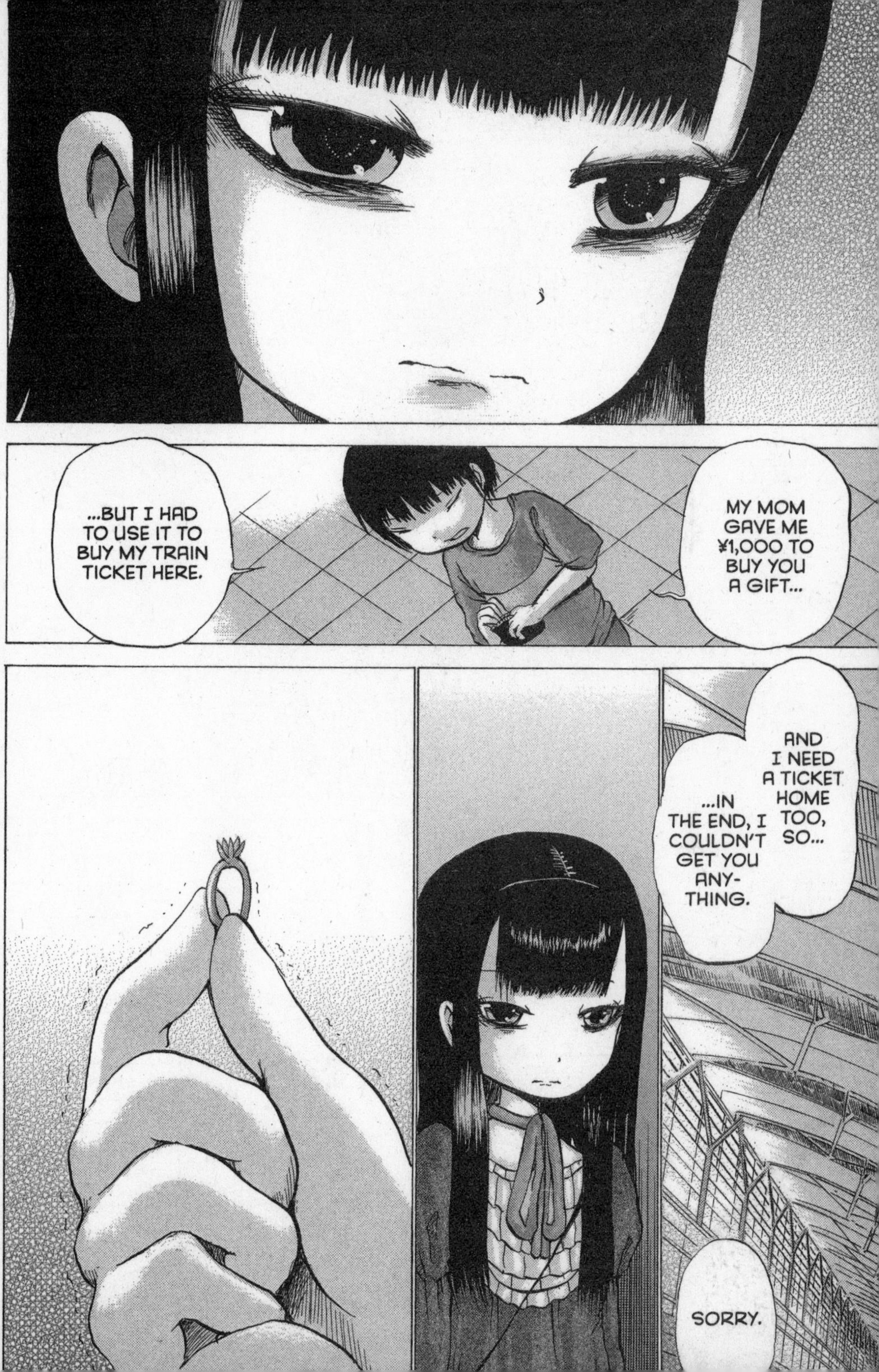
MY MOM GAVE ME ¥1,000 TO BUY YOU A GIFT...
...BUT I HAD TO USE IT TO BUY MY TRAIN TICKET HERE.
AND I NEED A TICKET HOME TOO, SO...
...IN THE END, I COULDN'T GET YOU ANYTHING.
SORRY.

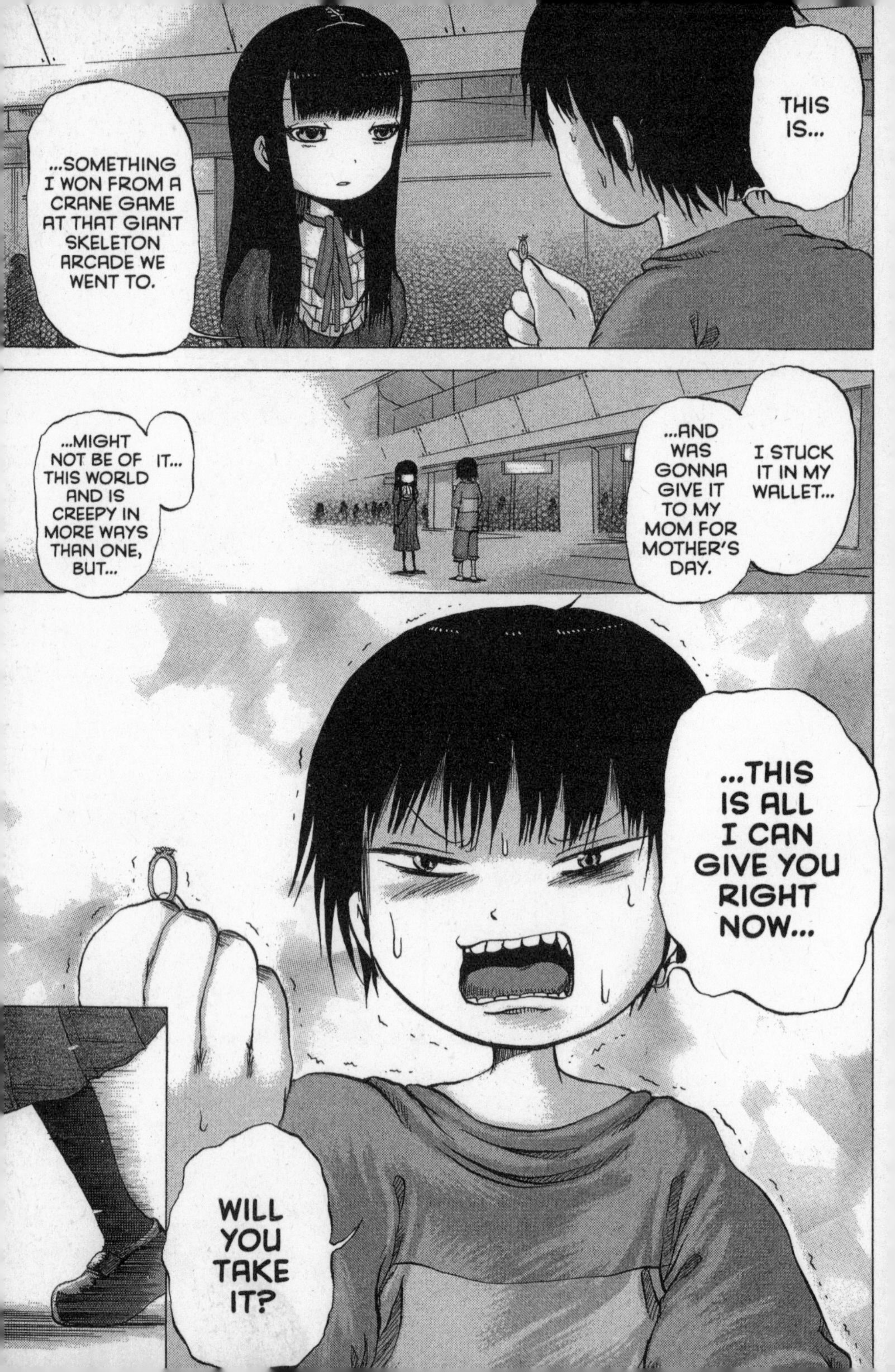
THIS IS...
...SOMETHING I WON FROM A CRANE GAME AT THAT GIANT SKELETON ARCADE WE WENT TO.
I STUCK IT IN MY WALLET...
...AND WAS GONNA GIVE IT TO MY MOM FOR MOTHER'S DAY.
IT...
...MIGHT NOT BE OF THIS WORLD AND IS CREEPY IN MORE WAYS THAN ONE, BUT...
...THIS IS ALL I CAN GIVE YOU RIGHT NOW...
WILL YOU TAKE IT?

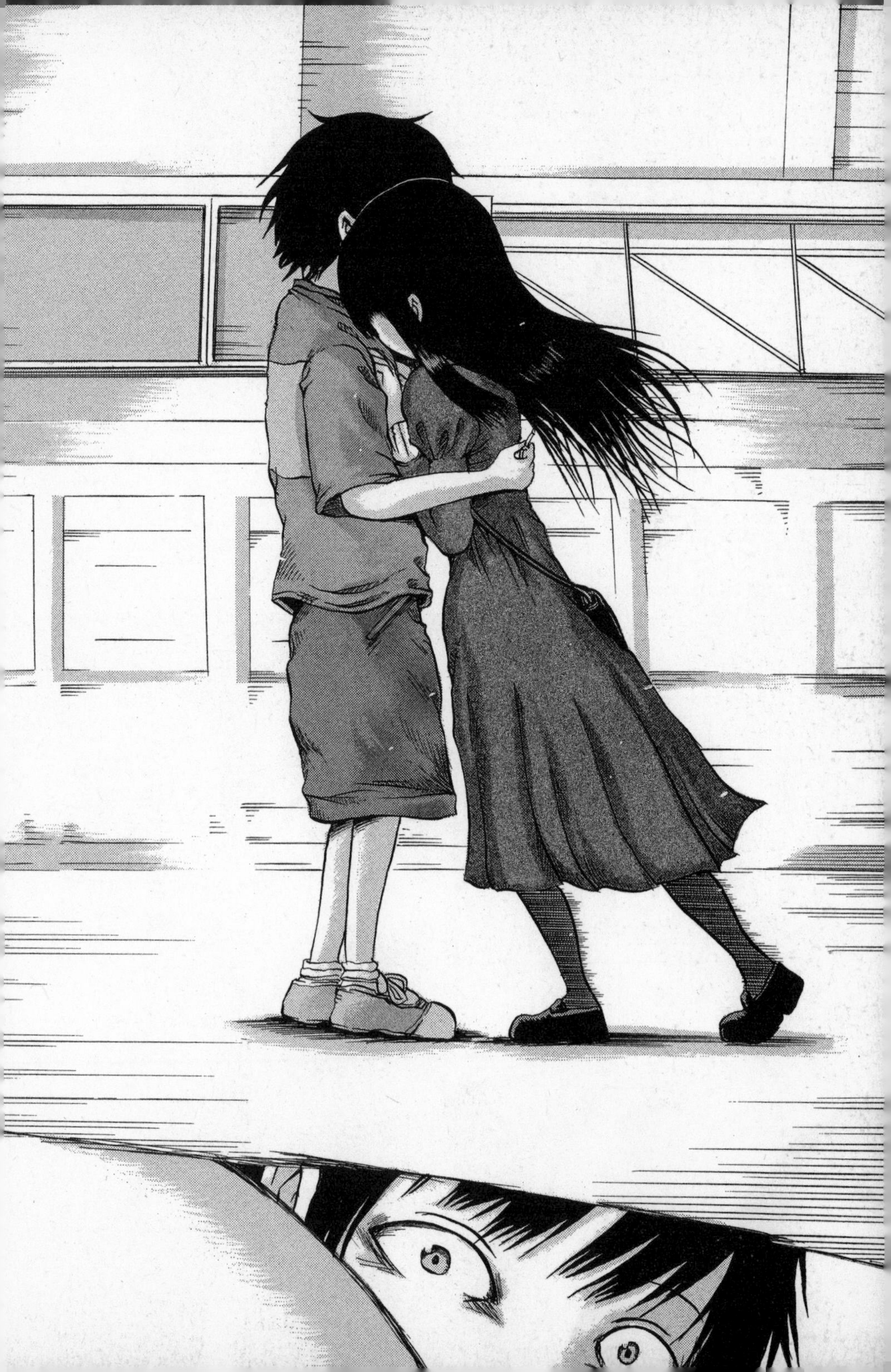

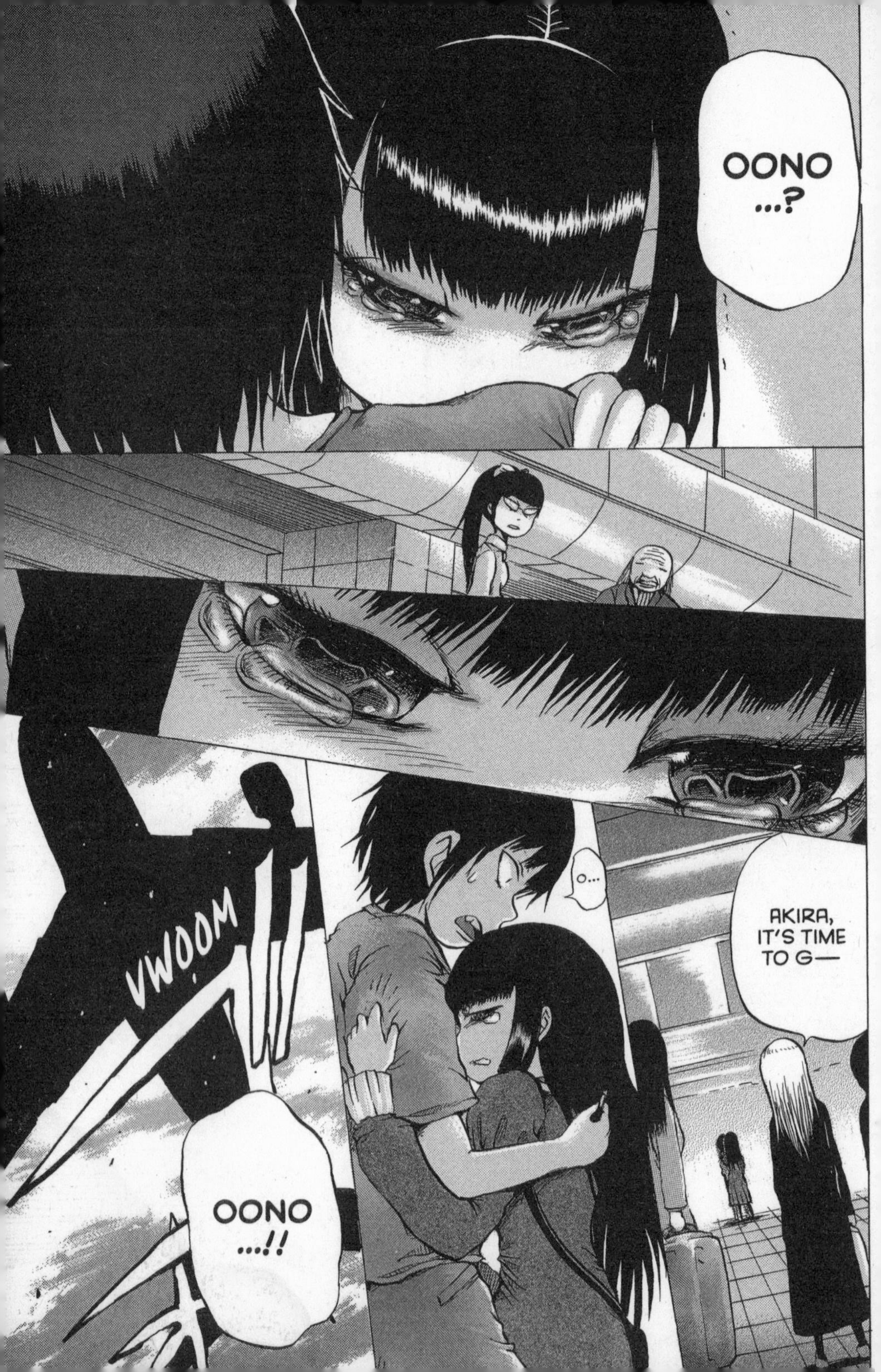
OONO ...?
AKIRA, IT'S TIME TO G—
O...
VWOOM
OONO ...!!

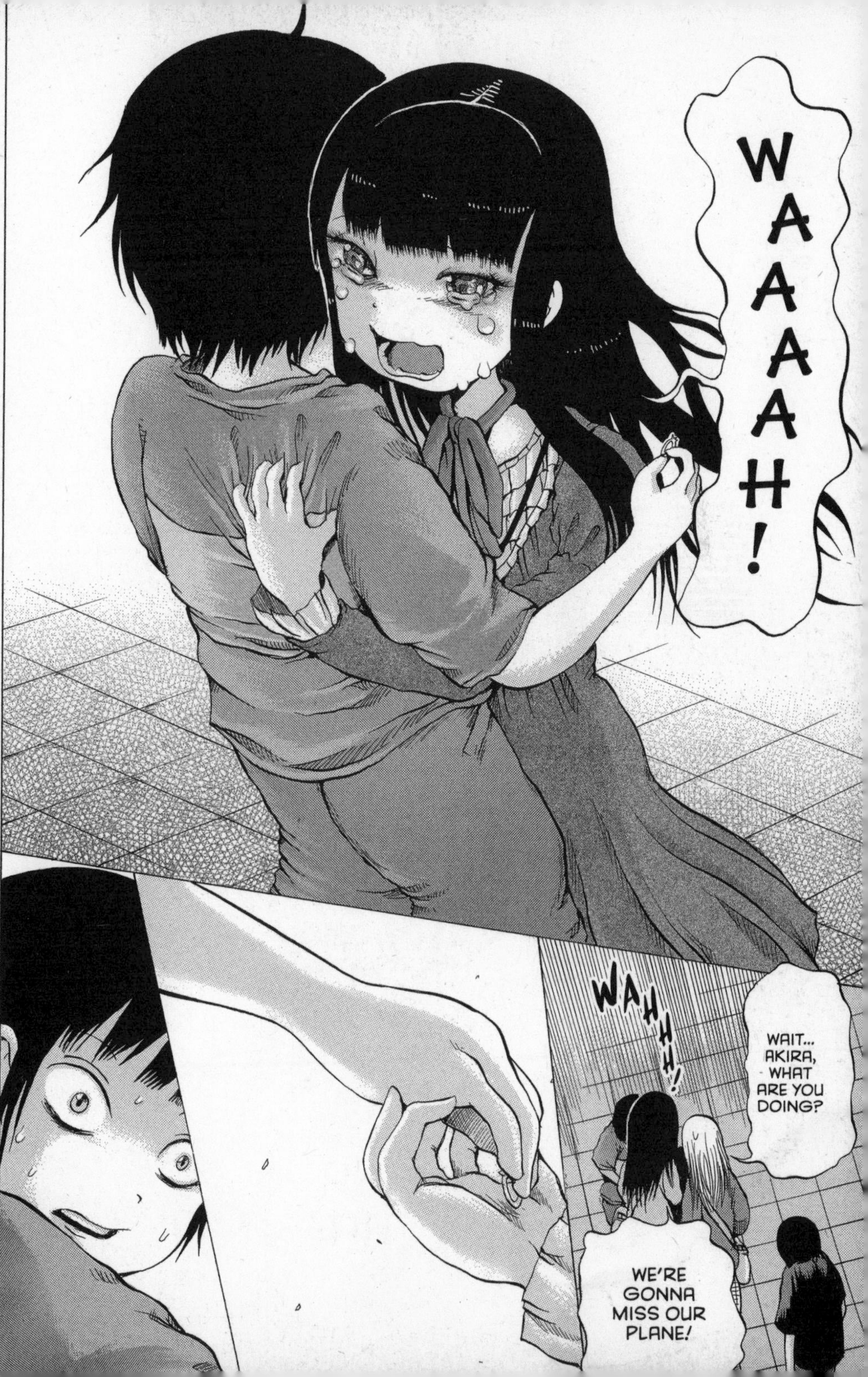
WAAAAH!
WAHHH!
WAIT... AKIRA, WHAT ARE YOU DOING?
WE'RE GONNA MISS OUR PLANE!

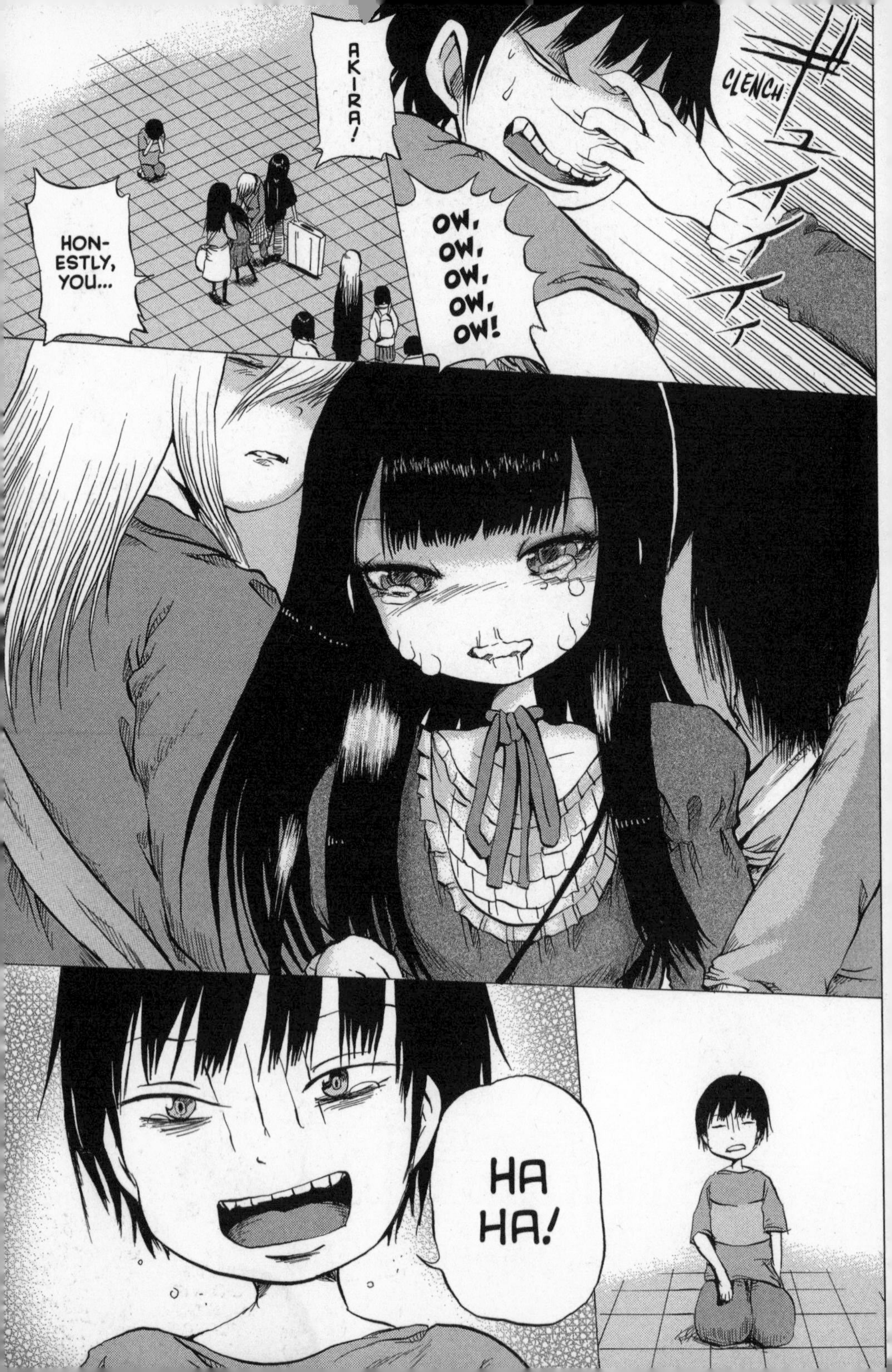
CLENCH
AKIRA!
OW, OW, OW, OW, OW!
HONESTLY, YOU...
HA HA!

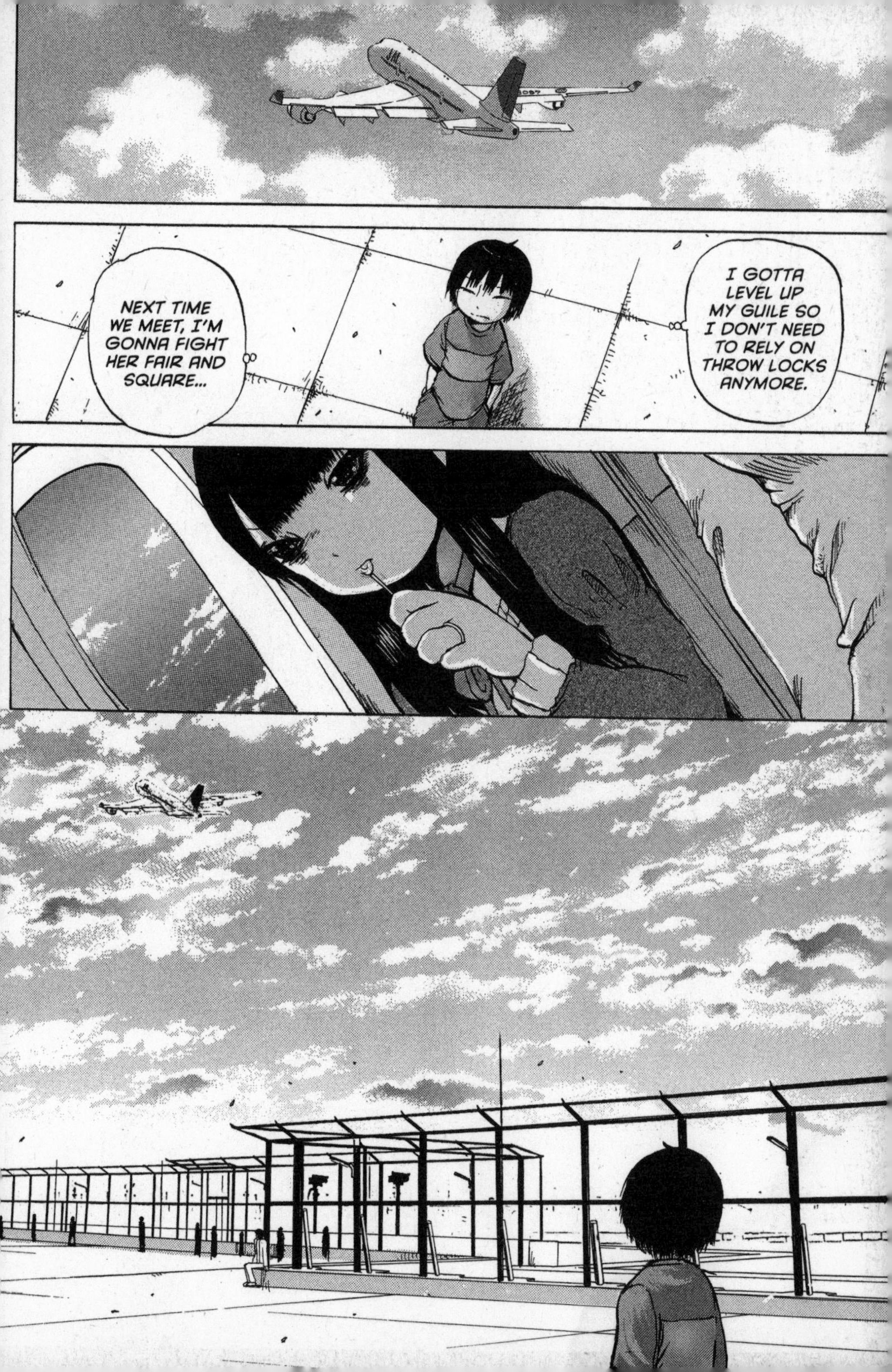
I GOTTA LEVEL UP MY GUILE SO I DON'T NEED TO RELY ON THROW LOCKS ANYMORE.
NEXT TIME WE MEET, I'M GONNA FIGHT HER FAIR AND SQUARE...

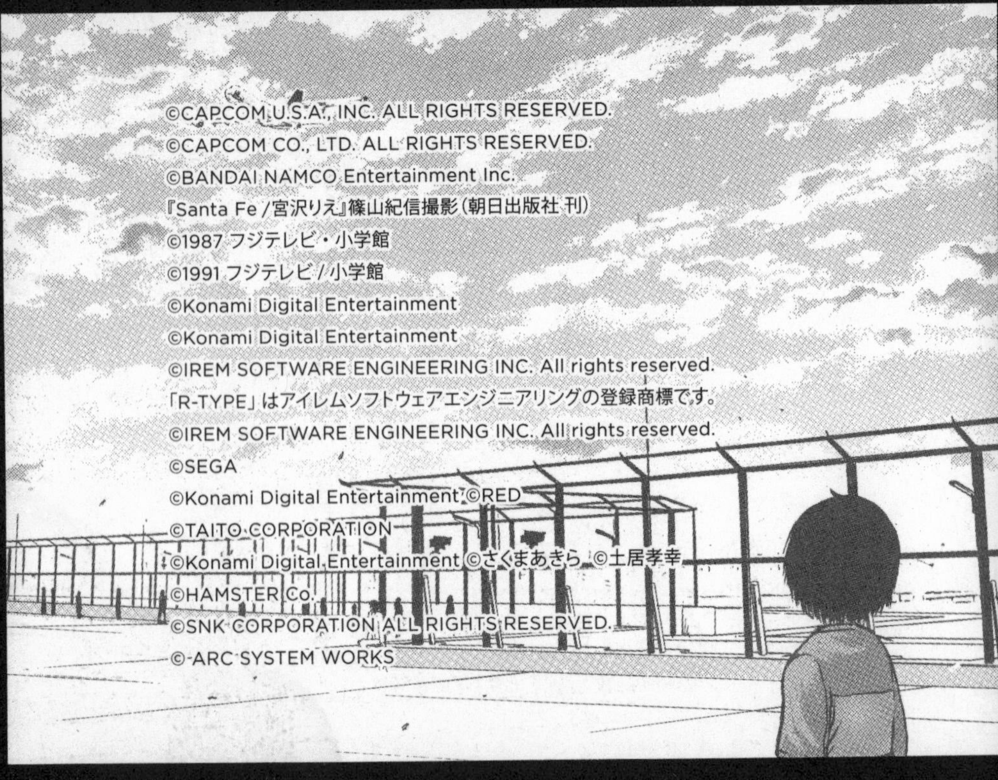

HI SCORE GIRL

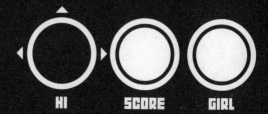

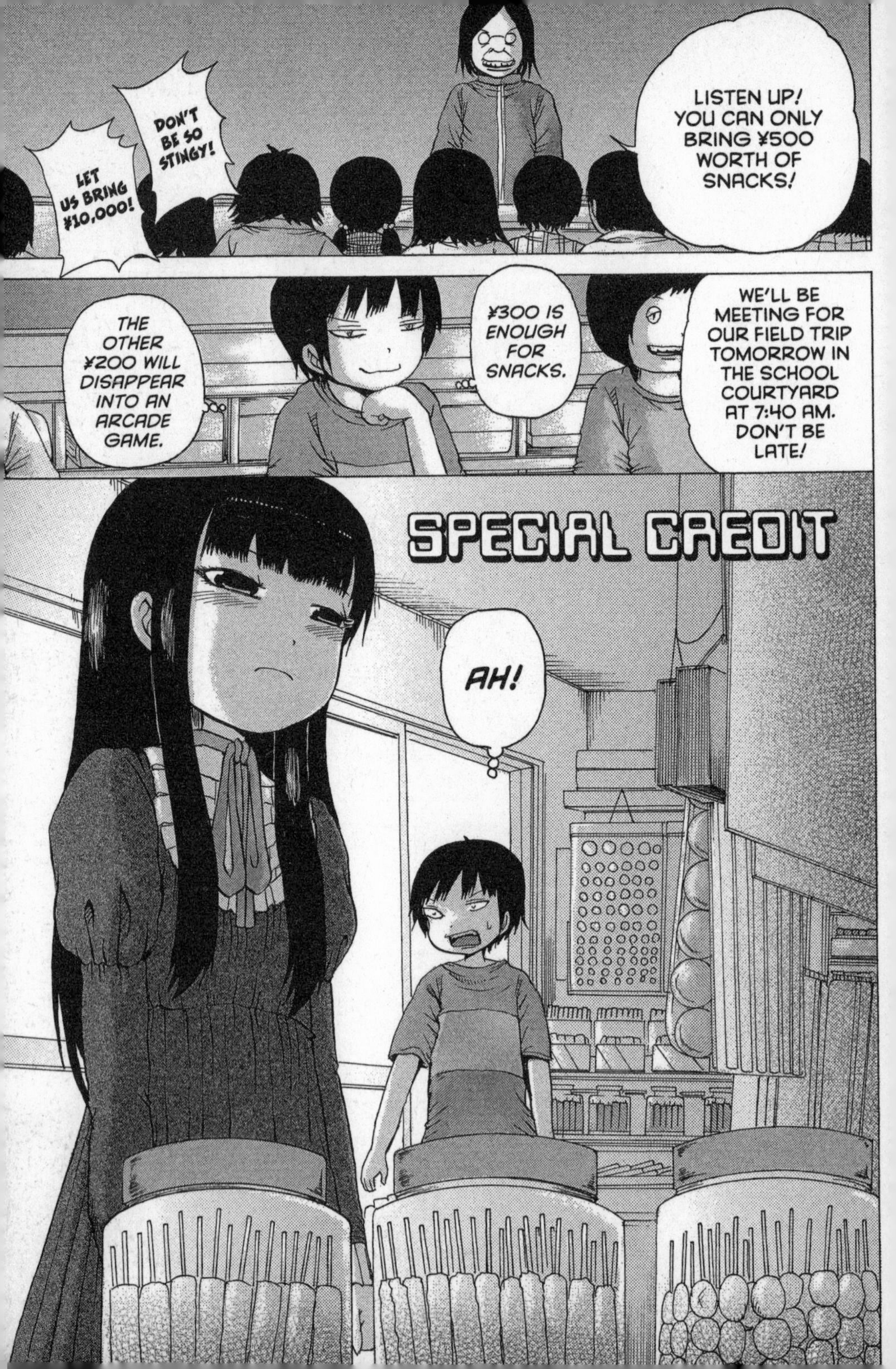
LISTEN UP! YOU CAN ONLY BRING ¥500 WORTH OF SNACKS!
DON'T BE SO STINGY!
LET US BRING ¥10,000!
WE'LL BE MEETING FOR OUR FIELD TRIP TOMORROW IN THE SCHOOL COURTYARD AT 7:40 AM. DON'T BE LATE!
¥300 IS ENOUGH FOR SNACKS.
THE OTHER ¥200 WILL DISAPPEAR INTO AN ARCADE GAME.
SPECIAL CREDIT
AH!

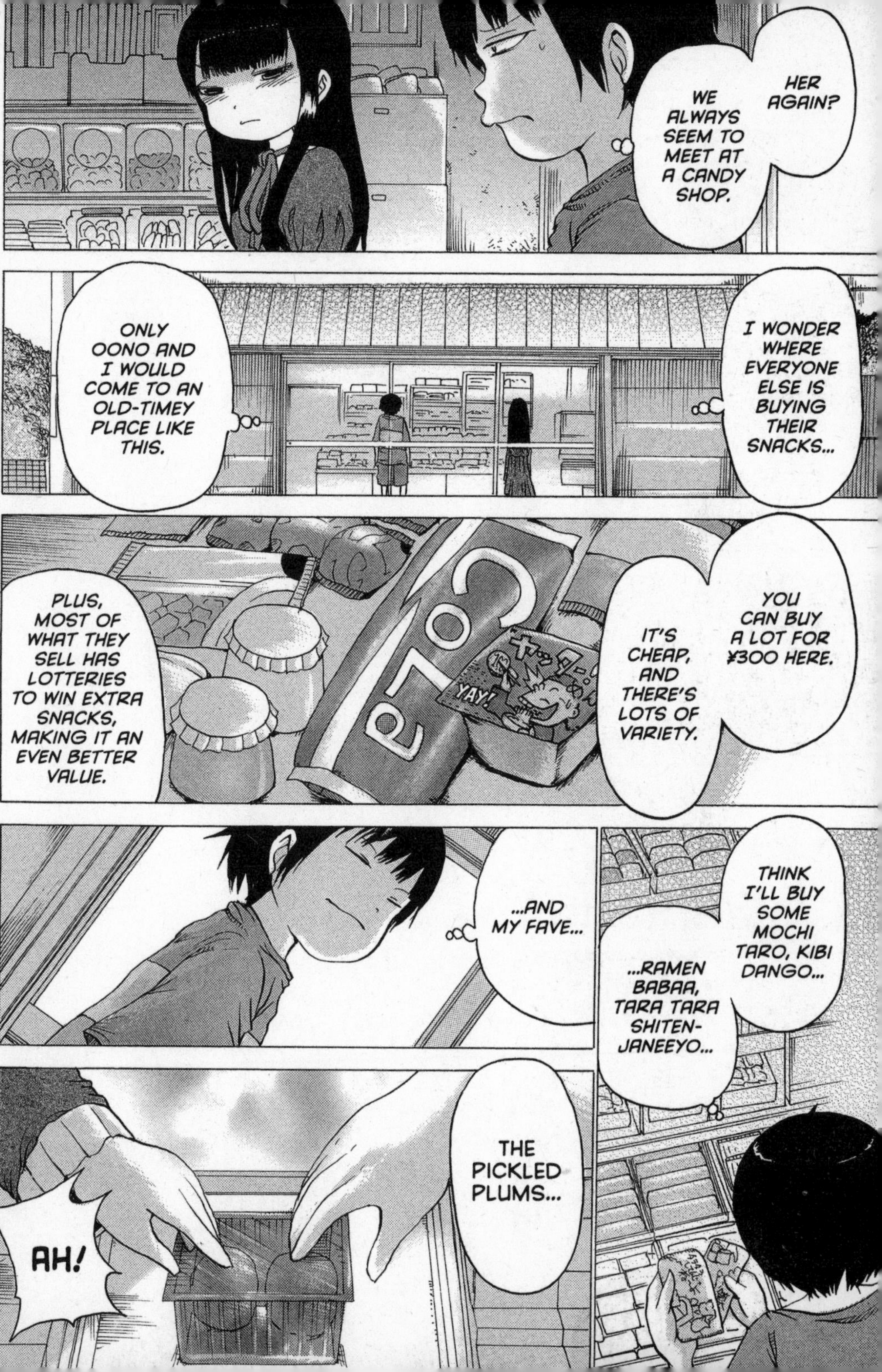
HER AGAIN? WE ALWAYS SEEM TO MEET AT A CANDY SHOP.
I WONDER WHERE EVERYONE ELSE IS BUYING THEIR SNACKS...
ONLY OONO AND I WOULD COME TO AN OLD-TIMEY PLACE LIKE THIS.
YOU CAN BUY A LOT FOR ¥300 HERE.
IT'S CHEAP, AND THERE'S LOTS OF VARIETY.
YAY!
PLUS, MOST OF WHAT THEY SELL HAS LOTTERIES TO WIN EXTRA SNACKS, MAKING IT AN EVEN BETTER VALUE.
THINK I'LL BUY SOME MOCHI TARO, KIBI DANGO...
...RAMEN BABAA, TARA TARA SHITEN-JANEEYO...
...AND MY FAVE...
THE PICKLED PLUMS...
AH!

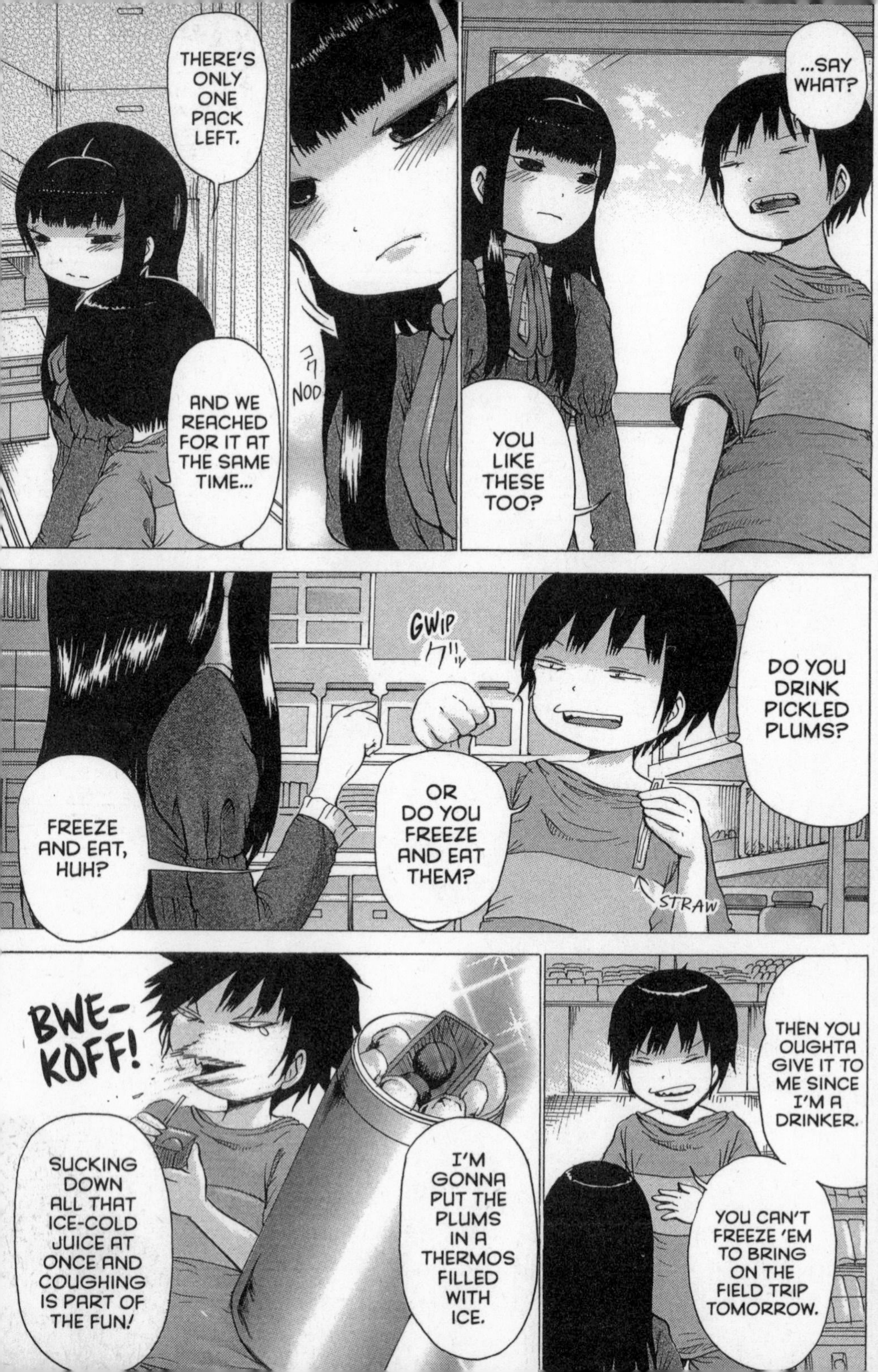
...SAY WHAT?
YOU LIKE THESE TOO?
コク NOD
THERE'S ONLY ONE PACK LEFT.
AND WE REACHED FOR IT AT THE SAME TIME...
DO YOU DRINK PICKLED PLUMS?
GWIP グッ
OR DO YOU FREEZE AND EAT THEM?
STRAW
FREEZE AND EAT, HUH?
THEN YOU OUGHTA GIVE IT TO ME SINCE I'M A DRINKER.
YOU CAN'T FREEZE 'EM TO BRING ON THE FIELD TRIP TOMORROW.
I'M GONNA PUT THE PLUMS IN A THERMOS FILLED WITH ICE.
BWE-KOFF!
SUCKING DOWN ALL THAT ICE-COLD JUICE AT ONCE AND COUGHING IS PART OF THE FUN!

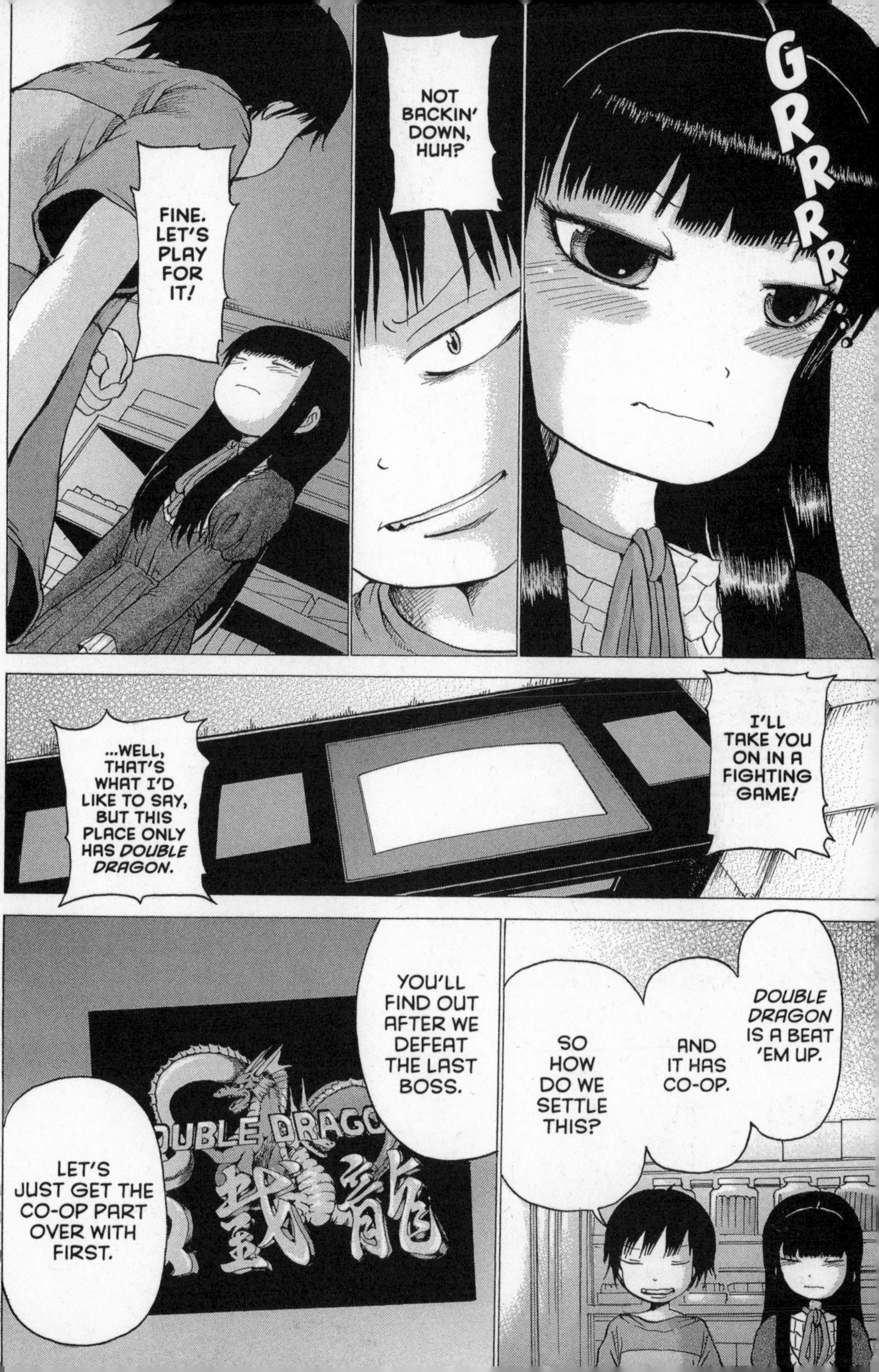
GRRRR
NOT BACKIN' DOWN, HUH?
FINE. LET'S PLAY FOR IT!
I'LL TAKE YOU ON IN A FIGHTING GAME!
...WELL, THAT'S WHAT I'D LIKE TO SAY, BUT THIS PLACE ONLY HAS *DOUBLE DRAGON*.
DOUBLE DRAGON IS A BEAT 'EM UP.
AND IT HAS CO-OP.
SO HOW DO WE SETTLE THIS?
YOU'LL FIND OUT AFTER WE DEFEAT THE LAST BOSS.
LET'S JUST GET THE CO-OP PART OVER WITH FIRST.

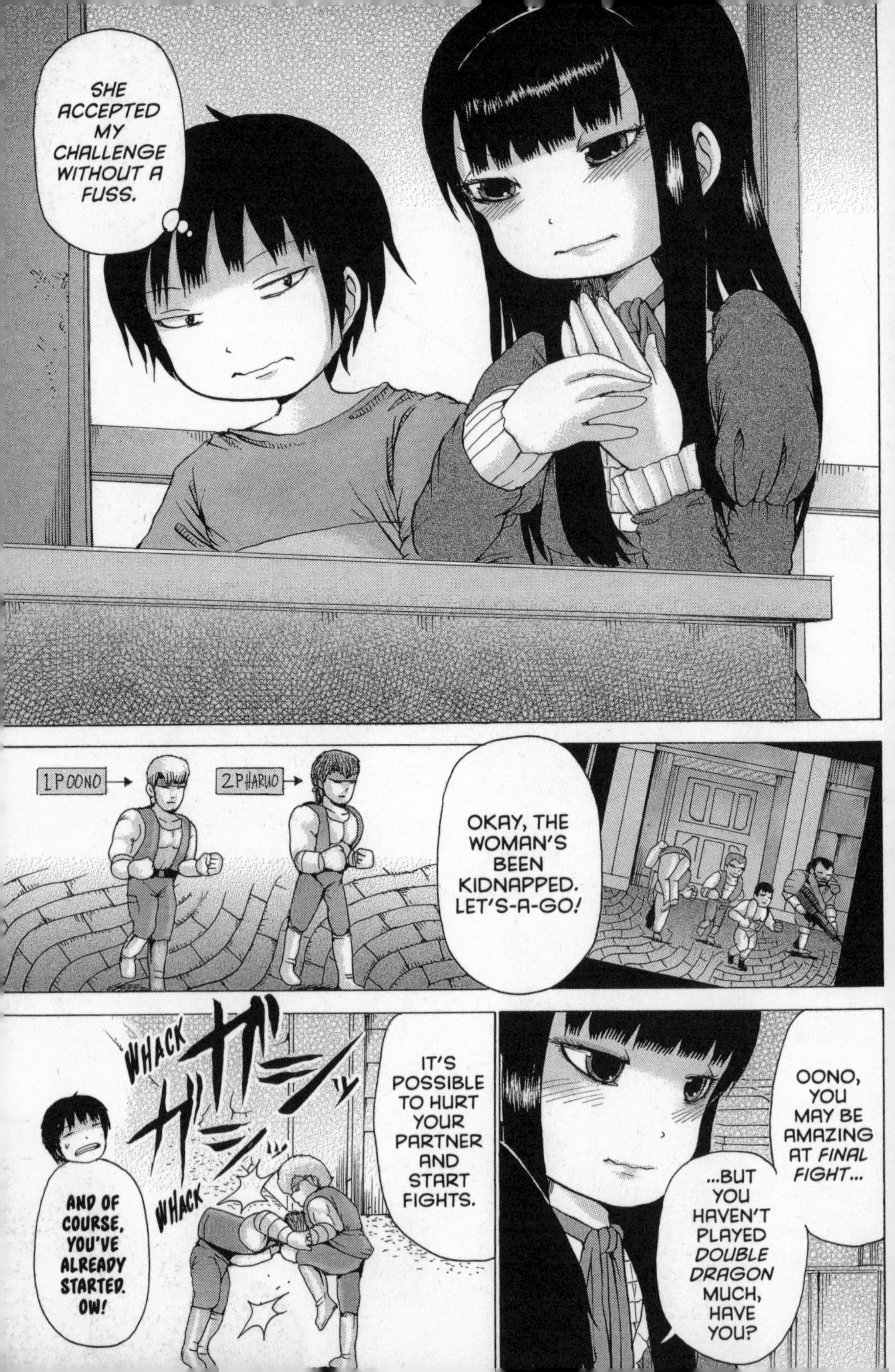
SHE ACCEPTED MY CHALLENGE WITHOUT A FUSS.
OKAY, THE WOMAN'S BEEN KIDNAPPED. LET'S-A-GO!
1P OONO
2P HARUO
OONO, YOU MAY BE AMAZING AT *FINAL FIGHT*...
...BUT YOU HAVEN'T PLAYED *DOUBLE DRAGON* MUCH, HAVE YOU?
IT'S POSSIBLE TO HURT YOUR PARTNER AND START FIGHTS.
WHACK
WHACK
AND OF COURSE, YOU'VE ALREADY STARTED. OW!

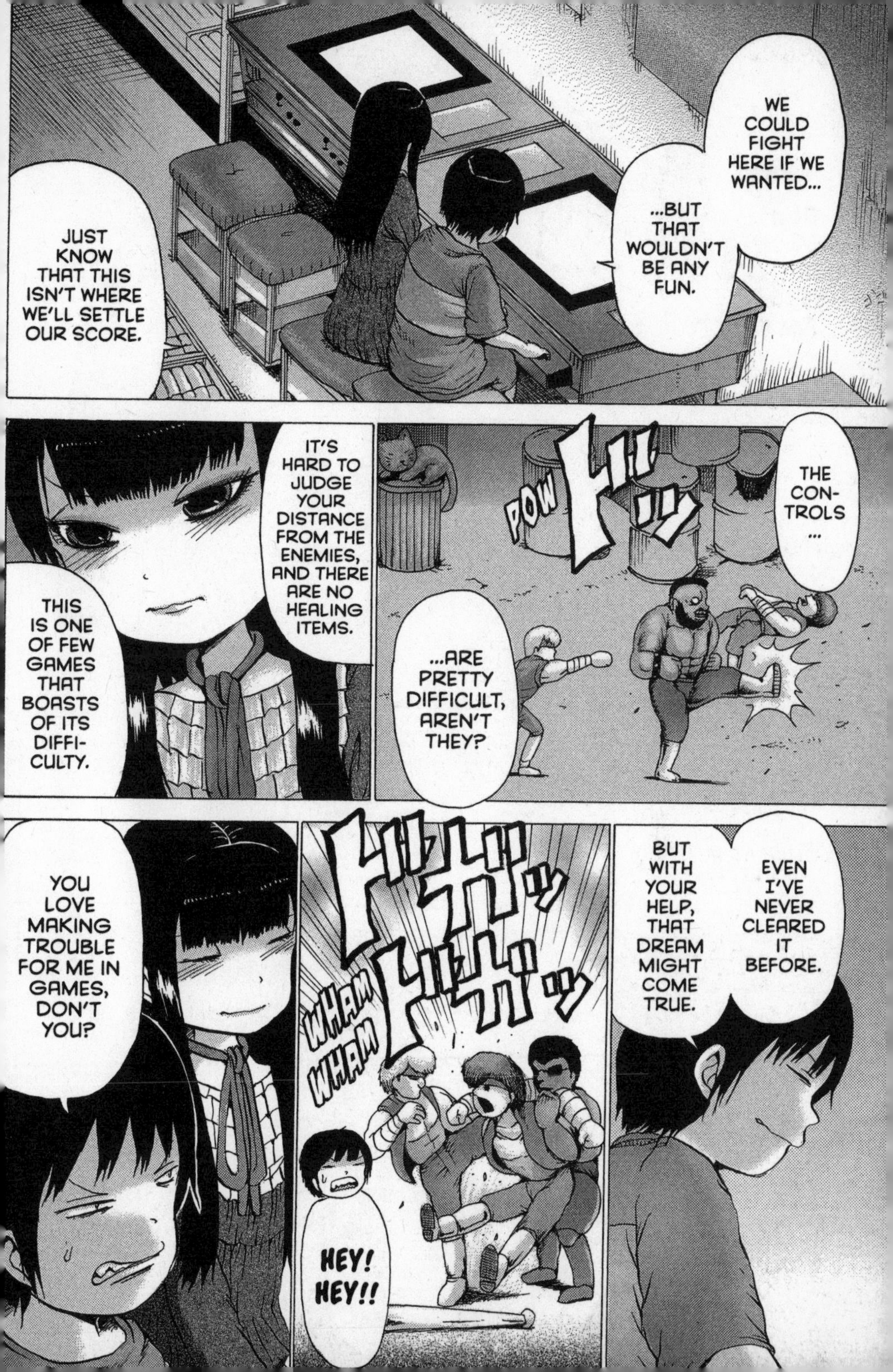
WE COULD FIGHT HERE IF WE WANTED...
...BUT THAT WOULDN'T BE ANY FUN.
JUST KNOW THAT THIS ISN'T WHERE WE'LL SETTLE OUR SCORE.
THE CONTROLS...
POW
...ARE PRETTY DIFFICULT, AREN'T THEY?
IT'S HARD TO JUDGE YOUR DISTANCE FROM THE ENEMIES, AND THERE ARE NO HEALING ITEMS.
THIS IS ONE OF FEW GAMES THAT BOASTS OF ITS DIFFICULTY.
EVEN I'VE NEVER CLEARED IT BEFORE.
BUT WITH YOUR HELP, THAT DREAM MIGHT COME TRUE.
WHAM WHAM
HEY! HEY!!
YOU LOVE MAKING TROUBLE FOR ME IN GAMES, DON'T YOU?

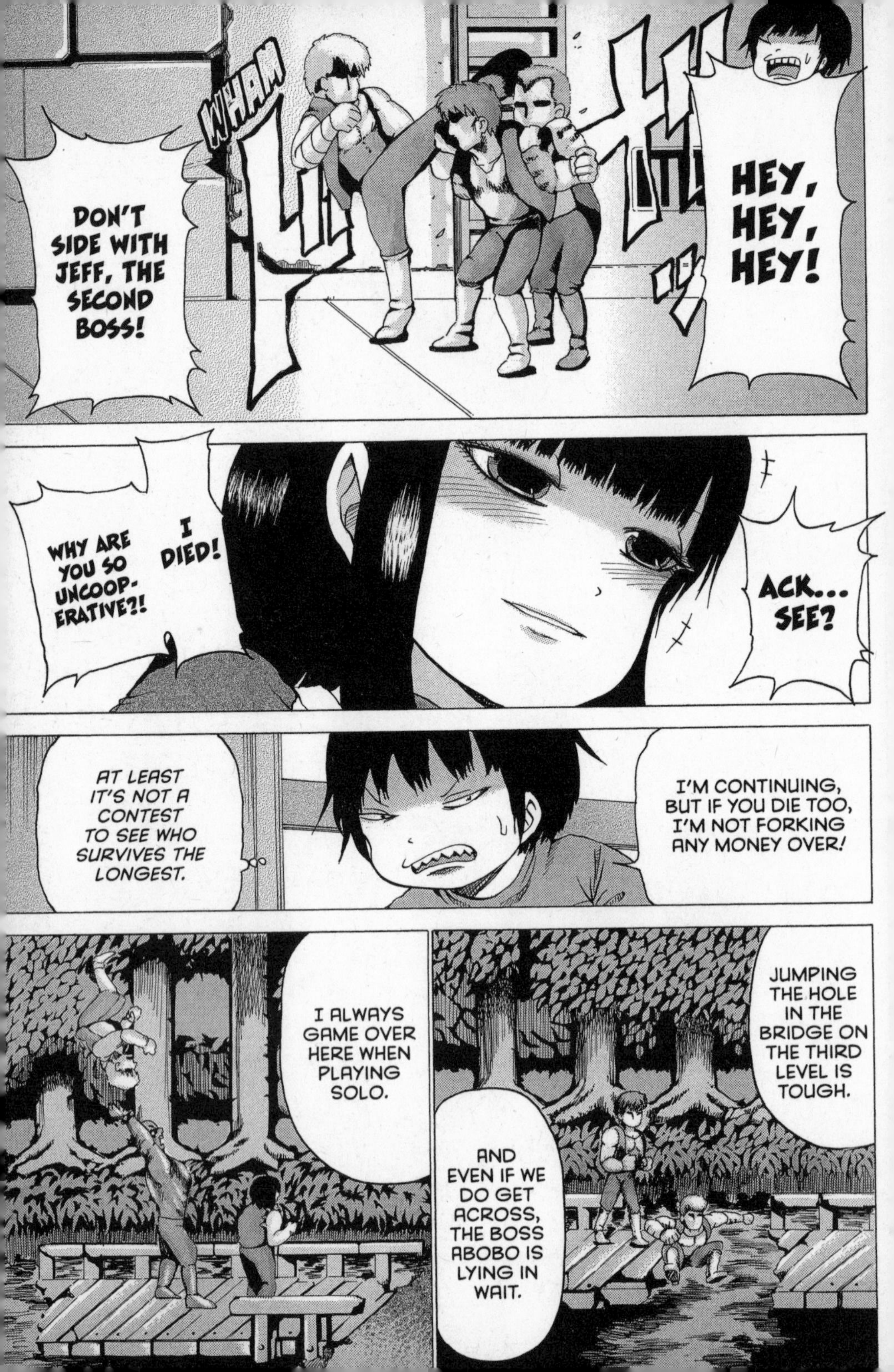
HEY, HEY, HEY!
WHAM
DON'T SIDE WITH JEFF, THE SECOND BOSS!
ACK... SEE?
I DIED!
WHY ARE YOU SO UNCOOP-ERATIVE?!
I'M CONTINUING, BUT IF YOU DIE TOO, I'M NOT FORKING ANY MONEY OVER!
AT LEAST IT'S NOT A CONTEST TO SEE WHO SURVIVES THE LONGEST.
JUMPING THE HOLE IN THE BRIDGE ON THE THIRD LEVEL IS TOUGH.
AND EVEN IF WE DO GET ACROSS, THE BOSS ABOBO IS LYING IN WAIT.
I ALWAYS GAME OVER HERE WHEN PLAYING SOLO.

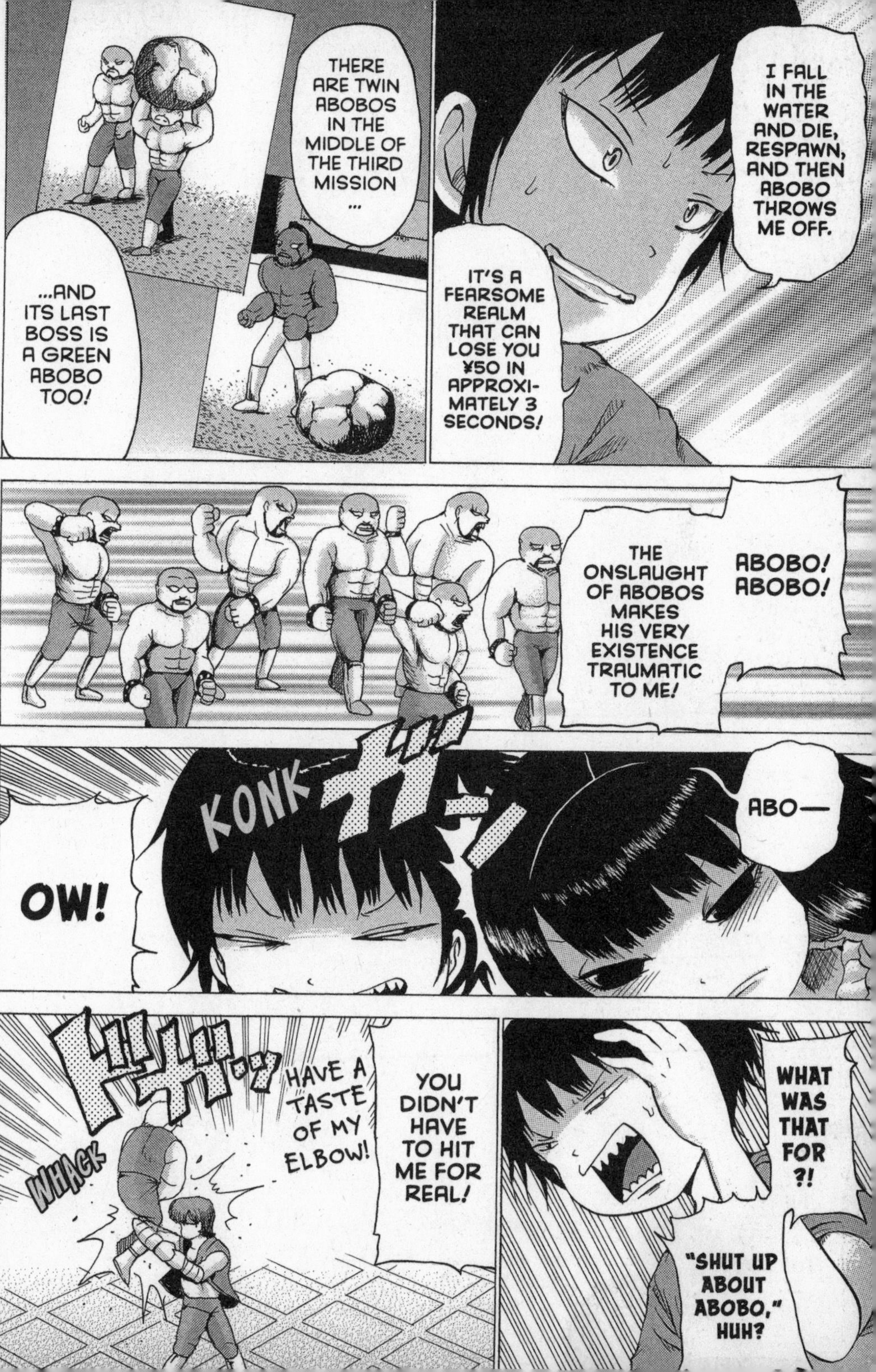
I FALL IN THE WATER AND DIE, RESPAWN, AND THEN ABOBO THROWS ME OFF.
IT'S A FEARSOME REALM THAT CAN LOSE YOU ¥50 IN APPROXIMATELY 3 SECONDS!
THERE ARE TWIN ABOBOS IN THE MIDDLE OF THE THIRD MISSION ...
...AND ITS LAST BOSS IS A GREEN ABOBO TOO!
ABOBO! ABOBO!
THE ONSLAUGHT OF ABOBOS MAKES HIS VERY EXISTENCE TRAUMATIC TO ME!
ABO—
KONK
OW!
WHAT WAS THAT FOR ?!
"SHUT UP ABOUT ABOBO," HUH?
YOU DIDN'T HAVE TO HIT ME FOR REAL!
HAVE A TASTE OF MY ELBOW!
WHACK

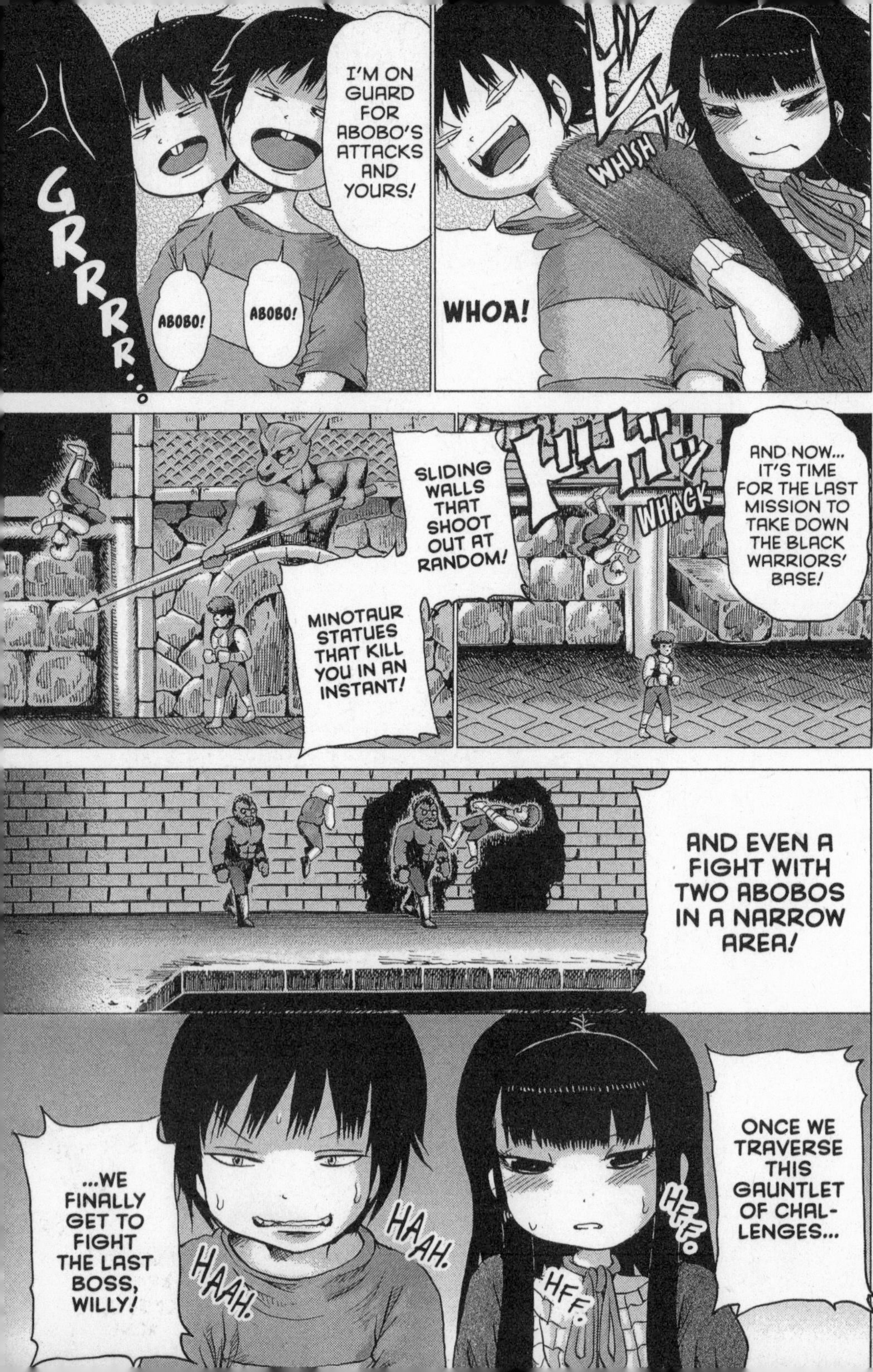
WHISH
WHOA!
I'M ON GUARD FOR ABOBO'S ATTACKS AND YOURS!
ABOBO!
ABOBO!
GRRRR...
AND NOW... IT'S TIME FOR THE LAST MISSION TO TAKE DOWN THE BLACK WARRIORS' BASE!
WHACK
SLIDING WALLS THAT SHOOT OUT AT RANDOM!
MINOTAUR STATUES THAT KILL YOU IN AN INSTANT!
AND EVEN A FIGHT WITH TWO ABOBOS IN A NARROW AREA!
ONCE WE TRAVERSE THIS GAUNTLET OF CHAL-LENGES...
HFF.
HFF.
HAAH.
HAAH.
...WE FINALLY GET TO FIGHT THE LAST BOSS, WILLY!

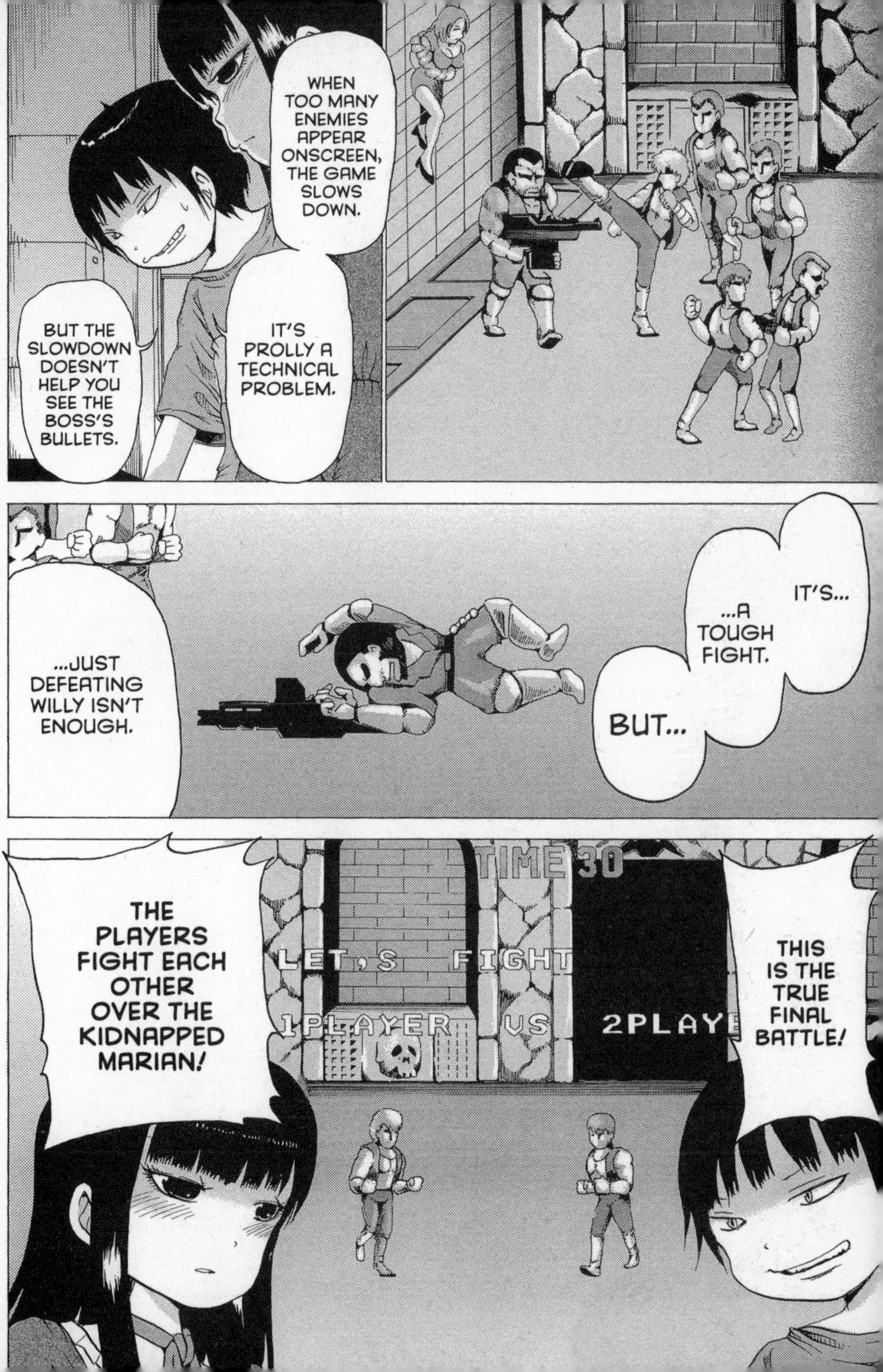
WHEN TOO MANY ENEMIES APPEAR ONSCREEN, THE GAME SLOWS DOWN.
IT'S PROLLY A TECHNICAL PROBLEM.
BUT THE SLOWDOWN DOESN'T HELP YOU SEE THE BOSS'S BULLETS.
IT'S...
...A TOUGH FIGHT.
BUT...
...JUST DEFEATING WILLY ISN'T ENOUGH.
THIS IS THE TRUE FINAL BATTLE!
TIME 30
LET,S FIGHT
1PLAYER VS 2PLAYE
THE PLAYERS FIGHT EACH OTHER OVER THE KIDNAPPED MARIAN!

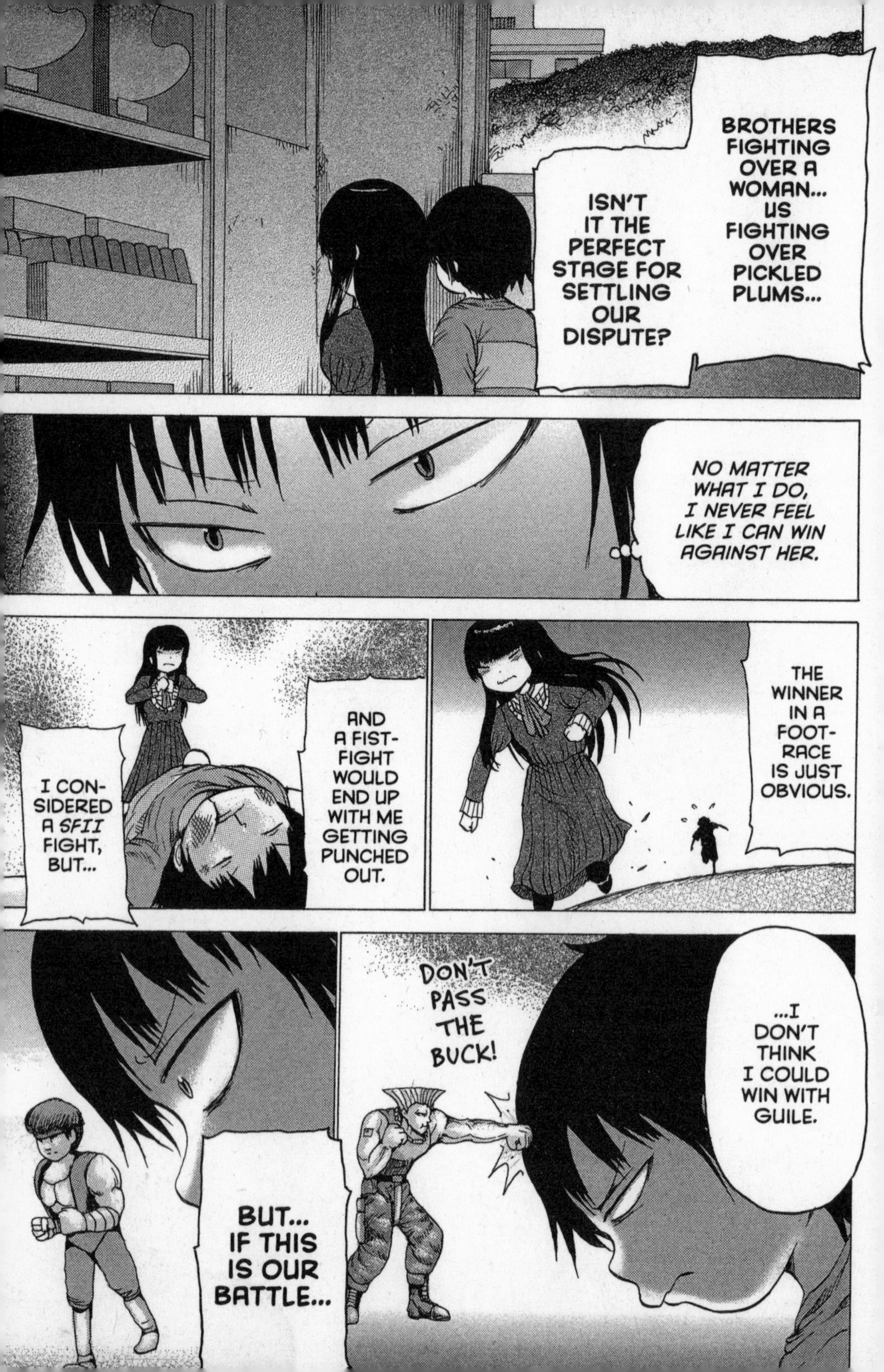
BROTHERS FIGHTING OVER A WOMAN... US FIGHTING OVER PICKLED PLUMS...
ISN'T IT THE PERFECT STAGE FOR SETTLING OUR DISPUTE?
NO MATTER WHAT I DO, I NEVER FEEL LIKE I CAN WIN AGAINST HER.
THE WINNER IN A FOOT-RACE IS JUST OBVIOUS.
AND A FIST-FIGHT WOULD END UP WITH ME GETTING PUNCHED OUT.
I CONSIDERED A *SFII* FIGHT, BUT...
...I DON'T THINK I COULD WIN WITH GUILE.
DON'T PASS THE BUCK!
BUT... IF THIS IS OUR BATTLE...

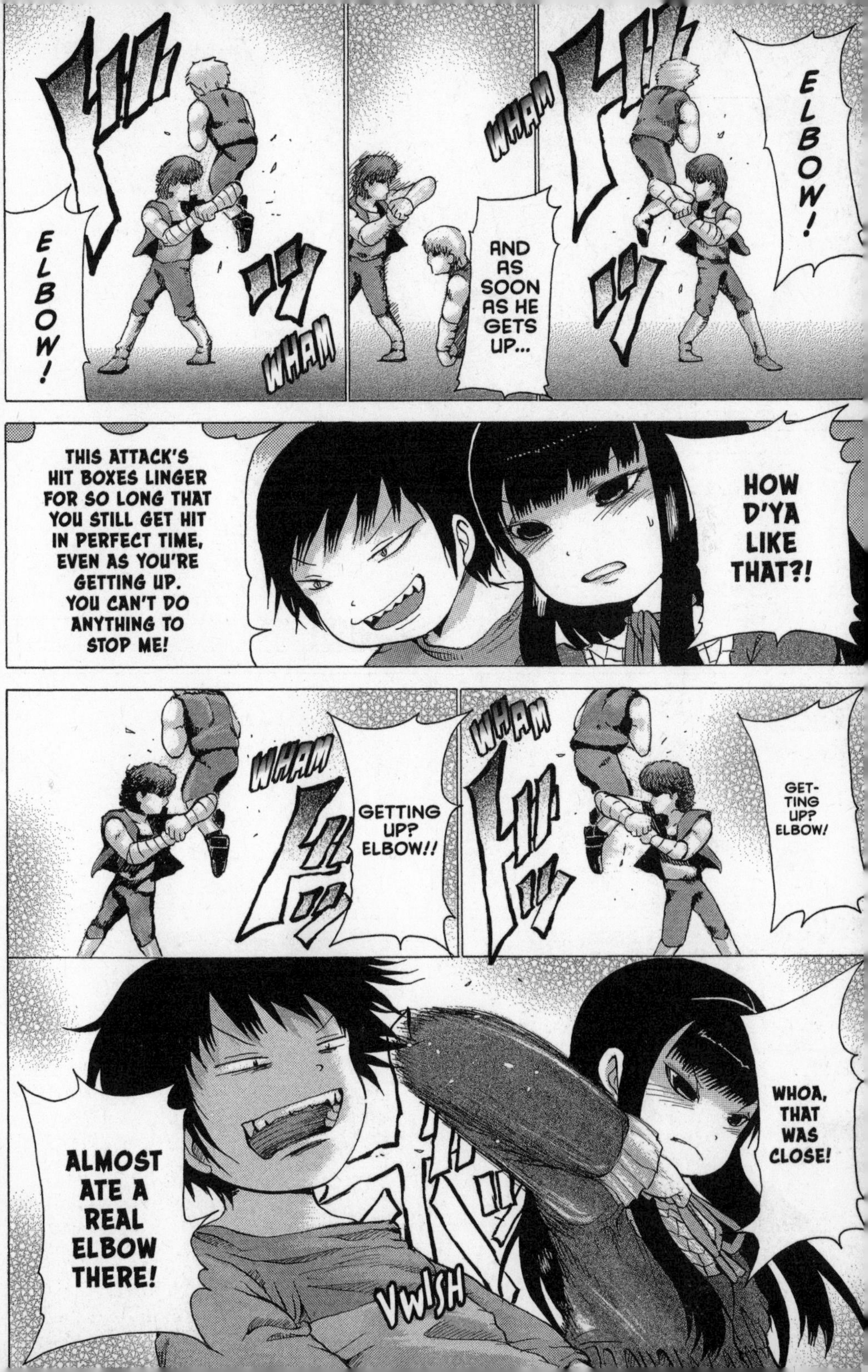
ELBOW!
WHAM
AND AS SOON AS HE GETS UP...
ELBOW!
WHAM
HOW D'YA LIKE THAT?!
THIS ATTACK'S HIT BOXES LINGER FOR SO LONG THAT YOU STILL GET HIT IN PERFECT TIME, EVEN AS YOU'RE GETTING UP. YOU CAN'T DO ANYTHING TO STOP ME!
GET-TING UP? ELBOW!
WHAM
GETTING UP? ELBOW!!
WHAM
WHOA, THAT WAS CLOSE!
ALMOST ATE A REAL ELBOW THERE!
VWISH

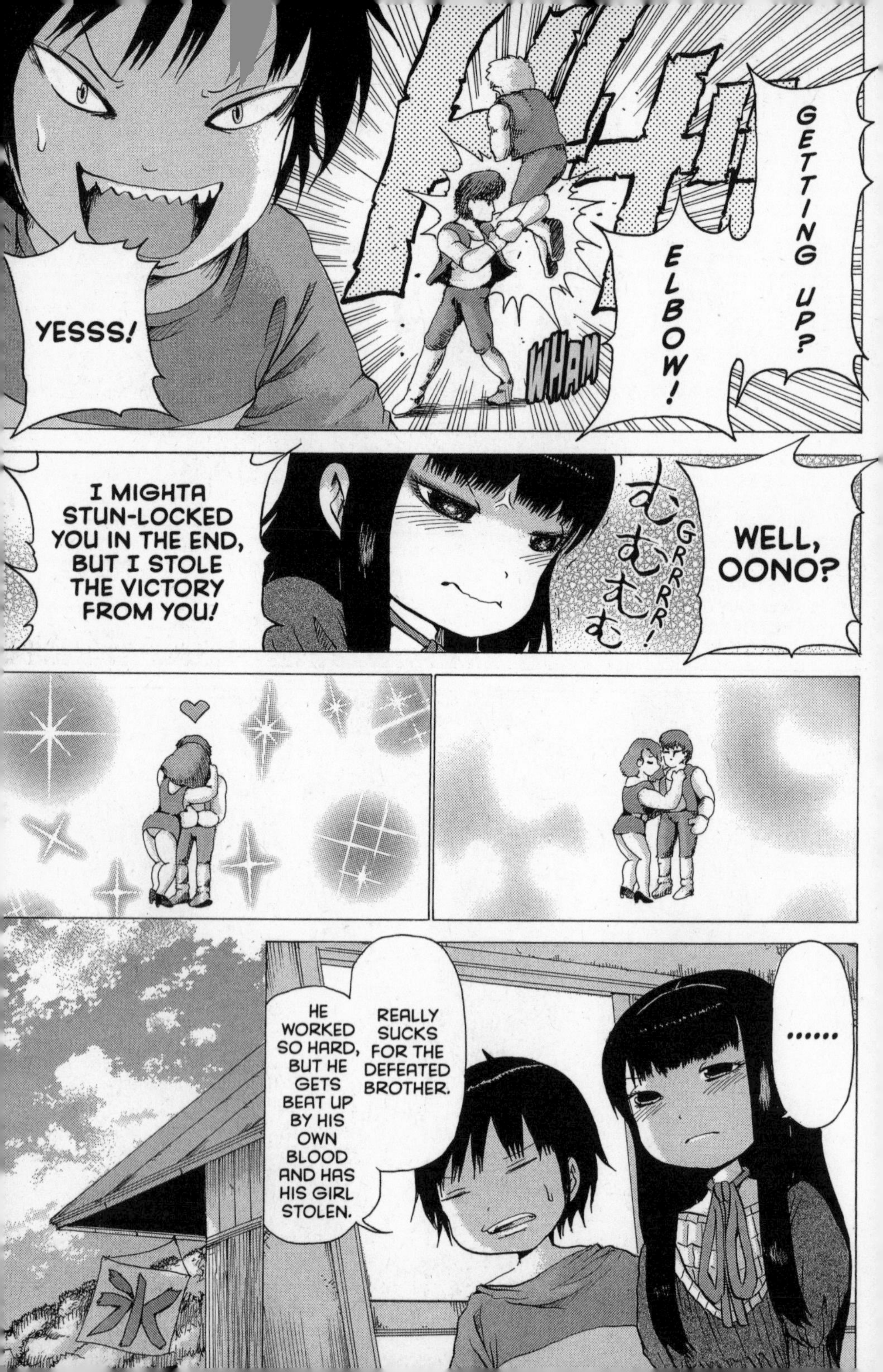
GETTING UP?
ELBOW!
WHAM
YESSS!
WELL, OONO?
GRRRR!
むむむむ
I MIGHTA STUN-LOCKED YOU IN THE END, BUT I STOLE THE VICTORY FROM YOU!
......
HE WORKED SO HARD, BUT HE GETS BEAT UP BY HIS OWN BLOOD AND HAS HIS GIRL STOLEN. REALLY SUCKS FOR THE DEFEATED BROTHER.
氷

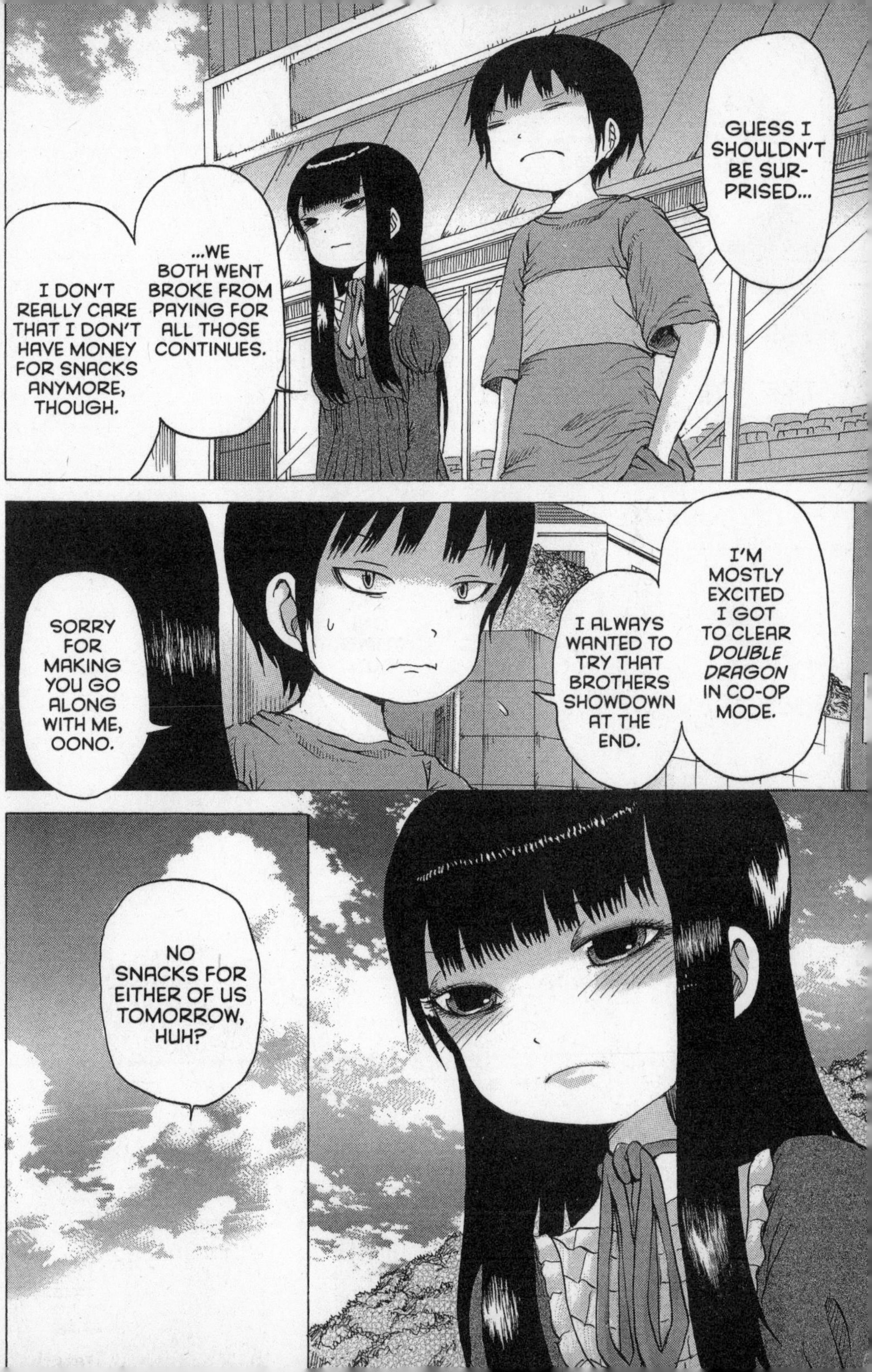
GUESS I SHOULDN'T BE SUR-PRISED...
...WE BOTH WENT BROKE FROM PAYING FOR ALL THOSE CONTINUES.
I DON'T REALLY CARE THAT I DON'T HAVE MONEY FOR SNACKS ANYMORE, THOUGH.
I'M MOSTLY EXCITED I GOT TO CLEAR *DOUBLE DRAGON* IN CO-OP MODE.
I ALWAYS WANTED TO TRY THAT BROTHERS SHOWDOWN AT THE END.
SORRY FOR MAKING YOU GO ALONG WITH ME, OONO.
NO SNACKS FOR EITHER OF US TOMORROW, HUH?

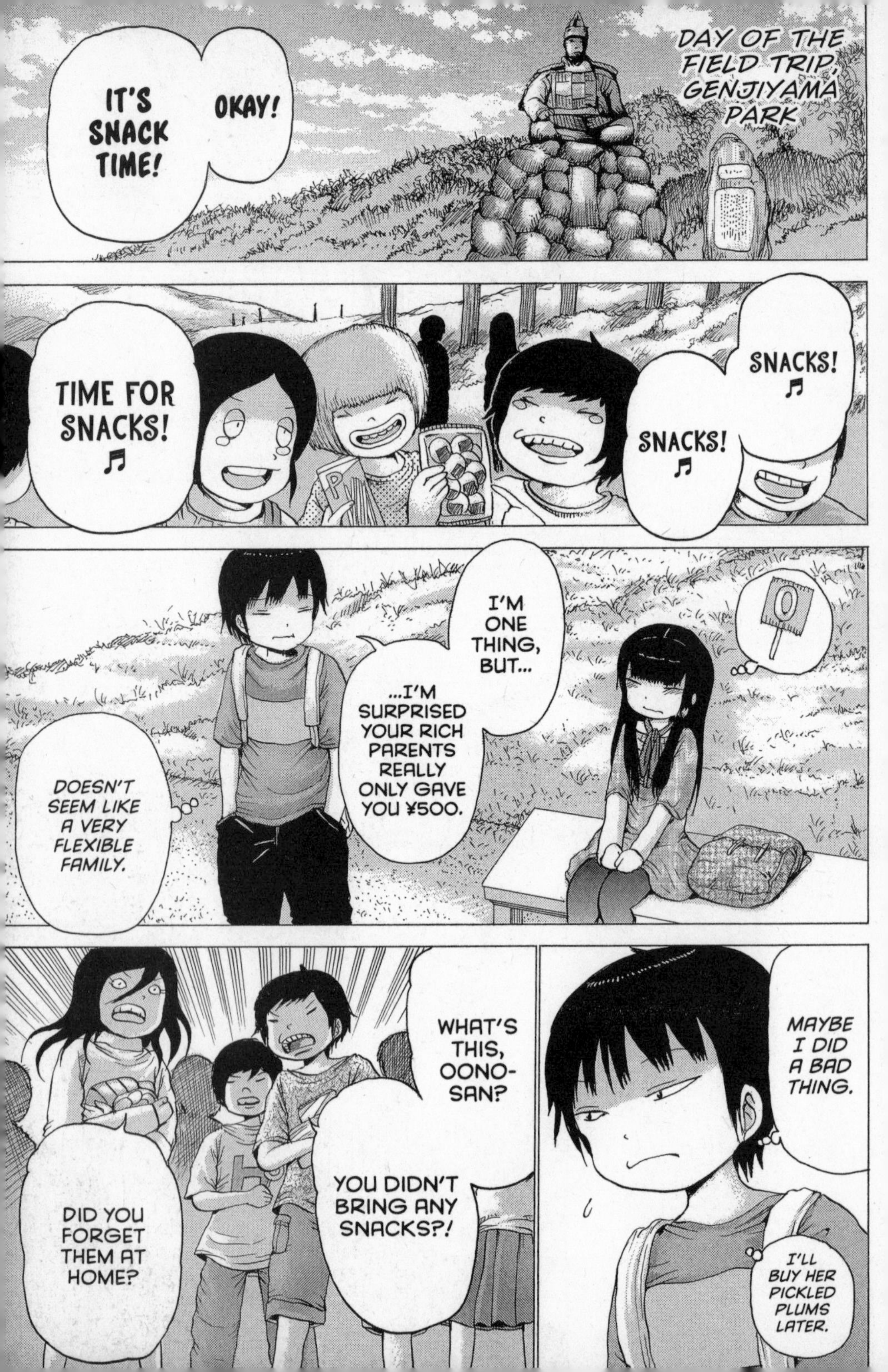
DAY OF THE FIELD TRIP, GENJIYAMA PARK
OKAY!
IT'S SNACK TIME!
SNACKS! ♫
SNACKS! ♫
TIME FOR SNACKS! ♫
I'M ONE THING, BUT...
...I'M SURPRISED YOUR RICH PARENTS REALLY ONLY GAVE YOU ¥500.
DOESN'T SEEM LIKE A VERY FLEXIBLE FAMILY.
MAYBE I DID A BAD THING.
I'LL BUY HER PICKLED PLUMS LATER.
WHAT'S THIS, OONO-SAN?
YOU DIDN'T BRING ANY SNACKS?!
DID YOU FORGET THEM AT HOME?

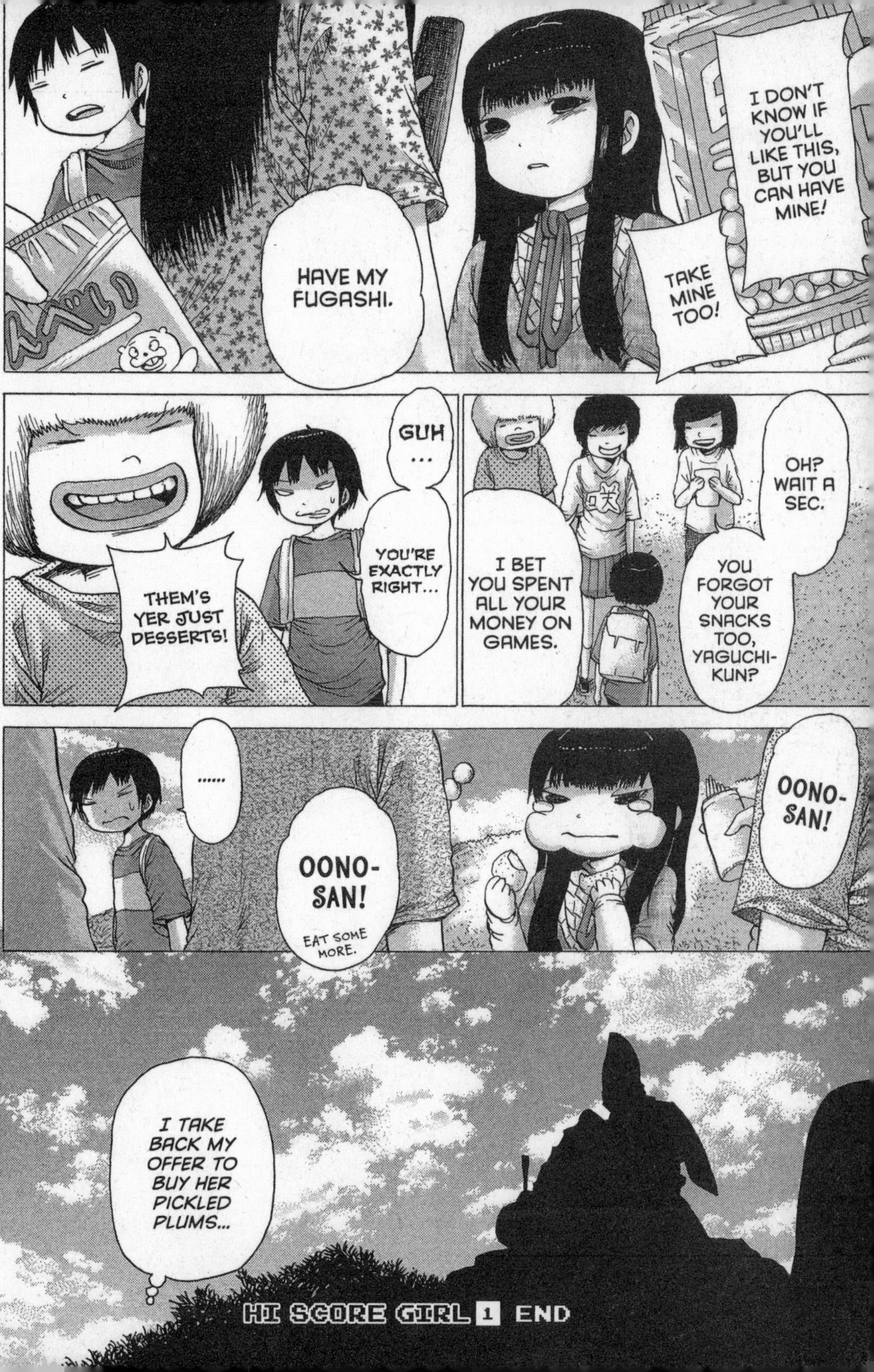
I DON'T KNOW IF YOU'LL LIKE THIS, BUT YOU CAN HAVE MINE!
TAKE MINE TOO!
HAVE MY FUGASHI.
OH? WAIT A SEC.
YOU FORGOT YOUR SNACKS TOO, YAGUCHI-KUN?
I BET YOU SPENT ALL YOUR MONEY ON GAMES.
GUH ...
YOU'RE EXACTLY RIGHT...
THEM'S YER JUST DESSERTS!
OONO-SAN!
OONO-SAN!
EAT SOME MORE.
......
I TAKE BACK MY OFFER TO BUY HER PICKLED PLUMS...
HI SCORE GIRL 1 END

HI SCORE GIRL

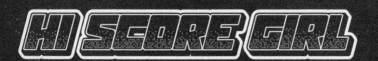

TRANSLATION NOTES

PAGE 19
Gamest was a Japanese video game magazine that specialized in arcade games. It ran from 1986–1999.

PAGE 25
Strip mahjong is like strip poker, where one removes an article of clothing upon losing. It was popular digitally, and the game screen would show images of nude women when the player won.

PAGE 35
Rie Miyazawa's *Santa Fe* nude collection was part of a trend in '90s Japan, during which the nation's pornography laws seemed to relax. Many productions began to show uncensored pubic hair as a result.

PAGE 35
Hoichoi Productions was a creative group representative of the "bubble era" of Japan. From 1987–1991, they found explosive success with three films known as the "Hoichoi Big Three," giving rise to a trend of similar movies.

PAGE 36
The **Famicom** and **Super Famicom** were released as the NES and SNES abroad.

PAGE 65
The **PC Engine** was released as the TurboGrafx-16 abroad.

PAGE 82
The **PC Engine GT** was released as the TurboExpress abroad.

PAGE 120
Liverleaf is the name of an earlier manga by Rensuke Oshikiri.

PAGE 123
The term "**game brain**" was originally coined by Professor Akio Mori in his book *The Terror of Game Brain*.

PAGE 126
A **paddle** is a game controller with a round wheel used to control player movement.

PAGE 170
This page features an assortment of Japanese snacks.

PAGE 173
The original line is *Rettsurago*, a line from the 1971 manga *Rettsuragon*, by Fujio Akatsuka.

PAGE 184
Fugashi is a sweet Japanese baked good that is covered in brown sugar.

HI   SCORE   GIRL

BEHIND THE SCENES OF PAGE 14 OF 6-CREDIT

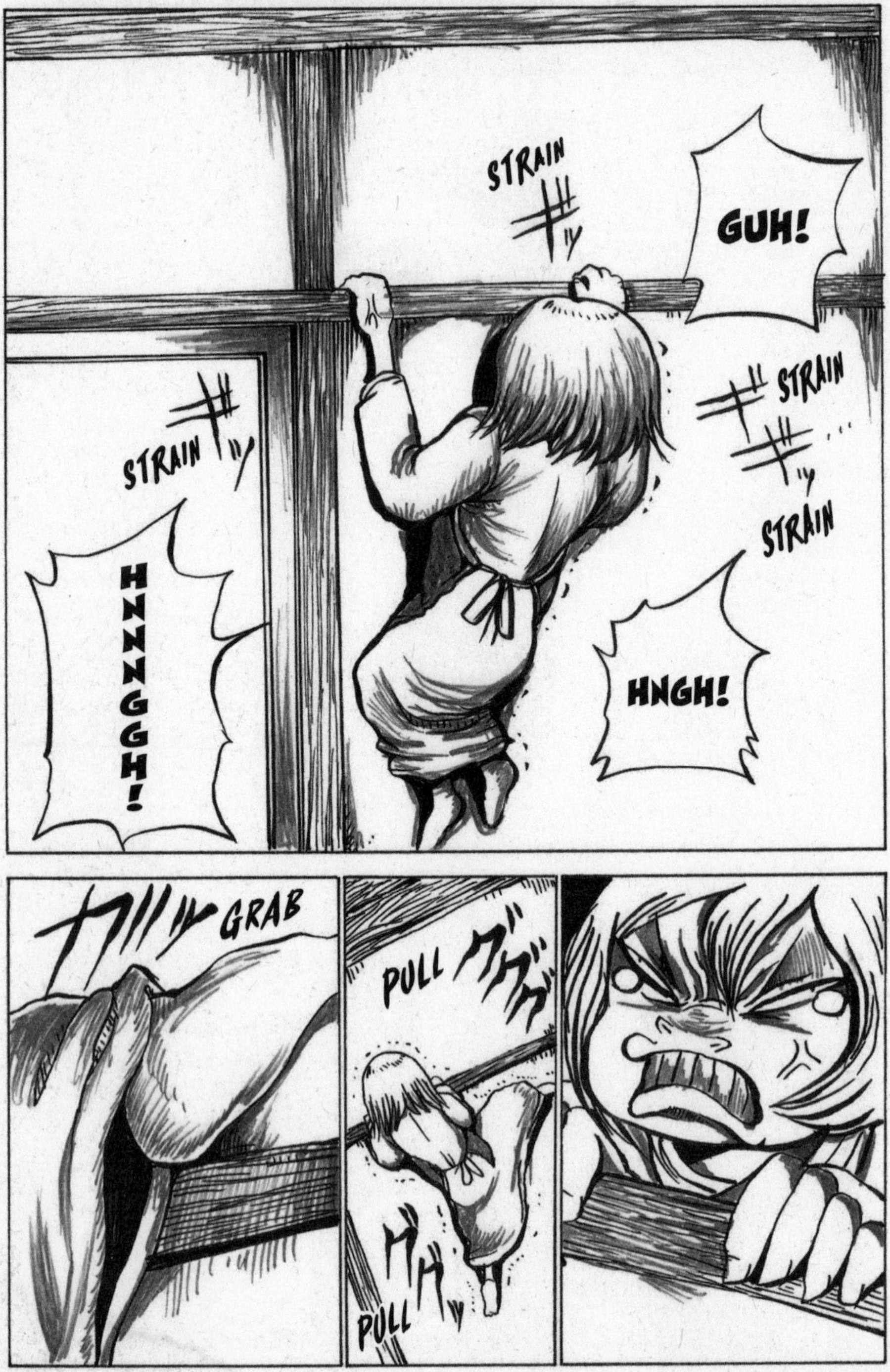
STRAIN
GUH!
STRAIN
STRAIN
HNGH!
STRAIN
HNNNNGGH!
PULL
PULL
GRAB

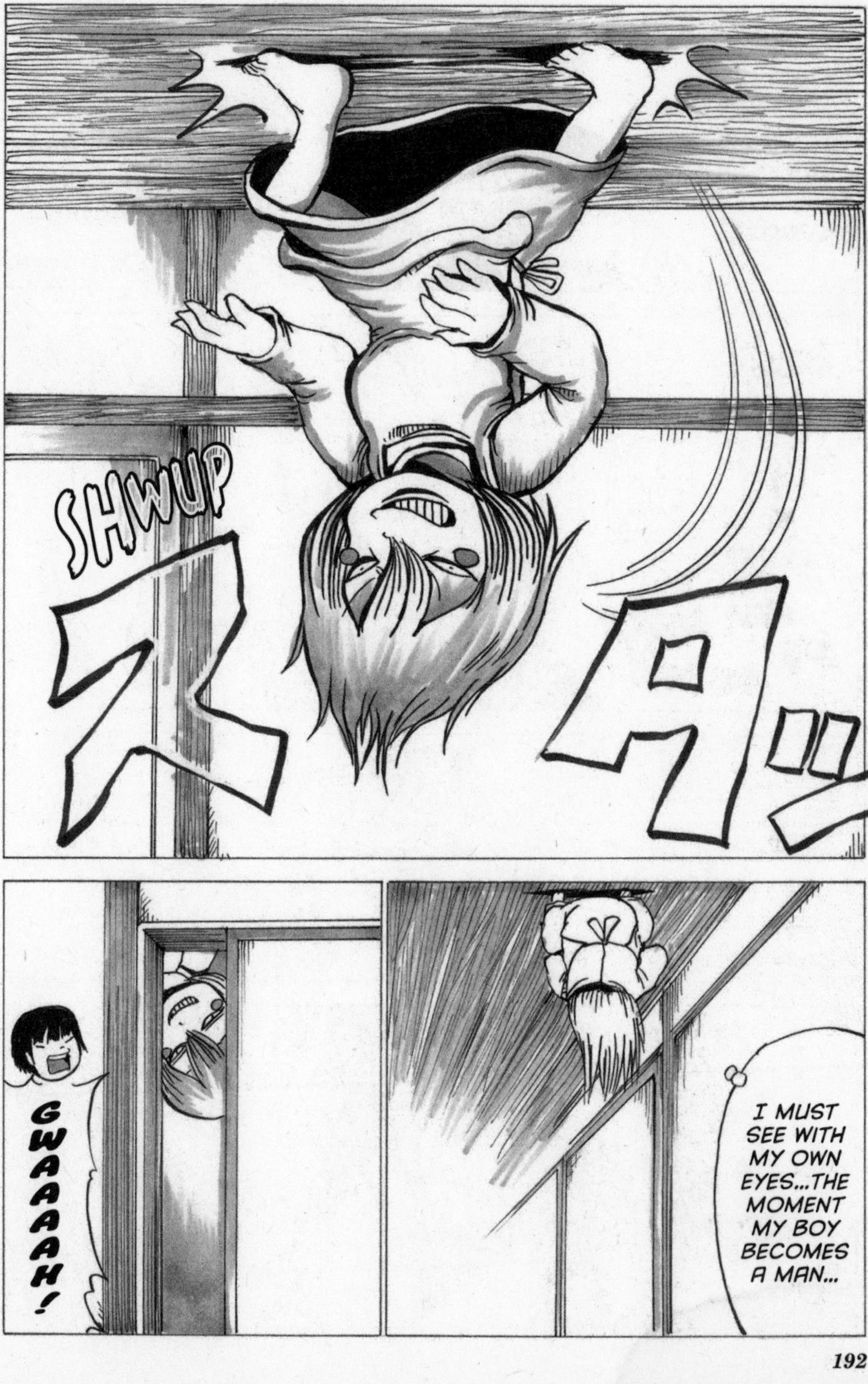
SHWUP
スタッ
I MUST SEE WITH MY OWN EYES...THE MOMENT MY BOY BECOMES A MAN...
GWAAAAAH!

BEHIND THE SCENES OF PAGE 24 OF 7-CREDIT

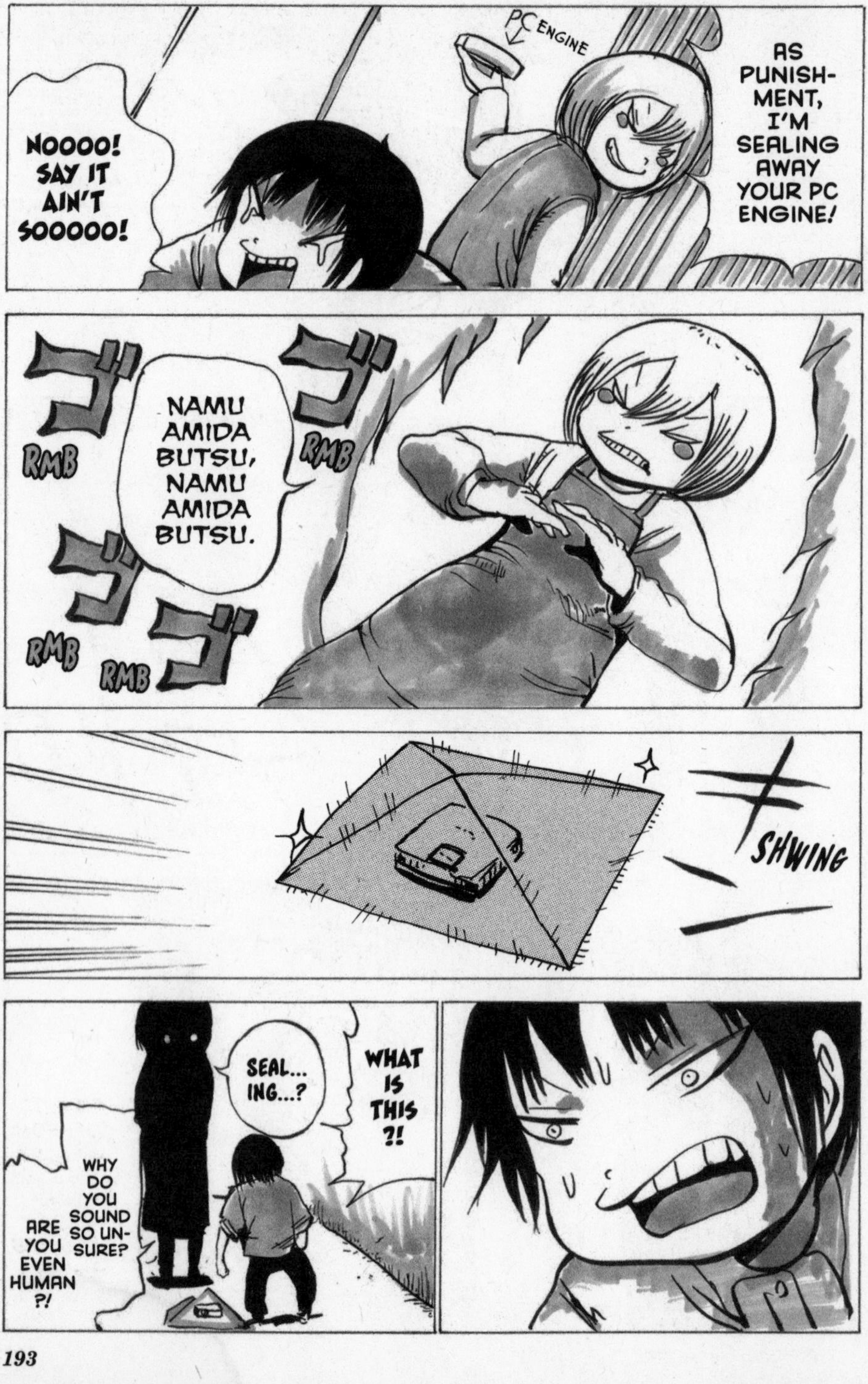
AS PUNISHMENT, I'M SEALING AWAY YOUR PC ENGINE!
PC ENGINE
NOOOO! SAY IT AIN'T SOOOOO!
NAMU AMIDA BUTSU, NAMU AMIDA BUTSU.
RMB
RMB
RMB
RMB
SHWING
WHAT IS THIS?!
SEAL... ING...?
WHY DO YOU SOUND SO UNSURE?
ARE YOU EVEN HUMAN?!

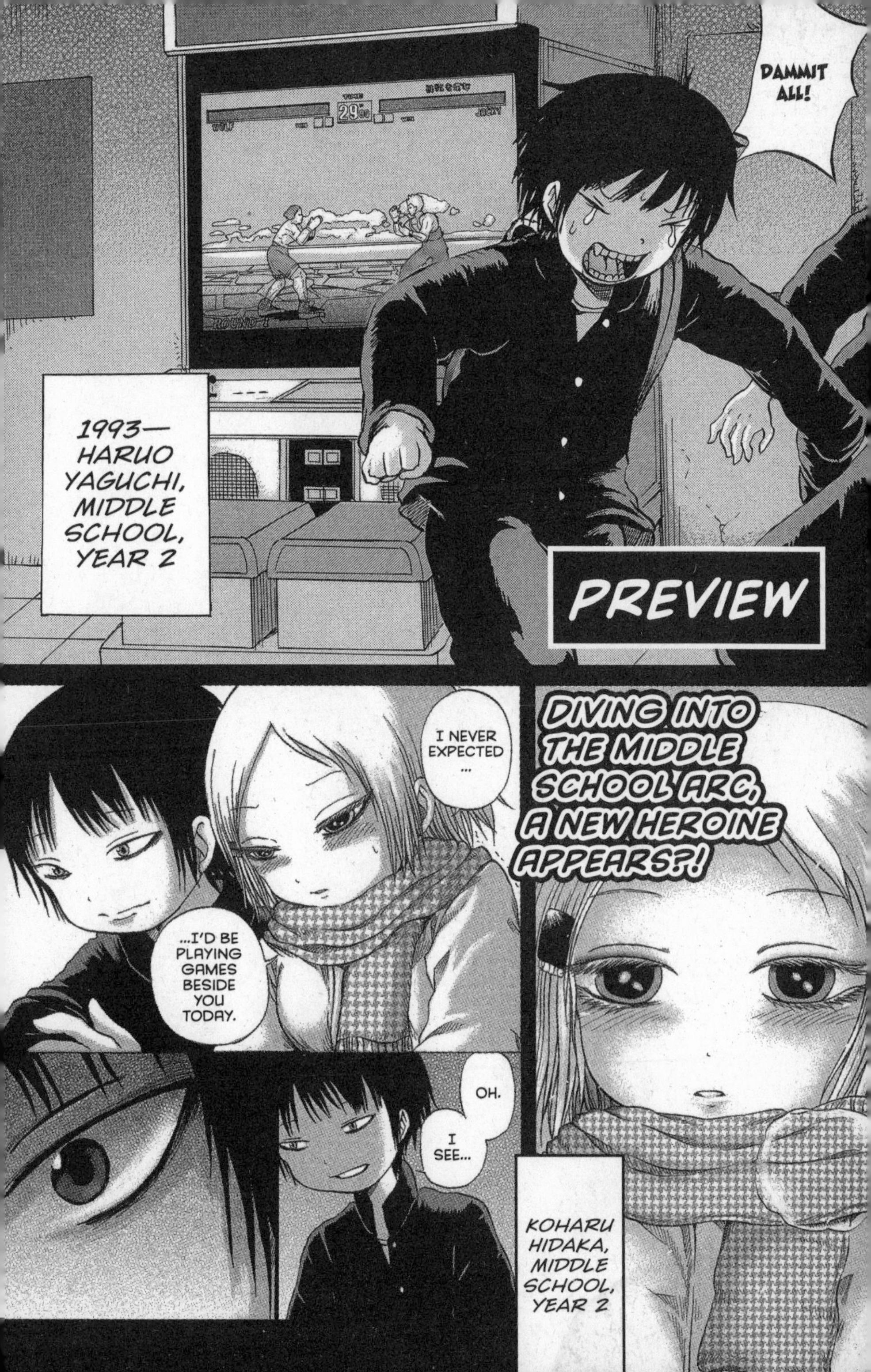
DAMMIT ALL!
1993—HARUO YAGUCHI, MIDDLE SCHOOL, YEAR 2
PREVIEW
DIVING INTO THE MIDDLE SCHOOL ARC, A NEW HEROINE APPEARS?!
KOHARU HIDAKA, MIDDLE SCHOOL, YEAR 2
I NEVER EXPECTED ...
...I'D BE PLAYING GAMES BESIDE YOU TODAY.
OH.
I SEE...